BOLD EXPLOITATION

BOLD EXPLOITATION

Tom Hansen

2023

Bold Exploitation is a work of fiction based upon real events and locations. Certain dialogue and characters were created for the purposes of fictionalization. All dialogue by well-known professional athletes, political figures, and religious leaders, are products of the author's imagination and not to be construed as real. Some businesses and organizations are real but only used to support this novel's fictitious nature. In all other respects, any resemblance to actual persons living or dead, events, or locales is entirely coincidental.

Unified Global Press
4106 N. St. Elias
Mesa, AZ 85215

Unified Global Press is a division of Educational Video Training Concepts, LLC.

ISBN: 979-8-9889662-1-0

Printed in the United States of America

Cover Design by Luke Hansen

This book is dedicated to coaches, teachers, moms, dads, and everyone who teaches the principles of being a good sport. John Wooden, UCLA's renowned basketball coach, believed athletes should play fair, respect their opponent, and be gracious in winning and losing.

For your reading pleasure and reference,
a cast of characters chart is included in the appendix.

"Golf is a game of respect and sportsmanship; we have to respect its traditions and its rules."

Jack Nicklaus
Professional Golfer

*Talent is God-given. Be humble.
Fame is man-given. Be grateful.
Conceit is self-given. Be careful."*

John Wooden
UCLA Basketball Coach

Author Note

Bold Exploitation serves two purposes: a sequel to my first book, ***Seminole Bend***, and a prequel to my last book, ***Bend of Honor***. When you're done scratching your head, read on. If you haven't read either book, it won't interfere with your enjoyment of *Bold Exploitation*. The plots are different, and there are references to scenes and characters in *Seminole Bend* and *Bend of Honor* that create a link to the new storyline.

For those who remember *Seminole Bend*, I hope you will enjoy reading that hero Willy Banks is back again, trying to solve an even more baffling mystery.

Bend of Honor looked hard at the possible influences of sports gaming on the National Football League. As a prequel to that novel, *Bold Exploitation* does the same to a different professional sport, but in a more mind-boggling way.

And lastly, readers of my first three novels, *Seminole Bend*, *Gila Bend*, and *Bend of Honor*, have inquired why I didn't use "bend" in the title. Hmmm. Good question!

PROLOGUE

October 26, 1991

The cowhide leather cover was sewn together with 108 hand-woven stitches. Its circumference was nine inches and weighed slightly more than five ounces. Atlanta Braves pitcher Charlie Leibrandt tossed it sixty feet six inches to home plate at a speed of only seventy-three miles per hour. However, because it was Charlie's signature pitch, the knuckle-curve ball twisted and dipped more than a gymnast on uneven bars. When Kirby Puckett connected, it appeared to be a can of corn, an easy pop-out to the shortstop. But the ball traveled eerily in slow motion over the leftfield fence for a walk-off homerun setting up an exciting Game Seven in Minneapolis the next night.

Outside on October 26, 1991, the Twin Cities were covered in clouds and chilled in forty-six-degree temps. Inside the Metrodome, it had been a perfect seventy-two at gametime, but as Kirby touched home plate in the bottom of the tenth inning, the frenzy warmed the stadium to well over eighty degrees. The homer hankies created a whiteout more blinding than any blizzard had ever blanketed The Land of Ten Thousand Lakes. The Braves fans' trademark tomahawk chop would be silenced for one more night. The Minnesota Twins would look to become World Champions for the second time in five years.

Father Max grinned in the eighth row of the leftfield bleachers as he inspected the homerun ball he had just caught using the leather glove he wore for parish picnic softball games. Then he handed the souvenir to a seven-year-old boy sitting in front of him. The boy's dad about collapsed from awe at the priest's bigheartedness and thanked him profusely. Father Max flipped up the five-inch metal cross he had sewn into the pocket of his glove and kissed it. Fans beside him wondered how the ball stayed in his glove after hitting the cross. Regardless, Father Max's prayers for a Twins win seemed to have worked.

During an interview on *ESPN* an hour later, Braves' owner, Abbot Tunley, accused Minnesota management of turning on a massive air conditioning blower located near the rafters behind home plate just as Kirby Puckett stepped into the box. He complained that the fan slowed Charlie Leibrandt's speed on the pitch and that Puckett's ball got caught in an artificial air current that caused the game-winning homerun.

Twin Cities newspapers and sports analysts nationwide had a field day with Abbot's sour grapes interview. Embarrassed by how the media portrayed him, Tunley hired an atmospheric scientist to conduct a velocity pressure test to find the total force exerted on a baseball within the Metrodome. The multibillionaire paid the Twins one million dollars to run the experiment before fans began rolling in for Game Seven. Minnesota owner, Carl Pohlad, gladly accepted the money. Unfortunately for Tunley, his handpicked scientist couldn't find evidence of wind current tampering.

Meanwhile, gamblers in Las Vegas were scratching their heads. Why were the odds against the Twins winning Game Six? Yes, they were down three games to two, and the Braves could clinch the World Series with a victory, but it was a home game in a must-win situation for the Twins. Pitcher Scott Erickson was twelve and two and had just as great a year as the Braves' Steve Avery. And the Twins played exceptionally well in the Hubert H. Humphrey Metrodome. Regardless, their moneyline odds had been +117. A $1,000 bet would net the gambler $1,117.

But Vegas oddsmakers were incredibly stupendous, and most wagers favored Atlanta. Talk around the sports bars was that the Twins would choke. However, Kirby Puckett wasn't a good listener when it came to naysayers. Puck stepped confidently into the batter's box in the bottom of the tenth with the count at two balls and one strike. He dug into the dirt with his right cleat, erasing the slight trace of limestone chalk that separated him from the umpire. He pounded the plate with the end of his bat, visualizing that one quality swing in the bottom of the tenth and Jack Morris would be dueling John Smoltz for all the marbles on October 27th. Charlie Leibrandt affirmed the sign from catcher Greg Olson, stretched, and delivered.

Father Max lightly touched his large cross and looked up to heaven.

CHAPTER ONE

Fall 2007

Eric Mann lived in the back seat of a thirty-year-old Plymouth Duster that had more rust than paint. The two-door coupe automobile sat covered in palm fronds hidden behind a patch of cypress trees in the Loxahatchee Slough Natural Area of South Florida. The 340-horsepower V8 was a gas-hogging monster, and the carburetor, transmission, and suspension were on their last legs. The vehicle worked fine when Eric was young, but the Manns didn't take it too far because Eric's daddy, Jim, couldn't afford the gas. Then the motor started pinging and rattling. Soon, the seventy's muscle car died when they drove home from St. Max's Catholic School at the North Palm Beach County Airport. Jim pulled over, put his head down in his hands, and cried.

The Mann family didn't own a cell phone—couldn't afford that either. They were homeless and had been that way since Eric could remember. The patch of swampy woodlands was their roost. Other than many cypress trees, their view was that of an abandoned citrus handling tractor with a rickety boom hoist left by the Everglades Fruit Company when they ended operations due to the westward expansion of residences in Palm Beach County.

The day the Mann's car broke down, Jim and Eric pushed it two miles to their swamp home while Jim's wife, Dora, steered the vehicle in neutral.

Several folks drove by them but didn't offer to help. A few teenagers in a Chevy pickup slowed down, opened their windows, and laughed. Then they tooted their horn several times as they tore off, screeching their wheels on the asphalt and kicking up dust like bulls in a rodeo. A gravel rock hit Mann's windshield, shattering it into the shape of a spider web. It was the fourth huge crack in the glass since they owned the vehicle, none of which they had the finances to repair.

A few feet from the Duster, Jim had built a small shack with a raised wooden floor out of used orange crates to sleep in while Dora and Eric slept in the car. The foundation for the shanty was made from chipped concrete secured from dumpster bins at the nearby Mirasol Country Club, where multi-million-dollar homes were being constructed daily. The Manns had obtained a full-size mattress from the North County Transfer Station, better known as the Military Trail dump, and bought a can of Raid in a futile attempt to keep the bugs out of the bed.

The concealed camp had a fire pit to stay warm in the winter and was used for cooking food their daddy hunted with a homemade bow and arrow. Fortunately, plenty of white-tailed deer, wild hogs, hares, and storks wandered by. Sometimes, an unsuspecting muskrat would be looking for cattail and become the Mann's dinner. Jim was in tough competition with the Florida panthers to see who could claim the meat first. Should an alligator want to partake in the contest, Jim conceded and hightailed it back to the car. But there were always plentiful largemouth bass and bluegills if Jim decided to fish in the slough. Park ranger Willy Banks was the only person who knew the Manns lived in the swamp. He gave them two old coolers and brought ice several days a week to keep things cold, but most of the food had to be thrown away because there wasn't enough room in the ice chests. The family ate wild gooseberries, blueberries, and mayhaw for breakfast.

Dora would take Eric and sell fruit twice weekly at a makeshift stand on Highway 786 and Jog Road. The City of Palm Beach Gardens allowed Dora to put up her table on Saturdays and Sundays for two hours at midday. Jim did not let Dora beg for money, but peddling wild berries seemed like an honest business.

*****

May 1997 (Ten years earlier)

After graduating from Seminole Bend High School in May 1997, Jim worked for the US Sugar Company in Belle Glade. He began as a freight train brake operator but quickly moved up the ranks to engineer. US Sugar owned and operated an extensive rail network throughout Florida's sugar cane fields, serving their mills in Belle Glade and Clewiston. Unfortunately, in the fall of 2001, Jim was sipping coffee on the job and didn't notice a cane harvesting truck stalled on the tracks. The truck's driver was frantically trying to restart the motor when the train struck the Mitsubishi's cab, killing the driver and two workers. A month later, Jim was found guilty of manslaughter and spent most of 2002 in the Loxahatchee Road Prison. His small trailer in Pahokee was confiscated and sold to provide restitution to the families of the dead sugar cane employees.

Dora was seven months pregnant with Eric at the time of the accident. When the court took away her trailer, she was forced to find a new home. It was then that she found religion. Father Frank at St. Mary's Catholic Church in Pahokee offered to convert a small storage room in the basement for Dora to live in until Jim was released from prison. Sister Nancy delivered Eric on a shaggy rug in the bathroom because Dora couldn't afford to go to the hospital.

While cleaning up garbage along the Beeline Highway with an inmate crew of fifteen, Jim gazed to the southeast and found what would become his next home. Beyond a patch of cypress trees was an unkempt orange grove overtaken by yellow and purple nutsedge and papyrus. Jim was an avid hunter and fisherman, and he was sure Dora could become a prolific gatherer. Yes, he would raise his family in this tropical paradise and live off the land. No more lawyers, judges, or juries to interfere with his life! His Plymouth Duster would make a suitable place to sleep and escape the torrential summer rains that saturated South Florida. An old dirt road led to the grove used by the Everglades Fruit Company back in the day. The entrance off the Beeline was marked with a sign that read "**PRIVATE PROPERTY – KEEP OUT!**" Everglades Fruit must have put it there, and no one thought to take it down after the company moved on. Following his release in October 2002, Jim, Dora, and Baby Eric moved into the slough.

It was a stroke of luck when Ranger Banks offered Jim a job with the US Fish and Wildlife Service in November. He would be responsible for repairing and maintaining the hiking and biking trails in the area. Not only would Jim be making the $5.15 minimum wage per hour, but he would also be getting a parking sticker for his car. He could enter and leave the natural preserve on the old Everglades Fruit Road without worrying about being fined for trespassing. Perhaps by the time Eric reached school age, Jim would have enough money to buy another trailer. There were plenty of places to settle down on Lake Okeechobee.

CHAPTER TWO

Winter 1982

Okeechobee County Deputy Sheriff Willy Banks received the Presidential Medal of Freedom award in 1982 for his investigative efforts that ended the worst domestic terrorist plot in American history. Ex-CIA agents Oliver Harfield and Ray Jackson had broken bad. They teamed up with Jackson's brother Roy, a South Florida rancher, to develop radar jamming devices and remote actuators that could control commercial planes from the ground. With the help of National Transportation Safety Board Lead Investigator Jake Tassett, the terrorists had caused two midair collisions in Florida, one in the Everglades west of Miami International Airport and the other over Lake Okeechobee. They also demolished a massive section of Gainesville's University of Florida campus. Harfield and the Jacksons were later killed, but Tassett was never found. Harfield had five illegitimate children he never knew and didn't want to know. His oldest son, Oliver II, grew up in a foster home near Murphy, North Carolina, after his mother abandoned him. Not wanting his name associated with a traitor and murderer, he changed his last name to Harwas when he turned eighteen. After high school graduation, he hitchhiked around the country and was never heard from again.

Willy had accepted a position in Washington, DC, with the FBI, but he hated living in the capital city. So, in 1995, he applied for a directorship position with the US Fish and Wildlife Service. The South Florida USFWS maintained the Everglades area from Lake Okeechobee to Key Largo. As a native of nearby Seminole Bend and a great American hero, Willy was a shoo-in for the job. His only request was that his office be located in Palm Beach County so he could fish the incredible waters of the Loxahatchee Slough each and every day. He lived with his younger brother, Otis, in a modest townhome within the gates of the PGA National Resort in Palm Beach Gardens.

Willy took a liking to Jim and Dora Mann from the day he first met them. The Manns had stopped at Willy's office to get permission to live in the Loxahatchee Slough Natural Area. It contradicted the policy, but Willy didn't have the heart to say no. A few months later, he offered Jim a job and a spare bedroom until Jim could afford a rental. Jim said yes to the employment offer but no to moving in with Willy. He was too proud to take handouts, a rare quality for homeless people.

*****

Eric Mann was born on New Year's Day in 2002 and was probably Florida's firstborn of the new year; however, Sister Nancy didn't think it was wise to report the delivery to the newspapers. People would wonder why Dora gave birth in a church bathroom instead of going to a hospital. It could trigger an investigation by the Florida Department of Children and Family Services.

Jim and Dora's parents had virtually disowned them after they ran off and got married the night of high school graduation. They each had one sibling, but neither stayed in touch with their immediate family. Dora insisted on having her son baptized, and Willy was asked to be his Godfather. When the Manns moved into the Duster, Willy Banks assumed the big brother role. Later, Willy became known as Grandpaw to Eric.

The US Fish and Wildlife Service owned a Cessna 172 parked at the North Palm Beach County Airport. It was at Willy's disposal for required trips to Tallahassee and Key Largo. Willy learned to fly the four-seater, so he didn't need a pilot. On a recent trip to the state capital, Willy noticed that a large hangar was being built next to his, and a sign out front said it was the future home of St. Max's Catholic Church. A place of worship using an airplane hangar for mass – very strange!

Pahokee was too far for the Manns to drive for Sunday service. Gas prices were high, and maintenance for the Duster was costly. So, Willy told Jim and Dora to go to the airport and see if they could find more information about the church being built. It was only about two miles from their home on the slough.

The day they visited, Dora thought she had discovered a goldmine. Father Jacob would be the new priest, and he was a wonderful person! After listening to Dora tell the story of Jim's train accident and subsequent arrest, the birth of Eric, and living in a car in the Loxahatchee Slough, Father Jacob felt bad for Dora and offered her a job. He had a vision of starting a small catholic elementary school on the church's premises, and he wanted to know if Dora would operate it. She would be the only teacher. Father explained to her that if a school was built in the parish, he could secure a five-million-dollar loan from the Catholic Charities Foundation.

Dora smiled and shook her head no. "Father, I only have a high school education. I can't be a teacher."

Father replied, "Dora, I can secure a grant to pay for your college degree online. How does that sound?"

Jim told Dora it was a no-brainer. She would be earning a small salary, and she could bring Eric with her when he started school. Perhaps they could afford a new trailer sooner than they thought. The church would be finished that summer (2007), and Father Jacob said the school could open in the fall.

Curiosity was eating at Jim, so he stopped by the priest's office and asked Father Jacob why the diocese would build a church in a hangar at the airport. Father said it was a temporary location until they could gather enough attendance data to construct a permanent cathedral. He explained it was Father Max's dying wish before passing in 1998 to provide a place of worship for the poor. The diocese wanted a place to serve migrant families working in the citrus groves and sugar fields. St. Max's Catholic Church would be named for the late priest.

*****

Fall 2007

The day the Duster broke down, Willy noticed Jim and five-year-old Eric struggled to push it up the Everglades Fruit Company path, so he quickly came to help. He used to wrestle alligators and bench-pressed 500 pounds back in the eighties. Now, Willy's arms were still the size of a ham, but his conditioning and endurance dropped with age. Still, pushing the old Duster to the camp was a piece of cake for the man who had held an AARP card for the past ten years.

Willy offered to pay for the auto repairs, but pride wouldn't allow Jim to accept his boss' generosity. He had saved some of his salary since starting with the US Fish and Wildlife Service. Still, Dora had just started teaching at the Catholic school and had little to show for her efforts. But without a car, she and Eric would have to walk to the church. Selling wild berries on the weekends would be on hold. Willy guessed fixing the car would cost around $3,000. Thoughts of buying a new trailer and relocating to Lake Okeechobee would end.

CHAPTER THREE

September 2007

Thanks to the five-million-dollar loan from Catholic Charities, the church was finished on time. The school was ready to begin educating students in September 2007. Father Jacob built a clergy house in the basement of the church to kick back, watch football, drink beer, and play pool. But in public, Father was a stickler for tradition.

Catholic uniforms were required and provided to the children free of charge. Girls received a white Polo shirt with the St. Max's logo. Shirts needed to be always tucked in. Girls also wore knee-length navy, gray, & white plaid skirts. They were given two pairs of calf-length socks and black Mary Jane shoes. Tennis shoes were supplied but could only be worn for PE and recess. The boys received two light blue Polos with the St. Max logo, navy chinos, black loafers, and tennis shoes.

Father Jacob gave Dora five new dresses, three pairs of shoes, and a makeup kit from Ulta. He asked her to go easy on the lipstick and eye shadow. Dora insisted on paying him; however, Father flat out refused to accept any money. He wanted to provide clothing for all the kids and the teachers.

After the Duster broke down and Dora and Eric began hiking two miles to and from school, Father bought them athletic gear and tennis shoes for their walking commute to the church. He converted a storage room into a bathroom with a shower for teachers; however, he let Eric use it, too. Neither complained about their homeless life–they were simply humbled by Father Jacob's generosity.

The first church service was scheduled for Sunday, July 20th, at 10:00 am. A few weeks earlier, Deacon Ollie was hired and placed in charge of recruiting and assisting Father Jacob with anything he asked. The deacon printed fliers about the new church and school and posted them in public places and grocery stores from Indiantown to Twentymile Bend and west to Port Mayaca. The first mass drew a crowd of fifteen: the Manns and twelve others from three families. Seven of those fifteen good Catholic folks would start school in Dora's mixed-age classroom. Eric would be in kindergarten, and the other six kids would be in grades one to five.

Father Jacob purchased a small yellow bus to transport students to and from school. All lived in rural areas served by gravel roads. Deacon Ollie would be the bus driver and cook breakfast and lunch for the kids. Dora worried about teaching six levels of instruction with no training in education. In fact, she had never even set foot on a college campus! Her online program from Ottawa University was set to begin in January.

Fifteen good Christians attended every Sunday for mass in August: the Manns who lived in the Loxahatchee Slough, the Carsons from Indiantown, the Johnsons from Canal Point, and the Butlers from Bryant. Phil Carson worked the front counter at the Dunkin Donuts in Indiantown, and his wife, Sue, cleaned the kitchen at Little Caesar's Pizza next door. Their children were April (fifth grade) and Mike (second grade).

Bill and Chris Johnson repaired trailers at the Lakeview Estates Mobil Home Park in Pahokee. Keith (fourth grade) and Karen (third grade) were their kids.

Robert and Rebecca Butler were unemployed and living on welfare since being laid off by the US Sugar Company a year earlier. Because it sounded better with their last name, Robert and Rebecca went by Bob and Becky, and their family included Ben (second grade) and Betty (first grade). After attending church together for a month, the families became best friends by the time school started in September.

After hearing how enlightening the homily was during Sunday mass, Willy and Otis Banks joined the church in December 2007, in time for Christmas services. The ex-sheriff's deputy and brother didn't think St. Max's could survive too long with a parish of seventeen. However, they were impressed by the church's beauty and guessed Father Jacob's clergy home in the basement was just as charming.

Father shocked everyone on January 1st, 2008, during the first mass of the new year. He proposed buying another hangar next door to the church and converting it into an apartment. Father said it would be used for needy families to live free of rent, and he offered four flats to the Manns, Carsons, Johnsons, and Butlers. Each family eagerly accepted the priest's offer, and he said the construction would commence the following week.

Willy was amazed! Not just at Father Jacob's generosity but how he could budget for this project using Catholic Charities' five-million-dollar loan. After completing the church and clergy home, buying a bus, and providing clothing and supplies to the school kids, you wouldn't think much would be left.

How would Father Jacob ever build a parish-subsidized apartment with only seventeen registered church members? And of them all, Willy was the only contributor to the weekly collection basket. Maybe he would hold a fundraiser at his home in PGA National. Plenty of wealthy professionals and retirees had nothing better to do with their money than play golf!

CHAPTER FOUR

January 2008

Otis Banks struggled to hold down a job his entire life. At sixteen, he dropped out of school and tried his hand at several trades but failed miserably. However, at home, he would do anything his brother Willy asked. Otis scrubbed the kitchen and vacuumed the whole house each day. He enjoyed waxing the car and taking Herr Hermann, the German Shepherd, for walks. After white shirts turned pink and perfectly fitted pants shrunk in the waist and inseam, Otis was told not to wash the clothes anymore! But all the neighbors loved Willy's younger sibling and placed him in charge of daytime security for the block watch. However, he wasn't allowed to carry a weapon.

Willy and Otis' next-door neighbor was Hugh Kraft, a golf pro who taught Jack Nicklaus his infamous fade shot. "No, no, no, Jackie! Don't square up your clubface at the address to hit a perfect fade. Open the clubface straight and aim slightly to your target's left."

*****

September 19, 1959

Hugh and Jack had been best friends at Upper Arlington High School in Ohio, and both were stars on the basketball and baseball teams for four years. However, their passion was golf, and Hugh and Jack caddied for tips at the nearby Scioto Golf Club on weekends and during summer break. The boys finished first and second at junior tournaments around the Midwest, with Hugh besting Jack most times. In 1959, Jack beat Hugh by one stroke in their first US Amateur Golf Championship at the Broadmoor Country Club in Colorado Springs. He dropped an eagle on the 433-yard par-four eighteenth green to win the match that had been tied since teeing off on the first hole.

The best friends celebrated their one-two victory by renting ten-speed bikes and riding up Pikes Peak the following day. The nineteen-mile climb to a 14,115-foot elevation was extremely strenuous yet stunningly gorgeous! All the while, they were thinking about the delicious donuts at the restaurant on top of the world. Coasting down the mountain without pedaling would be fantastic!

The boys boarded their ten speeds for the return trip with bellies full of powdered, glazed, and chocolate-covered pastries. Hugh's brakes gave out three miles from the summit, and he couldn't slow the bike. He lost control going thirty-five miles per hour and hit the front end of a red Corvette traveling thirty miles per hour uphill. Hugh's torso was launched over the Vette, landed hard on the asphalt, and rolled a hundred yards from his crushed bicycle. The ambulance took an hour to arrive, and Hugh was transported to a local hospital, where he stayed in a coma for a week.

When he awoke, Jack was at his side while the doctor gave him the bad news. Hugh was paralyzed from the waist down and would never walk again. Jack sat in a chair next to the bed and wept. Hugh felt worse for Jack than he did for himself.

"For my sake, make something of yourself!" Hugh told his friend. "You have the skills to be the greatest golfer of all time. Now go prove it to the world!"

Jack nodded contritely. In his heart, he knew Hugh was the one who should be making it big, not him. Jack covered his eyes with his hands to shield the tears. He thought that had he chosen Hugh's bike at the rental store, he would be lying on the hospital bed or, worse yet, in a cemetery.

"I need you to be my coach!" stated Jack matter-of-factly. "I can't win without you at my side."

"Jack, I can't even walk. What good would I be to you?"

"You know the ins and outs of the game. You could tell me what to do and what I'm doing wrong."

Hugh thought about it for less than ten seconds. "I'll do it! But you must fire me if I can't elevate your skills to be better than Arnie Palmer. That's the deal—understand?!"

Jack cracked his first smile of the day. "You got it!"

*****

October 1959

Neurologist Omar Cauldwin reviewed Hugh's medical file and prepared a physical therapy plan. However, upon examining him more thoroughly than the attending doctor, Cauldwin found some discrepancies in the original findings. The neurology specialist decided to conduct some more tests.

Two weeks later, Hugh received good news. He was diagnosed with Brown-Séquard syndrome. His spinal cord was damaged in the accident but not severed. Had Doctor Cauldwin not caught the misdiagnosis of Hugh's paralysis, there was a good chance he would have remained a paraplegic for life. However, Hugh defied all odds six months later and stood up from his wheelchair. He never regained his earlier mobility, but he could still play a mean game of golf.

Hugh's handicap ranged from zero to five during his entire career as Jack's personal coach. And Jack gave him a ten percent cut of all his tournament winnings. When his book on perfecting the golf swing was endorsed by Tiger Woods, Hugh became a multimillionaire.

*****

January 2008

Willy invited the Manns to a backyard barbeque at his house in January 2008. Otis befriended young Eric, and the two played games all afternoon. At Willy's request, Otis and Eric knocked on doors at PGA National residents' homes the following Saturday to raise money for the church and school.

Hugh Kraft invited them into his house and, without hesitation, promptly wrote a check for $100,000. Then he asked Eric if he would like a quick golf lesson at the driving range.

Eric was giddy with excitement! Otis asked if Hugh would mind giving him a few pointers, too. Hugh smiled and said, "Sure, Otis! You're my favorite neighbor!"

Eric caught on quickly. Otis—not so much. Eric had a natural swing that reminded Hugh of Jack Nicklaus. After minor adjustments, Eric drove the ball over 150 yards straight as an arrow! Not bad for a boy who had just turned six years old!

Seeing another opportunity to create a world-class golfer, Hugh offered to give weekly lessons to Eric for free. Jim and Dora were thrilled but weren't sure the Duster would survive long enough to provide transportation to PGA National, say nothing of the gas price. Also, Eric would need clubs, a bag, balls, shoes, and tees if he ever played golf regularly.

Hugh smiled and said he would have everything Eric needed during his first lesson.

CHAPTER FIVE

June 2008

Deacon Ollie was ashamed to admit it, but deep down, he believed he was a sinful man. He drank too much alcohol and gambled too much, as well. Several times a year, he would vacation in Las Vegas, return to St. Max's, and spend an hour in the confessional with Father Jacob. With kind words of absolution, Father forgave Ollie of his Jack Daniels abuse at the Flamingo, slot machine woes at Harrah's, and poker losses at Treasure Island. But the deacon never confessed to the abundance of money won in the sportsbook each year. It seemed it was the only place in the casino where he could win. This year he netted thousands of dollars betting on the National Football League, College Softball World Series, and the Cricket World Cup in England. However, to relieve his guilt complex, the deacon donated the majority of his winnings to St. Max's. It didn't seem like much, but Father Jacob claimed those donations helped speed up some of his parish projects.

The apartment complex next to the church on the airport grounds was completed in June 2008. That was a minor miracle for Father Jacob, who professed scriptural miracles every day. The building had eighteen three-bedroom, two-bath units—six on each of the three floors. As promised, the Manns, Carsons, Johnsons, and Butlers moved first into rent-free homes. They were overwhelmed by the generosity of their priest. But they were stunned when Father gathered them into the apartment's lounge for another incredible offer.

The priest wanted to know if the men would like new jobs. All would be paid $500 a week, much more than they were currently making. First, he needed a head of transportation. That person would also assume the duties of bus driver for the school. Now that all the current parish families were living on campus, the primary responsibility would be for field trips. However, the position would also require someone to regularly transport Bibles from the Port of Miami to the church. Father planned to give the books to the homeless and the poor.

Jim offered up his services for that task. He was sure Willy would give him time off from repairing hiking and biking trails to work part-time for St. Max's. Because Phil Carson helped stir batter at Dunkin Donuts, Father Jacob thought he should be the head chef for the parish. Phil smiled from ear to ear when he heard the offer. Thanks to his trailer-repairing skills, Bill Johnson would become the head of maintenance for the church and the apartment building. And Bob Butler was asked to be the head of security for the complex.

Jim Mann told Willy and Otis about the jobs and expressed his excitement for his family's revived life. A new home and career just like that! Father Jacob was truly a gift from heaven! Otis wished he could have been the assistant head of security.

Willy wasn't an accountant but had questions about where all the money came from. There were still only seventeen church members, so weekly contributions were minimal. Catholic Charities' five-million-dollar loan was huge, but Willy guessed that the fund would soon be depleted and needed to be repaid. Door-to-door requests for handouts at PGA National would result in some nice donations, such as the $100,000 gift from Hugh Kraft; however, those would likely be only one-time benefactions. Father Jacob and Deacon Ollie were terrific men of the cloth. Still, Willy thought they were clueless about managing the church's business.

*****

Father Jacob purchased a two-year-old used Ford Econoline seventeen-foot box truck from U-Haul. Jim helped him scrape off the U-Haul decals and repaint it white with St. Max's Parish logo on both sides. He was excited about his first trip to the Port of Miami but wondered why Father would buy a truck when the small school bus could transport the Bibles to the church. Father Jacob explained that the truck would also be used to deliver food to the poor on Thanksgiving, Christmas, and other days during the year.

There were no time restrictions on Jim's trip to Miami. Basically, when he drove there, that was all Father Jacob required that day. Jim had never traveled much and never outside of Florida. When he was a kid, his parents would take him to watch alligators leap for chickens tossed by workers at Gatorland in Orlando or to see the mermaids at Weeki Wachee Springs State Park. They couldn't afford to go to popular attractions like Disney World, Universal Studios, or Busch Gardens. So, Jim decided to make the most of his weekly excursions by visiting Little Havana and Miami Beach. Maybe he would get up early and venture to Everglades National Park to fish or Pennekamp State Park near Key Largo and learn to scuba dive.

Jim's first trip to the Port of Miami didn't go as planned. His GPS routed him correctly to Dodge Island but ended at the Carnival Cruise Line's parking lot. Jim could see gigantic cruise ships destined for exotic places he could only dream about. So, where were the cargo ships? An unfriendly police officer abruptly directed him to the South Florida Container Terminal. Jim spoke to Abdul Fareesh at the front desk a few minutes later.

Father Jacob had told him the Bibles would be arriving on the MV Gulf Streamer, a cargo ship from Nassau. Abdul punched keys on his computer, gave Jim a surreptitious glance, and excused himself.

"Please have a seat," said Abdul. "I'll be right back."

Jim noticed that the clerk gave him a secretive look but thought nothing of it. "Okay, no problem."

He grabbed the latest *Sports Illustrated* off a worn-down table, then sat on a plastic chair and flipped through the pictures. Ten minutes later, Abdul returned with a tall man wearing a pair of black designer dress pants, a long-sleeve starched white shirt, and a tie with a Stars and Stripes metal clasp. The man stopped at the front desk and stared at Jim without saying anything. Jim looked at the intimidating man. Paranoia set in, and he quickly returned his focus to the magazine. "What's going on?" he thought to himself.

"What's your name, son?" said the man in a deep voice.

Jim hesitated, then replied. "Jim Mann. I'm here to pick up some Bibles. Who are you, if I may ask?"

"The name's Dale Maglia. I'm head of US Customs for the Port of Miami. Come to my office. I have some questions for you."

Jim was taken aback. He remembered being arrested after the train he was conducting collided with the sugar truck years ago. Jim wasn't a troublemaker, but he felt like a criminal right now and wasn't sure why.

"Is there a problem, sir?" Jim uttered meekly.

"I'm not asking you, Mr. Mann. I'm telling you. You need to come to my office now."

Jim put the magazine on the table and followed Abdul's lead to the director's office. Maglia brought up the rear and kept a close eye on Jim.

"Close the door on your way out, Abdul," ordered Maglia. The clerk nodded and left the room. The director then motioned to a leather chair in front of his desk, and Jim plopped down quickly. If nothing else, the man was unsettling!

Maglia sat and opened a desk drawer. He pulled out a small recording device and turned it on. Jim's eyes opened wide. What was going on?

"So, you say you're here to pick up some Bibles. Is that right?" asked Maglia with a tone of skepticism.

"Yes, sir. There should be a crate with 120 Bibles on the MV Gulf Streamer," replied Jim delicately. He didn't dare show anger or frustration to Dale Maglia.

"And who did you say sent you to pick them up?"

"Father Jacob. He's the priest at St. Max's Catholic Church in North Palm Beach."

"What's Father Jacob's last name?"

Jim paused to think. He wasn't sure. "Uh, I actually don't know his last name. Sorry. Why?"

"I hope we've established that I would be the one asking the questions." Maglia glared at Jim, and Jim dropped his head.

"Yes, sorry again."

"So you're saying you work for a man whose last name you don't know? I find that very hard to believe."

"He's my church's preacher, sir. I guess I never thought to ask him his last name."

"Well, doesn't he sign your paycheck? Perhaps you could look at that!"

"I just started working for St. Max's. My job is to transport kids to and from the parish school and come here to pick up Bibles and other parish goods. In other words, I haven't been paid yet."

"How many members are in your church?"

"Uh, I think about twenty."

"Twenty churchgoers, and you pick up 120 Bibles a week?! What the hell kind of BS are you feeding me, son?!" Maglia's face turned several shades of red.

Jim fidgeted and wasn't sure what to say. "The Bibles are for the poor, sir. Father Jacob does everything he can for the homeless and others who need help to survive."

"I'm sure he does," remarked Maglia sarcastically.

Maglia did a complete one-eighty with his next question. "Where is Plana Cay, Mr. Mann?"

"Never heard of it. Why?" As soon as Jim asked why he regretted it. Maglia's eyes turned evil. "Sorry, sorry, that just slipped out! Sorry, sir!"

"Well, I'll tell you where Plana Cay is, son. It's a tiny Bahamian island in the West Indies. And it's uninhabited."

Jim was totally lost. What did Plana Cay have to do with anything? Why was Maglia telling him this? He hesitated before asking, "So very sorry, Mr. Maglia, but I'm not sure why you're pointing this out to me."

"Because according to the bill of lading, the crate with the Bibles originated from Plana Cay. Thus, I'm assuming the Bibles were manufactured in Plana Cay. The crate arrived in Nassau on a twenty-five-foot wooden vessel that barely had room for the four crew members. Not exactly ocean-worthy, huh?! It was transferred to the MV Gulf Streamer without inspection by Bahamian customs agents, a huge mistake when cargo arrives at the port from a company you've never done business with before. Just the fact that they saw a damn twenty-five-foot boat sailing in the Atlantic Ocean should make them want to inspect the contents! Unbelievable!"

"Yes, sir," spoke Jim abashedly, although he wasn't sure why he was embarrassed. He had done nothing wrong, and this narrative didn't make sense. "Do you think I could just take the Bibles and go? I'm just here doing my job, sir."

"Your Bibles? If you want your blessed Bibles, you'll need SCUBA gear. You see, the MV Gulf Streamer was sunk last night by a bomb. They are now resting on the sand at the bottom of the Bermuda Triangle! That is why you are sitting with me right now, Mr. Mann!"

"Why me?! What have I got to do with the sinking of that ship?!" That was two questions, but at this point, Jim didn't care. His fear was turning to anger.

"Perhaps nothing. Perhaps something. I'm questioning everyone who had cargo on the MV Streamer. I believe the bomb was in one of the containers, and quite frankly, yours is the most suspicious. After doing some checking, I found that Plana Cay was uninhabited. It also has no docks to load containers. Furthermore, the Bahamian government sold both the east and west islands to two investors back in the 1980s; however, the investors' names on the bill of sale for the real estate were wrong. Either there was a mistake in filing the paperwork, or the investors gave false information. So, do you understand where I'm coming from, Mr. Mann?!"

"Yes, I see that all you've told me sounds suspicious. However, I do not know where the Bibles were manufactured or shipped from. And, I'm also sure Father Jacob has no knowledge, either. He just needed the Bibles to distribute to the poor. You should be looking for the people who market the books, not the innocent folks simply buying them."

"Don't tell me who I'm supposed to be looking for, Mr. Mann! A ship sank last night in the Atlantic Ocean, and I'm trying to get to the bottom of it! Do you understand?!"

Jim had had enough. His fear turned to frustration. "If you are going to arrest me, do it. If not, then I'm out of here." He stood up and started walking towards the door. Maglia rose, pounded his fist on the desk, then leaned forward and peered with a dark shade of red on his cheeks.

"If I find that you had something to do with the sinking of the MV Streamer, son, you better hide! When I make an arrest, I don't mess around. In other words, you may need some bandages handy!"

Jim couldn't believe the customs director was threatening bodily injury, but he knew better than to speak further. He quickly exited the facility and ran to his truck, but it was gone! What's going on?! Jim turned, looked back at the building, and saw Abdul standing in the doorway with his hands on his waist. It looked like he was laughing.

"Are you wondering where your truck is?!" shouted Abdul from the South Florida Container Terminal entrance. "We impounded the vehicle. It's locked in our storage area."

Jim jogged back to the door. "Why?! There was nothing in it! I'm sure you've already looked!"

"Yes, true. But we are stripping it down, removing the panels and wheels, checking the chassis and other hiding places."

"What are you hoping to find? It's just an old U-Haul with nothing in it." Then a thought sparked in Jim's mind. "Do you have a search warrant?"

Abdul chuckled and pointed towards the entry to the parking lot. "Did you read the sign on the fence before you entered? It says, ***'WARNING: ALL VEHICLES ARE SUBJECT TO SEARCH.'*** We have court-ordered authorization to search any car, truck, RV, motorcycle, or even a bicycle with training wheels if we deem it necessary to protect the safety of our nation. You'll get all the pieces back when we're through. However, you'll have to do the reassembly!" Abdul chuckled louder and longer at that comment.

Jim didn't own a cell phone but needed to call Father Jacob. Abdul refused to let him use the SFCT's landline. Across Port Boulevard was the Norwegian Cruise Lines passenger terminal. Jim ran into the building but didn't see a pay phone. After telling a security guard that he worked for a church, the officer let him use his personal cell phone. Father Jacob picked up on the second ring.

"Father!" Deep breath. "Father!" Another deep breath.

"Jim? Is that you?" asked the priest.

"Yes, yes, yes, Father! It's me!"

"Relax, Jim. What's the matter?"

"I'm at the Port of Miami. I stopped to pick up our shipment of Bibles at the South Florida Container Terminal, and the customs agent forced me into his office. Last night, the MV Streamer was sunk by a bomb in one of the containers. The man, his name is Dale Maglia, thinks it was our shipment!"

"Our shipment?! Why our shipment?"

"Because the container originated on a tiny flatboat from Plana Cay, which it turns out is uninhabited! At least, that's what the bill of lading said. I'd never heard of Plana Cay, so I didn't know what to tell him. He kept asking questions, and I thought he would arrest me, so I left. But when I got to the parking lot, our truck had been impounded, and they were stripping it down, looking for something! They wouldn't let me call you, so I ran to the Norwegian Cruise Lines passenger terminal and borrowed a cell phone from a security guard. What do I do, Father?!"

"Okay, Jim, just relax. Everything will work out fine. Have faith in God, son. Wait at NCL, and I'll be there as soon as possible. Don't sweat this, Jim. It's not a problem."

Jim's anxiety was overwhelming, and he hung up without saying goodbye. Then he returned the phone to the guard and sat in the waiting area. What just happened? Jim couldn't wrap his head around it.

Father Jacob dropped Deacon Ollie off at the South Florida Container Terminal, then picked up Jim at NCL. They crossed the bridge onto the MacArthur Causeway and merged north on Interstate 95 before Jim came to his senses. "Uh, Father, where are we going? You forgot the truck."

"I hired a mechanic in Miami to reassemble the truck. Deacon Ollie will wait there until it is fixed and drivable. You don't have to worry about it."

"That could take a week or more!" exclaimed Jim. "What will he do in the meantime?"

"He'll stay on South Beach for as long as it takes. We'll get the truck back."

Jim barely spoke on the return trip to North Palm Beach. He had too many unanswered questions, most of which centered around money. More specifically, where were the church funds coming from? Without blinking, Father spent money boundlessly for a new parish, apartments for the homeless, Bibles for the poor, jobs for church members, a bus for the school, a truck to haul things around, and now, an expensive room in a hotel on South Beach for Deacon Ollie. Everything was for good intentions, but was there no limit? The loan must have dried up by now.

*****

July 2008 (two weeks later)

It was mid-July, and Jim had nothing to do but repair trails at the Loxahatchee Slough for Willy. However, St. Max's was still paying him $500 weekly. So far, no new members had joined the church, and no new students would attend school in the fall. Seeing everyone lived in the apartments, he wouldn't have to drive the bus until the kids took field trips. Deacon Ollie hadn't returned with the truck, so Jim's regular runs to Miami had been put on hold. That was fine because he didn't want to return to the South Florida Container Terminal anytime soon. In fact, he was apprehensive about ever going back there! But how else would Father Jacob get the Bibles for distribution? Maybe they could be shipped to Fort Lauderdale instead. Regardless, St. Max's didn't have a truck to transport them.

How much did Deacon Ollie's hotel bill on South Beach cost the parish? Jim kept his thoughts to himself, but he was puzzled. He spent most of his free time fishing the Loxahatchee Slough or watching Eric's golf lessons at PGA National.

CHAPTER SIX

June 2013

In June 2013, there were forty registered patrons of St. Max's Catholic Church. Four elderly men who had lost their spouses years ago lived in a rusty 1967 model Chevy cargo van near Canal Point. They saw one of the signs posted on an electric pole by Deacon Ollie, then drove to the church and registered for membership. Father Jacob immediately moved them into one of the apartments.

Meanwhile, the Martin County Board of Supervisors had ordered five homeless families to vacate their tent city on Jupiter Island. Willy Banks heard about the eviction and explained the situation to Father. As usual, the priest welcomed them into the church with open arms and helped each family move into one of the vacant apartments.

None of the twenty-one new parish members had ever seen the inside of a church or heard of the word Catholicism. Father would quickly baptize the entire lot, provide religious studies, then confirm them into the Catholic religion. The rest of the sacraments would follow as time allowed. Eight of the twenty-one were children with ages ranging from six to fourteen. They would all attend Dora's mixed-level classroom in the fall.

Father wanted to ensure that all his parishioners had jobs to keep them from begging on street corners, especially during the sweltering South Florida summer months. Because the church was located near PGA

National and other lush courses, Father wanted to raise money for the church by producing and selling something related to golf. Unfortunately, only a handful of the parishioners had ever played the game and those that did have handicaps higher than their grandparents' ages! However, Father had high hopes, big ideas, and spiritual guidance in everything he wanted to do. He believed his parish members could learn to make a new aerodynamic golf ball that flew further and more accurately than anything currently on the market.

Tommy Williams, a high school friend, designed balls for Titleist and was willing to consult with Father Jacob and his church members to construct something new and better. Golf was the hottest recreational sport in America. If the ball could have quality spin, distance, and drag, it might become a huge item in pro shops.

Father envisioned St. Max manufacturing and selling enough golf balls so the church could become self-sustaining someday. Shockingly, the Catholic Charities Foundation had forgiven St. Max's five-million-dollar loan because of the church's productive work for the poor and homeless. Instead, it supplied additional grant money to the parish for Father Jacob to elevate his ministry.

Since the Port of Miami incident five years earlier, Father used Port Everglades to import Bibles. Jim Mann would unload the boxes and leave them at the stairway door to Father's home beneath the church. Jim offered to carry them downstairs, but the priest was too embarrassed to let others see his abode. Empty beer cans and uneaten pizza were lying amidst dirty clothes and used paper napkins. Father would re-box the Bibles into smaller packages, and Deacon Ollie would deliver them to homeless shelters and poor neighborhoods around Lake Okeechobee.

*****

Tommy Williams met with Father Jacob and showed him a design plan and what would be needed to make the golf balls. He suggested two types of balls: a standard one to sell to the general public and a premium ball for professionals. Tommy detailed how both cores would be made from a magnesium alloy instead of the popular titanium. But the inside of the premium balls would have additional ingredients. Father's friend also recommended a new type of cover that would offer more strength and longevity than the current surlyn or balata types. Tommy worked with a plastics company that could create a new, durable surface that would be soft enough to insert microscopic holes inside the dimples. Those holes would aid in keeping the flight path straight, and the balls could slightly correct the golfer's inherent hooks and slices.

Father had a straightforward question. "Somebody in the golf business will need to approve the balls. Are they legal?"

"Would I design a golf ball for a Catholic priest that wasn't legal?" answered Tommy sarcastically. "I would probably end up in hell!" Father Jacob and Tommy both chuckled.

Tommy continued, "To be legal, the golf ball's weight and size must adhere to USGA specifications, and the golf ball's shape must be spherically symmetric. Also, a maximum permissible initial velocity can't be exceeded. Plus, there must be consistency in the golf ball's lift, carry and drag. Both the standard and premium balls will conform to those specs when it's all said and done."

Father Jacob called the bishop to get approval for raising church funds in such an unorthodox way. He briefly described the standard balls but indicated that the premium balls would be the real money maker. It just so happened that Bishop Bob Kaiser was about to tee off on the tenth hole at The Breakers Ocean Course when his cell phone rang. "Golf balls?!" asked the bishop quietly, not wanting the rest of his foursome to hear. "Well, Jacob, as long as you send me a dozen, then I guess it's a go!"

*****

August 2013

The ball's core was produced somewhere in the Bahamas. The spherical magnesium cast alloy consisted of aluminum, manganese, zinc, and planacalum. Only recently discovered and as of yet not charted by chemists or metallurgists, planacalum was what made the ball totally different from the rest. The unknown metal had strong ferromagnetic qualities and would expand and contract in heat or when struck with force. The core was made by pouring the molten liquid metal into a mold that solidified into a curved half-shell. Tommy Williams said a ferrofluid made from tiny magnetic fragments of iron, black oxide, kerosene, and oleic acid (to prevent clumping) would be injected into the half-shells, sealed, and rounded to perfection. Father was again skeptical of the liquid's legality if it were ever tested by the USGA.

"The formula is legitimate. Yes, the planacalum could raise eyebrows, but I will try and patent the ball before I submit it to the USGA for approval. If the ball is patented, they should approve it without question!"

"Obviously, the planacalum is the key to the ball's success," said Father Jacob. "If you don't get the patent, what is our Plan B?"

"We'll cross that bridge when we come to it. I know what I'm doing."

"Please don't take offense, Tommy. I was just asking."

Tommy's childhood dream was to become an inventor. He told friends that he was named after Thomas Edison, and many didn't doubt his namesake based on the wild things he used to create as a kid in his garage. He was debating leaving Titleist if this new venture panned out. Father explained that he couldn't pay anywhere near as well as Titleist, but Tommy didn't care about his stipend. The greater satisfaction was being teamed up with his old high school friend who was now —believe it or not—a priest!

While the ball's core was cast in the Bahamas, the moylyn cover was made in Barbados. Moylyn was a soft and durable plastic that Tommy Williams had invented during his free time after work and eventually patented. This would be the first time that it was ever used. Meanwhile, Jim Mann continued his frequent runs to Port Everglades to facilitate the importation of golf ball materials and Bibles. He became close friends with the port's operators.

Father Jacob acquired a third hangar at the North Palm Beach airport to build a golf ball factory. The parish now owned the church, school, apartments, and manufacturing plant. Tommy was given a parish apartment to use as his office and workstation.

A while back, Tommy met two aeronautical engineers on a golf course, and they immediately became weekly golf buddies. Their names were Mel Smith and Keith Malone. They impressed Tommy with intelligent scientific discussions while riding on golf carts or drinking beer in the clubhouse. Tommy thought their knowledge of aerodynamics could help significantly in the golf ball project. Father was skeptical that Tommy didn't know Mel and Keith's background besides what they told him while playing golf. But he trusted his friend to do the right thing. So based upon Tommy's recommendation, Mel and Keith were hired to oversee the product assembly. Both were honors graduates of the Massachusetts Institute of Technology. Because of that, Father gave them an excellent salary with health benefits. Plus, each was given one apartment next to the church. Neither was married and didn't need a three-bedroom unit, but they saw it as a great perk and moved in at once.

Tommy cautioned Mel and Keith to keep a low profile and try to avoid the parish members who were living in the apartments. "All the people who reside here, except us, are poor. It's best they don't know we were given a place to live for free. Especially try to stay away from the kids. We will have a lot of work to do, and children are naturally curious. If they interrupt us, we won't be able to get much done."

Father told Smith and Malone to hold down costs so the price of the golf balls would be competitive with Titleist, Taylor Made, and Callaway. He wanted to set the initial price tag at thirty-five dollars per dozen. The marketing pitch would center around the profits going to aiding the homeless.

Shortly before school started in August, Tommy Williams created a prototype for Smith and Malone to follow. Father Jacob approved the design and flew to New York to meet with Ursula Vero, the CEO of the nation's largest distributor of golf equipment, Golf Country Superstore. She was a good Catholic and was thrilled to help Father in his new adventure. She offered to sell the balls in all of GCS's 252 stores across the United States, with all the profits going to St. Max's. Father had to mass-produce the balls and get them to GCS's four distribution centers in

Atlanta, St. Louis, Denver, and San Francisco. That would be the next mountain to climb for the church.

Every unemployed church member offered to work in the factory or drive to the distribution cities. Still, none had any experience with mass production or operating a truck. Father contemplated renting a twenty-six-foot U-Haul and hiring a parishioner to journey to the four distribution points whenever enough golf balls were manufactured to fill the cab. But after crunching the numbers, he thought buying another used truck from U-Haul might be best. Deacon Ollie was sent to negotiate a good deal for St. Max's, and he returned with a 2004 Ford F-650 with 203,000 miles on it. The price was only $8,000, but it needed new tires, a transmission, and who knew what else.

The truck's bed also needed reinforcements, so Father dished out another $1,500 for steel planks. What he didn't know was that the gross vehicle weight went from 25,808 pounds to 26,010, which meant the operator would need to have a commercial driver's license. By law, 26,000 pounds was the cutoff point. Although the planks were non-returnable, Father thought replacing them with lighter wood reinforcements was best. He was about to make the switch when Otis Banks told him he had a CDL and would love the job. He obtained the special license in 1988 and used it only once; however, he continued to renew it every five years before it expired.

*****

Otis didn't tell Father Jacob about his one and only experience driving a commercial vehicle, and Father never asked. The priest was ecstatic that he wouldn't have to remove the steel planks now that he had found someone with professional trucking experience. Little did he know that Otis' one trip ended with him getting fired. In the summer of 1988, after six months of training at a semi-truck school, he had been hired to transport frozen fish, shrimp, crab, and lobster from a processing plant in Delray Beach, Florida, to a distribution center in Houston, Texas. He was contracted to make the journey in less than twenty-four hours. It was a seventeen-hour drive, which would have allowed for seven hours of rest along the way.

Unfortunately, Otis accidentally turned off the freezer switch in the cab as he left the factory. It was summertime in the deep south, and temps were in the nineties. The humidity neared one hundred percent. Otis was ticketed twice on the Florida turnpike for speeding, once on Interstate 10 near Pensacola for reckless driving and another time in Houston for going the wrong way down a one-way street. Because of the police stops, Otis didn't have time to rest. He had not slept for the past forty hours when he arrived at the distribution center. Although he was dead tired, he became wide awake from the stench of a semi-truckload of spoiled seafood upon opening the door to the cab.

Fortunately, Pisces Fish Company had insurance to cover the spoiled cargo. And luckily for Otis, his brother Willy was an American hero. Without Willy's knowledge or even asking for it, the Federal Motor Carrier Safety Administration reluctantly suspended Otis' license for a year instead of pulling it permanently. They thought they were doing Willy a favor by helping out Otis. Willy paid his brother's fines for his tickets but had no idea Otis could renew his license when it expired. Willy wasn't aware that Otis still had a CDL until he discovered that his brother would be driving for St. Max's. Willy thought he should tell Father Jacob about the seafood incident, but Otis needed a second chance in life. Hopefully, this opportunity would be successful.

CHAPTER SEVEN

September 2013

The cores and the covers needed to assemble the golf balls arrived at Port Everglades from San Juan, Puerto Rico, on a cargo ship named the MS Progress. The Progress departed San Juan twice weekly and stopped in Havana, Nassau, and Miami before docking at Port Everglades. Then it turned around and headed back to San Juan using a reverse itinerary. Unfortunately, the cores and covers did not arrive simultaneously and often didn't come in the same shipment as the Bibles. That meant Jim Mann needed to make recurrent runs to Fort Lauderdale to gather all the pieces for the factory.

It was a lengthy process training the workers to do their jobs. They had to insert the cores inside the covers and seal them perfectly. Once the workers began assembly, they packaged six dozen balls daily or thirty dozen weekly. The golf balls that weren't perfect would become X-Outs and be sold to local driving ranges for minimal profit.

The golf balls were complicated to make. First, the cores were centered within mold cavities, then the moylyn covers were placed around them and held together by pins. Molten thermoplastic was injected into the moylyn, and the heat and pressure caused the material to join with the center and form dimples. The pins were retracted as the plastic cooled and hardened, and the finished balls were removed.

Rough spots and the seams on the molded covers were abraded. Then, two coats of paint were applied to the balls uniformly. Next, they were stamped with St. Max's logo and sealed with a clear coat of polyamide epoxy for high sheen and scuff resistance. Finally, the balls were placed in large dryers and packaged in boxes for shipment.

Every adult church member except for Willy and Otis and the four directors, Phil Carson (head chef), Bill Johnson (head of maintenance), Bob Butler (head of security), and Jim Mann (head of transportation), pitched in and were paid equally: $500 per week. The jobs helped form comradery among the church members. Lifelong friendships resulted, all part of Father Jacob's master plan.

Although not very comfortable, the factory workers used plastic tables and chairs. The first team centered the cores inside the mold cavity and pinned them on the moylyn covers. The balls were then passed to another group to inject the molten thermoplastic. The third group lightly sanded the rough edges and seams, and the last painted the balls.

Once the balls were completed, they would be turned over to Mel Smith and Keith Malone for quality control and the final touches were applied. The two engineers would delicately puncture tiny holes inside the dimples. That was a crucial part of Tommy Williams' creative design to make the balls fly further with better accuracy.

Smith and Malone lived in two apartments on the top floor of the three-story complex next to St. Max's church, but they were rarely seen because that's the way Tommy wanted it. They completed the golf ball process in a vacant apartment next to their own. The church members knew two people were finalizing the golf ball production but had never met them. Some parishioners took offense to that setup. There was plenty of room in the makeshift factory, so why would they be allowed to do their jobs in the comfort of a three-bedroom apartment? Did they believe they were better than the rest?

Smith and Malone would then turn the golf balls over to Deacon Ollie, who would place them in boxes with St. Max's logo etched on the cover and seal them with cellophane. Golf Country Superstore donated the raw materials for boxing, sealing, and shipping to the parish.

Father Jacob's goal was to have 500 dozen balls ready by Christmas. CEO Vero said the boxes must be at the distribution centers by November 1st to make that happen. The intent was to have Otis on the road with the old U-Haul by October 20th. Working overtime, the assemblers easily met that deadline; however, Smith and Malone's finishing touches slowed the process. No one knew why other church members weren't allowed to help the engineers puncture holes in the dimples. In fact, no one except Smith, Malone, and Tommy Williams was even permitted to enter the apartment. Many in the congregation wanted to tell Father Jacob that they felt slighted, but they believed it wasn't their job to do so.

*****

Bill Johnson and Jim Mann reinforced the truck's bed with steel panels and replaced the tires and transmission. Plus, they added a new fuel pump, radiator, and hoses. The parts for the repairs were costly, but Father Jacob didn't have to pay for labor. As with the last truck purchased to make runs to Port Everglades, Jim painted the old U-Haul white and then embedded St. Max's logo on both sides.

On October 19th, Otis was raring to go! Willy decided that riding with Otis on the first cross-country adventure was best to ensure everything went as planned. The truck was loaded with all 500 boxes of balls, and there was plenty of space for more. If the balls sold successfully, the truck would be filled to capacity during future trips. If they were all purchased, St. Max's would gross $17,500. But subtracting fuel costs and paying $500 per week to the assemblers and even more to Smith and Malone, the parish would lose money. Willy did the math as Otis pulled out of the North Palm Beach airport. He shook his head in disbelief. This project didn't make sense. It was insanity! Couldn't Father Jacob see that?!

But Willy Banks was the only one who seemed to be bothered. Everyone in the parish was high-fiving, waving to Otis as he turned north on the Bee Line Highway. Otis smiled and saluted in return.

CHAPTER EIGHT

October 2013

Each level of St. Max's apartments had six three-bedroom and two-bathroom units. The entire ground floor and four flats on the second floor were occupied by church families, meaning twelve of the eighteen units provided living spaces. Deacon Ollie lived with Father Jacob in the church basement until the priest suggested he move into a top-floor apartment next to the flat that was being used to finalize the golf balls. The deacon would stay there until the apartment was needed for more homeless folks.

Mel Smith owned a black Porsche 918 Spyder, and Keith Malone drove a deep blue Hennessey Venom GT. Both engineers kept the vehicles in an airplane hangar they bought together on the other side of the airport from the church. Between the two parked cars was their co-owned Cessna Citation X, the fastest private jet globally. Equipped with two high-powered Rolls-Royce turbojets, the plane could reach 717 miles per hour.

Before Willy departed with Otis, he asked Jim Mann to repair a small pedestrian section in the Sweetbay Natural Area north of the airport. There was a paved loop trail off the beaten path where a boardwalk had collapsed during a recent storm. Sweetbay was only a mile or so from the apartments, so Jim could easily walk there. Bob Butler, Father Jacob's head of security, was bored and asked Jim if he could use some help. Jim was thrilled to have some company, and the two headed to the boardwalk early on Wednesday, the 22nd of October.

They returned late afternoon and saw a shiny black Porsche rolling down Aviation Road. The driver looked like one of the new golf ball engineers, but neither Jim nor Bob could believe it. Why would the guy make a pittance working for St. Max's if he could afford a luxury sportscar? Jim and Bob decided to follow the car. They were tired from a long workday but could still jog and keep out of sight.

Mel Smith opened the hangar door and was greeted by none other than Keith Malone, who was waxing down a Hennessey Venom GT. A Cessna Citation X was next to the car, looking like an eagle ready to take flight.

Bob and Jim glanced at each other with their mouths wide open. "What the hell?" asked Bob timidly. "Those are the men we ran into when we were looking for Deacon Ollie. The deacon introduced us and said they were hired as consultants to oversee the golf ball manufacturing. Do you remember their names?"

"Yeah, I'm pretty sure they're Mel Smith and Keith Martin. No, wait a minute, I mean Keith Malone."

"You don't suppose this is Mel and Keith's hangar, do you?" replied Jim.

"Couldn't be. How could they afford those cars? Both cost nearly a million dollars! And if that's their jet, it's probably in the range of twenty million!"

"Your right," said Jim. "Those cars and jet couldn't be theirs!" Silently stunned, Jim tossed around several thoughts in his head. "But if they do own them, I wonder if Father Jacob knows about it."

Bob shook his head. "No way! He certainly would be appalled if he knew that his two engineers were multimillionaires, seeing he has dedicated his life to helping the poor and homeless."

"Do you think we should tell Father?" asked Jim hesitantly.

"Well, I think he has a right to know. I'm the head of security, so I will be the one to tell him."

"I don't think this is a security issue, but I'll be happy to let you do it. I only hope Father doesn't fire Smith and Malone. The whole golf ball project could end up down the drain."

"Yeah, you're right," responded Bob. "Maybe this is none of our business, or anybody else's, for that matter. Perhaps we should keep this our secret."

"Yeah, I think so, too. Let's get back. I'm getting hungry!"

CHAPTER NINE

October 2013

The drive to Atlanta was supposed to take ten hours, given that the old U-Haul's top speed was sixty miles per hour. But factoring that the truck only got four miles to a gallon meant that Otis had to exit twice for gas. And furthermore, each fill-up had to include pastries! At each stop, his body's fuel was a small thermos of coffee and four apple fritters. Thus, the filling station needed a Dunkin Donuts within 300 yards. He was determined to navigate the entire trip west on only leavened fried dough and caffeine. The ten-hour driving time was one thing, but the fuel refilling and potty breaks added another two hours. Otis' large stomach began growling just north of Macon, and his focus on the road faded. After swerving over the center line and nearly ramming three passing cars, Willy ordered him to pull off the freeway. He took over the wheel for the final hour, and the brothers checked into Motel Six at 8:00 pm. From that point on, Willy would do much of the driving.

The drops at the Golf Country Superstore distribution centers were easy. The truck was backed up to the large shipping platform, and GCS employees did the rest. It never consumed more than twenty minutes in each of the four cities to unload 125 boxes. Otis and Willy were always back on the road sooner than they anticipated. Otis couldn't wait to find the next Dunkin Donuts.

Although the truck had a new transmission, radiator, hoses, and fuel pump, the engine began pinging, and the chassis rattled incessantly as the U-Haul approached Monteagle, Tennessee. Willy told Otis they needed to slow down because the truck was too old to maintain full-throttle speed up and down the Appalachian Mountains. He was worried about what might happen when they reached the Rockies. Unfortunately, the U-Haul succumbed to the odds before arriving in Missouri and had to be towed to an all-night truck stop in Mascoutah, Illinois, where mechanics adjusted the ignition timing and replaced the spark plugs and wires.

Willy was embarrassed when he called Father Jacob to report that the repair bill would be $1,500, including the tow. And the fuel costs seemed to be much higher than what they had in the budget. But Father just laughed and told him everything was okay. Before departing from North Palm Beach, the credit card he gave Willy had a good-sized limit, and they need not worry. Father Jacob reminded Willy that the profits from the golf balls would cover the costs. Willy wasn't so sure!

Using midgrade fuel and slowing down to fifty miles per hour increased the mileage to seven per gallon. But the higher cost of the fuel probably offset the gain in mileage. Regardless, Otis and Willy successfully dropped 125 dozen balls in St. Louis, Denver, and San Francisco well before the deadline. Golf Country Superstore could now sell them for Christmas presents to slicers, hookers, and hackers everywhere.

Willy was not looking forward to bringing the U-Haul back to Florida. He was told to wait in San Francisco for instructions on the return trip. Father Jacob may have some places to stop on the way back. Willy was confused about where those locations might be and, worse, how far out of the way he and Otis may have to go to get there.

Shea Hansen owned and lived in a four-unit apartment building on Vallejo near the Lyon Street Steps with a gorgeous view of San Francisco Bay and Alcatraz Island. Looking west past the Presidio, the residents also had a glimpse of the Golden Gate Bridge and, directly below them, a peek at the touristy Fisherman's Wharf. Incredibly, none of the apartments were currently leased. Perhaps because the rent was $6,500 per month. When full-timers weren't living there, Shea rented them out as AirBnb units at

$1,200 a night. Willy was surprised when Shea called and offered him and Otis the opportunity to stay for free until Father Jacob gave instructions for the return trip home. Like Ursula Vero, the Golf Country CEO, Shea must be a good Catholic!

But how in the world did Father know her?

*****

November 2013

Father told Willy and Otis to rest in San Francisco for a couple of weeks before making the long haul east. Otis was thrilled to death, but Willy was apprehensive. He didn't believe Shea was offering the ultra-luxury apartment for nothing. Maybe it was discounted, but Father must be paying something for the rental. Willy didn't want to eat up all the profits meant for the poor and homeless. Regardless, the Banks brothers did as they were told.

To avoid expensive parking costs in the city center, Father told Willy and Otis to leave the truck in the long-term area at the airport. They dropped off the U-Haul, took the BART back to the city, and walked a few miles to the apartment. During their two-week stay in the City by the Bay, Willy and Otis visited all the tourist sites: Alcatraz, the Golden Gate Bridge, Coit Tower, Lombard Avenue, and the rest. Because Otis loved seafood, they ate at Fisherman's Wharf every night. But after one day of hiking up and down the streets of San Francisco, Otis had enough. He and Willy would ride the streetcar or take an Uber to their destination from then on. They were racking up quite a bill, but every time Willy called Father, the good priest told them they would be reimbursed. No problem! Have a great time, he would say to them.

On the last day in San Francisco, Willy saw a Golf Country Superstore across North Point Street from Ghirardelli Square. He went inside to see if they had begun selling the balls. Sure enough, dozens were displayed on a large table in front of a poster: ***"Exceptional Golf Balls for Christmas! The golfers in your family will love the design and have a blast on***

the course! And most importantly, all proceeds will go to helping the poor and homeless! Only $35 a dozen!"

Willy decided to help St. Max's cause and buy a dozen for Eric Mann, who was becoming an exceptional young golfer. He paid the cashier and called for an Uber. Otis wanted a bucket of shrimp at Bubba Gumps for dinner, but Shea had told them she was cooking Thai food for the boys on their last day. Otis worried that the curry would be too hot, and he would have stomach pains all the way back to Florida.

Shea's apartment building had a metal detector monitored by a security guard at the entrance. She wanted no weapons brought into the building and had signs posted clearly on the doors. Willy was surprised when the alarm rang as he entered with Eric's golf balls. The security guard insisted that he inspect the box even though the cellophane was tightly sealed around it. Being an ex-cop, Willy didn't hesitate to let the guard open the package.

Obviously, there was no weapon in the box. After closely inspecting one of the balls, the guard said the machine usually does not go off unless an unfamiliar item is detected. Cell phones, watches, and jewelry never trigger it. The guard asked Willy if he could cut open the ball to check the inside.

"Sure!" exclaimed Willy. "Go for it! I just hope my young friend Eric understands why he is only getting eleven balls!"

"Oh yeah, sorry about that." The guard motioned Willy and Otis to follow him into a maintenance room. On a table in the room was a combination vise designed to securely clamp all shapes of objects. He put the ball inside the grips and braced it tightly. Then he removed a coping saw from a drawer and carefully cut into the golf ball's moylyn cover. Soon the saw contacted the solid core, and the blade broke.

"Damn," said the guard. "What is this ball made of? It busted my blade, and I don't have another one!"

"Well, as I remember, I think it's some sort of cast alloy made from several metals, though I'm not sure what metals were used. And I'm pretty sure that inside the shell is a liquid."

"That alloy concoction must be setting off the alarm. It's something not recognized by the metal detector's data bank. You better leave the balls out here because I don't think Miss Hansen would allow something that sets off the alarm into the building."

"I understand. But I'm really curious about what that alloy is made from. If it sets off your alarm, chances are good that it would set off an alarm at airport security. And plenty of golfers check their clubs and balls when they travel. If their bags are removed before being loaded, it would be bad for our business. Is there a hardware store nearby? Perhaps they would have a metal identification testing kit."

"Hey, now that I think about it, I'm sure I've seen one of those kits at Electro Eddy's. It's a small store a few blocks away on California Street. Suppose you have them give me a written okay that the golf ball isn't made from a dangerous metal that could explode into shrapnel or, God forbid, some sort of nuclear device. Then I can let you through." He winked at Willy. "How does that sound?"

"Well, thanks! That helps a lot. I'll Google the store's location and be back as soon as possible." Willy then turned to his brother. "Otis, go to the apartment and ask Shea to hold off on dinner for a while."

Otis nodded, and Willy headed to Electro Eddy's.

*****

Eddy Gambo owned Electro Eddy's. The store was 500 square feet at the most. He was the owner, operator, and only employee of the business. Eddy wore a stained pink t-shirt, white cutoff corduroy shorts, and brown flip-flops. He sat on a stool at the counter fixing some sort of gadget with a tiny screwdriver. His ultra-thick glasses made his eyes appear to be the size of tangerines. Willy was pretty sure Eddy couldn't see anything without the spectacles attached to his head. Without looking up, Eddy said subtly, "Can I help you, dude?"

Willy wasn't sure he wanted to do business with Eddy until he noticed a crooked picture frame on the wall. Inside the protective glass was a page cut out of a yearbook from the Galileo Academy of Science and

Technology. Seems Eddy Gambo was not only the valedictorian but also voted Most Likely to Succeed!

"Wow!" exclaimed Willy as he pointed to the picture on the wall. Then, speaking rhetorically, he added, "So, you must have been quite the student, I do say! Galileo is well-known as a great high school. I've even heard about it in Florida!"

Eddy didn't even look up from the gadget he was fixing. He nodded gently, then quietly replied, "You have, have you? So, can I help you?"

"Where did you go to college?" asked Willy excitedly. "You must have had offers from the Ivy League schools, Stanford, Cal-Berkeley, and the rest of the top universities, right?!"

"Sure did," said Eddy. "But I chose to skip the fluff and just get to work, so I opened this store after high school. Glad I did, too. Instead of spending six or eight more years of boredom in the classroom, I now skateboard in the Presidio, surf at Pacific Beach, and play acoustic guitar in my flat each night. Which, by the way, happens to be right above us." Eddy pointed to the ceiling, and Willy instinctively looked up. "And, by the way, I'm closing soon, so please tell me what you need."

"Oh, yeah." Willy handed Eddy the golf ball. "I understand that you have a metal identification kit in your store. Can you tell me what kind of material this is underneath the cover?"

Eddy scraped off the moylyn cover from the core, rolled it around in his hands, then placed it in a vise over some dirty rags. He then went into a closet and returned with a kit full of tools, gadgets, and chemicals. He poured three chemicals into a one-ounce bottle, swirled it gently, and then carefully dropped some of the solution onto the golf ball's core. Magically, a dark blue spot was displayed on the metal. "The ball has aluminum, which I suspected when I felt it."

"Aluminum," stated Willy, baffled. "Well, okay, but why did that set off the security alarm at our apartment? Aluminum is a common element. The guard said the alarm system didn't have the metal in its database."

"Hold your horses, dude! I'm not done yet!" Eddy then mixed up three different chemicals and dropped a tiny bit onto the core. Nothing happened. Without looking at Willy, Eddy said, "There's no titanium. That is weird. Most golf balls today have titanium in them, don't they? I'm not a golf connoisseur by any means, but I've read that many balls are made with titanium."

"So, how does this test work?" Willy was confused as he didn't understand what Eddy was doing.

"I have to mix various solutions to test for certain metals. Basically, it's a process of elimination. Each solution I make can only test for one element."

"So this could take hours, right? I mean, how many different kinds of metals are there?"

"You mean, besides stainless steels, low alloy steels, nickel and cobalt alloys, plated coatings, brasses, and bronzes?"

"Huh?!" Willy was perplexed. Eddy laughed, and Willy grinned. He was happy to see some kind of emotion from the educational superstar.

"Okay, dude, so here are the elements I'm testing for: aluminum, carbon, chromium, cobalt, copper, gold, iron, lead, magnesium, magnesium silicide, manganese, molybdenum, nickel, silver, sulfur, titanium, tungsten, vanadium, and zinc. That's all of them, in alphabetical order, I might add!" Eddy laughed again.

Willy was impressed! Eddy was a genius! How could he mix solutions, test, and spit out all that information without referring to anything? Willy didn't think he could do that himself, even if he followed it step-by-step on YouTube!

Eddy mixed solutions and tested for each metal on the list. When he was finished, he glanced up at Willy. He stated, "It's a magnesium alloy consisting of aluminum, manganese, zinc, and some strange metal that I can't identify. And, by the way, where did you get this? I'm not much of a golfer, but this isn't the kind of stuff generally found inside golf balls."

"Uh, well, it was made in a church back in Florida."

"Complex metal golf balls made in a church? Right! And Teslas are produced in Elon Musk's grandmother's basement!" responded Eddy sarcastically. "This golf ball is certainly illegal for sports use if you ask me."

"What the hell does that mean?" Willy was dumbfounded.

"It means the alloy used in the core is made from military-grade material. And, the unknown metal is extremely ferromagnetic."

"What does that mean? Ferromagnetic."

"Oh, come on, dude!" replied Eddy, spittle shooting out between his lips. "Did you learn nothing in your high school science classes?! Ferromagnetics are substances with abnormally high magnetic permeability, a definite saturation point, and appreciable residual attraction and hysteresis. They are also strongly attracted to both poles of magnets. Contrastly, paramagnetic materials are weakly attracted to a single pole. Ya dig?"

Willy didn't understand a word of Eddy's explanation and wasn't about to admit it! "So, well, yes, that makes sense. But is there anything else about the ball you think makes it illegal?"

"Yep! The core has pin-sized air holes all around it. What are the holes for? I'm guessing they don't go all the way through to the center, or the liquid in the middle would leak out. I'm assuming they are short holes used to relieve pressure on the metal alloy if it expands in the heat, like on a hot day or something. Trust me, this is advanced technology. It wasn't made in a church!"

"Well, Eddy, you're wrong about that! The people who assembled this ball are homeless and have little education. I watched them make it!"

"Sorry, man, but you're wrong. This alloy is used in supersonic fighter jets. You need to watch *Top Gun* and learn something from Tom Cruise! You're lying to me, dude! This golf ball wasn't made in a church by homeless folks!"

"Eddy, you're obviously a brilliant man," stated Willy firmly. Then showing some anger, he needed to stand up for his friends back home. "But you are the one who's wrong!"

Eddy shook his head in disgust. He had had enough of Willy's stubbornness. Why was the man even here? It was time to close shop and head to the Presidio. "I can assure you that this golf ball is unusual. How's that sound? Now, if there's something you would like to buy or have me fix, what would it be? It's closing time, dude."

Although he was shocked, Willy knew it was time to leave. But he needed one thing. "Would you please write a note for a security guard at my apartment and tell him that this golf ball is not a weapon?"

Eddy chuckled again. Then he scribbled on the back of a napkin he got from Starbucks that morning. He wrote on the coffee-stained, wrinkled paper with blueberry scone crumbs embedded, "This golf ball is not a weapon – Eddy Gambo, CEO."

Willy chortled at the CEO part of the signature, then thanked Eddy. But as he turned to leave, Eddy coughed and cleared his voice. "That will be twenty dollars, sir."

Willy was stunned but didn't want to argue. He opened his wallet and gave Eddy a crisp Andrew Jackson. When Eddy didn't say thank you, Willy noted sarcastically, "You're welcome . . . dude!"

*****

"Eddy Gambo is a nut case!" laughed Shea. "He even made the front page of the *San Francisco Chronicle* when he turned down full rides to Harvard and Stanford. What high school valedictorian does that? Skip college? Huh?"

They were eating Pad Thai in Shea's apartment. Willy loved the stir-fried rice noodle dish, especially the scrambled egg and peanuts. On the other hand, Otis picked out the shrimp and gave the rest to Bella, the cat. He asked if Shea had any Hamburger Helper in the pantry.

"I admit that Eddy is a weird guy," replied Willy, "but he seems pretty sharp when it comes to metals." Willy told Shea about the ball's core being a military-grade alloy. When he finished, he wished he hadn't said anything about it. Willy really didn't know Shea, and as an ex-cop, he knew better than to give out information to random people.

A few minutes after finishing dinner, Willy received a call from Father Jacob. The priest said he wanted them to stop in New Mexico on the way back to Florida. Willy and Otis were leaving in the morning. Their route would now be south on I-5 to Bakersfield and then cut over to I-40 for the eastern trip home.

Father didn't say where in New Mexico, but he would tell the boys before they entered Arizona. He also didn't say why they would stop in The Land of Enchantment. Strange!

CHAPTER TEN

November 2013

St. Max's golf balls sold out quickly throughout the United States. By the time Black Friday rolled around, you couldn't find them in a store. People buying Christmas presents were delighted they could find something to put under the tree that helped provide money for the poor and homeless.

Ursula Vero called from her Manhattan office and encouraged Father Jacob to produce more balls. She was confident they would sell. Father explained that the parts shipments used to make the balls were slow, and he didn't have enough employees to assemble them. Ursula offered to send some of her factory workers to Florida to increase production; however, she wanted a cut of the profits.

According to online reviews, golfers who had purchased the first few dozen balls in Georgia had seen a marked improvement in their game. Plus, the ball's cover never seemed to scratch or get dinged up. Miss Vero saw the balls' potential skyrocketing Golf Country Superstore stock prices if she could get a piece of the action. Ursula would undoubtedly be the queen of Wall Street by the end of the year!

Meanwhile, Willy and Otis were shacking up in a dumpy six-room motel in Blister Rock, New Mexico. The town's population was seven! Two families. That was it! How the dusty pit stop received articles of incorporation was beyond Willy's imagination! Milton Davis was the mayor, chief of police, and owner of Milton's Service Station, all wrapped into one. Morton Davis operated Morton's Route 66 Motel of Glory, which was about as glorious as ketchup spilled on a white shirt.

*****

The night before

The previous night, the boys slept in Holy Spirit Catholic Church on the north edge of Clines Corners, New Mexico. The U-Haul's engine started to sputter when they accelerated onto I-40 the following day. Twenty miles later, the Ford F-650 blew a head gasket. Otis managed to plod the truck to the SR3 exit but couldn't make it uphill to the stop sign. Fortunately, Milton's was just around the corner, so Willy pushed while Otis steered in neutral.

Holy Spirit Catholic Church was a tiny structure built from mud, sand, and straw adobe bricks in the early 1850s. The shape resembled a cruciform, and the church had a small steeple. Inside were glorious stained-glass windows, definitely the highlight of the building. There were eight rows of pews separated by an aisle. The church could hold ninety-six people if they were packed in well. The parish served a rural area of New Mexico, and most of its members worked on ranches.

Father Jacob directed Otis and Willy to go to Holy Spirit Church. Father never said why, but he explained that Holy Spirit's priest, Father Michael, was a friend and would be expecting them. They arrived late on November 5th. No motels were around, so Father Michael offered to let them sleep on the padded pews of the mini cathedral. He fed them green chili stew and Frito pie that he cooked himself. Otis ate three helpings.

In the morning, after munching down a breakfast burrito with Piñon coffee, Father Michael asked for the package that Father Jacob said was in the truck. Willy was confused by Father Michael's request and said he was certain the container was empty. He knew of no such package.

"Father Jacob told me there is a hidden compartment behind the front seat," said Michael. "It's on the floor in the back of the cab."

"Oh, that," replied Willy. "I thought it was a tool chest for the truck. So, you're saying there is a package inside?"

"That's what Father Jacob told me, son."

Willy went out and opened the compartment. There were no tools whatsoever. However, there were four square, twelve-by-twelve-inch boxes wrapped in brown paper. Willy grabbed one from the chest and handed it to Father Michael. He wondered why Father Jacob hadn't mentioned them.

"Thank you, Mr. Banks."

"You can call me Willy, Father. Any chance you could tell me what's in the box?"

"Oh my!" exclaimed Father Michael. "You don't know?!" He opened the box and removed a solid, crystal-clear glass cross with beveled edges. It featured an intricate Jesus sculpture encased inside to give a three-dimensional effect, and it sat on a wooden base about four inches thick. "It's a Christmas gift from Father Jacob."

"Well, okay," responded Willy. "That sounds like our priest! He would have us drive out of our way from San Francisco to deliver presents for him. Father is a very kind-hearted man!"

"Yes, indeed he is, Willy. I've known him for most of my life. He has friends everywhere who he would give his right arm to help. You're lucky that he's your pastor!"

*****

Mayor and Chief of Police Milton Davis knocked on Room One at Morton's Route 66 Motel of Glory. Otis rubbed his eyes as he opened the door. He had slept in that morning, and now it was close to noon. Willy was exercising by hiking several laps around town. Blister Rock wasn't known for its fitness facilities!

"Mr. Banks," muttered Milton, "perhaps you should sit down, sir."

"OMG!" blurted Otis. "This must be serious. The only time anyone ever called me Mr. Banks was when my teachers sent me down to the principal's office. Okay, okay, come on in!" There were no chairs in the motel rooms so Otis and Milton sat on the edge of the bed.

"Your truck has a blown head gasket. It will cost you $3,000 for me to repair it. We need to get parts from Albuquerque, so it will take three days to finish. You want me to get started?"

"Hmmm. Well, okay, I guess. But I should ask my brother first."

Just then, Willy walked in with beads of sweat rolling down his forehead. "Oh, hi, Mayor. I'm assuming you're here with news of our truck repair."

"Please call me Milton. And yes, I have an estimate for you. I was telling your brother that you blew a head gasket. It will take three days to repair, and the cost is $3,000."

"$3,000!! Holy crap! The damn truck ain't worth half that!"

"So, I'm guessing you don't want to get it fixed, right? In that case, our expert analysis was only $350. We don't accept credit cards."

"Hold on!" Willy cried out. "That's highway robbery! And you don't take credit cards? Say what?! Is there even an ATM in this town?!"

"No, sir. And by the way, Morton doesn't accept credit cards, either. How will you pay for the motel room when you check out?"

When he and Otis checked in, Willy remembered that Morton had never asked for a credit card. That was strange, but he was too wound up to think about it. He told Milton that he would give him an answer shortly. The mayor/police chief left and went back to the garage.

"How much cash do you have, Otis?" asked Willy.

Otis fumbled through his pockets and peeked into his wallet. "Ah, I got $6.14."

"Well, that's just great! I only have $43. The room costs $28.64 with tax. That leaves us with a little over twenty bucks!" Willy paced the room for a few moments. "Okay, I need to call Father Jacob. We are way over budget with this trip!"

Willy punched in the parish number, and oddly, Mel Smith answered. "Willy! What's up, man?! Where are you two?"

Willy paused for a moment. He hardly knew Mel Smith, yet the engineer spoke like they were close friends. "Why are you answering the church's landline? Oh, forget it. I don't have time. We're stuck in the middle of nowhere in New Mexico. The truck blew a head gasket, and the repair shop wants $3,000 to fix it. In cash, no less! And first, we ain't got $3,000. And second, our options are limited. The U-Haul won't run, and there's nowhere to take it if it did! We could probably tow it back to Albuquerque, but that might cost even more. Don't know what to do! Can I talk to Father Jacob, please?!"

"No need. Leave the truck and catch a ride to Albuquerque airport. Then fly home."

"That will be expensive! I think I should get Father's approval first!"

"Don't sweat it. The sale of golf balls will cover it."

"That's impossible! I've done the math. We're losing money big time!"

"Your math's incorrect. Hey, I got to go. I'll see you whenever you get here!" Mel hung up, leaving Willy dazed.

"So, what's up, Bro?" asked Otis quietly.

"That's the question of the day, Otis."

*****

"A ride to the airport and your truck is mine?!" asked Milton incredulously. "Seriously?" Willy nodded affirmatively and shook hands with Milton. It was a done deal.

Willy snatched the three remaining Christmas gifts from the cab of the U-Haul and climbed aboard Morton's pickup. Not a word was spoken during the entire trip to the airport. He wanted Morton to know he wasn't happy with the deal, and the "silent treatment" appeared to be his best option to demonstrate his displeasure.

Two hours later, Willy checked the wrapped boxes and the boys' suitcases to Palm Beach International. He and Otis played a game of Yahtzee while waiting at the gate for their American Airlines flight to Dallas. After a quick change of planes at DFW, they arrived in Palm Beach a few minutes past midnight.

Their suitcases were delivered via the baggage carousel in a matter of minutes. The gifts for Father Jacob's priesthood friends were nowhere in sight.

CHAPTER ELEVEN

November 2013

"Confiscated! Why?"

It was almost 1:00 am, and Willy was standing in front of the American Airlines baggage service counter, trying to get what seemed like an easy answer. He would have to file a lost luggage claim for the three wrapped Christmas presents that never made it to Palm Beach.

"I'm not sure, sir," the customer service agent politely replied. "It just says on my computer that the three packages were not allowed onboard the aircraft. TSA agents took them after they set off the alarm going through security.

"They were crosses of Jesus! Are you kidding me?! Can I please talk to a supervisor?" It had been a long couple of days for Willy, and he was overly tired. His fatigue was getting the best of him.

"I'm sorry, sir, I really am! But our supervisor doesn't come on duty until 7:00 am. I'm the only one working tonight."

"Alright. I'll be back at 7:00 am." Willy turned, grabbed Otis, who was napping in a plastic chair, and walked briskly out the door. He was going to call for an Uber to save money, but he was too wasted to wait for one. He and Otis flagged down a taxi and were home by 2:00 am. They were sound asleep by 2:05.

*****

A few hours later

"It's okay!" Father Jacob patted Willy on the back. "They were just fun gifts for a few of my friends from the seminary days. You don't need to go back to the airport and speak to a supervisor."

Willy slept in the clothes he had worn on the airplane the previous night. They were wrinkled when he got up at the crack of dawn, but he didn't care what he looked like when he returned to the baggage claim office. But first, he needed to tell Father Jacob what happened. Willy had hustled to St. Max's Church and ran into the priest in the parking lot. Father was returning from a morning jog. Willy explained the situation to Father Jacob, who showed very little emotion. He certainly wasn't mad. But then again, Willy knew that good priests were always slow to anger.

"Father Michael showed me the glass cross with Jesus inside. It was expensive, and the other three shouldn't have been confiscated. I'm guessing a wayward TSA agent thought they would make great, free Christmas presents for his family!"

"Calm down, son," said Father Jacob with a relaxed smile. "You mustn't think bad of people. They were just things. Things can be replaced. Now, you look exhausted. Please go back to sleep. You did a marvelous job getting the golf balls to the distribution centers, Willy! Our entire congregation thanks you for that!"

"Well, okay, Father. But there is something I would like to chat with you about. Perhaps later this morning, if that works for you?"

"Why, most certainly, son! I'm always available for my parishioners!"

Willy smiled and returned to his house at PGA National. How would he approach Father with the financial concerns the golf ball project created?

*****

An hour later

Mel Smith and Keith Malone filed a flight plan, and at 8:00 am, the Cessna Citation X took off from North Palm Beach County Airport. Traveling at a cruising speed of 700 miles per hour, the world's fastest subsonic corporate jet landed at Albuquerque International Sunport at 8:40 am local time. TSA Supervisor Mark Renko was waiting for them when they entered his office at 9:00 am. Keith had called beforehand and set up the appointment.

Sitting spitefully on Mark's desk were three solid, crystal-clear glass crosses with beveled edges. All had an intricate Jesus sculpture encased inside and were perched on four-inch-thick wooden bases. Three opened and now empty boxes were on the floor next to the desk.

Mel walked up to Mark and shook his hand with a firm grip. "Long time no see, buddy! How do you like the wild west?"

"Beats the Washington rat race," replied Mark with a vague grin to Mel and Keith. "I own a hot air balloon, PXG golf clubs, and a Yamaha Raptor 700R all-terrain vehicle to keep me busy when I ain't bogged down with this damn job."

"I thought you came out here to retire," said Keith, chuckling. "But here you are, the head of the TSA for Albuquerque. What's up with that?!"

"My wife thought I needed a second life to offset all my fun!"

"Well, it's good to see you again," said Mel as he patted Mark on the back. "I couldn't believe our good luck when we researched and saw that you were the head of security over here."

"Yeah, okay. So, what the heck are these statues, and why are you here to pick them up? They were checked by a man named Willy Banks. And, by the way, the name Willy Banks is very familiar to me. Is he the same deputy sheriff from Okeechobee County that kept our country from a total disaster back in the eighties?"

"Yep, one and the same. Your memory is still very sharp, Mark. Perhaps a return to the bureau would make your wife happy!"

"Won't happen. So, tell me. What exactly are these statues, and why were they in Willy Banks' possession? Then, pray tell, why are you here to pick them up?!"

"They are precisely what they look like—expensive Christmas gifts for priests. Willy is now retired and drives a truck for our pastor, Father Jacob, back in Florida. These were presents for three of Father's seminary friends. Unfortunately, Willy's truck broke down near here, and he had to fly back to Palm Beach. Because these were special gifts, Keith and I offered to come here and get them. We plan to deliver them to the priests after we leave here."

"Okay. Well, first question. Why didn't this Father Jacob just ship the statues to his friends? Seems it would be much cheaper than hiring someone to drive across the country and deliver them in person."

"We make golf balls at the church and sell them to raise money for the homeless and poor. Willy delivered dozens of balls to the Golf Country Superstore warehouses in various cities. He finished and was heading back to Florida, so Father thought he could hand-deliver the presents himself."

"So, second question." Mark's face became serious, and he stared at Mel and Keith. "Why haven't you asked me why I confiscated the statues? I would think that would be your first question of me."

Mel laughed, "Because when the boxes didn't arrive in Palm Beach, we did a little digging to find out why they probably weren't allowed on the airplane. We guessed that the statues contained an element that wouldn't be recognized by your metal detector. We figured that the embedded Jesus form must be made from a new kind of alloy. We're sure that's what triggered your alarm."

"And when did you do all this research? Mr. Banks wouldn't have known the packages were confiscated until he arrived in Palm Beach around midnight. Yet, eight hours later, you were on your personal jet to Albuquerque. So, while most Floridians were sleeping, you made an 'educated guess' as to why the statues were confiscated. And, you also found that I was the TSA supe here. Have you given up sleeping? That story sounds a little fishy, wouldn't you say?"

"Oh, come on, Mark! Really?! Our friend Google can find answers in a matter of seconds! You know that! Anyway, Father Jacob jogs each morning just before dawn. Willy drove to the church to tell Father what had happened. He said he would return to the airport and find the status of the statues. But Father told him not to worry. It was no big deal.

"Keith and I go to morning mass most days. Today, Father Jacob told us about the statues after the prayer service. I have a brother in Los Angeles that I haven't seen for a year, so I decided to kill two birds with one stone. I could fly out here and pick up the statues, then go to LA and see my bro. Keith decided he needed a vacation, so he tagged along. He'll be sipping Mai Tais on the beach in Malibu this afternoon. Shoot, Mark, if you've got some personal days coming, you're more than welcome to join us!"

Mark laughed. "Yeah, as if that is going to happen! Okay, listen. You two were the CIA's and FBI's top consultants for aeronautical advice. Looking at your Citation X, you've obviously made a haul working in the private sector. I can't help but think you're BSing me a bit, but at this point, I don't care or even want to know why. You're good, honest guys, and I trust you both. Go ahead and take the statues and enjoy your beach vacation. But when I come to see you in Florida, I fully expect you to comp me three rounds of golf at Sawgrass!"

"You're on, buddy! We look forward to your visit!"

Ten minutes later, the Citation X rose west above the scattered clouds. Mel waited until the jet was out of Mark Renko's sight before banking to the east. The air traffic controller began to panic and squawked repetitive orders into his mic. The filed flight plan was for the next stop at Los Angeles International Airport, and the Citation was heading in the wrong direction.

Malibu Beach would have to wait for another time.

CHAPTER TWELVE

November 2013 (The next day)

"You did what?!" screeched Tommy Williams. Deacon Ollie lowered his head in embarrassment. "Those are my premium balls. We planned to sell them directly to professional golfers and make a mint!"

"Yes, I know. I'm very sorry," said Ollie dejectedly. "What else can I say?"

"Well, for one thing—"

Mel cut Tommy off. You don't scold a deacon for making a simple error. "That's enough! It was a mistake, that's all. It's not the end of the world!"

Mel and Keith made stops at Holy Family Catholic Church in Dallas, Texas, St. Joe's in Jackson, Mississippi, and St. Mary's in Augusta, Georgia, before returning to Palm Beach late last night. They hand-delivered Father Jacob's gifts to his priest friends, who were overwhelmed with joy at Jacob's thoughtfulness. There were still two Sundays before Advent, but receiving a Christmas gift anytime during the year was special.

Mel and Keith were tired from their previous day's cross-country travel adventure. Still, they met in Deacon Ollie's apartment for coffee and donuts at the request of Tommy Williams. He was storming mad!

"We need to get that box of a dozen balls back. Do you know where they ended up?" Tommy started pacing. Mel and Keith shook their heads in disgust at Tommy's unwarranted demeanor.

"I'm pretty sure they were in the group going to San Francisco," replied Ollie downheartedly. "The premium balls have a gold 'SMP' stamped on the bottom of the box. St. Max's Premium, you know. But that's the only difference in packaging between the regular balls and the premium. Maybe we should put them in a different colored box or something."

Mel glanced at Tommy and asked, "So what's the harm? One box of extra-good balls got mixed in with the other boxes of really-good balls. Deacon Ollie feels bad, so what purpose is this chastisement serving? Okay, so move on."

"It's what's in the core!" exclaimed Tommy. "The middle of the premium ball is extremely expensive! This can't happen again! Oh, come on, you all know that!"

"Okay," said Ollie calmly. "I'll call the San Francisco warehouse for Golf Country Superstore and see if they can locate the box and return it to us."

"That sounds great!" nodded Mel. "Now pass me another donut or two, please!"

*****

December 2013

On Christmas Day, Willy gave young Eric Mann the box of balls he bought from Golf Country Superstore in San Francisco. On the bottom, in gold letters, was stamped ***SMP***. Willy had never looked close enough to see that the dozen balls he purchased from GCS were slightly different than the rest he had delivered to Atlanta, St. Louis, Denver, and San Francisco. One of the St. Max's balls was missing because Eddy Gambo, aka Electro Eddy, had destroyed it while testing the core metals. Willy replaced it with a cheap Srixon Brite Red ball that he said he did on purpose so Eric could "add a little color" to his game. Tacky!

On New Year's Day, 2014, Eric turned twelve years old. Hugh Kraft, Eric's golf coach, treated him to a round at PGA National's Champion Course. Most professionals consider it one of the most challenging eighteen holes on the PGA Tour. The Champion is perilous, with tricky winds constantly wreaking havoc and water penalty areas hidden throughout that muddle the minds of even the world's best golfers. Hall of Famer Wayne Siebold and his son Troy joined Hugh and Eric on the crisp winter day in South Florida. Siebold, nicknamed Phenom, was a basketball and golf All-American at the University of Wisconsin.

Eric was beaming with pride! Thanks to Hugh's generosity, he now owned a spanking new Titleist bag, Ping clubs, all-leather Footjoy shoes, a Taylor Made Tour Preferred flex glove, a Garmin Approach S62 GPS watch, and three dozen Titleist Pro V balls. Hugh was astounded by Eric's natural ability, and how the youngster could implement his coaching techniques at once. He hoped to live long enough to watch Eric dominate the pro circuit.

Wayne Siebold was skeptical of Hugh's review of Eric's abilities. He was somewhat annoyed, thinking Eric would slow down the foursome and hold up players coming up from behind. Only the best should play The Champion Course. His skepticism lasted a grand total of five minutes.

Eric was told he would tee off last because the other three golfers would hit from the blacks, better known as the tips. Wayne said Eric should play the white tees, which were two steps easier than the back tees. Eric didn't respond immediately. He wouldn't argue with a Hall of Famer and past pro champion.

Troy teed off first and sliced it into a palmetto bush used as a barrier for the driving range. He played a provisional that rolled off the fairway about 150 yards from the green. Hugh went next and, using a three wood, placed the ball a little right of center, fifty yards from the pin. Wayne drove with a three-iron, and the ball landed two feet from Hugh's. Eric made his plea as the three were heading off the tee box.

"Please, Mr. Siebold, I would like to hit from the blacks. If I mess up, I promise to play the whites the rest of the day."

Wayne chuckled, but Hugh inserted, "Give him one shot, Speedboat! What's the harm in that?!"

"Okay, you're right," said Siebold, nodding. "Go ahead, kid. Make my day!"

Hugh laughed. "Clint Eastwood, you're not, Siebs! Stay away from the movies!" Hugh was a lifelong friend of Siebold's, so he called him by three names: Wayne, Speedboat (his nickname on the circuit), and Siebs (his nickname in college).

Meanwhile, Eric stepped up to the box, inserted his tee, placed the Srixon Brite Red ball he got from Willy on it, took a few practice swings with his Ping G425 Max Driver, then stepped up to hit. But Hugh cut him off.

"Hold on, Eric! What's up with the red ball? Use one of the Titleists I gave you."

"I want to play this one," said Eric. "I want Grandpaw Willy to know that his was the first one I used."

Hugh rolled his eyes, although Eric didn't see it. "Well, okay, I just wanted you to have the best ball for the best course. That's all."

"Thanks, Mr. Kraft. I just want to do this for Willy."

Eric readdressed his ball but didn't bother with another practice swing. He adjusted his body so his legs were shoulder-width apart and his knees slightly bent. He envisioned a straight line leading from his ball to the hole and aligned his legs and shoulders to parallel this line. Eric pulled the club astern with a firm grip, shifted his weight backward as he rotated his chest, then swung with a controlled arc around his body. His club changed direction at the top of the swing, and on the way down, Eric shifted his weight back to the front.

The Brite Red ball soared straight as an arrow down the fairway, landing slightly left of center due to the dogleg right. The drive was 265 yards, only fifty back from Wayne and Hugh: A fantastic feat for a twelve-year-old! Wayne and Troy's mouths were agape with stupefaction! Hugh patted Wayne on the back and proclaimed, "I told you so."

Unfortunately for Eric, the sandtrap that wrapped around two-thirds of the green was where his second shot landed. Hugh and Wayne chipped on, and their balls sat only a few feet from the cup. Meanwhile, Troy's approach hooked left and also ended up in the sandtrap. He buried his first trap shot near the edge and still needed a wedge to get out onto the green.

Whereas most beginners would be intimidated by a bunker shot, Eric confidently approached his ball. He arranged his grip to have a flat clubface, opened his stance, and positioned the ball inside his lead foot with most of his weight on that leg. Then, as Hugh had instructed many times, Eric cocked his wrists early in the takeaway and swung quickly as he kept the club face skyward. The ball lifted with a sprinkling of sand out of the trap, landed gently onto the green, then rolled about fifteen feet from the cup.

Troy was the furthest back, but his putting skills were the best part of his game. He played the angle perfectly and dropped the putt. But with his penalty shot and two digs out of the sand trap, he ended the first hole with a triple-bogey seven.

Eric went next after studying Troy's roll. Playing the distance and shape of the turf perfectly, his putt dropped in for par. Both Wayne and Hugh walked over and gave the boy a hug. Not many preteens shoot par on their first hole at The Champions. Few lifetime golfers can even par half the holes on that course!

Wayne and Hugh made their short putts and walked to the second hole with birdies under their belts. Hole two was a hundred yards longer and ten times more challenging than one. Water, trees, doglegs, sandtraps, and residential houses were the perils of mishitting. For novice golfers, this should be a par ten!

Troy teed off first, ignoring honors and golf etiquette for time's sake. Not trusting his driver, he used a pitching wedge and landed the ball 106 yards away but placed it immaculately in the middle of the fairway after the immediate dogleg left. Hugh suggested that Eric play the ball like Troy, but the rookie had a better idea. He pulled out his driver and hit a drive 256 yards directly to the straightaway, narrowly missing the tops of trees that would have doomed him. But he now had an undeviating shot to the green, 198 yards to the pin. Hugh and Wayne used their three-irons and landed their balls again in the middle of the fairway, but they were ten yards behind

Eric. The youngster was beaming with pride that he outdistanced two pros on the second drive of his life! And his self-esteem ballooned when his fairway two-iron shot stopped six inches from the cup. He had missed an eagle by a half-foot but graciously settled for his first birdie! Wayne and Hugh parred the second hole, and Troy ended with a double-bogey six.

For the next three hours, Eric misplayed only a couple of shots, and when the foursome headed to the tee box on eighteen, he was two strokes behind Wayne and one behind Hugh. Troy was a distant fourth, fourteen behind Eric. But the signature hole was not for the faint of heart. The par five, 560-yard gem was plagued with two doglegs, eleven sandtraps, water all up the right-side fairway, and, to top it off, three alligators sunning themselves in the rough!

Wayne and Hugh had honors for the final hole. Both hit astonishing drives of 300 yards, landing in the middle of the fairway. Eric knew he didn't have the strength to hit that distance, so he aimed right to have a better angle for his next shot. The drive was 223 yards, but it was sitting on the fairway with an unobstructed view for his approach. The alligator family was perched ominously fifty yards to his right. Troy bested Eric by twenty yards, so Eric was out and had to hit next.

Eric's three-wood shot landed a foot from the 150-yard marker, a 212-yard approach sitting dead center on the fairway. Wayne and Hugh had watched the boy all afternoon and were stunned. But hitting that last shot almost put them over the edge! With water and sand traps dotting the landscape near the hole, Wayne and Hugh played short irons and landed a few yards behind Eric. Hugh's third shot landed on the green, but Wayne's flew into the right-side sand trap, about twenty yards from the pin.

Hugh smiled and patted his buddy on the back. "Just what I needed to catch you, my friend!"

"Pretty confident for an old crippled fart, wouldn't you say?" Wayne chuckled back at Hugh.

Eric pulled out a seven-iron and landed his ball within ten feet of the pin for the eleventh time today. Troy played out because he didn't have a chance at winning the round; thus, he could sit back and watch the match unfold to its conclusion. He finished with a respectable fifteen over par for an eighty-seven. The two ex-pros told Eric to finish as well. Eric dropped another birdie, ending the round with an incredible one over seventy-three. But more importantly, if Hugh missed his putt, he would tie him, and if Wayne struggled in the trap, he might even tie for the match!

Hugh was sixteen feet from the pin, and Wayne jokingly said, "Putt your damn ball and get it out of my way."

Although he knew it wasn't legal to do so, Hugh decided to get at his friend's ire. "Okay, Siebs, I think I'll take you up on that! Might as well put the pressure on you rather than me!" Sixteen feet on a green was nothing for Hugh. He dropped the putt for a birdie, ending his round at even par, seventy-two.

Eric felt disappointed but was still excited about finishing only one stroke from his mentor. Secretly, he hoped Wayne would botch his sand shot, and perhaps he could beat the one-time PGA MVP. But Wayne did what he did best, hit the shot of the day in the clutch. His ball floated high and rolled tenderly into the cup. His birdie on eighteen left him with a one-under-par, seventy-one.

Wayne, Hugh, and Troy gulped down a pitcher of Corona in the clubhouse while Eric drank a Coke. But Wayne wasn't celebrating his victory. Three toasts were made to Eric, the true star of the day.

Walking out to their cars, Wayne approached Hugh and pulled him to the side out of earshot of anyone. He gestured to Eric, "Hey, my friend, you have a gold mine there. The boy could make you a fortune. Would you be interested in an agent partnership?"

"Doubtful, Speedboat. I'm a rather greedy guy!"

CHAPTER THIRTEEN

January 2014

Tommy Williams filed for a patent on his new golf balls on January 4, 2014. He was required to prove that the St. Max's balls were structurally different from others already on the market. Titleist had five patents, including one that Tommy designed without receiving credit. Even though he wanted to patent every component of the ball, he decided to submit just two ingredients that made his ball different: Planacalum in the core and the moylyn cover with holes.

Two weeks later, Tommy received his rejection letter in the mail. No one in the US Patent Office had heard of planacalum or moylyn. And he couldn't get a patent for those elements because metals and alloys are created by nature; thus, they can't be patented. The person who discovers new chemicals can get credit for the discovery, even have his name attached to it, but cannot get a patent. Tommy was a man of little patience. He wasn't about to partake on a long journey to get a simple patent. It was more important to make a lot of money.

"There's an empty apartment up on the top floor near your office apartment," said Mel Smith to Tommy. They drank coffee with the deacon and Keith Malone in the church school lounge. "I'm sure Father Jacob wouldn't mind that you lived here, too," said Mel.

Just then, Jim Mann and Bob Butler entered the lounge for coffee, then sat in the back of the room. Not knowing Jim and Bob very well, the others became cautious. They weren't sure they should speak in front of them.

Deacon Ollie glanced at Jim and Bob, then spoke up, "Well, hold on, Mel. These apartments are supposed to be for the homeless. Having Tommy up here with us would be nice, but I doubt Father Jacob would want to use up another space. And seeing he and Tommy were good friends in high school, Father might have trouble turning him down. So, I wouldn't put him on the spot by asking. That's all I'm saying."

"Well, I think –"

Tommy cut Mel off. "Hey, don't sweat it. I'm happy living in my condo on Riviera Beach. Why would I leave the beach life for airport life? No brainer!"

Jim and Bob were appalled at Tommy's wealth declaration but were not invited guests, so they just sat, sipped coffee, and listened.

"Yep," uttered Keith. "That makes sense. But we need to move on. We should discuss Ursula Vero's proposal now. All five hundred dozen balls sold out; the feedback has been awesome! People bought them mostly as Christmas gifts for friends and relatives, but now those who have played a round or two with the balls say they're fantastic! Look at this review on the Golf Country Superstore website: *'Best darn golf ball ever! Flies longer, straighter, and has an amazing soft touch on the green!'* All the reviews have five stars. That's incredible! But now Miss Vero wants a piece of the action."

"How so?" asked Deacon Ollie. "This is the first I've heard of her wanting an allotment."

"Simple, Ollie," replied Mel. "She wants to buy us out."

"Buy us out? How? Our factory is makeshift with unskilled laborers. That is crazy!"

"She doesn't care about our factory or homeless workers," explained Mel. "She just wants the formula for the standard ball and will make it in her own plants."

"And I say we don't do it!" exclaimed Tommy. "I may not get a patent, but I am not giving up my secret to success. And another thing, my word is final! You and Keith seem to forget I hired you as consultants to oversee manufacturing, not the other way around!"

"You recommended us to Father Jacob. That doesn't make you our boss!" said Keith. "But let's get back on track. If our premium ball fails to meet our goal, Miss Vero would probably pay you millions for the standard ball's formula and offer you a job, too. Why would you turn that down?"

"Because I could make more, in the long run, manufacturing the standard balls myself and blow Titleist out of the water. Plus, I firmly believe we will be successful when we find professionals to use our premium balls. Are you getting my drift?"

Jim and Bob were clueless about the conversation. What were they talking about? Everyone else took a sip of coffee while pondering Tommy's statement. Mel stood up and began pacing the room in deep thought. "Well, that's why we're really here anyway—right? Our plan is centered around the premium balls. So, what's the harm in selling off our standard balls?"

"We need to prove the effectiveness of the standard balls to create a name for ourselves. It's the only way to market the premium balls."

"How much is Vero offering?" asked Ollie. "You talked to her, right Keith? Perhaps the money would satisfy Father Jacob's goals."

"She's offering two million. Cash deal. We provide her with the formula and sign a covenant not to compete. I believe that clause would include us manufacturing the premium balls. In other words, we could be permanently out of the golf ball business. Then we would need a Plan B! And one other thing, Ursula wants to continue to use St. Max's name."

"What do they mean by Plan B?" whispered Bob to Jim. Jim shook his head. He didn't know.

The deacon saw Bob and Jim murmuring, then said to the group, "So what she's really saying is she wants to advertise the balls as beneficial to the homeless and poor in order to sell more! But because it's a cash deal, she has no plans to support St. Max's mission whatsoever! Pathetic!"

Keith responded immediately. "So, let's see if she'll negotiate. Instead of a cash deal, we take a cut of each ball sold. She's selling the balls now for a hair less than three dollars each. How about we get fifty cents of that or one-sixth of whatever price she puts on the balls?"

Tommy stood red-faced and shook his forefinger at Keith. "I created these golf balls, and I'm the one who decides how they're sold! Case closed, gentlemen!"

"Well, actually, the case is still open," broached Mel. "We can't sign a compete clause. We must sell the premium balls to professionals and use the St. Max's trademark."

"And to do that, we need to keep producing standard balls," said Keith. "I'll call Miss Vero and tell her we're not interested in her offer. Do you all agree?"

"Don't burn any bridges, Keith," voiced Mel. "We still need Golf Country Superstore to market the balls."

"No fears. I'm the sweetest guy I know," chuckled Keith.

*****

A few days later, Jim Mann and Bob Butler were again having coffee in the makeshift teachers lounge of the church school. Actually, it should be called the teacher lounge (singular) because Dora Mann was still the only teacher on the staff. Regardless, the Mr. Coffee machine brewed the best java on the parish grounds. Starbucks donated the coffee to the church; in return, Father Jacob prayed for them. He also gave them a receipt at the end of the year so they could deduct the contribution on their tax forms.

"What exactly do Mel and Keith do all day?" asked Jim. "Father hired them to oversee the golf ball assembly production, but I rarely see them in the factory. They spend most of their time in the apartments."

"Becky says the same thing. She works in the factory and doesn't interact with Mel or Keith most days. I guess most of the parishioners are on the same page. They all want to know how much Father is paying them. They know it's different from what the rest of us are getting—$500 a week."

"That's because they have a college education. But that's beside the point. We're not manufacturing enough golf balls to make much of a profit.

And we don't have enough people to produce more golf balls." Jim stood and paced around the room with his coffee mug. "In retrospect, I think we should have told Father Jacob what we saw in the hangar."

"You mean the corporate jet and two fancy, expensive cars? Father must know about it, right?"

"I'm not so sure. Father seems quite naïve when it comes to spending church funds. Regardless, that's not the question of the day. I would still like to know where those two made their money and why they chose to quit whatever they were doing to come here. It smells a bit fishy if you ask me!"

"Well, I'm the head of church security, Jim. What if I use my official duties to check them out? It's not like I do much else around here anyway!" They both laughed.

"Okay, sure. Why not? Right? Do you think we should involve Willy, too? He used to be a cop and quite a good one at that!"

"Let's see what I come up with first, Jim."

"Okay, then. If you need my help, feel free to ask."

A moment later, Deacon Ollie entered the lounge. "Jim. Bob. How are you men doing today? Thought I'd drop by for the best coffee around!" Ollie smiled broadly as he stirred cream and sugar into the coffee he had just poured.

"My, Deacon, you sure are in a good mood today!" said Jim. Then he added jokingly, "Did you win the lottery, or what?"

"Close to it! I've got tickets for next year's Super Bowl in Miami! Can you believe it?!"

"Holy cow!" shouted Bob. Then thinking about who he was talking to, he said, "Oh, sorry. I'm sure cows aren't holy. Anyway, how did you get tickets for next year? This year's game hasn't even been played yet!"

"A rich friend from college owns an island and a glorious estate in the Caribbean. He has some sort of connection with the NFL. I called him just to chat about old times, and out of the blue, he offered me two tickets for the next season's championship game!"

Ollie sat down, and he, Jim, and Bob talked football for a half hour. Jim was dying to ask Ollie what he thought of Mel and Keith but decided against it. He didn't want to spoil the moment. Then they finished their coffee simultaneously and placed the mugs in the sink. Dora would clean them later—she always did. Just another thankless task a schoolteacher does for the love of kids!

CHAPTER FOURTEEN

March 2014

The International Conference of Catholic Deacons was held March 2014 at the Cathedral Church and Minor Basilica of St. Patrick in Melbourne, Australia. Father Jacob encouraged Ollie to attend, and the deacon was ecstatic. He had never traveled to The Land Down Under.

As a bonus, the Cricket World Cup happened to be playing at the Melbourne Cricket Grounds. Ollie loved watching matches on *ESPN* and looked forward to being at the game. Father had pulled some strings with Archbishop Martin from the Melbourne Archdiocese and got tickets to the World Cup for his deacon. Ollie decided to show up early to place some bets on the match. A mini-sports book was located next to the concessions in the stadium. Perhaps one day, that simplistic method of gaming will happen in America.

Jim Mann saw Father give Ollie a St. Max's corporate Mastercard for his travels. Where was the money coming from to send the deacon to Australia? Where was the money coming from to run the entire church?!

Otis Banks had just returned from delivering the second load of golf balls to the Golf Country Superstore warehouses. A brand new, one-ton Chevy cargo van had been purchased after the U-Haul was abandoned in New Mexico. It held 1,000 boxes of a dozen balls, so the journey grossed another $17,500, meaning proceeds for the two trips totaled $35,000.

Expenses were slightly less because the van got eighteen miles to a gallon of gas. And because it was new, there were no repairs.

Willy had refused to go with his brother on the trip. He was appalled that Father Jacob had purchased a new van. It would be cheaper to ship the balls via UPS. Otis survived the cross-country adventure with no speeding tickets or accidents. Thank God. And yes, Father did thank Him for that!

Jim told Bob Butler about the credit card and sending Deacon Ollie to Australia. The head of security wrote it down in a spiral notebook right after his logged entry about buying the new cargo van. Bob called it an evidence notebook to keep an eye on Mel and Keith. He suspected the two aeronautical engineers were responsible for most of St. Max's expenses. To get the big picture, Bob decided to log all the church's expenses, regardless of if they were used for the golf ball project. The notebook was Willy's idea. Jim and Bob were now using Willy as a consultant.

Without notifying Father Jacob, Willy had installed several hidden cameras around the parish grounds and rigged them into the head of security's apartment. If motion was detected from midnight to 6:00 am, an incessant pinging rang next to Bob's bed. Becky hated it! At 2:00 am one day in early March, the security alarm beeped in Bob's apartment, waking him. Groggily, he walked over to the computer screen that was divided into twelve sections—one for each of the cameras.

Three people were leaving the apartment building with suitcases. They didn't get into a vehicle. Rather, they walked down the airport road heading towards a hangar. Bob zoomed in. It was Mel, Keith, and Deacon Ollie. Where were they going in the middle of the night?

*****

Wearing only his underwear, Bob hustled out of the apartment and followed the three men as they went into Mel and Keith's secret hangar. They loaded their belongings into the Citation X, then prepped the jet and rolled it onto the deserted runway.

Knowing that the deacon was planning a trip to Australia, Bob surmised that perhaps Mel and Keith were flying him there. But if that was true, Father Jacob must be aware of the hangar and jet. Deacon Ollie would have indeed told him about it, right? And if Ollie had told him about the hangar and jet, he certainly would have mentioned the expensive cars. Still, was there really anything wrong with Mel and Keith being rich beyond imagination? Maybe they had accumulated wealth in their previous jobs and were now retired and committed to serving the Catholic religion. Bob looked up as the Citation X zipped into the starry sky, then turned southwesterly.

"Sorry about the late, ah, I mean early call," whispered Bob into the apartment's landline. He was hoping not to awaken Becky and hoping even more that Willy would not be upset. It was 3:00 am.

"What is it, Bob?" asked Willy, half asleep. "This better be good!"

Bob told Willy about Mel, Keith, and Ollie taking off in the jet, each carrying a suitcase. "I'm not a certified sleuth just yet, Willy, but I find this very suspicious. Am I wrong?"

"Let's hope so. I'll stop by this morning, and we can chat."

*****

"Son, the Diocese of Palm Beach audits our books annually," Father Jacob told Willy as he sipped coffee. They were having a chat after the morning prayer service. "Our loan has been forgiven because of our efforts helping those in need. I appreciate that you are worried about our financial state, but rest assured, we are doing God's work in the black. Yes, I knew about Mel and Keith's fast jet and fancy cars. And I sent Deacon Ollie to the conference in Melbourne. I didn't have a problem with expenses after Mel offered to fly him there in the Citation free of charge."

"Sorry, Father, I didn't know that the Catholic Charities Foundation had forgiven the five-million-dollar loan! That's tremendous! And all because of your excellent work for the homeless and poor."

"No, Willy, what we all do for the homeless and poor! You and all our parishioners are in this together!"

"So, let me try and understand what you told me this morning." Willy paused to think. He wasn't sure he wanted to say anything more because he didn't want to appear to be grilling the priest. "The Catholic Charities Foundation will provide continual financial support to St. Max's as long as we continue to go above and beyond what other churches do. Things like asking for donations, selling golf balls, operating a free school, and providing shelter for homeless families. That's truly wonderful, Father!"

Willy stepped to the sink, washed his mug, and added, "Well, I need to go to work. Thanks for the coffee."

"Anytime, Willy! You're always welcome to stop by for a chat!"

As he entered the US Fish and Wildlife Service pickup truck and cranked the engine, Willy sat for a moment and pondered his conversation with Father Jacob.

Something about it didn't feel right.

CHAPTER FIFTEEN

March 2014

The Melbourne Cricket Ground had its own gambling station, and similar to horse racing, one could bet on the match while attending the game. Fortunately for Ollie, the 2014 Cricket World Cup was being played on March 28th, which happened to be during the week of the deacon's conference. Archbishop Martin had secured tickets for Ollie at the request of Father Jacob, and he had no problem with St. Max's deacon attending a match or two.

Ollie was a huge cricket fan, perhaps even more so than professional baseball in the United States. But he was an even bigger fan of sports gaming and was sure that his hopes for eternal life were being challenged by the devil. Regardless, he decided to skip one additional conference session to gamble on the final match between New Zealand and Australia. Ollie would ask for forgiveness ten times to make up for that evil deed!

Australia entered the game as the favorite and won by seven wickets for a fifth World Cup triumph. But that wasn't the wager Ollie placed. Instead, he laid $50,000 on a player-specific bet—the top batsman. He picked Aaron Finch, the Australian team captain, to hit five or more "sixes" during the match. In cricket, when you hit a ball out of the boundaries of the field without it touching the ground, it's worth six runs and is therefore called a "six." Aaron hit five during the inning in which he logged a century in an amazing demonstration of strength and athleticism. Ollie scooped up $300,000 in winnings and placed his original bet of $50,000 into the collection basket at St. Patrick's, making sure Archbishop Martin saw the donation. The leader of the Melbourne diocese was overwhelmed by Ollie's generosity!

Meanwhile, Mel and Keith rented a Corvette convertible and drove the Great Ocean Road to take photos of the Twelve Apostles, a collection of limestone stacks off the shore of Port Campbell National Park. Then they would try their hand at deep-sea fishing in Port Fairy. Mel and Keith would pick up Ollie at the end of the deacon's conference and shuttle him back to America.

But first, they needed to meet with Bushman Jack in the Outback.

*****

Two of Aaron's sixes bizarrely hit an Australian flag hanging from the fence behind the boundary wedges. Two others landed squarely on a New Zealand flag. The last six struck the Victoria state emblem between the national banners. The captain was showing off for the home crowd! The fans were going wild!

The odds of Finch hitting five sixes or more were six to one. The chances of that happening were meager, but then again, if anyone could accomplish the feat, it was Aaron. Interestingly, only one wager was made on that bet—Deacon Ollie's.

Kangaroo Sportsbetting general manager and head bookmaker, Art Minter, was beside himself. He set the initial odds, but all bets were adjusted based on opposing wagers, which minimized the sportsbook's risk. With their commission, they were assured they would make a profit. However, when only one person bet, the house assumed the opposite outcome. Art had never experienced a case where only one wager occurred!

Still, how could he lose a sure-win bet?! To encourage more gambling, Art petitioned the gaming commission to allow a higher maximum stake for the final game of the World Cup. The commissioners agreed to up the ante limit from 20,000 Australian Dollars to 75,000 for this match only.

Minter thought Ollie's bet would be an easy seventy-two grand of Australian Dollars (50,000 US Dollars) for his business. He wished now that he had lowered the odds on Finch; however, the payout would have been too low for anyone to risk the bet.

Thanks to offering many possible wagers, Kangaroo Sportsbetting still came out ahead for the day. However, the house simply blew the Finch "sixes" bet, which lowered the company's profits. Art Minter would need to polish up his resume and peruse the job ads tomorrow.

*****

Mel and Keith's head nets were covered in gnats five minutes after the hike to Ayers Rock summit began. Better known in Australia as Uluru, the climbing path is only a mile long but very steep and treacherous. The first section has a chain to hold on to, and only those with a death wish ignore using it. The strenuous ascent takes about two hours to complete, barring a fatal slip or heart attack. Rumor has it that the trail will close to tourists by the end of the decade because Uluru has been sacred to the Anangu people for tens of thousands of years and climbing disrespects their culture. Today, Mel and Keith were alone on the blazing red rock's path.

Bushman Jack was the world's greatest scientist. Based on an average of five IQ tests, Jack scored a 263, landing him even with Ainan Celeste Cawley, the Singaporean child prodigy who, at the age of nine, was able to recite Pi to 518 decimal places and thoroughly memorize the periodic table. But whereas Cawley eschewed science and became an acclaimed filmmaker at age twelve, Bushman Jack developed a company in 2002 called GenomeAtHome, where DNA testing could be done to research ancestry from the convenience of your living room. Unfortunately, even though Jack was a scientific genius, he was a failure when it came to marketing a business. He could not secure a grant and thus had to rely on bank loans for the start-up. His vision was clear, but he was two years ahead of his time. No one believed a complicated deoxyribonucleic acid test could be performed at home by someone scientifically clueless.

Jack declared bankruptcy on New Year's Eve in 2002 and went to work for geneticist Spencer Wells. With Jack's research leading the way, Wells received a grant from *National Geographic* and launched the *Genographic Project*, the first primary direct-to-consumer genetic testing kit. Its mission was to analyze historical patterns in DNA to understand migration and shared genetic roots.

Wells became a celebrity inventor and was featured in various magazines and newspapers. Not once did he mention Jack's name in any article. Wells was bound and determined to accept all the credit, although none was his own doing. Disgusted, Bushman Jack resigned and returned to work for International Intelligence and Inquiry (III), where he had served as head of meteorology and geologic studies after graduating from Dartmouth in 1986. Triple I, as it was known, was an agency that provided intergovernmental advisory assistance to global intelligence agencies, including the CIA, MI6, and Mossad.

Triple I provided a secret laboratory for Jack at the summit of Ayers Rock. It was disguised as a cave and couldn't be seen overhead from airplanes or helicopters. There was no better place on Earth to study the physics and chemistry of the atmosphere, including its interactions with the Earth's surface. Bushman Jack completely understood natural phenomena and was a maestro when making predictions based on scientific interactions. He was an invaluable expert for the spy agencies he served.

Mel and Keith knew Jack from playing rugby against him in college. He had been a monster of a hooker with tremendous strength and power to make big hits and hold up the scrum. But he also maintained a cool head and had perfect timing to accurately throw a ball into the lineout. Thanks to Jack, Dartmouth destroyed MIT in every game. However, his friendship with Mel and Keith grew once they realized how smart he was, especially in science and technology. They would meet at a bar in Concord monthly to chat, not about girls or sports, but about what they learned in school. Boring!

Staying in touch throughout the years, Mel and Keith knew Jack was stationed in the Australian outback. The trip to Melbourne was their opportunity to see their buddy in action. However, only Mel and Keith knew where Bushman Jack's secret laboratory was located. Their friend let that one slip.

Jack greeted his longtime buddies with Gatorade and a hug that significantly squished their innards. They retold Ivy League jokes and caught up with each other's family and friends. An hour later, they got down to business.

*****

"So, you invented drones that can circle the globe with the most advanced miniature telescopic high-definition camera attached." Mel hadn't asked a question, but Jack nodded without comment. "Is the camera better than NASA's best?"

Bushman Jack chuckled before answering. "My drones put NASA to shame! The cameras are more powerful, and the lens is ultra-sharp. Plus, the drones can cruise 150,000 feet above the Earth's surface."

"That's thirty miles high! How do you refuel them?"

"I invented an onboard fuel cell that automatically recharges using solar and atomic energy. When the cell detects power drainage, the drone is programmed to fly to the outer layers of the atmosphere. The ionosphere contains an abundance of electrons, ionized atoms, and molecules that resupply the fuel cells. The sun's energy is also tapped from the lower layers of the atmosphere. A full cell can power the drone for 50,000 miles, or twice around the equator, without recharging."

"Damn!" blurted Keith. "Did you patent the drone?"

"I'm done with patents, my friend. After Spencer Wells stole my DNA research, I've had it with the politics of inventions. I have three drones, all of which I made by hand in a warehouse not far from here in the Great Sandy Desert. I hired ten Aboriginal people to help me assemble them."

"The camera," stuttered Mel. He couldn't believe what Jack was telling him. "Exactly how powerful is it?"

"Let's put it this way—it's actually a telescope. I can get a super clear picture from a distance of 100,000 feet."

The technical jargon continued like a ping-pong match until Mel and Keith needed to leave. Finally, Mel asked, "Do you need more drones to cover the parameters of our mission?"

"Well, yes, I think that I do. What I need to know is how long you will drag this out. Seems to me you could move right now and wrap this up with no one getting hurt."

"It must be red-handed, Jack. It must be a certainty. Right now, we're just playing the game."

CHAPTER SIXTEEN

April 2014

Eric Mann played in his first youth golf tournament from April 15th to the 18th of 2014. The matches were held at Breakers West Country Club in West Palm Beach, a premier course in the Southeast. The Breakers Junior Open was supposed to be for kids aged thirteen to fifteen, but Hugh Kraft talked officials into letting Eric compete at age twelve. The young golfers played from the standard men's tees instead of the championship tees, 6,690 yards of pure frustration for those who couldn't hit a straight ball. Eric wasn't one of them.

His fourteen-under-par finish broke the tournament record by eleven strokes! The next nearest competitor was sixteen back. Eric was so far ahead that he played with only irons and a putter on the last round. He left his driver and woods in the clubhouse. This was Hugh's idea so Eric would be challenged and focused on the fourth and final day.

The *Palm Beach Post* sports section had a quarter-page picture of Eric receiving his championship trophy. Reporter Gibby Collins asked him about his secret to success, and Eric humbly replied, "I want to thank God first. I was just lucky, that's all. The other players were excellent and should also have their pictures in the paper. Plus, I wouldn't be here if it wasn't for my coach, Mr. Kraft. And thanks to my parents for letting me play."

Deacon Ollie showed Father Jacob the newspaper article, and both men were beaming with pride. Who knew that one of their young parishioners was a fantastic golfer?! And he thanked God. What a wonderful young man!

"Father," the deacon whispered, "are you thinking what I'm thinking? We need to make sure Eric is guided by the Holy Spirit if he decides to be a professional golfer someday."

"Yes, Ollie, I was thinking the same thing. I will have a heart-to-heart chat with him."

*****

"Eric, from what I hear, you have the ability to make a career out of golf. Is that right, son?"

Father Jacob and Eric were sitting in a pew in the back row of the church. The priest patted the boy on his knee. "I would like that, sir," said Eric with a wide smile. "But I'm not sure I'm good enough."

"Well, I believe that with the help of God, anything is possible. As long as you don't forget that, you can be anything you want to be!"

"Yes, Father, I will never forget what you said."

"Good boy! And Deacon Ollie and I are here to help you along the way. We have a plan to get you started."

"A plan? What do you mean, Father?"

"I would like to bless your golf balls before each match. How does that sound?"

"Sure. That would be awesome! Thank you, Father!"

"I was wondering if you would be willing to do one favor for the church. Would you play your rounds with our new St. Max's Premium golf balls and endorse them? It would help us raise money for the poor and homeless. You know that would be for a good cause, right?"

"Yes, sir. It surely would! I would happily endorse the St. Max's balls, but I'm not sure my endorsement will do much good. I'm just a lucky golfer, that's all."

"Eric, don't ever undersell yourself. Have confidence in your skills, and let God lead the way. Blessing the golf balls will be a good start and help ensure you are a believer. Let the Holy Spirit guide you, son."

"Okay, Father, I will. I'll pick up my golf balls from you before each tournament. Thank you very much!"

"You are most certainly welcome, Eric. And good luck and Godspeed on the golf courses!"

*****

"He wants little Eric to be the face of St. Max's Premium balls?!" questioned Tommy Williams disdainfully. Deacon Ollie had just delivered the news that Father Jacob wanted the youngster to be his celebrity endorser. "Huh?! The kid's only twelve years old!"

Williams, Keith Malone, and Ollie drank coffee in Mel Smith's apartment. The deacon finished his cup and excused himself. He had better things to do than listen to Tommy Williams rant and rave.

"Calm down, Tommy," said Mel. "From what I read in the *Palm Beach Post*, Eric sounds like an up-and-coming superstar."

"But Jordan Spieth and I are buddies from my time working at Titleist. He just won the Masters! I'm sure I could get him to endorse our premium balls. Who better to be the face of St. Max's?!"

"We can't use St. Max's Premium balls until they are approved by the USGA. That's going to take some time, right? If they decide to dissect our balls, we're screwed. They won't know what moylyn is or planacalum, either. You need to find some way to patent those first."

"I can't patent new chemical elements! I've already tried. But I have a different idea. Now hear me out before you say no. Okay?"

"This should be good," replied Malone sarcastically. "Will I need Kleenex for my tears of exaltation?!"

"The USGA tests ten balls, and each one must be identical. The weight and size must adhere to USGA specifications and be spherically symmetric. When struck by a robotic club, the balls cannot exceed the maximum permissible initial velocity, and there must be consistency in the lift, carry and drag. If all that happens, they won't bother to dissect the ball."

"But they could cut it open and see what's inside, right?" asked Mel.

"Sure, they could do anything they wanted, really."

"How do you plan to get around the moylyn cover and planacalum interior? You can't risk that they won't look inside. If they do, we're out of business for good!"

"We take ten of St. Max's standard balls and replace the cover with a soft cast urethane elastomer. Titleist uses that cover—but guess what? I hold the patent! We then extract the planacalum from the core and replace it with synthetic rubber mixed with bits of legal elements. I think a combination of tungsten, titanium, and acrylate would work just fine. We then prick holes into the dimples to resemble our original St. Max's balls. So, what do you think?"

"Okay, you asked," responded Keith. "I think you're out of your mind. Sure, the core ingredients would be legal, but the ball wouldn't fly as far or straight as St. Max's balls. Someone at the USGA would get suspicious. They would wonder how we would market such a cheap ball to professional golfers!"

"The people who do the testing probably could care less. They probably don't even play golf! They're just some engineers with only one goal—making sure the balls are legal."

"Too many 'probablies' for me! What do you think, Mel?"

"Okay, so I tend to agree with both of you. Keith, you're right. This is a risky move. But then again, Tommy is right in saying there may be no other option to get the balls approved for professional play. I think we give Tommy's plan a try. We've come too far to stop now. How long will it take to have the balls ready?"

"We can't tell the other parishioners what we're doing, so the three of us must create the balls ourselves here in my lab. They must be perfectly consistent with each other. I will design and test several prototypes to see which is the best. But we should be able to have them ready to send to the USGA by June 1st."

CHAPTER SEVENTEEN

May 2014

Father Jacob startled the entire forty-two parishioners during the May 31st Sunday service. "Please pray for Deacon Ollie's return to good health. He has an undisclosed condition that will keep him from being with us on a regular basis. Hopefully, the deacon will be around more often than not, and I ask you to welcome and comfort him on the days he is here."

"Do you think it's cancer, Dad?" whispered Eric to his father, Jim.

"I don't know, son, but the best medicine is prayer, no matter his health problem."

"We should get the congregation together and provide meals for him," said Dora.

"Father Jacob told me about it before church this morning," responded Jim. "He asked me to take over some of Ollie's tasks. From what I understand, the deacon isn't going to live in his apartment here. I'm guessing he's gone to some specialty hospital for treatment. Maybe the Mayo Clinic up in Minnesota or something."

"That's a shame. How can we show our support if we don't know where he is?"

"Maybe if the treatment works, Father Jacob can tell us where Ollie is staying."

"Let's pray that the treatment is successful!"

"Amen to that!"

*****

June 2014

"They now have a machine in their hangar that hits golf balls into a canvas wall. The canvas is laced with all kinds of wires." Bob Butler had secretly broken into Mel and Keith's hangar. He installed a camera on the ceiling where it was difficult to see. Bob showed Jim and Willy Banks a taped recording from the previous night.

"I think they must be testing the St. Max golf balls," stated Willy. "What's the problem with that?"

"It was recorded at two in the freaking morning, Willy! Why were they working all night? And why don't any people in the factory know about that thing? It looks pretty expensive to me! I wrote it down in my journal, but I thought you should both know. Father keeps spending money like it's going out of style!"

"Yes, you're right about that, Bob," stated Willy. He was about to leave when Jim stopped him.

"One other thing," said Jim. "Dora and I were cleaning up Ollie's apartment yesterday, and we found this unopened box addressed to him at St. Max's Church."

"Okay, so what? You sound like it's some sort of crime to get mail."

"No, not mail sent to Palm Beach Gardens. But this box was for pickup at Port Everglades."

"And what's the problem with that?" Willy was late for work and needed to move on. He didn't mean to be rude.

"Well, it's my job to pick up supplies at Port Everglades. So why did Deacon Ollie get this box instead of me?"

"Maybe he happened to be in the area and picked it up. It was addressed to him anyway! You're making a mountain out of a molehill, Jim!"

"Why would the deacon be in the area of Port Everglades? Okay, I know you're in a hurry, Willy, so let me get straight to the point. I think we should open the box and see what's inside."

"It doesn't belong to us!" snapped Willy. "There happens to be a law against that! Now return the damn box to Ollie's apartment and get ready for work. I need you in the slough by nine to widen the trail." Willy slammed the door as he left. Bob and Jim stared at each other momentarily, making sure Willy was out of earshot.

"I think we should open it," said Bob meekly.

"So do I," muttered Jim.

CHAPTER EIGHTEEN

June 2014

"The box is full of plastic cylinders. I count fifty-four of them. Each has a recessed hole in the bottom of it," stated Jim as he turned one around in his hand.

"They look familiar," said Bob. "But I can't place it. Where have I seen these things before?"

"Well, I think they look like cups for golf greens. Do you have a ruler handy?"

"Yep, right here in my desk." Bob grabbed a wooden measuring stick that was mixed with pencils and pens in the middle drawer. He handed it to Jim.

"The diameter is four and a quarter inches. The depth is five inches. I can't turn the ruler, but the hole on the bottom appears to be about three-quarters of an inch. Hey, fire up Google for me, please."

Bob opened the Chrome web browser on his computer. "What do you want me to search?"

"Measurements of a golf hole cup." Bob typed it in and pressed enter. Within seconds, Google responded with a drop-down list of possibilities, but one appeared on the screen with no hyperlink: *Golf Hole (Golf Cups) have a regulated diameter of 4.25" (108 mm) and total depth between 4"-6" (101.6-152.4 mm).*

"There it is in black and white," stated Jim. "They're golf hole cups. What would Deacon Ollie want with fifty-four of them?"

"Three rounds of eighteen holes each would be fifty-four cups. That's very strange! He's got exactly enough for three rounds of golf."

"You don't suppose Father Jacob is going to build a golf course, do you?" asked Jim. "Why else would he want golf cups?

"It wouldn't surprise me. If he thought it could raise money for the poor and homeless, he might give it a try!"

"Still, why did Deacon Ollie pick up the package at Port Everglades? I could have easily gotten it during one of my trips. And why was it addressed to Ollie? None of the other packages I got had his name on them. They were just labeled St. Max's Church."

"Who knows?! My bigger concern is that Father is planning on building a golf course. There's no way the Catholic Charities Foundation would fund that expense!"

"We don't know for sure that's what he's planning, Bob."

"But if not, why does he need fifty-four golf cups?"

"Let's ask Father Jacob. He'll tell us. What do we have to lose anyway?!"

*****

"You opened a box addressed to Deacon Ollie? Shame on you two. Not only is that illegal, but it's also sinful." Father Jacob was scolding Jim and Bob in a soft, loving tone, the way he always spoke. Still, he was getting his point across, and the men dropped their heads in embarrassment. They were in Father's office at the back of the church.

"We're very sorry, Father," apologized Jim. "Please forgive us, sir. We were just helping clean up the deacon's apartment for him during his absence when we saw the box. I noticed it was picked up at Port Everglades, and I was curious why Ollie got it, not me. So, we opened—okay, Father, you're correct. Sorry again! We had no right to look in the box."

"All is forgiven, Jim. Is there anything else?"

Bob and Jim glanced at each other afraid to say more. But the box wasn't the main issue. Jim decided to ask. What the heck?!

"Father, are you planning on building a golf course to raise money for the parish?"

Father Jacob blurt out in laughter. "Son, the box was addressed to Deacon Ollie. Sure, he used the church's shipping location at Port Everglades, not his apartment. I'm not sure why he did that. But I think I know what he wanted with all those golf cups: he mentioned building a miniature putt-putt course for the folks living in the trailers over in Pahokee! He made some money gambling and wanted to give something back to the poor. Ollie has a good heart, wouldn't you say?!"

"Yes, Father!" affirmed Bob. "He's a wonderful man! Jim, we need to move on and stop bothering our priest! I'm sure he has a ton of things he needs to do!"

Jim nodded, and Father stood up and patted the men on their shoulders. "You're not pestering me, boys. Remember, I will always make time for my parishioners!"

Jim thanked him and said he would rewrap the box and return it to Deacon Ollie's apartment.

Bob and Jim didn't say anything on the way to the deacon's flat. But after placing the box on the counter, Jim asked, "So, are you satisfied with Father's explanation?"

"Not yet. I'm going to drive over to the Pahokee trailer court this afternoon. I'd like to see if there is space to construct a fifty-four-hole putt-putt course. Wanna come?"

Jim chuckled. "No, I can't. I have to widen a trail out at the slough. But you make a great investigator, Bob!"

Bob smiled. "Yes, sir, that's why I'm the head of security!"

*****

"Myra Rother's the name. And yep, I'm the head cheese in this here mousehole. I run the show, and like you, Bob, I'm also the security boss! So, how can I help ya?"

Bob Butler had knocked on the door of the first trailer he saw after entering the trailer court. The sign on the door's window said *Office*. An elderly lady answered, and Bob introduced himself as the chief security officer for St. Max's Church. The gal had short white hair, apple red lipstick so thick it had smeared onto the bottom of her nose, and skin so astonishingly tanned and wrinkled that her age couldn't be determined. Too many years in the Florida sun will do that to you!

"Hi Myra. So, you are the head cheese of a mousehole—now there's a figure of speech that will have you guessing! You must have a way with words. Anyway, the deacon of our church is a tall, rugged sort of fella with a kind heart. I was wondering if you've ever met him. Has he ever been out this way?"

"Can't say if he has," replied Myra. "No, wait a minute. You be talkin' about Number Thirty, ain't ya? He be the fella that put up signs on our electric poles. He was trying to get folks to go to that church you work for. You say he's a deacon. What da heck is a deacon?"

"Signs on electric poles. Yes, yes! That would be him. A deacon is an ordained minister who helps a priest. Did you ever speak to him?"

"Well, of course! I speak to him every month! Got to if I want my rent. You say he's an ordinary minister?"

"Ordained. Never mind. You said your rent?" questioned Bob. He was puzzled. "What do you mean rent?"

"Ain't you never gone to school, son?! Rent is what someone pays you to live on their property!"

"Yes, I know what rent is. I mean, what does rent have to do with our deacon?"

"My oh my! You're not exactly the sharpest razor blade in my shaving kit, now are you, Bob?! The man rents trailer number thirty. And he's a good man. Never is late with what's due."

"Our deacon is renting a trailer from you?!" Bob was flabbergasted.

"Are ya deefe, son?! Yep, and Harry gives a prayer service for us in the rec hall when he's here."

"Harry? No, ma'am, his name is Ollie, not Harry."

"No, it ain't. It's Harry. You think I don't know my own tentacles?"

"You mean tenants? Are you sure we're talking about the same person? You said he came here putting up signs for St. Max's, right?"

"Yep, that's what I said. I got a picture of him in my desk. Got one of all the folks who live here. I don't know any last names, so I just take down their first names and paste a Polaroid picture next to it in my rent book."

Myra showed him the picture of the man in unit number thirty. It was certainly Ollie. Bob couldn't wrap his head around it. He was speechless. Why would Ollie rent a trailer in Pahokee using the name Harry? And why would he need to rent a trailer when the deacon has a perfectly good apartment next to the church? But that's not why he came, and Bob could see that Myra wanted to wrap up this conversation and get back to her soap opera on the TV.

"Uh, okay, thanks, Myra. Ah, just one last question, and I'll be out of your hair. "Did Harry ever mention building a miniature golf course somewhere out here?"

"You mean one of them putt-putt things? Nope, never said anything to me. Why ya askin'?"

"Oh, no reason. Thanks, Myra. Hope to see you again! Have a nice day!"

As Bob drove back to Palm Beach Gardens, he knew he needed to tell Willy about the deacon's trailer. But that meant Willy would realize Bob and Jim opened the box after he explicitly told them not to. Being the head of security was a thankless job!

CHAPTER NINETEEN

June 2014

"What is it, gentlemen? Church starts in an hour, and I must brush up on my sermon."

Willy, Jim, and Bob were again meeting with Father Jacob in his office. It was Sunday, June 21st, and Willy hesitated to have this get-together but decided it was best to take the lead on the conversation. Jim and Bob were worried about being excommunicated!

"I won't beat around the bush, Father. Bob drove to the trailer court in Pahokee to see if they had any plans to build a miniature golf course, and quite frankly, they didn't. But even more surprising was he found out that Deacon Ollie rented a mobile home there using the name Harry. We weren't sure if you knew that, which is why we're here."

"The deacon's medical treatments aren't going well, and this is what you boys are concerned about? None of you have asked how Ollie is doing. That's rather narrow-minded, I must say! But I'm in a hurry, so let me get to the point. First, Ollie's middle name is Harry, and he likes to use it sometimes on legal documents. I don't know why and it's none of my business. And yes, I knew the deacon rented a trailer in Pahokee. That's where he lived before he moved into his apartment here at the airport. He told me the rent was so low that he wanted to keep the trailer as a storage unit. I don't know why they have not heard about the putt-putt course he wanted to build. With his bad health, I assume Ollie postponed the project until he felt better. Now get your families and find a pew in the church. You all have some transgressions that need forgiveness!"

Father stormed out of the room. Bob and Jim were stunned and didn't know what to say. Willy shook his head and stood to leave. Then he turned to Bob and Jim and scolded, "You just couldn't leave well enough alone, could you?! I've never seen Father Jacob upset before today. Now put this issue to rest, got it?!"

"Wait a minute, Willy," inserted Jim. "I know we didn't follow your directions, but you must admit that much of what we are saying about Deacon Ollie is suspicious. I've read about your heroics that saved our country from disaster in the eighties. If those accounts are accurate, I don't think you put the issue back then to rest. You pursued the investigation right up to the bitter end. But now you want us to just relax. That's a hard pill to swallow!"

Willy ignored Jim's comments, exited the room, and stopped halfway down the hallway. He knew Jim was right. He knew this whole thing sounded fishy. Willy wanted to protect Bob and Jim from getting into something too deep, seeing neither had any police training.

But Jim's words had cut like a knife. Had Willy listened to his boss back in the eighties and not pursued leads, America might be governed by a criminal organization today. Chances were slim that Deacon Ollie would be involved in some type of coverup—he was a good man guided by his religious faith.

Willy needed to prove Jim and Bob were wrong, but the only way to refute their notions was to investigate a little further. He turned around and walked back into Father's office. Willy then took a deep breath and smiled.

"Okay, boys, let's do this."

*****

Later that night

That evening, Bob snuck back into the deacon's apartment, opened the box, and took out a golf cup. He resealed the box and went to his car where

Willy, his brother Otis, and Jim were waiting. Bob didn't want to wake his wife, Becky, or their kids, Ben and Betty, by meeting in his apartment. And Willy thought Otis might be able to help in some way, although he wasn't sure how.

"Why did you want a golf cup?" Bob asked Willy. "We all know what one looks like."

"It's called evidence tracing," replied Willy matter-of-factly. "During an inquiry, sometimes things aren't what they appear. The cups were the reason we first suspected Ollie was doing something suspicious, so technically, the cups were evidence. Does that make sense?"

Even though none of the men understood what Willy meant, they all nodded 'yes.' No one was going to admit to investigative incompetence!

"What's next?" asked Bob.

"What's next is what we shouldn't do," replied Willy uneasily. "We need to see what the deacon has stored in his trailer. That means breaking and entering. It's a crime in all fifty states and every country worldwide. You all need to think about that before we go to Pahokee. If anyone wants to back out now, I will totally understand."

"I'm in!" yelped Bob, Jim, and Otis in unison. And it wasn't planned.

Bob laid the golf cup on the dashboard of his 1994 Chevy Cavalier. The car had 209,655 miles on it. The tires had been on the vehicle for the past 82,147 miles. Two of the four doors rattled. The driver's seat had a spring sticking out of it. You get the picture! Cramming four bodies inside wasn't easy. Trying to be comfortable on a journey was impossible. For the last three months, the air conditioner hadn't been working. The heat and humidity in Florida in June could be unbearable, even at night.

All four men rolled down their windows using the cranks on the doors. Bob couldn't afford a used car with power windows. Then, a strange thing happened when he turned the key in the ignition.

The golf cup flew from the dash and clung to the driver's side mirror outside the car.

CHAPTER TWENTY

June 2014

"What the hell was that?!" shrieked Bob. He reached out the window to grab the cup, but it was stuck to the metal casing around the mirror. Willy walked around to the driver's door, then yanked the cup off the mirror. He opened his hand to examine the cup, and it shot to the door and clung hard.

"It's possessed!" yelled Otis. "We should get away from here!"

"Calm down, brother!" said Willy. "It's not possessed. But it's obviously magnetized."

"It's made of plastic," stated Jim. "How can plastic be magnetized?"

"I'm guessing the plastic coating covers a metal interior that must be used as a weight to keep the cup sturdy on a green. But something turned it into a magnetic force. It happened when Bob started the car. Turn off the car and see what happens."

Bob turned off the ignition, and the cup fell to the ground. Then he started it back up, and sure enough, the cup jumped from the asphalt and clutched to the chassis. He shut down the car, and again, the cup fell off.

Willy took a pocketknife from his pants and began to shave the plastic off the cup. What he saw startled everyone in the car. The inside was a metal that had tiny electric wires running through it.

*****

The following morning

"They're designed like golf cups," stated Mel firmly, "but they are used to determine the exact circumference, balance, and roll of St. Max's golf balls. I have a simpler question: What do you think you're doing? You're an ex-cop, Willy, and you know better than to open someone else's mail and packages!"

Willy dropped his head in embarrassment. Mel was right. Bob, Jim, Otis, and Willy had decided to wait until morning and get Mel and Keith's take on the metallic cup. They were now being scolded in Deacon Ollie's apartment, where Willy had taken them to see the box and have a chat.

"Yes, you're absolutely right," said Willy sheepishly. "But can you explain how they work?"

"The magnetic force surrounds the ball while the electronics measure the ball's dynamics under pressure. We test every ball before we package them. Any that don't meet our standard of excellence become X-Outs, and we sell them to driving ranges."

"Okay, so I don't understand any of that physics jargon, but it sounds legit," inserted Bob. "My question is, why did Father Jacob tell us they were golf cups that Ollie would use to build a miniature putt-putt course?"

"Because the deacon mentioned doing that a while back, but it never materialized," said Keith. "Father was mistaken. But knowing him the way we do, he was probably upset that someone had opened the deacon's package without Ollie knowing about it! He's got a pretty good grip on sin, you know!"

The room became silent. Keith was right, and they all knew it. They had jumped to the wrong conclusion and now sat red-faced and uncomfortable.

Jim decided to break the ice. "We're sorry. And I just want to say that I'm impressed with how we're testing and perfecting St. Max's golf balls. If I golfed, I would want to use a quality ball that I knew had been thoroughly examined before being sold. That's a credit to both you and Tommy Williams, too!"

"Thank you, Jim," said Mel smiling. "Now, if you folks don't mind, we have a lot of work to do."

*****

"Well, that settles that!" declared Jim.

"Yessiree!" proclaimed Otis. "Us investigators solved that mystery!"

Bob wasn't so sure. Something was bothering him, but he couldn't pinpoint it. "We didn't solve anything, Otis. Mel and Keith explained it all away. Willy, what do you think?" All eyes turned to their de facto leader.

"First things first. Opening that box was wrong. If we were actual detectives, we would have to present our suspicions to a judge, who then would give us a court order to open the box. But that's all in the past now. Mel and Keith's clarification made sense. If you make anything in this world and demand quality, you scrutinize it to ensure it's as good as possible. All great companies put their products to rigorous tests: Mercedes Benz, Apple, Sony, and even Titleist. Our golf balls are no different, and I appreciate that our paid engineers are conducting meticulous trials."

Willy stopped talking abruptly and walked to the window. He stared at the airport runway like he was in a trance. "I think you have a 'but' you want to add to your statement about quality testing, Willy," said Bob. "Tell us what you're thinking."

"What doesn't make sense to me is the number of cups in the box. Fifty-four. Why not fifty or sixty—a round number? It would be easier to figure costs for products packaged in tens."

"Perhaps we should contact the manufacturer and find out," voiced Bob. "The bill of lading said the company was TST Industries in the Bahamas. As head of security, I would be obliged to make that call for y'all!"

"Bob's a pretty good poet, too!" grinned Otis. "Isn't he?!"

*****

After church on Sunday, September 6th, 2014, Bob called the group together for a meeting in the school's teacher lounge. Monday would be Labor Day, and the day after would be St. Max's kids first school day. Dora Mann was busy preparing her room for Tuesday, and Jim lent a helping hand. He took a break to hear what Bob had to say.

"Sorry, but I'm a couple of months late getting back to y'all. TST Industries doesn't have a website. Nor do they have a listed phone number, but they do have a fax machine. I found the fax number by paying the online Yellow Pages twenty dollars for a search. I didn't know the Yellow Pages cover the US, Canada, Mexico, and the Caribbean Islands. Learned something there! Anyway, how does a business make money these days with no website or phone number?!"

"They must market only by word of mouth, I guess," replied Willy. "TST Industries must have built a strong client base through the years. Did you get any more information about the company?"

"Well, yes," said Bob. "That's why it took me so long to get back to you guys. After what I learned from the Yellow Page search, I hired a lawyer to follow up and get me as much information as he could find."

"What?!" exclaimed Willy. "Where did you get the money to hire a lawyer?"

"Okay, well, that's a small problem. He didn't ask for a retainer, so we owe him $10,000." Everyone in the room gasped. "I know, I know. That sounds like a lot, but it was a flat fee that included as much travel as he deemed necessary to get us our information!"

"And where do you propose we find the money to pay him?!" growled Willy.

"Let's worry about that later. He gave us until October 1st to pay the bill. Anyway, here's what he came up with. TST Industries is registered in Plana Cay in the Bahamas. The lawyer couldn't travel there because he wasn't able to find any public transportation to the island. But he discovered that TST has bank accounts in Nassau, the Cayman Islands, Switzerland, and Macao."

"You can stop right there, Bob! You say they have bank accounts in the Bahamas, the Caribbean, Europe, and Asia. Oh my God! What's the company's net worth?"

"Converted to American currency, it's nearly a trillion dollars!" Another gasp from the group!

"And if one of the banks is in Switzerland, you can bet they are hiding money! Swiss banks are closed-mouth! How did St. Max's Catholic Church start doing business with TST? I mean, how the heck did they ever find them with no advertising, website, or even a phone number!?"

Jim was fidgeting with a pen. He was tapping it on a table, making an annoying noise. Bob noticed that his friend looked very unsettled. "What's the matter, Jim? You appear a bit anxious!"

"You said the company was headquartered in Plana Cay. You also said there is no public transportation to the island. Well, that's because the island is uninhabited."

"That's impossible!" declared Willy. How could they manufacture products if no one lived there to work in the factory? Who told you the island had no residents?"

"Let's just say a person I don't ever want to see again who happens to work at the Port of Miami. I'm not sure he was right about the island being uninhabited, but there's certainly one thing I do know."

"What's that?" asked Bob. Everyone's eyes were focused on Jim.

"The Bibles we imported to give to the poor and homeless were shipped from Plana Cay."

*****

The US Fish and Wildlife Service provided their South Florida Division a $100,000 discretionary stipend yearly. As the director, Willy Banks could use the funds however he deemed appropriate. He decided to pay lawyer Marvin Zayer the $10,000 fee he was owed for his research on TST Industries. Willy would work overtime and pick up a second job as a night security officer to repay the borrowed money.

Willy looked at his calendar. He had three weeks of vacation coming up next February. He planned to travel to Plana Cay and find out precisely how TST operated. Willy hoped the island offered deep sea fishing, hammocks, and beach bars stocked with rum.

CHAPTER TWENTY-ONE

October 2014

Eric Mann won three USGA-sanctioned junior golf tournaments in the fall of 2014. Hugh Kraft had pushed Jim and Dora into letting their son play, even though he would miss some school and travel to Texas, Georgia, and South Carolina. That was the only way Eric could receive a ranking, which was the next step to going pro. He was the only player to shoot under par for each thirty-six-hole tournament. His handicap was now an amazing negative six! After winning the final match at Hilton Head, Eric became the first twelve-year-old to be ranked number one internationally. It was especially incredible because he zoomed to the top without ever being previously ranked.

The bad news was a golfer couldn't compete at the PGA pro level until he or she turned eighteen. That meant Eric needed to wait another six years to become eligible. He could continue playing in junior tournaments, but Hugh was worried that his young protégé would eventually become bored, seeing his competition wasn't anywhere near Eric's skill level.

Hugh appealed the minimum age requirement to the Professional Golfers Association. He had a signed affidavit from Wayne Siebold, who strongly supported making an exception for allowing Eric to compete. Hugh then asked his buddy Jack Nicklaus to write a letter in Eric's favor.

The PGA executives found themselves in a quandary. If they allowed one underage player, would they have to enable all of them? What if Eric was all hype and choked on the pro circuit? They could all lose their jobs.

Hugh proposed a challenge. If Eric could shoot at least par on the Old Course at St. Andrews in Scotland, the PGA would allow the boy to enter the pro circuit. To make it more interesting, Hugh said Eric would not be allowed to play a practice round: He would need to be evaluated on his first try.

The PGA execs laughed. There was no way a young kid could shoot par on the Old Course. Many pros found that task nearly impossible! After a quick chat, they consented to Hugh's proposition. But Eric would need to play in January when the temps in St. Andrews averaged forty-four degrees. There was a chance it might be snowing on the day he played. That was a risk he would need to accept. Hugh reluctantly agreed.

*****

December 2014

Father Jacob had made it a ritual to pray for Eric before golf matches and bless his St. Max's Premium Golf Balls in holy water and touch them with a small cross. The youngster and his parents believed the blessing was why Eric performed so well during the amateur golf tournaments. After the last Sunday in Advent (December 20th) service, Father was told about Eric's upcoming trip to Scotland. During the December 27th service, Father asked the congregation to pray for Eric. First, for safe travels to the United Kingdom, and second, for a masterful performance on the Old Course in a few weeks.

Mel and Keith weren't Catholic; thus, neither had ever gone to Sunday mass at St. Max's. They dropped in on a few daily prayer services just to show their faces. Father Jacob was concerned that his two engineers weren't living a Christian life, so he convinced them to attend mass during the Christmas season. Keith insisted they sit in the back so they could make a quick exit! The birth of Jesus was a miracle that Mel and Keith accepted willingly. Hearing about Eric playing the course where golf was invented for the chance to become professional raised their eyebrows!

The engineers and Tommy Williams met with Father and told him they would fly to Scotland to watch Eric's tryout. They cautioned Father not to tell anyone in the parish, especially Eric and his family. There was no need to make the kid nervous! The engineers wanted a firsthand examination of the St. Max's Premium Ball and its performance under harsh conditions. Mel would bring a drone along to record the ball's flight path. Father blessed the three with safe travels.

*****

Shortly after Christmas

While Mel, Keith, and Tommy were becoming faux Christians, Hugh Kraft flew Eric to Whistler, British Columbia, to play several rounds of golf in the snow. What better way to prepare for Scotland in January?! They would hack away at the Arnold Palmer-designed Whistler Golf Course. In the summer, the par seventy-two, 6,722-yard course is a breathtaking panorama of wide fairways, gentle streams, and picturesque lakes bordered by magnificent cedars and firs. However, in the winter, the frozen lakes draw ice fishermen from all over Canada, and often the sportsmen are stranded in their warming shacks while blizzards blow perilously through the mountains.

Wayne Siebold offered to help Hugh train Eric, and he flew them to Vancouver International Airport in his private jet. Had pro golf not worked out for him, Siebold planned to be a commercial pilot. They rented a four-wheel drive Jeep Wrangler from the airport, which proved to be a smart move. Fifty miles north on Highway 99, better known as the Sea to Sky Highway, it began to snow, and the roads were slippery. The final thirty-four miles to Whistler took three hours as cars slid everywhere in chaotic disarray! Sirius Radio struggled to hold on to a satellite signal. Eric and Hugh were forced to listen to Wayne's elephant and knock-knock jokes to pass the time.

They finally pulled into the Nita Lake Lodge a few minutes before midnight on December 28th. And despite the late hour, a group of workers had hung around to get Wayne's autograph. Rumors about his arrival began shortly after he booked his reservation. All the diehard golf fans on staff waited seemingly forever for him to make his way up from Vancouver. Eric and Hugh headed to the three-bedroom suite and crashed as Wayne was getting writer's cramp in the lobby!

The next morning, the temperature was ten below zero, so Wayne and Hugh decided to sleep in and wait a day or two for the weather to warm up a bit. Eric took advantage of his free time by renting ice skates and snowshoes from the hotel and making his way to Nita Lake. With no coaching, Eric mastered the winter sports regardless. The next day, he talked Hugh into letting him try downhill skiing on Whistler Mountain. He loved it so much that he dreamt about chucking golf and becoming an Olympic skier.

On New Year's Eve, it was time to practice. The temps had risen into the low twenties, and although it would be windy, at least snow was not in the forecast. Due to the snow already on the course, Hugh had ordered the golf balls painted black. The course executives told them they could chip onto the greens, but putting was prohibited. They didn't want a lot of foot traffic on the delicate areas. That was not a problem—putting through snow would be ridiculous! Wayne and Hugh promised to pay for any repairs that may be necessary.

All three showed up at the first tee in down-filled jackets and warm leather gloves. The practice range was off-limits because the resort had put in an ice rink for youth skating and hockey. Hugh taught Eric a variety of stretches for cold-weather sports. He then gave him a baseball bat to loosen up his swing. Eric felt like he was bound by tape. Wayne emphasized that he must use his entire body the same as he would in warm weather golf. Using no club, he showed him how to rotate his upper and lower torso while providing lift with his legs. This wasn't going to be easy!

Finally, Eric brushed snow off the area he was going to stand, grabbed his driver, and teed up his black Titleist. His swing was irregular, and he didn't keep his head down as he struck the ball. The Titleist hooked wickedly to the left and landed in a grove of tall pine trees. Hugh and Wayne were only there to coach, so Eric played alone. He teed up a provisional and hooked it worse than his first ball. The youngster was frustrated and pounded his driver into the ground. Then realizing that was unsportsmanlike, he turned and apologized to Hugh and Wayne. Both smiled and gave him a hug.

As tears streamed down his cheeks, Eric whimpered, "I can't do this with a winter jacket, long underwear, and gloves. I feel too restricted."

"There's no such word as *can't* in pro sports, son." Hugh was working on Eric's positive attitude. "You can say *you haven't yet.* In other words, you can tell me you haven't learned to hit well yet wearing a winter jacket, long underwear, and gloves. Okay? Now, tee up another ball and imagine you are in Florida wearing a Polo. The last two shots you were using only your arms. You need a smooth, whole-body stroke like usual. Remember, power comes from your legs. Take a few practice swings with your eyes closed. Don't hit the ball until you are sure your mechanics are excellent!"

Eric teed up his second provisional, then did precisely as his mentor advised. He took eight practice swings before addressing his ball. The contact with the Titleist was perfect, and the ball sailed into the frozen air with incredible velocity. It landed 230 yards in the middle of the fairway but stopped almost on a dime. The cold air deadened the flight, and the snow halted the ball's progress. But it was an excellent shot, and Eric jumped up high, then ran over and gave Wayne and Hugh another hug!

Eric was 150 yards from the pin. He bent down, brushed the snow around the ball, and was about to pick it up and place it on the clearing when Hugh yelled at him. "What exactly do you think you're doing, young man!"

"Nothing. I'm just moving my ball from the snow, that's all. Why?"

"Because that would be a two-stroke penalty. You need to hit the ball where it lies. You can clear snow for your feet, but you must address the ball where it is."

"I can't—." Hugh raised his hand to cut him off, then shook his head no. Eric didn't need any words; he knew what Hugh was thinking. "Okay, okay. Yes, I can, and I will make a great shot!"

Eric pulled out a five iron from his bag, stepped up to the ball, took twelve practice swings, and landed the ball in the dead center of the green. Hugh and Wayne stared at each other in disbelief! Because putting wasn't allowed, Eric picked up his ball and walked to the next tee. He had never played Whistler before, but he managed to hit fifteen of the eighteen holes in regulation. His confidence level and that of his mentors were sky-high. Tomorrow Eric would turn thirteen years old, and the future was brighter than the sun!

Hugh didn't find it necessary to play any more rounds at Whistler. Instead, he wanted Eric to work on specialty shots from various course areas. Hugh taught him how to purposely hook and slice the ball because those shots would be needed in the pros. He also had Eric play with left-handed clubs for those times he wouldn't have a quality swing right-handed. Then, after nine hours of practicing in the snow and cold, it was time for a steak dinner, birthday cake, and hot chocolate. Tomorrow, they would drive back to Vancouver and fly home to Florida.

But tonight, Eric wanted some alone time to celebrate his new life as a teenager. There was an ice fishing rental shack behind the lodge. It was midnight, and of course, no one was working. Eric didn't think anyone would mind if he borrowed an ice auger, a pole, and a bucket of minnows. He dressed warmly and snuck out of the hotel unseen. The rental shack was unlocked because, in the past, the hotel found no need to lock it. First, the gear was antiquated with old-style equipment. Second, who stole ice fishing gear in Whistler?!

Nita Lake Lodge was situated on the southern tip of Nita Lake. Eric struggled to carry the auger, pole, and bait to the shore. He placed the gear on the sand and tiptoed onto the ice. What a thrill! Walking on frozen water! You can't do that in Florida! He decided to run and slide in his padded snow pants. Eric pretended to be a baseball player stealing second base.

He hustled back to the shore, grabbed the gear, and walked about fifty yards on the ice. The auger had an eight-inch blade and looked simple enough to operate. Unfortunately, Eric didn't know that drilling with a hand auger required proper form. His knees touched each other, so his base wasn't solid. He should have used an open stance and kept his feet shoulder-width apart. But his biggest mistake was not wearing ice cleats.

Eric hunched over the handle, and his top hand wiggled from side to side as he applied pressure while turning the screw. He kept losing his balance but didn't give up. The blade swiveled between the ice at an awkward angle. When it finally broke through, the auger and Eric splashed perilously into the freezing water!

The sudden chill dulled his senses. Eric let go of the auger and scrambled to find the ice layer. As he came closer to the surface, the weight of his clothes pulled him down. His mind began playing tricks, and he became confused. His hand grabbed the edge of the ice next to the hole, but he didn't have the strength to pull himself out. Finally, Eric realized that this was where he was going to die. He loosened his grip on the edge and was ready to float to his death under the ice when two strong hands grabbed his jacket and yanked the boy up.

Eric began to shiver and regain consciousness. He was face down, sliding across the ice, when he tilted his head up and saw the person with a grip on his jacket. That man was lying face down, three inches from his own head. And behind the man who held the grip on his jacket was another man standing with his hands grasped on the feet of his hero. That person was pulling Eric and the other man away from the ice hole.

When all three were far enough away from the ice break, the two men huddled Eric to try and warm him up. Then one lifted him into his arms and rushed him back to the hotel. They entered a room on the first floor, quickly removed Eric's wet clothes, then wrapped him in blankets. The man who had done the pulling put a thermometer in Eric's mouth. His temperature read eighty-nine degrees. The boy was suffering from moderate hypothermia.

Eric fell asleep in an SUV and awoke in a hospital bed. When his vision cleared, he saw the two men who had saved his life sitting in chairs. Although they wore wool beanies pulled down to their eyes and scarves covering the bottom of their faces, they looked very familiar. Eric thought he had seen them in church or around St. Max's in Florida.

When Eric was fully conscious, the two men introduced themselves. "Hi, Buddy. I'm Roy, and this is Rick. We'll be heading out now that we know you're okay."

"Hey, wait a minute. I feel like I know you guys. Have we ever met?"

"No, son. I'm sure we haven't met. We're on the road crew here in Whistler. When it snows, we run the plows. We were going to work last night when we noticed you on the ice. You should never go on the ice alone."

The two men stayed as far back as possible from Eric in the hospital room. Eric was still trying to make out their faces, but all he could see was their eyes, nose, and mouth. "Yeah, yeah, you're right. I'm very sorry for putting you guys through all this. But thanks for saving my life!"

"Well, we'll be going then. Take care of yourself, young man!" They padded out to the hallway and closed the door.

A nurse saw them heading to the exit and yelled, "Hey, where are you going?! We need you to help us identify the kid! He has no identification on him, you know!"

"Sorry," said Roy, "but we don't know the kid, and we need to get to work. We have no idea where he came from or who he belongs to."

"But you two are heroes! You saved him from drowning! I think the newspaper should take a picture and run a story."

"That's okay, ma'am. We don't want any attention. We did what we had to do, that's all. Anyone would have done the same thing." With that, Roy and Rick exited the building. After getting in their SUV, Roy pulled out a disposable cell phone. He had several in the car's glove compartment.

Not wanting the person he was calling to answer the phone, Roy punched in the Slydial phone number. With this service, he could leave a voicemail without talking to the person. After listening to a mandatory Slydial advertisement, Roy left a blunt message at 6:30 am. "Eric is in Room Nineteen at the Whistler Emergency Health Care Center. He is fine and recovering from hypothermia."

*****

January 2015

Hugh and Wayne awoke at 7:00 am to pack and prepare for their trip back to Florida. Hugh opened Eric's door to wake him, but he wasn't in his bedroom. Wayne was in the suite's small kitchen making a pot of coffee when Hugh asked, "Hey, where's Eric? Have you seen him, Wayne?"

"Well, if he ain't here, he's probably down in the game room playing video games."

"You think he would get up early just for that?"

"Sure thing. He doesn't have a PlayStation or Xbox at home."

Hugh decided to go to the game room and check. Leaving the room, he picked up his cell phone and noticed that he had a voicemail. After listening to it, he muttered, "What the hell!"

"What is it?" asked Wayne.

"Someone left a message that Eric is in the emergency hospital. He is recovering from hypothermia!"

"What?! Huh?! Are you sure?! Who left the message?"

"I don't know, but we must get over there fast. We'll pack later!" Hugh and Wayne grabbed their coats and dashed for their rental car.

*****

Eric was sipping his third cup of hot chocolate. A bowl of chicken noodle soup lay empty by his bed. He was covered in blankets but seemed to be wide awake and alert. He had just finished apologizing profusely to Hugh and Wayne for sneaking off and falling through the ice. They were just thankful Eric was still alive and kicking!

"You said those two guys who saved your life were Roy and Rick?" asked Hugh. "And you think you've seen them before at St. Max's?"

"Yeah, I think so," replied Eric meekly. "But they don't go to church much. I thought I've seen them go into our apartment building sometimes."

Hugh pulled Wayne aside out of Eric's earshot. "Is he hallucinating from the cold, or could this be a legit coincidence?"

"Two guys from Palm Beach Gardens taking a ski trip to Whistler could happen, I guess," replied Wayne. "But aren't the folks who attend St. Max's kinda poor? I didn't think they could afford a trip like that. Seems strange to me."

"Yeah, me too. And then, to be on the ice in the wee hours of the morning makes it even less coincidental. We need to call Eric's mom and dad and tell them about him falling through the ice and to let them know that he's okay. I'll ask Jim if he knows a Roy and Rick that go to St. Max's."

*****

"He's fine, Jim!" emphasized Hugh, trying to assure Eric's dad and mom that their son would be well soon. "And don't worry about the hospital costs—I've got that covered, too." Hugh had called Father Jacob's phone at the church because the Manns still had no cell. Father was in the back of his office, listening to the conversation.

"Who did you say saved his life?" asked Jim.

"Eric said their names were Roy and Rick, and he's seen them around the church. Do you know any St. Max's members with those names?"

"No, there's no one in our church named Roy or Rick. Was Eric sure about that?"

"Well, not really. The hypothermia could have been playing with his mind. Anyway, we'll be heading back to Florida as soon as the doctors release your son. Eric looked impressive playing on the frozen, snowy golf course. I'm so looking forward to Scotland! See you soon!"

"Yep, thanks, Hugh. Please have a safe journey back to Florida."

When Jim hung up, he and Dora both cried. Were they pushing their son too hard to be a pro golfer? The close call on the ice could have been tragic. Father Jacob walked over and gave them both a hug.

"I'll continue to say prayers for Eric."

CHAPTER TWENTY-TWO

January 2015

PGA officials in St. Andrews set a date for Eric's chance at fame to January 28th, 2015. It was a Wednesday, and the Old Course would be closed to the public due to bleacher repairs. British administrators apologized to Hugh after they told him there would be pallets of wood and various mechanical equipment and tools on the edges of some fairways. Hugh asked for a different date, but the PGA said no. And not only did they refuse to reschedule, but they also noted that the manmade mess on the course would be in play. Eric wouldn't be allowed a free drop if his shot ended up in a pile of lumber!

Father Jacob gave Eric a dozen St. Max's Premium Golf Balls he had blessed. Although Hugh wanted Eric to play with Titleist Pro Vs, Eric refused. He believed a higher power would lead him to shoot the necessary par to secure a place on the PGA circuit. Wayne Siebold told Hugh to let Eric use the balls the boy wanted. Golf required confidence, and that's what Eric needed most. Besides, a little help from heaven couldn't hurt anyone!

Because Eric wouldn't be allowed a practice round, leaving a week or so early was unnecessary. Eric was pleased—he didn't want to miss much school anyway. He was the top student in his mother's class, after all! Hugh just wanted to make sure Eric would recover from jet lag. The PGA officials said they would allow him to walk around the course without his golf clubs. It was better than nothing!

Jim and Dora Mann escorted Eric to Wayne Siebold's private jet after school on Friday, January 23rd. With the time change, they would arrive in Edinburgh early on Saturday morning. From there, they would rent an SUV, drive the fifty miles to St. Andrews, and then check into the Old Course Hotel. Eric jokingly asked if the famous grand hotel offered ice fishing!

Wayne's hydraulic fluid warning light blinked as they were on the runway ready for takeoff at North Palm Beach County Airport. Perhaps the jet had a small leak in the lining. He needed to check the system but was hesitant to fly the aircraft back to his hangar at Palm Beach International. They taxied off the runway, hoping that Marcus Aviation could help them check the hydraulics. Unfortunately, Marcus closed at 5:00 pm, less than an hour ago.

Jim mentioned that Mel and Keith had a hangar and remembered an abundance of mechanical devices inside. There was a window on the door to the hangar, and Wayne said he could look inside to see exactly what equipment they had before bothering them. Eric wasn't sure who Mel and Keith were, but he kept his fingers crossed that they would help Wayne. He was itching to get to Scotland.

After peering through the glass, it was likely that the two engineers were gone: Their jet wasn't in the hangar.

*****

The next morning

Marcus Aviation opened on Saturday at 8:00 am. After a thorough test, it was determined that a loose electrical wire in the cockpit was causing the warning light to flicker. The repair would take a couple of hours. At 10:00 am, Hugh, Wayne, and Eric were airborne en route to Edinburgh. They touched down in Scotland on Sunday at 1:00 am. The car rentals were closed for the night and wouldn't reopen until 7:00 am, so the golfers slept on the plane.

Maneuvering the SUV on the left side of the road was a small challenge for Hugh. The built-in GPS offered the three a shortcut to slash a few miles off their drive. Big mistake. After traversing the Queensferry Crossing Bridge, Hugh exited the M90 freeway at Inverkeithing and headed east. The four lanes quickly gave way to two lanes, then to one lane for two-way traffic! Places to pull over to allow oncoming cars and trucks to pass were few and far between. Twice, Hugh had to back up a hundred yards or so to find an area that would let vehicles by. And without his morning coffee, trying to visualize using a roundabout the wrong way was adding to his ever-increasing headache! Trying his best to not be a backseat driver, Wayne offered no advice but had a firm grip on the dashboard!

Hugh had randomly selected the Old Union Coffee Shop near the campus of St. Andrew's University as his GPS destination. It was 11:00 when they arrived, which was an excellent time to find a seat in the busy café. Mass started at 11:00 at St. Salvator's Chapel next door. The coffee-drinking college kids moseyed out of Old Union and into the church, leaving plenty of open tables in the cafe and streetside.

Wayne hadn't played in the British Open for many years, and he was becoming less recognizable to local fans as time passed. That was just fine with him. He was too tired from the long flight and perilous road trip to St. Andrews to sign autographs. While Eric drank a Coke, Hugh and Wayne ordered large lattes with three extra espresso shots. They all nibbled on wonderful homemade scones.

Eric was daydreaming while his coaches were discussing plans for the week. Suddenly, he dropped his scone and gazed at three men seated at a table in the back corner of Old Union. Hugh glanced at Eric and asked, "What's the matter, son? You look like you've seen a ghost!"

Eric pointed at the men and replied, "Those guys there in the corner!"

"What about them?" asked Wayne.

"It's Roy and Rick and some other guy. You know, the ones who saved my life when I fell through the ice in Whistler!"

CHAPTER TWENTY-THREE

January 2015 (A moment later)

"Excuse us," said Hugh calmly. "May I ask your names?"

Hugh and Wayne stood in front of the three men sitting in the corner. Eric was wedged protectively between his two coaches.

"And who may I ask is inquiring?" replied one man in a soft British accent.

"My name is Hugh, and this is Wayne. I'm guessing you know the young boy here in between us."

The man glanced at Eric, then looked away immediately. "I'm sorry, I don't know the lad." He turned to his friend sitting next to him. "How about you, Johnny?"

"No, Egbert, I dunno him either."

The third man shook his head no but said nothing.

Eric took a step forward, but Hugh grabbed the collar of his shirt and held him in place. "You're lying!" yelped Eric. He pointed at the two men. "You're Roy, and you're Rick. And you saved my life a couple of weeks ago in Canada!"

The two men blurted out a laugh. Their friend sat with a stern look on his face. Then, the first man, who appeared to be the leader, said, "Sorry, laddie, you think we saved your life in Canada?! We ain't been anywhere over the big pond. Though, I wish we could take credit for such an act of valor!"

Hugh started to pull Eric back. "Okay, sorry, gentlemen. There must have been a mix-up. You folks have a nice day."

Eric shook free from Hugh's grip and stepped to the men's table. "I'm not wrong, and you know it! And I've seen all three of you around our church! Why do you pretend not to know me? Why did you leave the hospital in Whistler so fast? Why can't you see how thankful I am for saving my life?!"

"Sorry, laddie, but you're mistaken, that's all. We must look like this Roy and Rick you speak about. But I can assure you we've ne'r set foot in Canada. And we ne'r seen you before, especially at a church."

"No! You're lying! I know—"

Hugh and Wayne both pulled Eric away from the table. They paid their bill at the counter, then left in a hurry. Eric dropped his head and started crying as he walked out the door.

The man who had done most of the talking at the corner table whispered to the other two, "What now? The kid recognizes us."

*****

Their suite at the Old Course Hotel, Golf Resort, and Spa was owned by Jack Nicklaus and aptly named The Golden Bear Retreat. The PGA purchased the extra-large room for Jack as a retirement gift in 2005. Nicklaus and his close friends used it every year. Being Jack's best friend, Hugh was told he could stay there as long as he wished, and daily food, drinks, and midnight snacks were all graciously comped by the Golden Bear. The hotel combined two rooms to make the suite for Jack, and it was on the top floor overlooking the seventeenth green.

Being overly tired from the delayed flight, jet lag, and harrowing drive to St. Andrews, Hugh, Wayne, and Eric crashed for the rest of the afternoon. After they awoke, it was too late to hit some balls at a local driving range. The PGA wouldn't allow Eric to practice on the Old Course or its driving range before he teed off on Wednesday.

After a scrumptious dinner of Cullen Skink, wild grouse stewed in a casserole, and a Clootie Dumpling for dessert, all three were coaxed into an after-dinner cocktail to lighten up their caloric meal. The dumpling, made from dried fruit, sugar, spices, flour, milk, and a secret ingredient the waiter refused to mention, was boiled in a cloth known as a clootie. It settled in their stomachs in an indigestibly heavy way! The waiter suggested a wee dram or two of Dewar's Whiskey for Hugh and Wayne and an Irn-Bru for Eric. Although Irn-Bru did have a small amount of alcohol, the waiter said it was very slight and indistinguishable.

When it was time to head back to their suite, Hugh signaled for the waiter to bring the bill. The waiter came and told him that Jack Nicklaus had taken care of everything. Hugh was grateful for his friend's generosity, but he repeatedly told the waiter it wasn't necessary.

"I'm sorry, Mr. Kraft, but I must follow the orders of the greatest golfer ever. The Golden Bear is Scotland's GOAT!"

"Yes, he certainly is the GOAT—in more ways than one! I can say that because we grew up together in Ohio and caused more trouble than we were worth!"

"Ohio? Is that where Mount Rushmore is? Sorry, my United States geography needs some improvement."

"No, but don't sweat it. My Scottish folklore needs improvement. I still believe in the Loch Ness monster! Anyway, you've been great, and I'll give you a huge tip beyond what Jack provides for you! But only on one condition—you must tell us the secret ingredient in the Clootie Dumpling."

"And what's in this drink of mine!" blurted Eric as the waiter grinned. "It tastes like pears, bubblegum, sugar, rust, blackberries, cough syrup, and a salty banana all mixed together!"

"Do you like it?" asked the waiter.

"Yuk! Not really! But at least I'm having an after-dinner drink with the guys!" Eric smiled at Hugh and Wayne.

"And you will say nothing to your mother!" exclaimed the pro golfers in unison.

The waiter laughed, then asked sheepishly, "Do you really want to know the secret ingredient in the Clootie Dumpling?"

"Of course!" Hugh cried out.

"Suet. It's suet. Okay, well, I should get back to work! Thanks for coming!"

As the waiter turned, Wayne held up his hand. "Whoa, whoa, whoa. So, you need to tell us what suet is!"

"Are ye sure? Perhaps you'd best be heading back to your room."

"Uh uh! Not so fast. What exactly is suet?"

The waiter fidgeted, then said coyly, "It's the hard creamy fat on the kidneys and loins of cattle and sheep."

Eric's face turned white, and he vomited.

*****

The following day

Eric played the impressive Dukes Course on Monday and Tuesday and used their driving range. The natural shrubland habitat of acidic soils and open, low-growing woody vegetation provided exciting rounds of perils and possibilities, something he would encounter at the Old Course.

Herb Kohler, better known in eastern Wisconsin as the Multi-Billion-Dollar Toilet and Bathtub King, owned the Duke's Course in St. Andrews and cheerfully offered it up for his close friend and sometimes golf partner, Hugh Kraft. The course has hosted the Scottish Matchplay, the Scottish Strokeplay, the European Amateur Championships, and the Scottish Men's Amateur Open.

In 2012, Herb and Hugh won a senior's amateur tournament at Kohler's prestigious golf course, Whistling Straits. PGA championships, US Senior Opens, and US Women's Opens have all been played at the Straits course on the shores of Lake Michigan. The design is similar to St. Andrews, where the game of golf was born. When Hugh told Herb about his young protégé, Kohler said he would offer up the Presidential Suite at the American Club for Eric if he played in the Ryder Cup scheduled for 2021.

"If I had a calendar that dated six years in the future, I would gladly write that down, Herb!" exclaimed Hugh. "But you can hold me to my word when I tell you Eric will play in that tourney! He'll be the number one golfer on the pro circuit in 2021!"

Monday's weather in Scotland was horrendous. The high temperature was thirty-two degrees Fahrenheit, and the winds blew at thirty-five miles per hour from the northwest. Eric shot a five over par seventy-six and sat dejectedly alone in front of the pro shop when he finished. Hugh and Wayne were in the bar strategizing what went wrong. Eric needed to shoot par at the Old Course on Wednesday. If today's round was any indication, he would fly back home to the US to play in amateur tournaments for the next five years.

Tuesday morning, Hugh, Wayne, and Eric walked the Old Course and discussed playing positions. The machinery and wood planks set along the edges of the fairway were nightmares! This would be much more than a test of Eric's skills; it would dig deep into whatever controls luck!

The temperature Tuesday was thirty-two degrees, with winds blowing at thirty-six miles per hour; however, there was light snow in the air. Eric stopped playing after fifteen holes at Duke's. He was already eight strokes over, and there was no way he would make that up in the final three holes. He didn't want to stop because he prided himself on never being a quitter, but Hugh convinced him that the cold, wet weather could be bad for his health. He didn't want Eric to catch the flu before the big day.

That night after dinner, Eric went to bed while Hugh and Wayne had a final brainstorming session in the pub. They decided to drink Guinness Stouts to bring a little luck of the Irish their way! The weather report for Wednesday was frightening. Temps would drop into the upper twenties, winds would increase to the low forties, and blowing snow was scheduled for most of the day. Even the construction workers were given the day off!

*****

"They are all in place and tested," announced the unknown man who had been sitting with Egbert and Johnny at the Old Union Coffee Shop the day

Hugh, Wayne, and Eric walked in. "Cameras and Wi-Fi boosters are installed on bleachers and flagpoles. I will control them here. I rented this room for the day."

The three men sat inside the Jack Cole Building in a small laboratory room at the University of St. Andrew's School of Computer Science. The lab was filled with video equipment, computers, large high-definition screens, sound equalizers and mixers, and virtually anything necessary to do hands-on research while pursuing a technology degree. To raise money, the University would rent the room to non-students for £1,000 a day.

"You're sure this will work?" asked Egbert cautiously.

"I have no reason to believe that it won't! I don't make mistakes, my friends!"

"Wow!" exclaimed Johnny. "Now that's confidence!"

CHAPTER TWENTY-FOUR

January 2015

"Remember what we talked about at Whistler." Hugh gave Eric a pep talk as they walked from the hotel to the clubhouse. "There's no time limit. So, approach your ball, visualize, and line up your shot, then take as many practice swings as necessary. Don't think about the cold, wind, or snow."

At Hugh's insistence, Eric was wearing only a wool sweater over a Polo and light golf pants. He was freezing! His tee time had been changed to 8:10 am. However, the sun didn't officially rise until 8:21. Bottom line, the PGA thought Eric didn't have a chance. They wanted this demonstration of futility over with as soon as possible.

There really wasn't a detectable sunrise on the morning of January 25th. The cloud cover was thick, which fortunately kept the temperature a bit warmer. Eric would tee off at thirty-one degrees with winds blowing from the Polar north at thirty-eight miles per hour. A light dusting of snow was swirling around the entire east coast of Scotland.

Wayne tried to convince Eric to use a Titleist Pro V instead of St. Max's Premium Golf Ball. But Eric refused because he knew the dozen St. Max's balls he had in his bag had been blessed by Father Jacob. He needed every bit of help from heaven on this blistery, miserable day.

Wearing leather gloves, down-filled jackets, and turtleneck sweaters over their long underwear, Clydell MacGavin and Fergus Brùn were the unlucky ones selected by the British PGA to accompany Eric and record his scores. They chatted a couple of minutes with Hugh and Wayne, then met Eric on the first tee and filled him in on the rules of the day.

Eric stretched out every muscle in his body. Then after teeing up his ball, he pulled out his driver and swung it about twenty times to loosen up his arms, legs, and torso. The PGA officials were yawning and sipping from their thermoses of coffee. They were already bored with their assignment of the day.

But when Eric drove his first shot 255 yards onto the iconic wide fairway shared with the eighteenth hole, Clydell dropped his thermos in astonishment. He and Fergus glanced at each other and shook their heads. What an opening shot!

Eric wasn't allowed to hire a caddy, and Hugh hoped his heavy bag full of clubs wouldn't wear the boy down by the end of the round. He walked to his ball, then pulled out an eight iron for his 120-yard approach to the green. Normally, he would have used a pitching wedge or nine iron, but the swirling wind was now blowing directly into his face, and he needed to clear the Swilcan Burn, or his round would most likely end shortly after it began.

The shot was perfect! It lofted gently over the burn, landed softly on the green, and rolled into the cup. Eric scored an eagle on the first hole! Only Tiger Woods had ever accomplished that feat during the British Open!

Hole two would be a more significant challenge. The first of several shared greens lay 453 yards from the tee box down a much narrower fairway. And to top it off, it was a blind tee. Wayne reminded Eric to play the right side of the fairway to avoid Cheape's Bunker on the left. But a poor shot could fly too far right and land in the gorse. The only way out of the massive yellow, pea-blossom-shaped flower bed would require a penalty. Hugh thought about covering his eyes. He wasn't sure he wanted to look.

Eric drove with a three-wood for control, and the ball landed 225 yards from the tee in the center of the fairway. But he still had 228 yards to go in three strokes to make par. Using his three-wood again, the ball appeared to be headed left and short toward the rough. Suddenly, it changed direction, landed on the fringe, and rolled onto the green.

Clydell wasn't supposed to comment, but he couldn't help himself. He looked at Fergus and exclaimed loud enough for all to hear, "How did he do that?! The ball fought directly through the wind!"

Fergus replied even more boisterously, "The kid just defied every law of physics I ever learned!"

Eric needed an uphill putt that would be difficult due to the undulating green. He hoped to get it close to the pin and tap in for par. Instead, the ball traveled in an s-curve and landed in the cup for a birdie!

Hugh whispered into Wayne's ear, "Impossible!"

"Perhaps improbable is a better word, my friend!"

Regardless, Eric was now three under par after two holes. His four observers were in shock!

As he readied to tee off on number three, the snow began blowing in all directions. Those in the know would say the weather had become a blizzard. Hugh and Wayne did their best lawyer imitation and tried to convince Clydell and Fergus to give the wind a few minutes to calm down. But Fergus' retort did hold some value, "If we wait any longer, the laddie will have to putt through the snow. Now you wouldn't want that, right?!"

Eric's tee shot was another gem. Playing smart, he waited for the wind to turn and blow from behind while he took ample practice swings with his driver. A short time later, a strong gust came up on his back, and Eric quickly stepped up to the tee and swung. The nature-powered ball lifted high and landed 253 yards down the fairway, avoiding treacherous bunkers on both sides. Then it rolled another thirty yards for an incredible 283-yard drive.

Eric sat only 115 yards from the pin, but the wind blew right to left. That meant the hazardous moon-shaped Cartgate bunker was posing a serious threat on the front left of the green. Wayne Siebold scored a triple bogey years ago during the British Open on this hole when his ball flew into the sand trap. He struggled to gently place it over the masonry face onto the green. The ball landed easily, but the green's fall-away section at the back right provided a challenging pin position. Wayne explained all this to Eric, then closed his eyes as the youngster approached his ball. He couldn't watch!

Eric played his wedge shot to the right, and the ball blew onto the green and rolled a few inches from the cup. He tapped in for another birdie. He was now four under par after three holes. Clydell and Fergus stepped back from earshot and had a loud disagreement. Hugh and Wayne had no idea what they were arguing about.

"It's about preserving Colin Montgomerie's record, damn it!" yelped Fergus, but not so Hugh, Wayne, or Eric could hear. Spittle was flying all over Clydell's face. "This here laddie will break the Old Course record if we finish the round. We can't have some thirteen-year-old American besting Colin's ten under sixty-two, now can we?! He is and was Scotland's finest golfer!"

"Are ye saying we cheat, Fergus?" asked Clydell.

"Nope. I'm not saying that. The boy is good enough to play in the PGA. Let's just end it now and say he qualified. Then the record stands, and a Scotsman still owns it!"

"We have to submit an eighteen-hole score. How do you propose we maneuver around that obstacle, Fergie?!

"Hugh and Wayne don't know we must turn in a scorecard. We just tell 'em that Eric has passed the test and will be allowed to play in PGA tournaments. They should be happy about that and not question us! Then we make up a scorecard showing Eric shot par and nothing more."

"So ye are saying we will be cheating after all!"

"Consider it just a little white lie. That's all! Look at it this way—we can get da heck off this frozen golf course and warm up with some coffee and Dundee cakes!"

"But this is a weighty decision, my friend. What we say will allow a thirteen-year-old kid to play professional golf! If we get caught, we'll make Dundee cakes for the rest of our lives instead of eating them! Our bosses are going to have a tough time believing all this!"

"If the laddie plays and breaks Colin's course record, don't ya think they'll have a tough time believing that anyway!"

Clydell was about to respond when he was tapped on the shoulder. "What's the holdup here?" asked Hugh. "Eric's getting cold waiting on you two!"

"Okay, okay. On to hole four!" Clydell and Fergus gave each other a scornful glare.

*****

"The boy's playing incredibly! Everything is working perfectly. He's four under par after three holes." The man making the call watched the round on his computer from closed-circuit cameras around the Old Course.

"That's great. But, at that rate, if he plays too well, the British PGA authorities will question the outcome and probably launch some kind of investigation!"

The phone call was being placed from St. Andrews, Scotland, to Florida.

"Yeah, you're right. Hmmm. A minor dilemma, that's all!" The man hung up. Eric was about to tee off on number four.

*****

The snow began to accumulate on the fairways and greens. Hugh had purchased a battery-operated hair dryer before leaving Palm Beach. He thought he could use it to warm Eric's hands if they got cold. Now he found a better use for it—melting the snow from the ground. Clydell and Fergus didn't know how to rule using a hair dryer. They decided to compromise and let Hugh only melt the snow on the greens. Eric would have to make his approach shots as the ball lay.

The weather appeared to fatigue Eric as the round continued. He bogeyed two holes and birdied two holes. However, he managed to par the other eleven holes and finished the game with a fabulous four under, sixty-eight. Clydell and Fergus breathed a deep sigh of relief. Colin Montgomerie's course record was still intact!

Eric Mann would now become the youngest player on the PGA Tour. The news spread like wildfire, so Hugh and Wayne rearranged their schedules to give Eric a chance to talk to the press. They thought the publicity would do him well and build his confidence. They flew Wayne's jet to Glasgow, Edinburgh, London, and Dublin for interviews on the BBC Sports Network, Sky Sports, and Eurosport Network.

While in Dublin, Guinness Brewery marketers approached Eric to become his official sponsor. But Hugh cut them off quickly.

"He can't even legally drink beer for another eight years. Give it a rest!"

CHAPTER TWENTY-FIVE

February 2015

When the private jet landed at the North Palm Beach airport at 10:00 pm on Sunday, February 1st, Hugh and Wayne were exhausted. But Eric was still, figuratively speaking, sky high! The British newspapers had featured him on the front page—not in the sports sections, but as the lead story for all news! He was enraptured with his newfound stardom and couldn't wait to see what the American newspapers and *ESPN* said about him.

But Eric's excitement lurched to a halt as Jim and Dora escorted him straight to the church. They had hugged him and didn't say why a late-night service was taking place. He was startled to see a big screen TV next to the altar. All the parishioners were in attendance except for Willy and Otis. They had been there most of the afternoon and evening because Father Jacob had rented the television for the Super Bowl. But now, everyone sat in tears listening to the WMFL newscast in Miami.

"Once again," said the announcer, "if you are just joining us, we have unfortunate breaking news coming out of Miami Gardens and Sun Life Stadium. Although it hasn't been confirmed, it appears that Super Bowl hero Billy West of the Reno Mountaineers, and his wife Carol, were killed when a news drone struck the windshield of the taxi that was taking them to the airport. The car lost control, crossed the median, and hit a semi-truck head-on.

"Billy's last-second heroics had championed the Reno Mountaineers to an improbable victory over the highly-favored Carolina Panthers. An hour before the accident, Billy had received the MVP trophy at midfield. The future Hall of Famer was forty-two."

St. Max's congregation hadn't left the church following the game's conclusion. Instead, Father Jacob thought the party should continue after Billy West had been honored at the fifty-yard line. The Reno quarterback was well-known for his strong faith and belief in God. They toasted Billy with beer, wine, and Crown Royal whiskey while listening to the post-game interviews. They were barely paying attention later when WMFL interrupted with the tragic breaking news.

Jim Mann cut through the somberness by raising his hand to speak like he was in school. Father Jacob noticed and called on him like a teacher would. "Yes, Jim. Do you have a question?"

"Didn't Deacon Ollie have tickets for the Super Bowl? I remember him telling some of us about it a year ago. Do you know if Ollie was well enough to go?"

"Yes, I believe you are right, Jim. He got tickets from an old friend from college who couldn't attend the game."

"Have you seen or heard from Deacon Ollie?" asked Dora. "He's been gone now for so long! How's he doing?"

"Sorry, I haven't gotten any recent news about Ollie. But I think now would be a good time to pray for him, as well as Billy and Carol West and the semi-truck driver. Everyone, please join hands."

*****

A week came and went with no mention of Eric's accomplishments in Scotland. The tragedy after the Super Bowl consumed the sports headlines around the world. The police investigations provided conflicting stories. Seems the drone that struck the taxi was owned by WMFL, and Miami's flagship news corporation was being crucified as a cheap Paparazzi organization that dangerously gathered stories by placing others at risk. It brought back memories of Princess Diana's 1997 car crash in the Pont de l'Alma tunnel in Paris. WMFL denied that the drone was theirs.

Finally, on Monday, February 8th, the *Palm Beach Post* ran a front-page story featuring their local teenage prodigy, Eric Mann. Unfortunately, the majority of the article talked about his coach, Hugh Kraft, and his other new mentor, Wayne Siebold. Three paragraphs were dedicated to Hugh's friendship with Jack Nicklaus, including Kraft's bicycle accident in Colorado that ended his professional career. Nothing was mentioned about how Eric grew up homeless in the Loxahatchee Slough and was provided shelter by Father Jacob in St. Max's apartments. However, several lines were written about Eric's father's connection to Willy Banks, the great American hero from the 1980s.

Jim and Dora Mann thought more could have been printed about Eric's remarkable golf success. But Eric didn't care. He just admired the photo taken of him inside the Old Course clubhouse, standing next to the full-size statue of Bobby Jones. He clipped the picture from the *Post* and tacked it on his bedroom wall.

All the boys in school wanted to be his best buddy. During recess, Eric became the leader of the pack, so to speak. He always chose teams for kickball, dodgeball, basketball, and whatever game was in style that day. Everyone wanted to be on his squad. And Eric always made sure there was no hierarchy of talent. He rotated his selections so that everyone had a chance to be picked first.

All the girls in school wanted to be his girlfriend. Eric checked all the boxes. He had good looks, a wonderful personality, and extraordinary athleticism. Not to mention he was well on his way to becoming the class *Most Likely to Succeed.* The young ladies were dreaming of marriage and family!

But Hugh was worried. Would all the publicity go to Eric's head? Would he lose focus on his golf game? Would all the demanding work eventually go up in smoke?

Not if Tommy Williams, Mel Smith, and Keith Malone had anything to say about it.

CHAPTER TWENTY-SIX

February 2015

Willy's vacation days were fast approaching. He had tried his darndest to find transportation to Plana Cay without luck. Travel agents just laughed, and all Madame Google could tell him was that the island was part of the Bahamas and uninhabited. "Impossible, it can't be!" muttered Willy to Otis as he pounded his fist on the computer table. He was just using his brother as a sounding board. "If TST Industries is headquartered there, the workers must live there too! Plus, they must have some kind of port. Jim said the Bibles were shipped from Plana Cay. What the heck is going on?!"

Otis didn't have a clue. He had never received a passing grade in social studies or geography before he dropped out of school. But he didn't want his brother to think he was stupid, so he replied, "Maybe the dock workers at Port Everglades could tell you. Don't they unload the ships?"

Willy looked at Otis for a long, curious moment, then said, "You might be right. I'll drive down to the port right now. My vacation starts next Monday, so I must figure something out."

"Mind if I tag along with ya, Bro?"

"Hustle up. Get dressed, and let's get going!"

*****

"Well, sorry, fellas, I can't tell ya where Plana Cay is. No, sirree." Stu Perkins, director of Port Everglades Port Authority, was shaking his balding-gray head. He was an unassuming octogenarian good ol' boy who should have retired twenty years ago. He was basically a glorified public relations specialist—there to make customers happy. "Dang nab it! I oughta know where customer's shipped junk comes from, right?! But it's funny you should show up on my doorstep today."

"Really," said Willy. "Why's that?"

Stu pointed at his computer. "Cuz of this here email that came this morning from Dale Maglia. He's the head of US Customs for the Port of Miami. Pain in the ass, SOB if ya ask me, but he runs the show down there. He put out some sort of alert about Plana Cay."

"An alert. What does it say?!"

Stu stared at Willy with a puzzled look. "Ah, what did ya say your name was again, young man? Billy Tanks?"

"Willy Banks. Willy with a ***w*** and Banks with a ***b***."

"Okay, son, but I'm not sure I can have ya see my emails, ya know. I'm a person of great authority, ya know. Seems emails are private. Back in the day, I wouldn't be showing ya my letters, now would I?"

"Yep, you're right, Stu. But reading me just one tiny email is no big deal." Willy paused for a minute to think. "Do you fish, Stu?"

"Do I fish?" asked Stu. "Do I ever!! I love fishing. Why?"

"I'd like to take you on a guided tour of the Loxahatchee Slough. I know where all the fierce-fighting largemouth bass and big Mayan cichlid are caught!"

"Yep, he sure does!" added Otis with enthusiasm.

"Man, oh man! I sure would love to do that!" exclaimed Stu. "And you wouldn't charge me nothin'?"

"Nope. Just read me that one little email from Dale Maglia, and we'll call it even!"

"Well, I guess that won't hurt nothin'. But I don't read aloud so well. So, if ya don't mind, I'll just print it out."

"No, problem, Stu. Thanks!"

At age eighty-seven, Stu struggled with technology. But he did know how to use the printer. Sometimes. He handed a copy of the email to Willy.

DATE: *Wednesday, February 11, 2015*
TO: *All Port Authority Directors*
FROM: *Dale Maglia*
US Customs (Port of Miami)

As you may remember, about seven years ago, the MV Gulf Streamer sank in the Atlantic Ocean while delivering cargo to the Port of Miami. Recovery efforts have been complex because an explosion onboard the Streamer shredded the hull into hundreds of pieces. Chemical residue found on various deck parts indicates that an unknown, volatile substance most likely caused the detonation.

This coming July, the statute of limitations runs out relative to prosecuting criminal actions related to the incident. Thus, I am submitting our findings to the FBI today.

We believe combustible material was placed in a shipment of Bibles originating from Plana Cay, Bahamas. Because of this, I am issuing this order: No cargo from Plana Cay will be allowed into the United States, and no ship will be allowed into a United States port if it has docked in Plana Cay.

This order will go into effect on April 1, 2015, if approved by the Commissioner for U.S. Customs and Border Protection (CBP). You will be notified by his office when the declaration becomes official. Meanwhile, the FBI will thoroughly investigate the sinking of the MV Gulf Streamer and releases its findings to the CBP and the Congressional Subcommittee on Maritime Crimes and Punishment.

Willy read the email several times. He knew St. Max's Church was importing Bibles to distribute to the homeless and poor, but he didn't know where they came from. Were the Bibles possibly manufactured in Plana Cay, the same island making the golf cups? Something wasn't right—that would be too much of a coincidence!

*****

On Monday, February 16th, Willy rented a 2000 Sea Ray 460 Sundancer with twin Cummins 8.3-liter diesel engines from Bongo Bay Marina in Ft. Lauderdale. The yacht's rental price was rather steep: $10,000 a day. Willy paid with his business credit card and hoped his bosses would sign off without questions. They trusted him and had never scrutinized his expenses. However, this one might raise an eyebrow!

Willy asked Jim Mann, Bob Butler, and Otis if they would like to join him on a Bahamas vacation. Willy confided his destination to Jim and Bob and asked them to keep it quiet. It was okay to tell Dora and Becky, but he didn't want anyone in the parish to know he was checking out Plana Cay for himself.

Jim and Bob told their wives that Willy offered to take them on a fishing excursion for a few days in the Atlantic Ocean. Dora and Becky were happy for their husbands, knowing neither Jim nor Bob ever had a real vacation. The men guaranteed they would bring home plenty of seafood, and the entire parish would have a surprise fish fry when they returned. But, as Willy had requested, they told Dora and Becky not to tell anyone in the congregation where they were going.

According to the yacht's built-in maritime GPS, their destination was 474 miles away. Willy guessed they could make it in sixteen hours at a cruising speed of thirty miles per hour. They left at noon on Monday and planned to travel through the night. Otis became pale, not from the motion of the ocean, but from thinking about being in the middle of the Bermuda Triangle at night. Weren't there devils lurking about underwater?!

The Sea Ray had two cabins and two heads. Jim, Bob, and Otis played cards on the kitchen table for a few hours after dinner, then crashed at midnight. Captain Willy stayed awake and navigated the relatively calm waters despite being extremely tired. He saw nothing but a few cargo and cruise ships the entire night. Willy prayed that his GPS was correct. The rental agent at Bongo Bay Marina had preprogrammed it; however, he had just guessed at the coordinates based on a maritime map. Plana Cay had two islands, an east and a west. The Sea Ray was headed for the western one.

Miraculously, the boat approached its destination just as the beautiful sunrise lit the Atlantic waters in bright orange, soft blue, and dull gray colors. Jim and Bob wandered up on the deck with coffee mugs. Otis was snoring in his cabin.

"You okay, Willy?" yelled Jim up to the cockpit. "Need anything?"

"I'm tired, man! How about some coffee?"

"What's next?" asked Bob.

"We'll circle the western island and look for a dock and anything that resembles civilization. If we don't see anything, we'll do the same for the eastern island."

For the next eleven hours, the yacht did just that. Willy even beached the boat on the white sandy shores of each island, and the men hiked around looking for signs of life. None was to be found. As sunset approached, they decided to take a break, anchor, and fish off their deck. They were between the two islands, only fifty yards from the west bank of the easternmost one. Luckily, Bob landed a snapper while Otis fought mightily and pulled in a grouper. The men decided to lift anchor and beach their boat for the night onshore. That way, they could grill their catch in the open air and dine amongst the Bahamian palm trees. Bongo Bay Marina had stocked the refrigerator with the basic food necessities. A wine rack was loaded with plenty of reds, whites, and roses.

That night, they all slept on towels on the sandy beach. All was peaceful until Otis began screaming, then running into the water to escape something that was obviously scaring him. "Guys, get up! We're being attacked by giant rats!!"

Not knowing what Otis was yelling about, Willy, Jim, and Bob scrambled into the ocean and stood beside Otis. They all stared back at the beach. In the distance, they could hear the frenzied scampering of little feet through the brush. Then they noticed the little varmints as the animals raced out of sight. Later, Jim Googled and discovered that the creatures were rabbit-sized rodents called the Bahamian Hutia.

Wednesday morning's skies were as gorgeous as Tuesday's sunrise. However, Willy was agitated. Jim, Bob, and Otis were waiting for their leader and captain to decide what to do today. Yesterday, they had circumnavigated both islands and found no sign of human life, say nothing of a factory. The enigma of where the Bibles and golf cups originated was even more mysterious. What was Willy's plan?

"Okay, the first thing on our agenda is fuel. The island of Mayaguana is thirty-two miles south of here. We'll gas up at Pirates Well, then head back and circle both islands again."

"Do you think we missed something yesterday?" asked Jim politely.

"We had to. Where did the Bibles and golf cups come from if the Plana Cays were uninhabited? We need to figure that out."

By noon, they were refueled and anchored just off the southeastern tip of the eastern island. All four men were on the deck searching the island through long-range binoculars. Willy said he would drive slower today and closer to shore. He climbed up into the cockpit, lifted the anchor, and navigated the boat with a small wake.

By motoring near the shoreline, Willy constantly moved sand particles with the Sea Ray's propeller. Midway around the island's northern half, Bob heard strange noises from the engine compartment. "Hey, Willy! Ya hear those screeching sounds?"

Willy turned the boat toward the open ocean so he could climb down below deck while the twin Cummins Mercruiser Diesels were working. What he saw shocked him. Both motors were smoking, pinging, and creaking. They were obviously overheating. Willy dashed up to the cockpit, killed both engines and then hustled back to the engine compartment.

It appeared that each of the twin diesels had cracked engine heads. The metal was warped, and parts had burst. Black smoke rose as oil was burning. Willy did a quick check of the impeller and found the problem. It was clogged with seaweed and sand. The cooling system had failed miserably.

Willy needed to beach the boat. He raced up to the cockpit and tried to crank the engines, but neither would start. Westerly winds blew the Sea Ray opposite the island and out to the open ocean. To top it off, Willy couldn't reach anyone on the emergency radio frequency. Otis had a panic attack thinking about dying in the Bermuda Triangle!

The depth of the Atlantic where the Sea Ray was drifting was well over 5,000 feet. The boat's anchor was useless. Willy, Jim, and Bob all tinkered with the warped engine head, trying to find a way to get it started. The Sea Ray was stocked with plenty of tools but no parts. They had twenty-five emergency flares, but Willy opted to wait until dark to use them.

Otis was told to stay in the cockpit and continue to try hailing someone on the radio. He was also to watch for any passing ship. As the boat blew in a northeasterly direction, Otis' vision length was slightly more than three miles. It wasn't long before the eastern Plana Cay island disappeared on the horizon. His efforts on the radio were futile. It just cackled with constant static.

At 9:00 pm, Willy set off the first flare. At midnight, he launched a second one. Evidently, the Sea Ray wasn't near a shipping lane. By 2:00 am on Thursday, the men were all sound asleep. They needed rest to clear their minds.

Willy awoke when he could tell the rocking had ceased, and there was no movement. The boat was tilting towards the starboard side. He could hear waves breaking next to the Sea Ray. He dashed out of bed and up to the deck where Otis was dead to the world, lying on a cushion. It was still dark. Willy's watch read 5:00 am.

The boat had been beached while they slept and was now resting on a sandy shore, half in and half out of the water. Willy climbed up the stairs to the cockpit and checked the maritime GPS. They were at 22°46 north latitude and 73°11 west longitude. Willy zoomed in on the map entirely. There was not supposed to be anything here! Yet, he and the boys were undoubtedly shipwrecked on an island!

Willy woke the others up and explained the situation. They quickly dressed and went onshore. Grabbing a couple of mooring ropes, the boys heaved the Sea Ray further inward, then secured the boat to a palm tree. Light was beginning to form to the east. Willy, Jim, Bob, and Otis stood in line with their hands on their hips, peering out at their surroundings. Where were they?!

The island didn't appear to be large. But it had something most other Bahamian islands didn't have—an elevation. It certainly wasn't mountainous, more like a few significant hills. What he saw made Jim curious, and he kneeled down, scooped up some sand, and rubbed it with his palms.

"What's the matter?" Willy asked Jim. "What are you doing?"

"Something is not right about this place. I'm thinking about what Dora explained to Eric a while back when she was helping him with his homework. The junior high kids are studying the earth's crust and its formation. I overheard her tell him that the Bahama islands largely consist of limestone rather than volcanic rock, unlike the Caribbean Islands."

"What's your point? I don't understand."

Jim didn't fully understand what Dora had described but repeated it anyway. "Dora said the Bahama Islands were formed millions of years ago when the earth's continent broke apart. There was a collision of rocks or plates out here somewhere, and those rocks rested in piles at the ocean bottom."

"That's just what I was thinking," inserted Otis.

"Be quiet, bro! I want to hear what Jim is saying!"

"In other words," continued Jim, "the land that now forms the islands was once under water and rose above the ocean as the continent shifted. Dora also told Eric that dunes formed when strong winds blew sand from the Sahara Desert as everything broke apart. But the dunes hardened and were worn down by the rain and sea."

"So, why are you bothered by that sand you're rubbing in your hands?"

"Because the Bahamian beaches should have bits of coral, sea shells, and limestone. This sand has tiny pieces of metal."

"Where did that come from?"

"That's the question of the day!"

CHAPTER TWENTY-SEVEN

February 2015

"Four people are standing on a beach at Plana Cay," declared Bushman Jack into his untraceable cell phone from atop Ayers Rock in the Australian outback. "Thought you might want to know."

"Which of the Plana Cays?" asked Mel Smith.

"The Plana Cay no one knows about. Why else would I be calling you?"

"How can that be?" yelped Keith Malone. "It's uncharted; nobody knows about it!"

"I'm guessing it was found accidentally. Perhaps by some wayward fishermen."

"Can your drone camera zoom in and get a sharp picture of them?" Mel and Keith were pacing in their apartment next to St. Max's Church.

"I already did that. As you know, my lens is incredibly crystal clear. Right now, I have only pictures of their backs. I'll move the drone around, get shots of their heads momentarily, and then forward the pics to you. I assume you want them texted to your secure phone, not your computer, right?"

"Yes, Jack, that's correct. Our computer system is not entirely secure."

"Give me about twenty minutes."

*****

"Let's make our way through the brush and climb that hill." Willy pointed to the high ground about a mile away. "Maybe from there, we can see what's on this island, and if an airplane flies overhead, we could signal it."

Willy and Jim were experts in forging paths through the wilderness back in the Loxahatchee Slough, so they led the way. From his training and experience, Willy knew the species of most trees and shrubs. He pointed out the Caribbean pine, red cedar, sea grape, mahogany, and candlewood trees. Then he touched the surface of a dense tree. "This is the national tree of the Bahamas. It's called lignum vitae, or in some parts of the world, a guayacan tree. It is the hardest wood known on the planet. The lignum vitae is also oily and can be used for steamship bearings, pulleys, and heavy machinery. Caribbean wood carvers use it all the time."

Otis decided to touch all the lignum vitae he could find on the way up the hill. On one, he noticed something on the trunk several feet above his head. As the others kept moving, Otis climbed the tree. An inscription had been carved into the wood:

Con gli occhi di Dio,
proclamo quest'isola per la Spagna.
Cristoforo Colombo
12 Ottobre 1492

Otis reached into his back pocket and took out his smartphone. He snapped a picture of the carving, then hustled down the tree. He stopped and yelled loudly, "Hey, Willy! Come back here! I found something you should see!"

Everyone turned around, but no one could see Otis. "Get back here, brother! We'll wait for you!"

"Maybe we should see what he found," said Bob.

Willy shook his head and muttered, "That boy will be the death of me!" Then he nodded to Jim and Bob. "Okay, backtrack, fellas. Let's see what he found."

When they reached Otis, he was on his haunches next to the tree holding on to a primitive knife.

"What's up, Otis?" asked Willy.

"Well, first, I climbed that tree and found this carved into the trunk." Otis pulled out his smartphone and showed the others the picture. "Then, while waiting for y'all, I saw this in the dirt." He displayed the knife.

"Holy crap!" shouted Jim as he pointed frantically at Otis' smartphone. "This was carved by Christopher Columbus on October 12th, 1492! Oh my God! This is where Columbus landed! Historians knew it was in the Bahamas, but no one knew for sure which island. It was this one! Holy cow!!"

Otis stared at the picture and scrunched his forehead. "He wasn't a very good speller. Shoot, I don't think he even spelled his own name right. And I'm not sure, but I don't think that's how you spell October, do you? What's all that other gobbledygook before his name and the date?"

"It's either Spanish or Italian. Columbus was from Italy, but he sailed for Spain. When we get some Wi-Fi, we can Google it. Google can translate anything!"

The excitement of discovering a piece of history lightened everyone's moods. They high-fived each other and slapped Otis on the back with words of congratulations. But then Jim noticed something on the knife Otis was holding. "Look at those black particles stuck on the knife. It's the same material that's in the sand on the beach."

"What's so curious about that?" asked Willy. "The ground here is mostly limestone, but we know there's something else in it. Like, for instance, that black junk on the knife."

"If that was the tool Columbus used to carve the inscription into the tree, it was probably made of iron. Otis, can I please take a look at the knife."

Otis gave it to Jim, and Jim shook it wildly. "What are you doing?" asked Bob. "I don't get it!"

Jim answered, "The black particles won't shake off. They stick to the knife like glue."

"So what?" Willy was getting impatient.

"It's just strange, that's all. The black particles in the dirt are magnetic. And very strong, I might add."

*****

"Damn!" howled Mel. The text from Bushman Jack came in with a clear drone photo. "It's Eric's dad and that guy named Bob who thinks he is a security guard for the church. Who are those other two dudes? I recognize them but can't place them."

"It's the great American hero from the eighties—Willy Banks," stated Keith sarcastically. "I think that's his brother with him. They go to church at St. Max's."

"So obviously, it's not some kind of random fishing trip, is it?"

"That would be way too much of a coincidence for them to fish and find Plana Cay."

"Now what?" asked Mel. He and Keith didn't see this one coming.

Mel texted Bushman Jack: "Please keep a close eye on them. Thx!"

*****

By 10:00 am, the group had reached the top of the hill. They had marked the tree that had the carving with a circle of rocks around the base and placed the knife in a satchel Willy found in the boat. He carried some tools, binoculars, snacks, and water in it. The bag was built from handcrafted leather and had a hidden compartment where Willy carefully stored the historic knife.

Everyone was given binoculars and told to search the grounds in all directions. Jim noticed a peculiar-looking prominent hill about a half mile from where they were located. The limestone they were standing on was white to gray in color. But as he zoomed in on the next hill, the limestone was almost black, with traces of yellow and red. Once again, thanks to Dora's lessons on geology, Jim thought that meant the ground was rich in manganese and iron. But how did that happen? He was sure the island wasn't volcanic, so where did those elements come from? The black was probably the unknown magnetic pebbles they had found on the beach and on the knife. But for this island to have manganese and iron, too, something was off. The Bahamas weren't known for their abundance of minerals. Mining here was simply not done.

Meanwhile, Otis saw something next to the beach about a half mile from their boat. It was located down the slope from the hill Jim was looking at. He mentioned it to the others, and they all focused on it.

Willy suggested they go down to the unknown structure and then up the next mound.

The ground on the new path they were blazing began to turn dark brown the closer they got to the adjacent hill. Then something bizarre happened—black particles from the ground started rising and clung to Willy's satchel. He opened the bag, took out the knife, then laid it on the dirt. Amazingly, the particles moved from the pouch to the blade.

"There is an incredible magnetic force between the black pebbles and iron!" exclaimed Willy. "What do you make of that, Jim?"

"I wish Dora was here! She knows a lot about geology and natural energy forces. But I would leave the knife just the way it is—with all those magnetic particles on it. Maybe those two engineers, you know, Mel and Keith, could tell us what it is. Or maybe they know someone who could tell us."

Willy put the knife back into the satchel, and the group headed down the hill until they came upon the structure next to the beach. It was a metal frame with rollers and sat on what appeared to be a railroad track. Attached to the frame were wooden planks.

"It's a rollaway dock!" blurted Willy. The tracks go into the water; look how long it is!" He pointed back to the hill. "Holy cow! Let's get a closer view!"

The tracks and dock gradually inclined from the shore to the hilltop about the length of two football fields. At the end was an electric pole with a switch box. Without asking, Otis walked up and was going to pull down the lever on the switch box, but Willy stopped him. "No, Otis! Don't touch that! We don't know what will happen."

"Uh, bro, I'm no mechanical engineer, but I think this here dock will go down to the water if I yank this lever."

"Exactly! But we don't want to do that until we know who made the dock—and where those people might be right now!"

Bob finally spoke up. "I just thought of something. This dock is 500 or 600 feet long. That length could work for a small ship. Is it possible this is the pier where the Bibles and golf cups are shipped from?"

"Could be," said Jim. "But why would they make it retractable?"

"Perhaps to hide it," stated Willy. "When retracted, it would be difficult for boats to see from the water."

"Okay," responded Bob. "If that's the case, why don't they want boats to see it?"

"I guess that's why we came here. We all believed there was something strange about Plana Cay being a manufacturing and shipping port. Now we accidentally land on this uncharted island, and this could be what we were looking for—the origin of the Bibles and golf cups. I'm not sure everything is on the up and up here. But to find out, we must carefully search the rest of this island. The key word is careful! I hope you all understand my drift!"

Otis began sweating and shaking. "Willy, I think we need to run back to our boat and get the heck out of here!"

"That's really not an option, bro. Our motor is broken."

CHAPTER TWENTY-EIGHT

February 2015

"They found the retractable pier and the electric box," said Bushman Jack. The drone flew at 15,000 feet, but the pictures it sent to his computer in Australia were high definition. "They are standing directly on top of the entrance."

"Is it possible no one knows they are there?" asked Mel.

"Doubtful. I'm sure there are security cameras everywhere. Someone in the hole would likely lock the entrance and disengage the outside electric box. Just guessing, but I think that if the men don't notice they are standing on a camouflaged door, they might be safe."

"Might?! Remind me, how does the door open, Bushman?"

"Hold on. Let me pull up previous footage on my computer." Jack searched his video files until he found what he was looking for. Then he watched and took notes. "The entrance is a twenty by twenty-foot steel plate four inches thick. When switched, it drops down five feet to ensure the fake plants and dirt have enough clearance. Then it slides backward, leaving a twenty by twenty-foot hole."

"Are you sure about the measurements?"

"My drone's camera has unique measuring capabilities. It's more accurate than the ruler on your desk!"

"Anything else you see inside the hole?"

"Just a portable conveyor belt to move products to the dock. And there are stairs, of course. The distance from the floor to the opening is twelve feet, which should be the base. They couldn't have gone much further down without hitting an underground water source seeping in from the Atlantic."

"Okay, thanks, Jack. Please keep an eye on them."

*****

Bob checked out the switch box to view the electrical connection. The lever that appeared to engage the portable dock could easily be switched. But the inside of the box was secured using a combination lock. The push button numbers were on the top. Bob couldn't tell how many digits the pin code needed to open it. Then he noticed a black button on the bottom of the box about the size of a dime. It also served some function, but Bob didn't know what that would be.

"Look here, guys," said Bob. There's a button on the bottom of the switch box. Maybe that's what expands and retracts the dock."

"Then what does the lever do?" asked Jim.

"I'm not sure. Perhaps we should pull the lever and push the button and find out."

"I can't say I'm for it, but at least we'll see what we're up against," said Willy reluctantly. "You all hide first. I'll engage the switches."

"I'm not good at hiding, Willy!" cried Otis. "Can I just go back to the boat before you touch that thing?!"

"No, that's not an option. You're staying with us, bro!"

Jim, Bob, and Otis spread out and hid behind palmetto bushes about fifty yards from the electric box. When he couldn't see them, Willy pulled the lever. Nothing happened. He shoved it back up, then yanked it down again. Still nothing. Then he reached under the box and pushed the button. Dead as a doornail! There didn't seem to be power running to the switches.

"Come on back," yelled Willy. "The lever and the button don't work. Nothing happened."

The three that were hiding rejoined Willy at the electrical box and stared at him.

"What now, Willy?" asked Bob.

"We search the island like we were going to do."

*****

They climbed through the thick, subtropical brush to the top of the hill, then viewed the island with their binoculars. No sign of civilization anywhere! There were three hills: the one they climbed first, the one they were now standing on, and another about a hundred yards to the east. The hills ranged from 150 feet to 450 feet in height. In Willy's estimation, the island was about three miles long and two miles wide.

Once again, Otis was the first to notice something unusual. Below them, to the opposite coastline from the dock, and about 200 yards east was a structure with a brown roof. Otis pointed it out, and everyone focused in with their binoculars. It appeared to be a hacienda only a few feet from a small cove. The men all agreed to trek there next. They patted Otis on the back. Jim nicknamed him "Hawkeye."

The group descended the mound to the Atlantic, then followed the coast eastward. At two in the afternoon, they came upon the estate they had seen from the hill. It was a gorgeous, expensive house built on concrete stilts at the water's edge. A large wraparound deck encircled the home. The terrace and siding were made of ipe wood, perfect for Bahamian exteriors because it resisted the blazing sun, torrential rainfalls, mold, mildew, and tropical insects. The roof was fake thatch fastened on Brazilian Walnut hardwood.

The cove protected the property from monster-size waves rolling in from the ocean. The group climbed wooden stairs to the deck. The back faced east and overlooked the Atlantic. Sunrises here must be amazing! There was an old kayak in one corner but no patio chairs or loungers anywhere in sight. The entrance to the house from the deck was a wall of glass that slid open on rollers. It was locked. The men shaded their eyes with their hands and peeked inside. The place was empty—no furniture on the floors or pictures on the walls. Whoever lived here must have moved. They would have left their belongings if this was some sort of winter getaway.

"Let's find a way to get inside," stated Willy. "Maybe there are some tools we could use to fix our boat."

"How about we just smash this glass?" asked Otis, smiling with pride because he thought he had it all figured out!

"We're breaking and entering, bro. I would prefer not to leave a bunch of evidence indicating our crime!"

The four walked around the deck, looking for another entry point. A piece of the dwelling's wood siding had chipped. Willy pulled the fragment back and noticed something peculiar. "Look closely! Underneath the hardwood is steel! Whoever built this place didn't want anyone breaking in! This must have cost a fortune!"

"So," responded Bob, "if that's the case, there's no way we're going to get inside!"

"We could still smash the glass," stated Otis firmly.

"Well, you may be right, Otis. We came all this way, and our boat needs to be fixed, so I would call our situation an emergency. Let's bust the glass wall."

"That might be easier said than done, boss," retorted Jim. "If the walls are impenetrable, it's doubtful the glass could be readily broken."

"Let's find out. We need to use that kayak as a battering device." Willy walked over and felt it with his hands. "It's heavy and made from rigid fiberglass."

The oceangoing kayak was made for two people and weighed about seventy-five pounds. Otis and Jim grabbed the left side while Bob and Willy grasped the right. From the back of the deck, they took aim at the middle of the glass wall, then charged as fast as they could. What happened next rivaled a scene from *The Three Stooges*. The front of the kayak came to a complete stop, and the four men flew forward upon impact. No one was injured, and the glass wall was still intact.

Willy stood, dusted off his t-shirt, and pounded the glass in frustration. "Whatever this is made from is stronger than the steel siding! We need a Plan B!"

*****

"They're at the estate and are trying to get inside," said Bushman Jack matter-of-factly. "Not having much luck, though."

"Can they get in?" asked Mel. He and Keith were once again pacing in the apartment.

"I suppose someone could get into anything if he or she knew how. But I doubt these four will be able to figure it out."

"Keep us posted, Jack!"

"Will do."

CHAPTER TWENTY-NINE

February 2015

"The boat is due back at Bongo Bay on Saturday by noon," said Willy. "No one will be searching for us until Sunday or Monday."

"How will they find us?" asked Bob. "We're on an uncharted island with a broken radio."

"And we're in the Bermuda Triangle, too!" exclaimed Otis. "The devil might be coming for us right now!"

Willy ignored his brother. "We may need to use the boat as a raft. But the oars that are in it don't seem to be long enough for serious rowing! We could cut down a lignum vitae tree and make four longer paddles—one for each of us."

"We don't have a saw, Willy," stated Bob. "And that wood is really hard!"

"There's an axe next to the fire extinguisher in the boat. It might take a while, but we could do it. We could also use our bed sheets for a makeshift mainsail. We're probably forty or fifty miles from Pirates Well, where we gassed up, and it would be southeast of here. The westerly winds from the Gulf Stream will help us out."

"But if we miss Mayaguana Island," feared Bob, "we'll wind up drifting all the way to Africa!"

"Our GPS is working fine. We'll need a good weather day, but we can do this!"

Jim had been oblivious to the conversation. He had a handful of the black metallic particles he scooped up from the sand and tossed them in the air. They fell gently back to the earth.

"What in the world are you doing, Jim?" asked Willy with annoyance. He couldn't understand why Jim was ignoring the planning session.

"Just thinking," responded Jim. "These particles are highly magnetic, right? Then why are they not clinging to the exposed steel plate in the wall?"

"Good question! But you look like you already have the answer. What's your theory?"

"I'm guessing that the wall lining is not made of steel. It is probably titanium or tungsten, something strong that is not magnetic. It had to have cost a fortune!"

"Okay, great. So what? It doesn't change the fact that we're stuck on this island. So, would you mind joining us so we can find a way to get out of here?!"

"I was just wondering if whoever built this place purposely used titanium because he knew it wouldn't attract those black magnetic particles in the sand."

"What are you getting at, my friend?"

"I think whoever built this house was a scientist studying the island's geology, mainly the black pebbles."

"And what's your point?"

"My point is the geologist may have lined his home with nonmagnetic materials because he knew that the black pebbles he was studying would cling to anything magnetic in the house. That would be a mess! It might have nothing to do with security."

"But why doesn't anyone know about this black junk?! Wouldn't you think if the geologist discovered a new metal, he would try to get it named after himself? The house is empty, which means he or she is gone. Why would he or she keep this discovery to him or herself?"

"Good question, Willy. I don't know the answer."

Willy paced for a moment, deep in thought. Then he turned to the group. "Perhaps these black pebbles could be used for something that might make the geologist big money! That would be worth more than simply having your name on the periodic chart!"

Otis, Jim, and Bob stared at Willy, waiting for him to complete his thought. But they all had a good idea about what the ex-cop was thinking.

"Call me Negative Nelly if you want, but I'm guessing these black pebbles are being used for something underhanded or illegal! And I will bet you that whatever it is, it's happening up on that hill by the dock."

Otis wasn't listening. He was afraid of what Willy intended to do. To keep his mind off it and ease his anxiety, he walked to the shoreline, picked up black pebbles, and stacked them in a clamshell he found. Then something startled Otis, and he jumped up.

Bob noticed him and yelled out. "What's the matter, Otis!"

"This here clamshell is smokin', that's what!"

"Otis, put the lighter down and get back up here!" ordered Willy. "We're leaving!"

"It ain't my lighter, bro! It's magic or something!"

Willy, Jim, and Bob ambled down to the beach. They were in no hurry to see the mischief Otis was up to, but they thought they would appease him anyway. They all stopped on a dime when they saw the clamshell. It most certainly was smoking!

"How in the world could those rocks be on fire?!" blurted Bob.

While Otis, Willy, and Bob kept a safe distance, Jim meandered cautiously to the shell. He examined it, then turned to the others. "It's not the rocks burning. It's the clamshell."

"Did you use your lighter on the clamshell, Otis?" inquired Willy.

"Nope! My lighter is still in my pocket where it's always been. I just piled the black rocks in the shell, and I saw smoke. I swear it, Willy!"

Jim kicked the pile of pebbles, then tossed water on the clamshell. The shell had a hole the size of a quarter on the bottom that had been burned through. "Those black particles, pebbles, or rocks, whatever they are, are extremely magnetic! Whatever they're made of must have ions or something that move around and cause friction. It's almost like they're nuclear or something!"

"Nuclear?!" asked Willy astonishingly. "That's totally inconceivable!"

"That's what scientists said when they discovered uranium," countered Jim. "But I have an idea."

*****

The men gathered black pebbles until sunset and piled them on a sand mound they had built underneath the house. They jammed the particles together, and the top of the pile touched the base of the home. Jim thought the energy from the rocks would burn a hole through the protective metal, and they could enter the home from below the deck. Unfortunately, Jim's theory didn't work.

The deck provided cover from the steady rain that began around midnight, but the ground felt damp. Strangely, the pile of black pebbles was warm. The group decided to sleep next to it for the night. It was a restless evening, to say the least.

Otis woke everyone up just after sunrise on Friday. "Hey, look at Willy's satchel. It's clinging to the pile of rocks!"

The others yawned and turned to see what Otis was feverishly pointing at. Sure enough, the bag was stuck on the side of the pile. Willy jumped up and was astonished. "How could that be?! I left the satchel on top of the deck last night!"

"It's the iron knife!" exclaimed Jim. "The magnetic pebbles drew the knife to it."

"From on top of the deck?! That's impossible!"

"Look at the tracks in the sand that the bag made. The satchel fell over the side and was pulled to the rocks by magnetic force."

"Wow! What is this stuff anyway?!" Willy yanked the bag from the pile, and his face turned red in distress. He spat on his hand to cool his fingers off. "Ouch, this is hot. I wonder why it didn't burn a hole in the floor?"

"Maybe it only burns seashells," said Otis. Bob and Willy looked away and smiled. Not wanting to embarrass Otis, they didn't respond.

But Jim wasn't smiling. "You know, Otis may be right."

"Huh?" Bob shook his head. "How could this burn through seashells but not even dent the house's metal flooring?"

"It's a chemical reaction. At least, that's what I overheard Dora explaining to Eric while helping him with his science homework. In other words, maybe whatever seashells are made of interacts with whatever these pebbles are made of. So, are y'all up for a junior high experiment?"

Otis perked up. "Yep! I loved junior high!"

"An experiment? What are you talking about?" asked Willy.

"Everyone gather as many shells as possible and bring them back here. When we have enough, we'll smash them and sprinkle the pieces onto the pile of pebbles. Then we can see if the chemical makeup of shells reacts with those black particles."

*****

The men crushed seashells with their shoes until they had enough pieces and powder for everyone to grab two handfuls. Jim directed them to circle around the black pile and, at his command, toss the material onto the pebbles. "Okay, on the count of three, everyone throw."

It was only a matter of seconds when the fire started, and sparks shot upward. Jim yelled, "Get the heck out of here! Quickly!"

They were only fifty yards away when the explosion occurred. Rocks, shells, wood siding, and metal flooring were spewed in all directions. Luckily, the men dove into the sand at the last second and weren't injured by the flying debris.

But now, the beautiful ocean estate was engulfed in flames. The men sat dumbfounded in the sand and watched it burn. There was nothing they could do to save the house.

CHAPTER THIRTY

February 2015

"Holy crap! They set the house on fire!" shrieked Bushman Jack into the cell phone.

"What?! How could they? The house had a layer of titanium and gypsum sealed all around it!" Mel was beside himself. He and Keith both panicked. "Why would they do that? What purpose did it serve them?"

"It may have been an accident. The camera recorded a huge explosion followed by flames. Let me rewind a bit. I've been sleeping and wasn't watching live." Jack scrolled backward through his hard drive. "Here it is. The group gathered planacalum nuggets and piled them somewhere underneath the deck. Then they picked up seashells and smashed them into small pieces and powder. And, you guessed it, they threw the dust onto the planacalum pile and ran like the dickens! Looks like it took only thirty to forty seconds before it exploded!"

Keith kicked the coffee table and punched his fist into the wall leaving a dent in the sheetrock. "How did they know calcium carbonate would create a chemical reaction with planacalum? I don't think any of them have much education. And let's say they did have some sort of science background; they would know that calcium carbonate is not flammable. So why would they hypothesize that the mineral makeup would cause planacalum to energize? Shoot, how do they even know about planacalum? It's only used in Tommy Williams golf balls!"

Mel walked up to Keith and grabbed his arm. "Calm down. We don't know for sure if the men knew anything about the molecular makeup of planacalum or the shells. They may have discovered it accidentally."

"Accidentally?! Are you kidding me?! They piled planacalum under the house and sprinkled on the calcium carbonate purposely! That doesn't sound accidental to me!"

"Yeah, you're right, Keith. But all that's behind us now. We need to look ahead."

Bushman Jack interrupted, "The drone has an interesting visual. There's a safe inside the house. It appears to have been hidden behind bookshelves and into the west wall. The wall has collapsed, and the safe has fallen to the ground. But it doesn't look like it's been destroyed. It must be made from extraordinary nonflammable material!"

"What do you suppose Jake Tassett had hidden in that safe, Mel?" asked Keith.

"I think we better find out."

CHAPTER THIRTY-ONE

February 2015

"What now, Willy?" asked Otis tepidly. He wasn't sure he wanted to hear the answer.

It was noon on Friday, the twentieth of February. The boat was due back at the marina in Ft. Lauderdale tomorrow. That wasn't going to happen. And it was doubtful that a search party would find the men on an uncharted island. The motor was beyond repair. It appeared the group had two choices: stay on the island, perhaps the rest of their lives, or try and row the boat to Mayaguana, forty to fifty miles away. The danger with staying wasn't lack of food; it was where to find drinkable water. They had a little over one hundred twenty-ounce bottles left on the boat. But that was it unless they could find a freshwater source on the island.

"I guess we're back to Plan A. We don't have time to make the long paddles, so we'll have to use the four oars that are in the boat. Then, we'll tie all the bedsheets together to create a makeshift sail that we can connect between the radio antennas on both sides of the cockpit. Obviously, we'll need a westerly wind to help blow us southeast, which is the direction we'll mainly be headed. We should wait until tomorrow morning so we can have the entire day to journey to Mayaguana. Let's go back to the boat and prepare it today."

They all nodded their approval, even though they knew the chances were slim they wouldn't get blown across the Atlantic Ocean to Africa. The men turned to head up the hill when Bob noticed something in the pile of burnt debris that was once a gorgeous oceanfront estate. "Hey, wait, guys! What's that?!" He pointed to a safe on the ground near where the back wall used to be.

"Hmmm," muttered Willy. "Let's check it out." Willy knelt next to the charred metal strongbox and brushed off some ashes. "It's a wall safe that fell when the home burned down."

"I think we should look inside of it," Otis said.

"Otis is right," stated Bob. "We've been trying to solve the mystery of who lived here. This could give us some clues."

Willy shook his head. "The safe is locked tight. It warped a little from the heat but did what it was supposed to do—protect the documents inside. We ain't gonna open it."

"You sure about that?" questioned Jim. "Why not try another dose of those black pebbles and seashells smeared on the lock?"

"Even if that worked, everything inside would be destroyed. But hold on, look at this." Willy pointed to several black particles in the sand moving toward the safe. "This strongbox must use a nickel solenoid to activate the locking mechanism."

"A nickelsole what?" asked Otis.

"Nickel solenoid. I learned this many years ago during police training school before I took the Okeechobee County Sheriff's Department job. Burglars are notorious for breaking into home safes using magnets. A solenoid is a long, thin loop of wire wrapped around a metal core that becomes a magnetic field when an electric current is passed through it. Solenoids can be used as electromagnets. You can detach the lock by waving magnetic stuff around in front of the safe. So, let's give it a try. Otis, I need one of your sweat socks."

"Uh, bro. They're kinda dirty and don't smell so great."

"Oh, for Pete's sake! I don't care—just give me a sock! Jim and Bob, get me a handful of those black pebbles."

Otis untied a tennis shoe, took off his sock, then handed it to Willy. Jim and Bob filled the stocking with the pebbles. Next, Willy tied it so the rocks wouldn't escape, then slowly waved it counterclockwise near the front of the safe. They all listened closely and could hear movement inside, then a moment later, a click. The door sprung open, and the men let out a cheer!

But their excitement turned to disappointment when Willy removed the only item in the safe: a sheet of paper with printed numbers and letters. Nothing else!

Willy gathered everyone together and showed them the printout. "What do you suppose this all means?"

BIBC-Nass-41379-Tassett-8976453570092*70094
BOSE-Gene-792231-Tassett-76100800748*81345
GCIB-BodT-4566547979-Tassett-88856723234*790213
HKMACINV-Jinw-396442-Tassett-20208080997*6984

"Gobbledygook, if ya ask me!" yelped Otis.

"People don't protect gobbledygook in their locked tight safe, Otis!" Willy put his finger on the sheet and scrolled down slowly.

"What are you doing?" asked Bob.

"Looking for commonalities with the numbers or some sort of pattern. And there's one that stands out. 'Tassett' is in each of the lines. I think it might be a name, possibly the person who lives here."

"What about all the rest of the numbers and letters?"

"Not sure what those are." Willy pondered momentarily, then added, "Not saying it's the same person, but Tassett is a name that I know from the past," uttered Willy cryptically.

"Who is it?!" asked Jim impatiently. "The tone of your voice seems to indicate that the Tassett you know is not someone respectable!"

"Not respectable would be an understatement! Back in the early eighties, Jake Tassett was the National Transportation Safety Board Lead Investigator after terrorists had caused two midair passenger jet collisions over South Florida. The villains also blew up a large section of the

University of Florida campus. The masterminds were Oliver Harfield and Ray and Roy Jackson. Tassett was suspected of aiding and abetting their plans. Harfield and the Jacksons were killed, but Tassett escaped the FBI and was never found. Rumor has it that he moved to a Caribbean Island with Judge Boone, a close friend of Roy Jackson, a wealthy rancher in Okeechobee County. The judge was known for turning a blind eye to Roy's criminal activities when he was on the bench."

"I was just a young kid when all that happened," said Jim. "But I remember talking about it in history class. What makes you think it's the same Jake Tassett whose name is on that list of numbers?"

"Just a feeling, that's all. Those numbers must be important, or they wouldn't have been kept in a safe. A simple filing cabinet would have sufficed. My guess is that they are foreign bank account numbers, and whoever owned this house was hiding his money."

*****

"They located the safe and have somehow broken into it!" exclaimed Bushman Jack. "The drone has a clear view, but the big guy is in the way. I can't make out what they found!"

"This whole thing is going to blow up in our faces!" replied Keith panicking.

Mel stared at Keith disparagingly. "Calm down. We don't know what they found. We just have to ensure they don't return to Florida before we finish."

"How do you reckon we'll do that?! Their families will be sending out search parties soon. We need at least another year to complete our mission!"

"No, we just need the boy to qualify for the Honda Classic right here in his hometown. How hard can that be?"

"How hard?! Are you kidding me?! He's barely a teenager! This is his first PGA tournament! This is a huge test! Will he even want to play if his father is lost at sea somewhere?! I'm a bit worried! Can't you tell?!"

"I have a plan," stated Mel firmly. "It will work."

CHAPTER THIRTY-TWO

February 2015

Father Jacob was praying and doing his best counseling, but Dora Mann and Becky Butler were fidgeting with dismay. It was Sunday before church, and the gals were squirming with fear. Jim and Bob were due back home yesterday, and neither had heard a word from them. The moms kept it from the kids, telling them one fib after another when they would ask where their daddy was.

Mel Smith had an appointment to see Father and had arrived early. He sat in a waiting area lounge chair, but the priest's office door was open. He could hear every word that was being discussed. Mel thought maybe he could help, so he knocked softly on the door and stood in the entryway.

"Ah, excuse me; I'm very sorry to interrupt. We've never met, but you may have seen me around the apartments or at church. My name is Mel Smith, and I am one of the engineers developing the golf balls. I overheard what you said, so I apologize again, but I would like to offer you my services. I would be happy to use my jet and deploy a search team. I would do this with the help of the Coast Guard. Leave it to me—I will take care of all the preparations.

"Oh, good gracious!" whispered Becky appreciatively. "You would do that for us?!"

"You are a good man, Mr. Smith!" added Dora with a wide smile. "My husband, Jim, and Becky's husband, Bob, have mentioned your name and said you own a private jet here at the airport. When do you think you could start looking?"

"I can get started immediately if Father allows me to miss church," grinned Mel. Father smiled back and nodded his approval. "First, I'll stop by the marina where they rented the boat and get as much information as I can about their possible whereabouts. Then, I'll make a call to a friend who's an officer in the Coast Guard. Lastly, I'll file a flight plan. I'm sure my partner, Keith Malone, will gladly help me. We should be in the air by 3:00 pm. Once it gets dark, we'll stay overnight in either Freeport or Nassau. That way, we can get an early start on Monday."

Dora and Becky teared up with joy. Father gave them both a hug, then shook hands and thanked Mel. They still weren't sure what they would tell their children.

"Our kids don't know you two," said Dora, and Becky nodded. "When everyone is reunited, we'll all get together for a celebration barbeque!"

Mel smiled and winked.

"God bless you, Mr. Smith," asserted the ladies in unison.

"And great good luck!" added Father Jacob.

*****

On Tuesday, February twenty-fourth, at 7:00 am, just off the first tee box of the Champion Course in Palm Beach Gardens, *ESPN*, *Sports Illustrated*, and *The Golf Channel* all had reporters lined up to interview Eric Mann. It was the opening match of a two-day preliminary seeding event for the Honda Classic. With a great round of golf today and tomorrow, he would become the youngest player to ever qualify for a PGA tournament. But Hugh Kraft wasn't having any of it.

"You all need to stay back behind the media rope, please!" he shouted to the reporters. Cameramen were snapping photos of the teenage protégé. PGA security arrived to ensure Hugh's request was granted. "Eric will provide interviews only after his two rounds of golf are completed. In other words, see you all tomorrow!"

There was groaning from the media folks, but Hugh didn't care. Eric needed to be focused entirely on his game plan with no distractions. The boy remembered his first time playing the Champion Course, which was the first time he met Wayne Siebold. Hugh developed a strategy based on the success Eric had had before.

Forty-eight unranked and low-ranked golfers would compete for the final four spots in the Honda Classic that began on Thursday. Hugh had studied Eric's opponents and guessed he would need to shoot no more than two over par to qualify. The weather was a beauty! Clear skies, low wind, and highs in the upper seventies! A perfect week for golf! Eric hadn't played in good weather for quite some time. Today, he wore a short-sleeve Polo with the St. Max's Premium Golf Ball logo on his left arm. Father Jacob had blessed the balls on Monday night.

Eric's drives were somewhat erratic. During his two days of preliminary action, he landed only twenty-six of the thirty-six holes on the fairway. But he never suffered a penalty shot for going out of bounds. Eric's approach shots were terrific in the eyes of the sports writers. Every single one was right on target, and in some cases, his irons outdistanced his driver. Then there were his putts. Eric putted only once on twenty-four holes. He played the line, elevation, and roll perfectly!

Eric's two-day total was 136, eight strokes under par. He finished first in the qualifying event and would be teamed in a foursome with Pádraig Harrington, Phil Mickelson, and Sergio Garcia during the opening round on Thursday. This was really going to happen!

*****

Mel landed the jet in Nassau, and he and Keith rented a large fishing boat from Bahama Bob's. They hadn't notified the Coast Guard because there was no need. Mel and Keith knew exactly where Jim, Bob, Willy, and Otis were located.

The foursome had set sail with bedsheets and oars on Saturday and had unsuccessfully fought off a strong westerly wind that blew them away from Mayaguana. They were now adrift in the Atlantic Ocean.

Fortunately, Bushman Jack's drone had them in its sights, and the flying robot's GPS had pinpoint accuracy.

CHAPTER THIRTY-THREE

February 2015

"The approval finally came from the USGA for the ten doctored St. Max's balls we sent them," said Tommy Williams. He was on his cell phone talking to Mel, who was heading back to Nassau on the fishing boat rental. He spoke quietly to ensure Willy, Otis, Jim, and Bob wouldn't wake up. Mel and Keith had tracked them via Bushman Jack's drone GPS. However, they purposely stayed a mile away from the four men's broken boat until they heard the news that Eric had qualified for the Honda Classic.

"None too soon! Eric couldn't play in the Honda with St. Max's Premium unless they were approved. So, our little trick paid off. It was a clever idea of yours to send the USGA St. Max's Standard Balls and replace the moylyn cover and the insides to get the approval. Does Eric have them in his possession? What time does he tee off?"

"Father Jacob blessed the balls this morning at 5:00 am. Hugh Kraft picked him up, and he's practicing now. His tee time is 8:26 am."

"Is everything all set?" Mel didn't need to ask that question. He already knew the answer. Bushman Jack's drone camera had recorded everything.

"Of course! And it has been set since Tuesday morning before the preliminary rounds. I spent three nights installing equipment and calibrating it. It worked like a gem during the qualifier. There's no reason to think it won't work this weekend."

"Okay, keep me posted." Mel hung up without saying goodbye. It was now or never.

*****

Otis, Bob, and Jim had given up hope last Saturday after the wind had blown them far off course. They needed to go in a southeasterly direction, but the strong gusts drove them straight east. Their oars and makeshift bedsheet sail were worthless in the rough seas! But the GPS had worked perfectly, terrorizing them when they saw they were being pushed further away from the Bahamas. Would they still be alive when their boat crashed into the rocks of Morroco? That was Otis' recurring dream, while similar nightmares plagued the others. However, Willy kept a positive attitude. He wasn't one to give up!

"Things could be worse!" stressed the one-time American hero. "The boat floats, and there's plenty of fish in the sea to eat. We just need to conserve our bottled water."

The men were stunned yet jubilant when Mel and Keith pulled up next to them on Wednesday in their rental. The two engineers tied the boats together and boarded the broken-down one.

"Oh my God! Praise the Lord!" exclaimed Jim. He and Bob recognized Mel and Keith. They wished they hadn't raised suspicions after seeing their expensive jet and cars in the airport hangar. "What are you doing here?"

"Hopefully, saving your lives! When no one heard from you, we offered to head up a search party. I notified the Coast Guard and Bongo Bay Marina of our plans. We saw your boat from the air a couple of nights ago and tried to get your attention, but there was no response. So, we landed in Nassau and rented this boat. And here we are! We radioed the Coast Guard letting them know they were no longer needed as we could pick you up. But we haven't called your wives because we wanted to be sure you were all safe first. We'll tow your boat back to Nassau. Bongo Bay said they would fly to Nassau from Ft. Lauderdale and pick it up there."

"We were on an uncharted island, and our radio stopped working. Somehow, it became permanently damaged. None of us could get cell service, either. But we discovered some amazing artifacts proving Columbus had set foot on the uncharted island. Although we never saw anyone, someone lives there. There's a long, retractable dock on one side of the island and a beautiful estate home on the other. Well, I should say, there used to be a beautiful estate home." Jim looked down and shook his head.

"What do you mean by that?"

"We accidentally blew it up and burned it down."

Strangely, Mel and Keith didn't even react to Jim's confession. There was no need. They already knew what had happened, but the group didn't know they knew.

"Well, our cell phones and boat radio work just fine," said Mel smiling. "I think you should call your wives."

Using three ropes, the men tied the stranded boat to Mel and Keith's rescue watercraft, then climbed aboard. As the vessels plowed through the ocean waves, Willy could tell the trip back to Nassau would probably take two or three days. Something bothered him about what Mel had said, but he didn't want to share it with the others. Instead, he kept to himself as he thought about what had happened this past week.

The first issue was Mel's statement that he flew over the stranded boat and tried to signal. Willy couldn't sleep and had been awake the entire time they were afloat in the dark Atlantic. No jet had circled overhead.

*****

On Thursday morning, Jim and Bob called their wives using Mel's cell phone. The ladies were ecstatic and relieved that their husbands were safe and on their way home. Dora and Becky were walking around PGA National with Father Jacob, watching Eric play. Dora told Jim their son's game was incredible thus far, and he was holding his own against the seasoned pros he was teamed up with. She also said Father Jacob had moved Sunday's church service to 6:00 am so the congregation could watch the final round. He was using church funds to pay for everyone's ticket. In the meantime, Father was constantly praying for Eric to play well.

Eric shot six birdies and twelve pars on Thursday, besting his foursome by two strokes. He finished with a six under par sixty-six, while the other three each ended the round with a four under par sixty-eight. Phil Mickelson caught up with Hugh Kraft in the clubhouse after the match. He was in awe of the teenage golf master!

"The boy's drives are great!" declared Phil. "But his approach shots are magically induced violators of the laws of physics! He can bend around a dogleg using either an imperious hook or slice. The ball wobbles like a Phil Niekro knuckleball, lands softly, and ends up near the pin. And Eric's putting is astounding! Did you teach him all this, Hugh?"

"I wish I could take the credit. But the truth is—Eric's a natural!"

CHAPTER THIRTY-FOUR

March 2015

"And finally, on what could be called a happy ending to a tragic event, Billy West will be memorialized during a pregame ceremony at the Pro Football Hall of Fame preseason game in Canton, Ohio, next July." ESPN reporter Earl Mason paused to regain his composure. He visualized the car crash that killed Billy and his wife Carol after the Super Bowl. "NFL greats Bart Starr, Joe Montana, and Dick Butkus will eulogize the tremendous quarterback and league MVP, then a full-size bronze statue will be unveiled and placed inside the Hall of Fame. Permission was granted by Commissioner Roger Goodell to waive the mandatory five-year waiting period for induction into the Hall. Following the commercial break, we will be highlighting Billy West's career. Please stay tuned!"

The ESPN news brief about Billy was broadcast on televisions across America, including one inside the Paradise Casino Sportsbook in Las Vegas. No one was paying attention as the gamblers were fixated on college basketball tournaments being played to determine who would qualify for the Big Dance, better known as March Madness. No one, that is, except Oliver Harwas, who had changed his last name to disassociate himself from his father, the notorious criminal Oliver Harfield.

He was betting a million dollars that Eric Mann would win the Honda Classic.

*****

Eric dominated the tournament Friday and Saturday with two eagles, six birdies, and twenty-eight pars. Heading into Sunday's final round, the youngster led the field, shooting ten strokes under par. Pádraig Harrington from Ireland, Daniel Berger from the United States, and Ian Poulter from England were all tied for second at seven under par. Once again, Eric was swarmed by sports reporters as he tried to head to the clubhouse. Unfortunately, Hugh had no means to stop them.

Because things would be crazy in the morning, Father Jacob called Eric into the church at 9:00 pm on Saturday to bless his golf balls for Sunday. Berger, a previous Honda Classic champion, was paired with Eric for the final round. They would tee off at 1:35 Eastern time.

Father Jacob was over the top with excitement! He invited his priest buddies from Clines Corners, New Mexico, Dallas, Texas, Jackson, Mississippi, and Augusta, Georgia, to attend the match. They were hesitant to come to Florida for two reasons. First, all had received beautiful gifts for Christmas each year from Father Jacob, and, embarrassingly, none had sent presents to him. And second, they would be leaving their churches with a substitute priest for Sunday mass. But all four men of the cloth showed up in Polos and sat in Father Jacob's block of fantastic bleacher seats on the eighteenth hole.

Next to them was Ursula Vero, the CEO of Golf Country Superstore, who had made a nice profit for St. Max's Parish selling the balls. But now, she desperately wanted a piece of the action. With Eric sponsoring the balls, her company's stock would soar sky-high! She hoped she could schmooze Father into a contractual agreement.

The priest also invited Shea Hansen to show his appreciation for hosting Willy and Otis in San Francisco when the brothers drove the first shipment of balls to GCS distribution centers. Behind the group of special invitees were the entire St. Max's congregation. Everyone that is, except for Willy, Otis, Jim, and Bob, who were still out at sea getting their boat towed to Nassau.

*****

Mel maneuvered both boats through Nassau Harbor on Sunday morning and docked them at Prince George Wharf around noon. Bob and Jim used Mel's cell phone to call their wives, who were sitting in the eighteenth-hole bleachers getting ready to watch the earlier round of golfers finish. A large screen projection system was set up nearby that followed the leaders' progress. Their anxiety level was heightened to new levels. With a victory, Eric would make his claim to fame—and be $1.1 million richer! Listening to the chatter of the congregation, it could be said that a group panic attack was materializing!

A representative from Bongo Bay Marina was in Nassau to make arrangements to fix the crippled boat and drive it home to Ft. Lauderdale. Mel called for a taxi to take everyone to the airport. He said he could return them to Palm Beach Gardens in time for Eric's tee-off. After a depressing week of frustrations, Jim was thrilled that he could be in the stands with his wife and friends cheering on his son.

An eight-seat passenger van arrived, and everyone hustled inside. Everyone except for Willy, that is. He said he needed a few days of rest on Paradise Island to recuperate after the past week's stress. Otis offered to hang with him, but Willy told his brother he needed some time alone.

While the others headed to the airport, Willy boarded the ferry to Paradise Island. He strolled down to the Reef of Atlantis Hotel and Resort, and wearing his torn blue jean cutoffs and tank top muscle t-shirt, he inquired about a vacancy. February was high season in the Bahamas, but the Atlantis had a top-floor suite available for $1,200 a night. Willy pulled out his company credit card and gave it to the desk clerk. Hopefully, he could devise a good excuse for expensing this trip to Paradise Island!

The clerk asked if he needed a bellboy for his luggage, but Willy said he was wearing the only clothes he had brought. Otis had taken his duffle bag from the boat and was bringing it back to their home in Palm Beach Gardens. Willy checked into his room and then went to the hotel's gift shop and purchased a toothbrush, toothpaste, shaving cream, a razor, swim trunks, and a floral button-down shirt with matching khaki shorts. The new clothes fit tightly, but Willy would make do.

He changed into his swimsuit, ambled down to Paradise Beach, and rented a lounge chair. Willy pulled the printout of numbers out of his pocket that he had taken from the safe at the burned beach home and tried to make sense of it. Today was Sunday, and the banks were closed. Tomorrow he would see if a bank employee could decipher the numbers. But the name embedded within each of the four codes haunted him.

Was Jake Tassett possibly still alive and linked to criminal activities? If so, someone's life was in danger!

CHAPTER THIRTY-FIVE

March 2015

Mel and Keith's jet touched down at the North Palm Beach County Airport at 1:45 pm. Otis had the keys to Willy's car, and Bob and Jim hopped in. A half-hour later, Bob and Jim were in the bleachers on the eighteenth hole sitting with their wives and friends. The large-screen TV was showing Eric putting on the first hole.

Meanwhile, Mel and Keith hustled to Tommy Williams' apartment, where he was fixated on the match. They hadn't been in Tommy's place for a while and hadn't seen his new equipment. *NBC Sports* was televising the Honda Classic, and there was a fifty-two-inch TV on the wall, but Tommy was watching it on his computer.

Mel pulled out his cell phone and pushed the camera app. "Hey, Tommy! I think I should record your setup. If you're ever going to get a patent for those golf balls, you need evidence to support how you measure their effectiveness. Tracking the golf ball's flight path on your computer and gathering weather data that could affect the ball's trajectory, distance, and roll is pure genius. Any problem with me filming that?"

"I told you I don't care about a patent. But if it makes you happy, go for it." Tommy didn't look at Mel or Keith as he was focused entirely on the final round of the Honda Classic.

Mel pushed the red button on his phone and began recording. He panned the room, then zoomed in on Tommy's controller desk. Williams could split his screen into eighteen small boxes and see each hole at PGA National. His keyboard looked like the cockpit of a large passenger airplane. Vertically down the right side were strange red buttons labeled ***IG 1*** through ***IG 20***. Tommy would push one of those buttons occasionally, but the purpose was unclear. Keith moved to the couch to watch the match on the TV but dosed off after ten minutes.

*****

Daniel Berger hung with Eric through the front nine. He matched him hole for hole with eight pars and a birdie. Rounding the turn, Berger was still three strokes behind. However, the twosome playing just in front of Berger and Eric (Pádraig Harrington and Ian Poulter) had both gained ground. Harrington had an eagle and a birdie on the front nine, and Poulter had two birdies. At the turn, the leaderboard displayed the following:

Mann, Eric (USA)	***minus 11***
Harrington, Pádraig (Ireland)	***minus 10***
Poulter, Ian (UK)	***minus 9***
Berger, Daniel (USA)	***minus 8***

All four leaders parred ten, eleven, twelve, and thirteen. Then, the gorgeous South Florida afternoon turned ugly. Dark gray clouds moved in quickly from the west and were directly overhead as Eric and Berger putted on thirteen. As Harrington stepped up to the tee box on fourteen, lightning zapped, and a mind-boggling clap of thunder boomed overhead. Suddenly, the digital leaderboard and large-screen TV on eighteen went black. An executive from *NBC Sports* ran in front of Harrington and waved his arms frantically. Power was out from Military Trail to the North Palm Beach County Airport. *NBC* lost its broadcast signal.

PGA officials temporarily stopped play, and the golfers were rushed in carts to the clubhouse to take cover. A downpour of rain drenched the grounds, and fans who didn't bring umbrellas crammed underneath bleacher overhangs.

In his unlit apartment, Tommy Williams' computer shut down. Mel continued recording on his cell phone but didn't know what to think. Keith was still asleep on the couch.

Meanwhile, at the Paradise Casino Sportsbook in Las Vegas, the massive screen tuned in to *NBC Sports* was now showing replays from great PGA tournaments from the past. A chyron at the bottom of the TV scrolled across: *The Honda Classic is currently on a rain delay.*

Oliver Harwas pounded his fist on the table, and his glass of Crown Royal on the rocks shattered into pieces on the floor.

*****

At 4:50 pm, players were carted back to their playing positions. Officials declared that all golfers would resume play at precisely 5:00 pm. Sunset was at 6:21, but hopefully, some lingering light would remain to finish The Classic. No one wanted to postpone the finale until Monday.

The fairways were drenched, and puddles were everywhere. According to Rule 16.1a, penalty-free relief was allowed when an abnormal course condition physically interfered with the player's area of intended stance or area of intended swing. However, PGA officials deemed the entire PGA National course, including fairways, sand traps, and greens, playable. Berger, Harrington, and Poulter were beside themselves, and all confronted the PGA officials with strong words of protest.

"There's no way hitting a ball out of a mud pit is allowed in golf, sir!" exclaimed Harrington, spittle flying through the air. "Are you out of your mind!"

The official responded to Pádraig's outburst with a grin. "I've golfed in Ireland, Mr. Harrington. All you good folks have over there are mud puddles. Does it ever stop raining on the Emerald Isle?"

Berger and Poulter used choice cuss words to the same official, who just shook his head and walked away. Meanwhile, Eric's eyes were wide open as he listened intently to his golf partners. After playing on ice and snow in Canada and during a frozen windstorm in Scotland, a puddle here or there didn't faze him. He only wished professional golfers would show some respect to the officials. They were just doing their jobs!

The power had been restored from Military Trail to the Beeline Highway by 4:20 pm. PGA National now had electricity, but the North Palm Beach County Airport was still dark. Because the radar was out, small planes and private jets were diverted a few miles southeast to Lantana. Florida Power and Light guessed the remaining grid would be restored by 6:00 pm. Little good that did Tommy, Mel, and Keith. They had no computer or television power to watch the rest of the match. Keith really didn't care—he was still snoring on the couch.

"Well, that's that," mumbled Mel. "I guess we're not going to see how Eric finished." He propped his phone up on the coffee table but forgot to turn off the recording.

Tommy responded, "It's too bad. Eric needed to finish first to have a chance at qualifying for the Masters in April. He hasn't played in enough tournaments to certify any other way."

"It ain't over 'til it's over! He still has the lead with only five holes left to play. And we could go to a sports bar to watch the finish."

"I'll stay here and wait for the power to return."

Mel looked at Keith lying on the couch, dead to the world. He shook his head and said, "I guess I might as well wait, too." Mel pointed at Keith. "I couldn't wake him with a sledgehammer to the face!"

*****

For time's sake, PGA officials decided to team up Harrington and Coulter with Berger and Mann for the finish. Because honors could not be established by combining the foursome, they would tee off based on their current scores. Eric would go first, followed by Harrington, Coulter, and Berger. The golfers plodded through the damp grass to the tee box.

Hole fourteen was a challenging 465-yard par four. The fairway doglegged left, and the entire right side was a water boundary. There were bunkers ready to eat balls that weren't perfectly struck. The green fell away on each side, making it a very difficult surface to putt.

Eric's drive was 240 yards, but it landed in the sand trap right of the fairway. Fortunately, the bunker stopped his ball, or it would have gone into the pond. Harrington, Coulter, and Berger placed their drives on the fairway near the dogleg. The balls weren't carrying in the humidity nor rolling much on the wet ground.

The sand trap was more like mud as Eric tiptoed into it with his five iron. He just wanted to get the ball back on the fairway with as much distance as he could muster. Eric needed to play out without getting underneath the golf ball. Wet sand could wreak havoc if he tried to play it that way. He centered the ball and pulled the club straight back as far as he could reach. His swing was smooth with an excellent follow-through. The ball carried about 180 yards and landed forty from the pin. But the other three golfers placed their balls perfectly on the green, each within fifteen feet of the cup.

Eric's chip landed in the middle of the green and rolled down the other side. And on a day when putting had been his strength, it took three more strokes for his ball to drop into the cup. Berger one-putted, while Harrington and Coulter two-putted. After fourteen, Eric's double bogey dropped him to nine under par, tied with Berger and Poulter. Pádraig Harrington now led at ten under.

Fifteen is a 179-yard par three, once again bordered tightly on the right side by water. Easy enough for a pro, but today after the storm passed, the winds picked up and made it a very tricky hole. The green is diagonal, running left to right. Eric couldn't remember how he played this hole when he went out with Hugh and Wayne Siebold, so he was happy to not have honors. He closely watched the swings of those in his foursome. They all pitched into the wind with high lofts, and their golf balls landed softly on the front part of the green and rolled left. Although they were over twenty feet from the pin, Eric knew he shouldn't try to get closer to the cup. Too much velocity and his ball would end up in a big bunker in the back of the green. Too little speed and his ball would end up in the pond. But Eric's main concern was the loft. He didn't have the strength to hit a ball 170 yards with a wedge. So he pulled out his six iron and hoped for the best. The ball carried perfectly, and Eric was ever so fortunate when the water-soaked green slowed his roll. He putted eight feet for a birdie while the others each parred fifteen.

Going into sixteen, Eric and Harrington were now tied at ten under. Berger and Poulter were one back at nine under par. The 434-yard par four was challenging for pro golfer wannabes because they would try to launch their drives over the dogleg water hazard and, you guessed it, ended up in the reservoir! Actual pro golfers knew to tee off with an iron onto the fairway before the pond, then hit another long iron onto the green. After the birdie on fifteen, Eric's confidence was restored. He played a pair of beautiful three-iron shots, and his ball stopped twelve feet short of the cup. But the other three golfers were equally flawless, and everyone two-putted for pars.

The seventeenth is a 190-yard par three over the water with a tiny heart-shaped green and a bunker in the back. Having rollover honors, Eric stepped up to the tee box and took a couple of practice swings. Hugh was watching from a distance like he had the entire day. Coaches couldn't be closer than fifty yards from their players once the match began. However, they could radio instructions to the caddie, who would then inform the golfer. Hugh noticed that a strong gust of wind was starting to blow. He wanted Eric to wait for it to die down, but his walkie-talkie's batteries were dead. He couldn't communicate with the caddie.

Eric's tee shot looked wonderful until the wind caught it and drove it into the pond. Hugh turned and walked away, stomping his feet. In Las Vegas, Oliver Harwas smashed a beer bottle on the floor and was escorted out of the sportsbook by security.

Eric teed up his penalty shot, and, this time, the ball landed ten feet from the cup. But he was lying three, and the others all placed their tee shots on the green. He handed his club to the caddie and asked him what Hugh thought. The caddie told him his walkie-talkie connection with his coach had broken.

*****

The power returned to FPL customers west of the Beeline Highway as the golfers walked to the green. Tommy Williams' computer booted up rapidly, and he quickly scrolled the eighteen boxes to find Eric. He pressed the ***IG 17*** button, and Mel picked up his cell phone and continued recording. Keith, who finally woke up, switched on the TV. All three listened to the announcers criticizing young Eric Mann for teeing off instead of waiting for the gust of wind to die.

"From what they're saying, I think Eric played a penalty stroke," stated Keith. At the bottom of the screen, the chyron says he's lying three while Harrington, Berger, and Poulter are all lying one."

Tommy kept punching the ***IG 17*** button, then shouted, "Damn!"

"What's the matter," asked Mel.

"Something may have happened to the system when the power crashed! The warning light came on when I pressed the ***IG 17*** button."

"I see the warning light. What does it say?"

"***Reverse function initiated.***"

"What does that mean?"

"It's something I invented to display the opposite angle on a green. If I can't fix it, all of the camera views will be inside-out. Long story. But now I need to get things back to normal."

"We all work together here, Tommy. You could keep us informed of your new inventions!"

Tommy turned away, closed his eyes, and thought to himself, "What they don't know won't hurt them."

*****

Harrington, Berger, and Poulter all two-putted. Each came within a couple of inches from the cup and tapped in. With a good putt, Eric would only lose one stroke. He had been putting exceptionally well, save for the three-putt on fourteen. His ball needed only to roll ten feet slightly downhill in a straight path.

Eric lightly tapped the putter. The ball moved perfectly toward the cup at just the right speed. Then it did something inexplicable—it stopped six inches from the cup and rolled backward uphill a foot! Huh?!

Meanwhile, Tommy tracked the path on his computer and kept punching ***IG 17*** until the warning light finally went off. Seconds later, ***Reverse Function Disabled*** flashed momentarily, then faded away. Relieved, Tommy mumbled "Whew!"

"How did that happen?" asked Keith as he sat straight up on the couch and peered at the TV. "Eric's ball was headed for the cup and turned uphill like it was way out of whack! I bet the moylyn cover is cracked, or the insides have become imbalanced. Something has got to be defective with his golf ball!"

"No!" yelped Tommy. "The moylyn cover won't crack, and the inside is fine. It was just a fluke! Now, watch the match or go back to sleep, okay?!"

Eric tapped in for a double bogey. Heading to eighteen, Harrington led the tournament with a ten under par, followed by Berger and Poulter at nine under. Eric was bringing up the rear with eight under par, but he was looking forward to the finish line. He never really cared if he won or lost—he was just thrilled to compete and be in the top four. And he knew his friends, family, and pastor would cheer him on as he finished the round.

PGA officials delayed teeing off on eighteen. They huddled and discussed the possibility of finishing the round tomorrow. The sun set two minutes earlier, and dusk was settling in. However, the rest of the field had completed their final matches, and *NBC* pleaded with Honda Classic executives to finish. It was now prime time in the East and delaying it to Monday would reduce viewership.

Money talked, and Daniel Berger was waved to the tee box. He had carryover honors from the fourteenth hole. The closing hole on the Champion Course had been lengthened to 604 yards for this year's Classic. The double dogleg par five can create a lot of excitement. Unfortunately, not so much for Berger. His four-iron tee shot landed in the middle of a bunker on the left side of the fairway. Pádraig Harrington was next. He hit a long five iron in the middle of the fairway and smiled. He could smell victory. Ian Poulter was next and squeezed a three iron between the bunkers and outdistanced Harrington by twenty yards.

With no radio communication between himself and Hugh Kraft, Eric wasn't sure of the best club to use for the final hole. But he was confident his coach would have told him to "go for it and leave it all on the grass!" Poulter's three iron went 250 yards, and Eric was sure he could match that with his driver. But he never thought that luck would be on his side, too. His drive landed a few feet behind Poulter's, but then the ball crazily bounced left in the same direction as the dogleg. It continued bouncing for another seventy-five yards—an amazing 325-yard tee shot, which was by far the longest of his life!

Berger pitched out of the sand trap onto the fairway but was still 300 yards from the pin. Harrington's second shot flew over the water on the right and avoided the bunkers, landing fifty yards from the hole. Poulter, trying to best Pádraig, landed his ball directly into the water on the right side of the green. He removed his cap and tossed it into the pond. With a one-stroke penalty for landing in the water and having to replay the shot, Ian knew the match was over for him. His next hit landed near Harrington's, but he was sitting with four strokes to Pádraig's two, an obstacle he knew he wouldn't overcome!

Berger was up next and landed his third shot five feet from Poulter's golf ball. But, already down a stroke to Harrington on the scorecard and back a stroke on the eighteenth, he knew his chances were slim, too. As dusk was evolving into darkness, Eric approached his ball. He was exactly 279 yards from the pin, and the longest he had ever played a fairway wood was 240 yards. He decided to play it safe with a three-iron.

But as he approached his ball, he heard Hugh's voice swirling around in his brain: "No guts, no glory!" Eric stepped back and surveyed the area. It was getting dark, and he couldn't make out much of anything. *NBC's* cameras, his golf partners and their caddies, that was about it. No Hugh anywhere in sight. But certainly, his coach was playing tricks inside his head!

Eric gave his club back to his caddie and asked for a two-wood. He could hear a chuckle or two coming from Harrington, Poulter, and Berger.

There was no way this thirteen-year-old kid was going to hit the ball on the green!

Eric's swing was perfect! He launched the ball with everything he could muster, but it got caught up by the wind and drifted to the right. There was no doubt in the golfers' minds it would end up in the water. Then shockingly, the ball turned into the wind and landed a yard short of the green. It took two bounces and finally rolled into the cup! The golf addicts in the bleachers never saw the shot due to the darkness, but they witnessed history in the making. Eric had scored a double eagle on the final hole, a first for the course, and finished the tournament at eleven under par! Now could he hang on for the win?!

Harrington, Berger, Poulter, and even Eric didn't know what had happened. They watched the ball take off but lost it visually in midair. The golfers all assumed that the ball landed in the pond. But when they heard the crowd roar, they knew something good had taken place. They were stunned when an official sprinted to them and told of Eric's incredible feat!

Harrington, Berger, and Poulter all chipped on the green. Berger dropped his long putt for a bogie six, finishing the tourney at eight under par. Poulter two-putted for par, completing the Classic with nine under. All Harrington needed to do was one putt, and he would tie Eric. But his fifteen-footer stopped an inch short, and the fans erupted again! The teenage rookie was now $1.1 million richer following his first PGA tournament match!

Tommy Williams high-fived Mel and Keith at St. Max's apartments.

Oliver Harwas' cheers woke up the entire Las Vegas Strip!

CHAPTER THIRTY-SIX

March 2015

Bahama Daddy Air was located adjacent to Jaws Beach in Clifton Bay. They owned three Cessna C-206 amphibian seaplanes. Two were used for private scuba diving charters, and the third was a rental. Willy asked to lease the seaplane but was told that due to rough seas, the rental was off-limits until Monday, March 2nd.

Willy left his pilot's license at home, but after asking around some of the tougher areas of Nassau, he found a hooligan counterfeiter who could produce any type of document needed—from passports to ID cards to, yes, pilot license certificates. Willy needed one with a seaplane endorsement. It cost him $5,000. The cash was wired from his bank in Palm Beach to the Bank of Nassau.

He picked up the money when the bank opened on Monday, then took a cab to Clifton Bay. The rental cost was a flat $1,000 per day plus fuel. Using his company credit card, he paid for two days. Once again, he hoped his bosses wouldn't notice.

Willy had flown plenty of small Cessnas but never a seaplane. How hard could it be? He was about to find out. As he attempted to lift off by transferring the support of the aircraft from the floats to the wings, the seaplane began to porpoise. Willy needed to maintain proper pitch angles but applied too much back elevator pressure. The stern of the floats dug into the water, creating a strong resistance. The owner of Bahama Daddy's covered his eyes. He couldn't watch!

Fortunately, Willy was a quick learner and figured out what he was doing wrong. Soon he was airborne and headed eastward. The flight plan Willy left with the rental agency said he was headed to Eleuthera. He told the owners he planned to scuba dive and camp on the island before returning on Tuesday.

Willy had plotted his course on a detailed map of the Bahamas he had purchased in Nassau. It listed typical prevailing wind and ocean currents, sea depths, and topography of the islands. But, as expected, it didn't show any landform northeast of the Plana Cays. Willy would have to make an educated guess when he reached that area. He flew over Tarpum Bay and Eleuthera, then turned southeast and headed for the Plana Cays. His heading took him over Cat Island and San Salvador Island. Willy listened intently to his radio, waiting for an air traffic controller to question why he was not sticking to his flight plan. But it never happened.

Due to the weight and drag of the C-206 amphibian aircraft, Willy cruised at only 125 knots. Surprisingly, he located the uncharted island about three hours after leaving Nassau. The retracted dock was his targeted landing spot. The landing itself was as shaky as his takeoff, but he managed to touch down in the water on the island's west side and taxi the plane to shore.

But when he stepped down onto land, three rather well-built, tall men greeted him. Each one was pointing a fully automatic AK-47 at Willy's head. The day that started out so well had gone south in an instant!

*****

After being hounded by reporters following his victory on PGA National's Champion Course, Eric was dead tired. He slept in on Monday until noon. His mother, who also happened to be his teacher, gave him an excused absence from class.

The last question he was asked before going home on Sunday night was from a sports reporter for the *Palm Beach Post*. "What will you do now that you are a millionaire?"

Eric smiled and didn't hesitate with his answer. However, it shocked everyone in the room! "I'm donating all the money to St. Max's Church for them to give to poor and homeless people living in Florida."

The astonished crowd who had stayed for the interview applauded loudly. Although Jim and Dora hoped to see a little of the money saved for their son's college education, they were pleased about the news. Father Jacob collapsed onto a chair and cried.

Two days earlier, Ursula Vero had reached an agreement with Father Jacob to provide free advertising and transportation costs in exchange for a twenty-five percent cut in the sales of St. Max's golf balls. Tommy Williams was bitterly angry, but Father had no choice. Vero said if he didn't sign a contract, then GCS would no longer sell the balls. Father didn't have time to find another distributor, so he agreed to the deal.

Ursula pulled out her cell phone and called her marketing vice president. "Doug! Eric won the Honda Classic! We need to jump on this right away. Make sure the entire world knows that St. Max's balls, sold by us, won the tournament! Then, we must sign Eric to an extremely long-term exclusive sponsorship for Golf Country Superstore! Don't fail me on this, Doug!!"

"I'll get it done, boss!"

*****

Willy tried to explain to his captors that he was just planning on scuba diving. When they didn't respond, he added that he didn't know the island was private property. When they still didn't respond, he offered to get back on his seaplane and fly away, promising never to say a word to anyone. The assault rifles didn't waver from his head.

The armed men led Willy up the path he had taken a few days earlier. It followed alongside the retractable dock for about 200 yards. They stopped at the electric pole with an attached switch box. The trio's leader punched several buttons on the top that appeared to be a combination lock. A green light lit on the box's side. The man then pushed a black button on the bottom of the box.

Willy was dumbfounded by what happened next. A twenty-by-twenty-foot steel plate four inches thick dropped down about five feet, then slid backward, leaving a twenty-by-twenty-foot hole. Willy noticed that the plants and shrubs on the plate were fake. Why hadn't he seen that a week ago?!

Willy was led to the opening, and the leader pointed his rifle at portable stairs, indicating that he should descend into the hole. Willy carefully stepped down about twelve feet to the floor. Next to him was a mobile conveyor belt. Willy glanced around and saw that the entrance was a hub, and four tunneled walkways veered off like spokes on a bicycle. One walkway was three times wider than the other two. Willy peered down the hall and watched a rollup door open. A flatbed mini-truck the size of a large golf cart exited and stopped. A man got out of the truck, touched something on the wall, and the door closed. He then entered a side door. Willy guessed the mini-truck was used for transporting goods from that room to the conveyor belt at the entrance. Behind that rollup door was most likely a small factory.

The second tunnel ended at another massive, roll-up steel door. A sign read ***DO NOT ENTER – MINERS ONLY!*** What was being mined? Yes, Willy was under a large hill, but if they were digging down, wouldn't they soon strike water? This place was only a few feet above sea level.

The third walkway had several doors along the hallway. Willy wasn't sure, but he guessed behind them were small offices or closets. Then a guard tapped Willy on the back with his rifle and nudged him toward the door at the end of the fourth walkway. The egress opened into a technology center loaded with computers and all sorts of devices Willy had never seen before.

Willy glanced this way, then that way, taking in everything he possibly could while being led to a storage unit at the far end of the room. His captors grabbed the cell phone from his pocket, pulled his thick arms behind his back, then tied ropes to his hands and feet. After that, they pushed him to the floor. They turned off the light and locked the door on their way out. Was anyone going to speak to him? Were they planning on leaving him in storage until he died?

In Willy's right front pocket was his trusty foldout knife that also contained a screwdriver, bottle opener, and other seemingly useless items. After taking his phone, the captors, surprisingly, hadn't frisked him. But getting the tool out of his pocket and opening the knife would be difficult in his position. However, the blade was spring-loaded, and one only needed to press a small button on the side of the tool to release it like a switchblade. Willy squirmed and wriggled on his hip until the knife finally sprang open, ripping a hole in his pocket. Fortunately, it firmly lodged in his pants, making it easier to cut the rope if he could writhe into position. With his sizable frame, that was easier said than done.

Eventually, the blade contacted the rope above Willy's wrists, and the big man was careful not to try and cut too deep. Small, shallow strokes were necessary to keep the knife in place. About three hours later, the Manila hemp rope had been bored, and strands of the natural fiber were shredded. From there, Willy jiggled free, then untied the rope around his feet.

The first battle was won, but getting out of the locked storage unit would be more difficult. The walls were made of steel, and there was a large bolt with a padlock on the door's exterior. Willy looked at the shelves to see what was stored in the small room. Perhaps something inside could help spring him loose. He saw nothing on the lower shelves. But as he gazed up to the top shelf, he noticed something he had seen before. A long time ago, in fact. It was during the time he worked with the FBI in Washington and helped wrap up the investigation of the worst domestic terrorist attack in United States history: the downing of two passenger airplanes in South Florida and the bombing of the University of Florida campus in Gainesville.

On the upper shelf were six radar jamming devices.

CHAPTER THIRTY-SEVEN

March 2015

Willy sat with his legs crossed on the floor of the storage room in deep thought. He pulled out the piece of paper found in the safe of the burnt estate on the beach. The numbers still didn't make sense, although Willy guessed they were bank accounts. But the letters ***T-a-s-s-e-t-t*** on each line began to clarify Willy's mind. It was radar jamming equipment used to crash the two airplanes in the early eighties, and Jake Tassett used his position as the lead investigator to cover up both incidents. He escaped prosecution and was never found. Supposedly he headed for a Caribbean Island with Judge Boone, who protected Okeechobee County criminals by handing down wrong verdicts. Willy was now sure Jake Tassett had lived in the beach home and owned this underground factory. Whatever was being produced here was most likely illegal and dangerous, if that was true!

Could Jake Tassett be in this factory now? Willy's mind was exploding! Then he heard a metallic jiggling sound outside the door. Someone was fiddling with the lock. To decoy, Willy placed the rope loosely around his legs and put his hands behind his back. The switchblade was open. This might be his one and only chance.

At 5:00 pm, one guard entered with an open can of tuna and bottled water. A second guard carried a large, empty plastic bucket that had been used to hold paint. The third guard was pointing an AK-47 at Willy.

The man with the gun spoke. "The tuna and water are dinner. Eat wisely. The container is a honey bucket. We'll have you empty it and rinse it out once a week. There's printer paper on the bottom of that shelf if you need to wipe. We're going to cut you loose now. Don't try anything stupid!"

It was now or never. Willy sprang up and kicked the unsuspecting guard in the groin with the power of a stampeding elephant! The man instinctively dropped the gun. Willy grabbed it and spun around in a flash. He moved the AK-47 back and forth from one guard to the next. Frightened, the two guards raised their hands high above their heads. Using the butt of the rifle, Willy knocked the third guard into a state of unconsciousness. That was probably much less painful than his groin injury!

As Willy backed out into the technology center, he uttered sarcastically, "I hope you enjoy sharing your tuna as much as you enjoy sharing the honey bucket! Use the printer paper judiciously. I'm not sure what happens when you run out!"

Carrying the AK-47 with its shoulder strap on his back, Willy closed the door, slid the bolt into place, and snapped the lock shut. Guessing the three guards were assigned to him, he doubted anyone else would be checking the storage room anytime soon. Unless, of course, they needed printer paper!

*****

Willy exited the technology center and moved slowly toward the entrance. At the hub, he looked down the hallway where the factory was located. A voice inside his head told him to get out of the subterranean pit of corruption while the getting was good! But strangely, no one was anywhere in sight. The tech room had been empty like it was when he was captured. There were no more guards to contend with or people walking around. Willy crept gradually toward the factory. The entrance was a steel-paneled roll-up door that was secured with biometric technology. The lone way in was to press a finger on the glass reader. Willy assumed that only factory workers and high-level administrators had fingerprints that would open the door.

Near the roll-up and off to one side was a room with mirrored glass about five feet long and three feet high. Willy had seen enough of those in his police days to know it was a one-way pane. Whoever was inside could see out, but outsiders couldn't see in. Was someone in there now? If so, Willy was working on borrowed time. Armed security guards would be here any minute!

Willy turned the handle and yanked the door. Oddly, it was unlocked. The room was about twelve feet by twelve feet. Inside was a stool beside a countertop with a cup of cold coffee. Whoever manned the booth was gone. Perhaps his shift was over for the day. Above the countertop was the one-way mirror.

Willy glanced around the perimeter. TV monitors were displaying all areas of the underground factory and offices. The cameras swung back and forth to cover a large space. This was obviously the main security room. On the counter was a paper pad with a five-column log entry:

DATE/ TIME/ PRODUCT/ DESTINATION/ SIGNATURE

Willy assumed that an authority figure filled in the data every time a product left the factory.

Willy rapidly examined the entries. Something left the factory today around noon. That must be what he saw on the mini-truck when he arrived. The other items were listed for the previous month, and all were on Mondays:

2/09/15:1342 Bible/ACT (PoFL/SMC)—CB
2/16/15:1114 Bible/ACT (PoSV/SMC)—RP
2/23/15:1405 GC/18 (PoGV/HFCC)—CB
3/02/15:1220 GC/18 (PoNO/SJC)—RP

Besides the date and time on a twenty-four-hour clock, nothing else made sense except for the word Bible. And even that was hard to understand in this context. Frustrated, Willy mumbled, "Someone smarter than me needs to figure this out."

He would have used his phone and snapped a picture of the log on his camera, but the guards had confiscated the cell. He was thankful they didn't find the pocketknife. Knowing time was slipping away, he tore the log off the pad, folded it, and tucked it in his pants.

Holding tightly to the automatic rifle, he emerged into the hallway and headed for the central exit. Still, nobody was anywhere in sight. Very curious! Willy wondered how many people worked here. Thinking back, he only saw the three guards and the man driving the mini-truck. Because of the cold coffee in the security room, he assumed another person was employed in the factory. But that was only five people! Where were the others?!

A button attached to a pole next to the main entrance needed no code to be punched. That lack of security was fortunate for Willy. He pushed the button, and the twenty-by-twenty-foot ceiling door dropped several feet to provide clearance for the fake plants and shrubs fixed to the top. The overhead door then slid aside and tucked itself away. Willy climbed the steps to the outside and looked around. The sun was setting in the west.

He hustled down the path next to the retractable pier. The seaplane was where he had left it. Willy started to climb in, then hesitated. He hopped down, stared at the top of the hill, and mumbled, "Nope. I'm not leaving here without him."

If Jake Tassett was on this island, he would find him and try to make a citizen's arrest. Chances were good that Tassett wouldn't come quietly. Willy decided that his best option was to hide the seaplane and observe the comings and goings of factory personnel for a week. According to the log, Mondays were the days products shipped out. If he could hide until the following Monday, he would be able to gather evidence and see what kind of boat was used. And if he was lucky, perhaps Jake Tassett would exit the hole.

Using a rope, Willy pulled the plane down the shoreline. It was difficult to see once the sun set. The moon provided his only light to navigate by. There was a small cove on the island's west end where Willy could hide the seaplane. With all the strength his colossal muscles could muster, he pulled the boat onto the beach and over a small sand dune.

Willy covered the plane with palm fronds. It was just past midnight when he finished. He would sleep inside on the floor of the cargo hold. Willy guessed he was about a half mile from the factory.

Sleeping was a challenge. The seaplane's floor was uncomfortable, and his mind was overwhelmed with anxiety. Were there security cameras hidden on the island? Did they know where he was? Would they look for him?

The AK-47 next to him was his security blanket!

CHAPTER THIRTY-EIGHT

March 2015

The crushed seashell powdered formula arrived in Edinburgh, Scotland, on Wednesday, March 4th. On Thursday, the Old Course was closed to golfers to prepare Scotland's historical icon for its annual soil treatment. Groundskeepers spread the mixture of calcite, aragonite, and limestone liberally on the fairways. The next day, the greens would be saturated with the same minerals. The rain and chemical formula would soften the soil and prepare it for fertilizer treatment in two weeks.

On Friday morning, the groundskeepers were supposed to remove the cups from the greens before spreading the formula. However, the head horticulturist, Bram Stewart, had just repositioned the pin placements yesterday and didn't want to damage the putting surface. As the sun rose in the east, he led a group of three workers onto the first hole to start the task. Bram hoped to have all eighteen greens covered with the formula before sunset. The wind blew calcite, aragonite, and limestone particles into the cup.

When they noticed smoke rising from the green, Bram and his three groundskeepers ran and dove for shelter in the sand trap, which saved them from serious injury. A minute later, the explosion could be heard throughout all the coffee shops in St. Andrews. The first hole's cup shot high into the air and landed in a narrow water channel next to the famed stone Swilcan Bridge. The blast covered Bram and his men in mud and grass from head to toe. Incredibly, there were now only seventeen holes left on the Old Course!

The first news reports from the BBC stated that terrorists had attempted to blow up the Old Course, and perhaps all of St. Andrews, using underground bombs. All golf courses in the area were closed immediately, as were public houses, businesses, and universities. Military personnel and armored tanks were rushed from Edinburgh and Glasgow to aid in evacuating the seaside town. London, Manchester, Birmingham, and other major cities throughout the United Kingdom were placed on high alert.

A tourist taking a picture of the Swilcan Bridge found the cup. When he heard the explosion, the frightened man accidentally held down the shutter, and photos were shot in continuous mode. His camera had captured the split second the cup landed in the stream. The stunned tourist covered his head with his hands in case another blast occurred. When nothing more was discharged, and the man felt safe, he reached into the water for the cup that had cooled enough for the man to pick up.

All golf cups have holes in the bottom for water to drain. However, the entire bottom of the cup was missing on this one. The thin sides were made from some sort of solid plastic. The tourist heard a faint buzz coming from inside the cup's walls. The man walked to his car with it. He thought a real piece of the Old Course would make an excellent souvenir for his fireplace mantle back in Toronto. When he opened the door to his rental, the cup fell out of his hand, bounced on the ground, and clung tightly to the car's frame.

"What the hell?!" muttered the tourist to himself. "Plastic isn't magnetic! There must be a powerful magnet inside the cup walls that can penetrate the plastic!"

The man decided he didn't want anything to do with the cup. He'd play it safe and buy a Polo shirt with the St. Andrew's emblem for his souvenir. He drove to the clubhouse to return the cup that was still clinging to the exterior of his rental, but he wasn't allowed to park in the lot. Yellow police tape was being wrapped around the entire course.

Winston Helms, the president of the British PGA, had an office in the Old Course clubhouse. He was standing outside with his hands on his hips, looking stupefied. The tourist didn't recognize Helms, but his blazer had a BPGA patch on the pocket, so the man knew he worked at the golf course.

"Excuse me, sir. I'm visiting here from Canada. I was taking pictures of the Swilcan Bridge when that golf cup landed in the stream next to me." The man pointed to his car.

"Golf cup? That's a golf cup?" asked Helms. He was confused. "How is it sticking on your car's frame if it landed in the water on the course?"

"I picked it out of the water. It dropped out of my hand when I opened the car door. It bounced up off the ground and clung to the frame like a magnet!"

Helms walked to the rental and examined the cup. It was just a cylinder with no top or bottom. "This is plastic! But it seems to be magnetic, like you said! How can that be?!" The men tried to yank it off the car but to no avail. The tourist retrieved a crowbar from his trunk and pried at the cup. It came off the frame but then stuck to the iron crowbar.

"Do you mind if I take the cup and your crowbar?" asked Helms. He slipped the tourist fifty British pounds. "Here, this should cover the cost of the crowbar if the car rental company wants you to pay for it."

The man thanked Helms, got back in his car, and made haste to Edinburgh. There was no reason to stay in St. Andrews. Everything was closed, and it appeared it would stay that way for several days.

CHAPTER THIRTY-NINE

March 2015

When the seaplane wasn't returned as contracted, Bahama Daddy Air waited the required three days, then filed a complaint with the Nassau police on Friday, March 6th. During their investigation, a photocopy of Willy's seaplane-endorsed pilot's certificate was examined and deemed a forgery. A warrant for his arrest was issued that afternoon, and an all-points bulletin was provided to the governments of every country within a 1,000-mile radius of Paradise Island. The Bahamian Navy and Coast Guard were put on instant alert.

Aries-Level (AL) priorities in the FBI are the highest criminal threats within the organization. Terrorist activities, civil rights violations, cyber crime, foreign influence, transnational organized crime, human trafficking, violent crimes, and criminal threats fall within this category. Mel Smith monitored Aries-Level FBI activity using a private app on his cell phone. On Friday afternoon, when the vibration indicating a notification was posted, he almost ignored it. The FBI's alerts were annoying to him.

But Mel was glad he didn't disregard this notification. He was flabbergasted that Willy Banks was accused of forging a government document and stealing a seaplane in the Bahamas. What was he doing back there?!

Mel speed-dialed Bushman Jack. "Willy Banks is back in the Bahamas! Can the drone find him? Check out Plana Cay."

"I'm on it! But I think you got bigger fish to fry."

"What's that supposed to mean?!"

"Have you heard the news out of Scotland?"

"No, what's up?"

"The entire first hole of the Old Course exploded this morning. No one was killed, but four workers were injured. MI6 is calling it an international terrorist threat. Great Britain is on high alert, and St. Andrews has been shut down and is now being evacuated. I have the drone locked onto the green, searching every square inch of the mud. No sign of the cup."

"Yeah, but how, Jack? How did it happen?"

"The investigation is just underway, but the BBC reports that the four groundskeepers were spreading chemicals on the green to loosen the earth before fertilizing it next week. They saw smoke rising and dove for cover in the sand trap."

"Let me guess—the chemicals were made from crushed seashells, right?"

"Yep. The drone found an opened package near the green. I zoomed in on the ingredients printed on it. Calcite, aragonite, and limestone."

"Damn!" Mel nervously paced the room. Keith watched him and shook his head. Tommy wasn't there as he had gone golfing for the day. "Okay. Let me know when you find Willy Banks." Mel hung up and stared at Keith, who was staring right back.

"Now what?!" asked Keith.

"We need to make a move!" replied Mel irritably.

"It may be too late. This could be checkmate!"

*****

On Monday morning, March 9th, a check from the Professional Golfers Association in the amount of $660,000 arrived special delivery for Eric Mann. He was in class at the time, but Dora allowed him to go in the hallway and sign for the envelope. That night, Jim explained to Eric that the IRS was withholding forty percent of the $1.1 million for tax purposes. But he also said that Eric would most likely get money back when he filed his 2015 taxes next spring, seeing he was donating it to St. Max's Church, a non-profit organization.

After wishing Eric and Dora a good night's rest, Jim turned on his computer. Since returning from the Bahamas, he had been intrigued that Columbus had landed on the same Plana Cay island he had last week. Jim didn't care about the expandable pier or the estate home that burned to ashes; he wondered why the island was uncharted. His Google search wasn't helping much, but then again, no history was recorded online in 1492.

However, a Portuguese historian's account of the Niña, Pinta, and Santa Maria's cargo caught Jim's eye. He claimed all three ships carried five hundred pounds of an unnamed ferromagnetic mineral mined in the Sierra Norte mountain range west of Seville, Spain. The historian believed the cargo would alleviate the fears of Columbus' crew. The magnetic reverse pull would keep the ships from sailing off the edge of the flat world, a belief shared by many sailors in the fifteenth century. All they would need to do was place the mineral on the Niña, Pinta, and Santa Maria's decks, and the ships would be pulled back toward the iron mines of Portugal.

The historian contended that after Columbus proved to his crew that the earth was round, there was no need for the mineral. Thus, they dug a hole in the Plana Cays and buried it. Meanwhile, the original mine near Seville continued to form more of the magnetic substance until it was blown up by the Iberian Anarchist Federation during the Spanish Civil War in 1936.

Jim was bewildered for two reasons. First, he didn't remember much from high school chemistry, but he was certain minerals couldn't reproduce! He Googled *mineral reproduction* and learned his knowledge was up for interpretation. If the earthen conditions were perfect, minerals could expand and form crystals. That must be what happened in Spain. Some of the substance was left in the ground and grew.

Second, Jim's confusion stemmed more when he tried to understand the purpose of destroying the mine. Why would anyone waste expensive bombs to level an area of Spain far from the fighting?

Then Jim pondered a different theory never written in history: Did the mine explode on its own? Was it possible that the black pebbles in the sand on the uncharted Plana Cay island were the same magnetic substance brought over by Columbus? Those rocks were indeed magnetic and definitely explosive.

The estate home on the beach was proof of that!

CHAPTER FORTY

March 2015

"The seaplane is hidden under palm fronds on the island's west side," said Bushman Jack as he forwarded the drone's pictures to Mel's computer. "Can't say how it got there, but there's no sign of Willy Banks. My guess is they've captured him and are holding him underground."

"Why would they do that?" asked Mel. "What purpose would it serve to let Willy live? I bet they killed him on the spot."

"Well, you may never have descended into the mine, but you're still the boss. Perhaps you should find out."

*****

Willy hid in the brush and watched two men pull the lever on the electrical pole. The retractable pier rolled out into the sea. In the distance, he could see a small vessel approaching. He wished he had binoculars!

It was Monday, March 9th, and Willy had camped in the seaplane for the past week. During the day, he would walk the half mile to the factory's entrance and hide fifty yards away behind thick shrubs, where he was now. Strangely, no one had entered or exited the disguised drop-down door until a few minutes ago when the pier was extended into the ocean.

On his hikes to and from the seaplane, he found three radar-jamming devices precisely like the ones on the shelves in the storage room where he had been locked up. They were camouflaged on the top of coconut palm trees. Brown wires ran from the jamming device to the ground. The wires wound around the tree's trunk and blended with the bark. Willy didn't have to climb the tree. Instead, he cut the wires at the base, then walked around the tree to unwrap them. Once that was accomplished, Willy yanked the device to the ground.

He was sure the radar jamming devices had been used on the island to ward off intruders. Willy remembered how the fishing boat he, Otis, Jim, and Bob had rented lost communications and GPS signals when it neared the uncharted Plana Cay island. Willy brought the jammers back to the plane. Hopefully, they would serve as undisputed evidence against Jake Tassett.

At 2:50 pm, the vessel docked at the pier. Willy couldn't believe his eyes: the craft was an old fishing boat about twenty-five feet long. It certainly looked like it had seen better days! In the stern, where the grouper, red snappers, and Chilean sea bass would usually be put on ice until the charter reached home, was a cargo hold. Only two sailors were onboard—probably the captain and first mate.

Willy observed closely as the conveyor belt moved four wood crates from the hole. The two men who opened the door pushed the crates that were on rollers onto the pier. From there, the men hustled downhill to the dock before the containers arrived. They joined the captain and first mate to lift the boxes onto the boat and into the cargo hold.

The captain signed something and handed it to one of the men from the factory. Then the captain went to the cockpit while the first mate untied the ropes from the dock and pushed off. The pier was retracted back to the top of the hill. Finally, the men climbed down the stairs into the hole and closed the false door. The entire ordeal took less than an hour.

Willy had planned to stay a week until the Monday shipment was gone. He hoped to find Jake Tassett, but the rogue ex-investigator for the FAA was nowhere to be seen. Willy debated staying a few more days to find a way to secretly reenter the factory and look for Tassett. Or another option would be to return to Florida and let the FBI handle the search. He needed a night to think about it.

Meanwhile, Willy was initially concerned about the buoyancy of the small boat now in the open ocean. But, then again, perhaps he needn't be. The cargo being shipped should protect the captain and first mate while navigating the dangerous waters of the Bermuda Triangle. Willy nodded as he remembered what was stamped in big red letters on the sides of the containers:

BIBLES

CHAPTER FORTY-ONE

March 2015

After school each day and on the weekends, Eric met Hugh Kraft at the PGA National driving range. The practice area was well-lit until it closed at midnight. Eric would golf until closing time, then come back to the apartment and do homework until the wee hours of the morning. Dora was concerned that her thirteen-year-old son and top student in her class was not getting enough sleep on school nights.

By winning the Honda Classic, Eric had taken the first step toward qualifying for the Masters Tournament in early April. Still, he needed a Top Ten finish at the Arnold Palmer Invitational to ensure a slot in Augusta. The API would be played from March 19th to the 22nd at the Bay Hill Club in Orlando.

Hugh tweaked Eric's swing and built his confidence. But his main task was to keep the persistently irksome toadies away from his protégé, which included autograph seekers, sports reporters, and Doug Cramer, one of three vice presidents at Golf Country Superstore. Cramer wouldn't give up on his goal of signing Eric to a long-term, exclusive marketing agreement for GCS.

*****

"Please, Father, pray for my brother's safe return!" pleaded Otis. Father Jacob was meeting with Otis in his St. Max's office. Otis told him Willy stayed in Nassau to relieve stress after the ordeal in Plana Cay. However, he hadn't heard from his brother since Sunday, March 1st, and he was getting worried. "He's been gone too long!"

"Calm down, Otis. I will most certainly pray for Willy. God will watch over him."

"Thank you, Father!"

"You're welcome. Please let me know if you hear from him."

Meanwhile, Willy found a pair of tools lying next to a palm tree that he believed was a message from God. It was an old shovel and pickaxe. Because of that discovery, Willy decided to stay on Plana Cay until he found Jake Tassett. He would dig a tunnel and enter the underground factory away from the main entrance.

*****

Eric was summoned to the Bay Hill Country Club guest waiting room early Thursday morning. He was astonished to see his dad along with Father Jacob standing there with a dozen St. Max's Premier golf balls in his hands.

Eric dashed to Jim, and they embraced. Then he looked at his priest. "Father, what are you doing here?!" called out Eric with a big grin.

"I wanted to watch the first round today, and your dad said I could catch a ride with him. Plus, I didn't give you new golf balls before you left Palm Beach Gardens. Here, I blessed these last night. Good luck, Eric. And remember, win or lose, you always make us proud!"

Eric took the balls and gave Father a hug. "Thank you so much for coming! What time did you leave?"

"We were on the turnpike at 4:00 am. Your fifty-year-old Plymouth Duster can still fly, and your dad has a lead foot! He would put Mario Andretti to shame!"

"Mario, who?"

Jim and Father Jacob chuckled. The famed racecar driver was well before Eric's time. "Never mind," said Jim. "Do your best, son. Mom will be coming up on Saturday with the Butlers. She's sad she will miss today and tomorrow because she has to teach."

Eric was teamed with Ben Martin and Zach Johnson for the first round of the Arnold Palmer Invitational. The greens at Bay Hill Golf Club were a big challenge for Eric. The Bermuda grass and grain pulled toward the sun, which meant it changed directions during the day. It leaned toward the east in the mornings and west in the evenings. Eric struggled reading the green due to the grain effect. Plus, the greens were firm, and Eric's flop shots would hit and release, making his putts a longer distance than he was accustomed to. Hugh got word to him via his caddie to use a bump-and-run chip with a pitching or sand wedge.

Still, Eric's drives were terrific, as usual! Though, he was lucky to par the first three holes. His putts appeared to be long, short, right, or left, but somehow became leaners and fell into the hole. Barely! Ben and Zach would look at each other and shake their heads when Eric's putts dropped in.

But the fourth hole gave Eric a fit. The pin placement had been changed since the practice rounds because a woodchuck had dug up and cracked the cup the night before. The hole itself was a 561-yard, par five, straight uphill. Martin and Johnson had both parred the first three holes, too, and they had honors carrying over from the first tee. Both hit drives nearly 290 yards. Eric knew better than to try and match their distance, but he thought he'd give it a go. Bad choice.

The youngster swung too hard and lost control. His ball veered right and landed in the creek. Hugh was furious and shouted in the walkie-talkie to the caddy, "Tell Eric to take it easy and play his game, not his opponents!"

With the penalty stroke, Eric re-teed and hit his third shot. It landed nicely on the fairway, 240 yards away, just before the dogleg left. But his fourth shot was a disaster! Using a two wood, Eric slightly pulled the ball, and it landed in the sand trap eighty yards from the pin. His sand wedge plunked the ball onto the undulating surface and it rolled off the right side of the green. He tried to putt from the fringe but misjudged the length of the grass and the direction of the roll. Eric finished with a four-over-par, quad bogey, nine. Martin parred the hole, and Johnson bogeyed.

Eric parred twelve of the last fourteen holes and birdied two of them. He finished the first round with a two-over par seventy-four. But he was four strokes behind Martin and Johnson, who both scored seventy. Making matters worse, Matt Every and Henrik Stenson shot sixty-eight, so Eric was sitting six strokes back of the leaders going into the second round.

Tommy Williams was furious as he slapped his computer. "Damn woodchuck!"

*****

For some odd reason, Eric couldn't figure out how to play the fourth hole. Those who play golf frequently call it a head game. If you think you can't make a shot, chances are good that you won't. Hugh coached him with diagrams, narratives from previous invitational winners, and a detailed flyover on YouTube. Yet he couldn't seem to build his confidence on the fourth hole. In the final three rounds, it was his nemesis. He tripled-bogeyed the fourth on Friday, double-bogeyed on Saturday, then triple-bogeyed on Sunday during the final round. Fortunately, he had plenty of birdies and two eagles to keep his score respectable. He finished in ninth place, tied with Kevin Na at thirteen under par, and he was six strokes back of the winner, Matt Every.

Eric wasn't happy with his performance. Regardless, he had qualified for the Masters Tournament in April. He wanted to win the green jacket so badly he could taste it!

CHAPTER FORTY-TWO

March 2015

Willy had been digging into the side of the hill for two weeks when his goal was achieved, but it wasn't the kind of fulfillment he had hoped for. The underground wall that enclosed the factory, mine, and offices was indestructible. It was a gold-colored metal with no corrosion from saltwater seeping upward. Willy guessed it was either brass or bronze. He knew from experience working in his garage back home that some brass material was partially magnetic due to its iron alloy components. But bronze was not magnetic. Willy surmised that Tassett, or whoever built the factory, wouldn't use ferromagnetic material because the unknown metal they were mining would cling to the walls.

The challenge now was how to get in. The wall appeared to be impenetrable and secure. The tunnel he dug was about forty feet long and three feet tall, only large enough for him to crawl through. Willy had little room to maneuver freely, meaning he couldn't take wide swings with the pickaxe. While Willy labored, he had reinforced the top of the tunnel with palm fronds and tree branches, but he still feared it would collapse with him in it. He wasn't sure a welding kit could penetrate the bronze wall even if he had one!

The further Willy went into the tunnel, the more difficult it was to breathe. He wiggled back and sat cross-legged outside the opening, thinking about his next step. It came to him immediately. He needed the black pebbles and seashells to create an explosion that would blow a hole in the wall. Not too much of either or the blast could kill him. He would need time to exit the tunnel once the elements were laid on the bronze.

Willy started back to the seaplane. He needed two containers: one for the rocks and one for the shells. After a few steps down the hill, he tripped and fell, hitting his forehead on the ground. He rolled over and lay on his back to catch his breath and regain composure. That's when he saw it. The sun was reflecting off something high up in the coconut palm tree. It had no cord wrapped around the trunk, so it couldn't be a radar-jamming device. Something else. Willy peered up and thought it looked like a camera. He ambled away from the tree, and it moved, pointing directly at him. He strolled in a circle, and it followed him. Without a doubt, it was a camera.

Willy then knew why no one had come looking for him. The guards he locked in the storage room had to be out by now. Everyone in the hole knew he had escaped. They had security cameras all around Plana Cay, so they would know where he was at all times. And this island was uncharted, so a search party was unlikely. But the guards must have known that Willy hid the seaplane. Why wasn't that a concern? They certainly wouldn't let him just fly out of here, right?

Willy had a sinking feeling in the pit of his stomach. He had moved the plane by pushing and pulling it through the water without starting the engine. He began to jog to where the seaplane was hidden. Willy cleared the palm fronds from the propellers, climbed in, and turned the ignition. Nothing! Not even a cough or a sputter!

Willy jumped down and opened the engine compartment. A quick glance inside told him everything. He pounded the fuselage with his fist, leaving a slight indentation in the metal.

Sure enough, the batteries were missing.

*****

Tuesday morning, March 24th, Willy scrapped his plan to blow up the tunnel. Instead, he decided it was hero time once again. He had plenty of experience solving crimes, and shoot, he was holding an AK-47 with a high-capacity magazine. It held ninety rounds, which should be plenty for raiding the factory. His goal was to break in, tie up everyone who worked there, and find Jake Tassett. He would arrest Tassett, find the seaplane batteries, then fly the crook back to Florida.

Willy made a surrender flag using a stick and one of his white sweat socks. He would go to the entrance, lay the AK-47 on the ground, look up at the trees where there would be security cameras, and wave the flag. Hopefully, the factory guards would open the entrance door to recapture him. He would quickly pick up the rifle, overtake the security team, and find Tassett. Voila! Just like magic, the great American hero would do it again!

But the best-laid plans often go awry. And this one did when Willy saw a huge cargo freighter anchor 300 yards offshore from the retractable pier. He hid behind a tree to watch and observe.

Six lifeboats were hanging from the sides of the merchant ship. In between each lifeboat were flatbed transport vessels. Four were lowered into the water and maneuvered to the cargo door. Containers were loaded onto the flatbeds, then motored to the pier. From there, twenty sailors from the freighter joined with four men from the factory to load the boxes onto the conveyor. One container was placed on the belt recklessly and fell off the pier halfway up the hill. The top was jarred open, and some contents spilled onto the ground.

One of the factory workers saw the box drop and break open. He shouted, "Just leave it! We'll get it later!"

An hour later, the remaining containers were inside the hole, and the fake entrance door moved back into place.

Willy was curious and didn't care if a security camera was locked on him. He sauntered to the broken container and removed the packaging list and some of the contents. The box contained curved, thin pieces of plastic and flat disks with holes. Willy was baffled.

He turned the pieces in all directions and tried to push them together like he was working a puzzle. Soon he gave up and decided to look at the packaging list secured inside a sealed transparent plastic folder. When he ripped it open, an instruction sheet fell out. It was assembly steps for putting the plastic pieces together. Willy quickly constructed one of the items. When assembled, it looked like a cup of some sort. Strangely, the curved sides were made of two pieces so something could be inserted in between. There were also two bottoms on the cup. Once again, it appeared that something could be wedged between the two disks. Willy thought he had seen something like it before but couldn't quite place it.

If Willy was going to be a hero again, he needed to understand what type of evidence the cup could be. And one other important mystery: the Plana Cay island he was on was uncharted, so how did the freighter know where to find it?

He squinted as he gazed at the ship. On the bow, he thought he could make out the letters that were painted in large, bold print:

REGISTRY: INDIA

CHAPTER FORTY-THREE

March 2015

"Here, Father. This is for the church." Eric handed the priest a check for $105,840, his net winnings for finishing in ninth place at the Arnold Palmer Invitational. "Dad said Uncle Sam gets to hold on to the other $70,560 until at least next April. I'm beginning to think Uncle Sam is my best fan!" Father and Eric both laughed.

"Many homeless families will be your best fans, Eric! Thank you for your enormous generosity, son! So, what's next?"

"The Masters in a couple of weeks. It's in Augusta, Georgia."

"You don't say! Father Bill at St. Mary's Church in Augusta is a good friend of mine. Perhaps he would have room for me in his parish home, and I could come to watch!"

"That would be awesome, Father, but I'm not sure you could get tickets now. I had a tough time getting tickets for Mom and Dad. It's one of the four major tournaments and the biggest one of the year."

"Well, son, I'll do my best to get in. Maybe Father Bill has connections. Hey, maybe both of us could bless your golf balls, seeing it's the biggest tourney of the year!"

"That would be grand! I hope you can get in, Father!"

*****

April 2015

"Golf Country Superstore is valued too high!" exclaimed Shea Hansen. "Their stock prices soared when the golf world discovered Eric Mann used St. Max's Premium balls, and they were the exclusive distributor. In other words, you waited too long!"

Oliver Harwas was sitting on the couch in Shea's San Francisco condominium complex, which was also her office. Surreptitiously, she was a corporate raider for many unscrupulous clients needing to invest their illegal profits. Many were criminals looking at serious prison time if caught. Oliver was one of them. Although Shea's job was technically legal, she still tried to maintain a secret lifestyle. Her income from successful takeovers was reinvested in the four-unit apartment building on Vallejo near the Lyon Street Steps. She rented by the month and sometimes daily as an AirBnb. Her neighbors had no idea she was a corporate raider.

Oliver got up and walked over to the enormous picture window with a spectacular view of San Francisco Bay and Alcatraz Island. "What's the current share price?"

"Thirty-one dollars a share. You would need roughly nine million outstanding shares to achieve significant voting rights. That would be $279,000,000. I assume you didn't win anything near that amount betting on the Honda Classic!" Shea grinned as Oliver frowned. "It's a shame, though. Before Mann won the Honda, the share price was eighteen dollars. That would have been a much easier takeover."

"You assume I only have gambling money. Trust me, I can secure billions in the blink of an eye!"

"I'm not saying you can't. I'm just advising you that raiding Golf Country Superstore might be difficult. First, we'd have to set up another shell company and do a takeover merger, like before. Obviously, we can't use your sullied name in the documents."

"Sullied?!" blurted Oliver as his face turned red. "There's nothing wrong with my name!"

"Other than you're one of the FBI's most wanted criminals! There's no way we'd get SEC approval with your name on the LLC!"

"Second, Ursula Vero will fight the acquisition tooth and nail. And lastly, by the time we put all this together, the share price could jump beyond fifty dollars!"

"You already have fake companies set up around the world ready to go! I will pay you to merge one of those so we can do this immediately!"

"That would cost you ten billion dollars. Can you afford me?" Shea's continual smirk was irritating Oliver.

"Give me your bank account number. I'll have it wired to you next Monday."

Oliver walked out and slammed the door. No smile, no handshake, and no goodbye.

*****

The call was placed somewhere in the Bahamas and received on Saturday, April 4th, somewhere in Florida. The recipient rarely used his cell phone because he wasn't sure if it was being tracked. But the caller claimed this was an emergency situation.

"We took the batteries from the seaplane so he can't fly it. But he's almost finished building a raft from bamboo. He took the floats off the aircraft and attached them to the raft's bottom."

"There's no way in hell he can navigate a raft that far out in the Atlantic!"

"Probably not. But he might get lucky, and someone will see him. Plus, he has one of our AK-47s."

"What?! How did that happen?!"

"Long story! And a crate fell off the conveyor belt. He saw the contents, though I'm not sure he knows what they're used for."

"A crate fell off the belt, and the man stole an AK-47?! What kind of chaotic operation are you running there?! One more screw-up, and you're done, Jimmy!"

"Sorry, sir. I promise our mistakes are over. I'm assuming you want us to kill him. Is that right?"

"I had you capture him to see who might come and rescue him. I needed to know who was aware of our activities. The people I guessed haven't made a move, though. So yes, don't let him get away on that raft!"

"Yes, sir. I will take care of it myself!"

*****

"You really don't think they'll let him go, do you, Mel?" asked Keith. The two had rented another boat in Nassau. They were now drifting in the open ocean a mile offshore with their powerful binoculars fixed on the island.

"He's got a rifle and has plenty of experience escaping perilous situations. So, we'll wait here and see what happens."

"If he does escape, what will we do?"

"We'll cross that bridge when we come to it."

CHAPTER FORTY-FOUR

April 2015

Oliver Harwas was a henchman for Burt Merriman, a mob boss who owned an island in the Caymans and an estate home on the bluffs in Wisconsin overlooking the Mississippi River. Merriman's cover was posing as a restauranteur, and he owned several famous Michelin three-star establishments in upscale cities worldwide. But his pièce de resistance was creating wealth via avaricious methods of greed. Fraud was his means to opulence, but more than that, it was his hobby! Merriman relished innovative practices of deceit and deception. Whenever he discovered a new fraudulent scheme, he implemented it for sheer enjoyment! The mob boss hadn't cared who he squashed on the way to the top! And Merriman never worried about his money or welfare because his right-hand man was Oliver Harwas!

Merriman was arrested several times for various charges but never spent much time in jail. His lawyers were highly paid and could find loopholes in every case, allowing the mobster to walk free. When a loophole couldn't be found, witnesses who would provide testimony against Merriman miraculously seemed to disappear before trial. Worried that he might be incarcerated when a financial decision needed to be made, Merriman signed a Power of Attorney for Oliver Harwas.

Years earlier, one of Merriman's corrupt business associates, Jake Tassett, had convinced the mob boss that professional sports could be manipulated in unethical ways and gamblers could make a fortune betting on players and teams who were unknowingly exploited. Merriman was ecstatic! This could be fun! He ordered Oliver Harwas to work with Tassett and make the scheme successful regardless of the costs.

But now Oliver needed money to raid Golf Country Superstore, and he didn't want his boss to know the whole truth. Using the Power of Attorney, Harwas temporarily changed the name of Merriman's financial holding company from Merriman Enterprises to OH Enterprises. Oliver was number one on the FBI's Most Wanted List, so he used his initials to hopefully avoid scrutiny down the line. When he completed the takeover, he would change the holding company back to Merriman Enterprises. Thanks to the POA, Harwas had complete control over the mob boss' properties, investments, and cash. But Oliver had to be very careful. Should Merriman scrutinize what Harwas did without his approval, he knew he would confront eternal darkness.

Oliver ended the debate in his mind with one overriding thought: ten billion dollars was a drop in the bucket for the kingpin. Knowing Harwas was a gambling addict, Merriman had given Oliver millions to wager on sports betting every year. Harwas was allowed to keep twenty percent of the winnings. However, he also had to give back twenty percent of the losses. Through the years, Oliver had accumulated a sizable personal fund, and gambling had become his hobby as well as his career.

On Monday, April 6th, Harwas wired ten billion dollars from OH Enterprises into Shea Hansen's bank account for the shell company that would initiate a hostile takeover of Golf Country Superstore. Then Oliver cashed in five million dollars to bet on the Masters. Should Harwas win, he kept twenty percent. Should he lose, he would be out one million dollars. Oliver loved his hobby because it aligned with his life's motto: No risk, no reward.

Eric Mann opened with 200 to one odds to win the Masters. In comparison, Rory McIlroy came in at eleven to two, Jordan Spieth at nine to one, and Bubba Watson at ten to one. However, Oliver believed Eric would perform like he did at the Honda Classic, so he was going to risk the entire five million on the child prodigy.

Harwas flew from the Caymans to his clandestine home in Florida. A few years ago, he created twenty fictitious names and provided each with fifty online sportsbook accounts. Harwas deposited $10,000 into each of those accounts. The $10,000,000 total was considered a loan from Burt Merriman, and Harwas was expected to pay it back plus $1 million in interest within one year. Oliver got lucky on his wagers and paid Merriman all he owed in six months. Meanwhile, each of his accounts now had over $20,000 in them.

None of the online sportsbooks asked for social security or bank account numbers. All they wanted was a valid credit card for Oliver's twenty aliases. Securing credit cards was an easy task. Banks fiercely competed for customers and handed out credit cards to any Tom, Dick, or Harry who roamed the streets.

Each online sportsbook company allowed for a maximum bet of $5,000. Using each of his twenty false names, Oliver placed five grand into each of his fifty online accounts for Eric to win the Masters. That ate up all five million of Burt Merriman's cash he had taken in the Caymans this morning.

But Oliver was greedy. He flew to Las Vegas on Wednesday to gamble some of his own money and watch the tournament on the big-screen casino televisions. Also, the sports betting limit in Vegas was $10,000 per wager. Harwas strolled confidently into twenty-five sportsbooks and laid down the maximum bet in each one. If Eric won, his $250,000 in total wagers would net him $50 million!

Oliver phoned his friend on the east coast from his suite on the top floor of the Bellagio Resort and Casino.

"Are you all set for Augusta?"

"Yep!" came the voice on the other end, who immediately disconnected the call.

*****

Trevor Muggins, Commissioner for US Customs and Border Protection, stamped the email from Dale Maglia with large, bold letters:

ORDER DENIED – DISREGARD!

Muggins shook his head and muttered to his secretary, "What was he thinking? Issuing an order before the investigation was completed is ridiculous! This is embarrassing to our agency!" Then he reread the email again:

DATE: *Wednesday, February 11, 2015*
TO: *All Port Authority Directors*
FROM: *Dale Maglia*
US Customs (Port of Miami)

As you may remember, about seven years ago, the MV Gulf Streamer sank in the Atlantic Ocean while delivering cargo to the Port of Miami. Recovery efforts have been complex because an explosion onboard the Streamer shredded the hull into hundreds of pieces. Chemical residue found on various deck parts indicates that an unknown, volatile substance most likely caused the detonation.

This coming July, the statute of limitations runs out relative to prosecuting criminal actions related to the incident. Thus, I am submitting our findings to the FBI today.

We believe combustible material was placed in a shipment of Bibles originating from Plana Cay, Bahamas. Because of this, I am issuing this order: No cargo will be allowed into the United States from Plana Cay, and no ship will be allowed into a United States port if it has docked in Plana Cay.

This order will go into effect on April 1, 2015, if approved by the Commissioner for U.S. Customs and Border Protection (CBP). You will be notified by his office when the declaration becomes official. Meanwhile, the FBI will thoroughly investigate the sinking of the MV Gulf Streamer and releases its findings to the CBP and the Congressional Subcommittee on Maritime Crimes and Punishment.

Muggins' embarrassment stemmed from the FBI report that indicated the FBI couldn't find a port or shipping dock on either of the Plana Cay islands. In fact, they couldn't find anybody on the islands save for a handful of campers on a scuba diving trip!

It was true that the original bill of lading showed a small flatbed vessel owned by TST Industries shipped the crate in question to Nassau, where it was transferred to the MV Gulf Streamer. However, in a classified report to Commissioner Muggins, the FBI concluded that the bill of lading was a counterfeit document and suggested it may have been forged by Dale Maglia himself. Interviews of Maglia's business associates and previous employees painted a picture of him as a loose cannon trying to move up the ladder of success. According to one dock worker in Miami, Maglia threatened to fire him for insubordination and told him that one day he would become the commissioner for US Customs and Border Protection. On that day, the entire Port of Miami staff would most likely lose their jobs.

The first week in April, Dale Maglia was terminated for deficient performance. He was last seen manning the deep fryer at Long John Silvers.

Because the case was dead, no investigation into TST Industries' foreign bank accounts ever commenced. But things might change if Willy Banks survived his bamboo raft journey back to Nassau.

CHAPTER FORTY-FIVE

April 2015

Pete Burns, the PGA of America Chief Executive Officer, opened an email from Winston Helms, the PGA of Great Britain President, on Wednesday, April 8th.

HELMS: *Pete, who manufactures the golf cups used on PGA courses worldwide? I'm assuming you purchase them in bulk to cut down on expenses.*

BURNS: *Sharma Plastics in Rajkot, a city in the western Indian state of Gujarat. Why do you ask?"*

HELMS: *You heard about the explosion on the Old Course a few weeks ago, right?*

BURNS: *Yes, most certainly! Devastating! How are things coming along?*

HELMS: *St. Andrews' businesses finally opened yesterday after MI6 gave the all-clear. London and the bigger cities have downgraded from high alert to cautionary status. MI6 believes it was an isolated incident. I'm not so sure.*

BURNS: *Why not?*

HELMS: *Just a gut feeling, that's all. The golf cup on the first hole was blasted into the air like a rocket! It landed in the stream near the Swilcan Bridge. A tourist found it and gave it to me. The bottom, or I should say bottoms plural, were missing.*

BURNS: *Sorry. I'm not sure what that means—the bottoms were missing. A golf cup only has one base.*

HELMS: *Yes, that's what I thought, too. Okay, this might be difficult for me to explain. Let me start by saying we dug up the other seventeen cups on the golf course to examine them. Each one had a double floor, base, bottom, or whatever you call it. In between was residue from a mineral substance scientists here in Britain had never seen before. Whatever that stuff was blew both bottoms off the cup on the first hole, which is why it burst out of the green.*

BURNS: *Wow! I wasn't aware that golf cups had two base layers!*

HELMS: *That's not all, Pete. It gets better. After slicing open the cylinders, we found that they were wrapped in electrical wires connected to a thin, bendable battery of some sort. The sides of the plastic cup also contained a tiny, flexible computer chip!*

BURNS: *Wires, battery, and a computer chip?! I don't understand! Help me out here, Winston.*

HELMS: *I wish I could! MI6 technicians claim the chip is a communications device typically used by terrorists. They circulate electricity around the cup remotely.*

BURNS: *For what purpose?!*

HELMS: *The minerals between the bottom layers are ferromagnetic.*

BURNS: *Meaning what?*

HELMS: *When turned on, the electrical wires produce a high magnetic field inside the cup, producing enormous heat. MI6 believed the matter in the base was heated and eventually exploded. But our British scientists had another theory. They thought something interacted with the unknown minerals to cause the blast. The scientists may have been right. It turns out our groundskeepers had just spread calcite, aragonite, and limestone on the green before the explosion. Chemical engineers hired by the British scientists tested their substance reaction theory using a different golf cup, and sure enough, it blew up, too. And it didn't need an electrical charge from the wires.*

BURNS: *If that's the case, what do the scientists think the wires and computer chip are for?*

HELMS: *They think terrorists can remotely melt the plastic using generated heat if they need to destroy evidence. MI6 had arrested the groundskeepers but released them yesterday after we explained to investigators that the calcite, aragonite, and limestone mixture is used yearly to loosen the soil before applying fertilizer. Our workers were just doing their jobs. So, that brings me back to my original question, Pete. You told me Sharma Plastics in Rajkot make the cups. MI6 will secure an international warrant to search their factory, looking for who knows what!*

BURNS: *Sure thing. But you said you had a gut feeling the cups were not an isolated event. What did you mean?*

HELMS: *MI6 believes a terrorist group plans to explode the cups at a PGA event to kill pro golfers. I think it would be wise to check the American PGA courses, just to be on the safe side.*

BURNS: *Good idea, Winston! I'll start right here at PGA National.*

HELMS: *Keep me posted! Thanks!*

*****

Hugh Kraft drove Father Jacob and Jim, Dora, and Eric Mann to St. Mary's Catholic Church in Augusta, Georgia, the night before the Masters commenced. Dora was excited that Spring Break fell during the same week as America's most famous PGA event. Hugh was skeptical of the habit Eric used before starting golf tournaments, but he didn't want to rock a boat that was sailing full steam ahead. He certainly believed and trusted God, but blessing Eric's golf balls was pure silliness!

Father Bill smiled widely and surprised everyone as he greeted them at the door, embraced Father Jacob, then pointed at the sidewalk and said, "How about we have a delicious dinner on me down at Sheehan's Irish Pub? It's only a block away."

Hugh grimaced. In less than twelve hours, Eric would be partaking in his life's most significant test of mental strength. He needed rest, not creamy mashed potatoes with cabbage! Hugh was displeased but didn't say anything.

Fifteen minutes later, the group sat at a large table in the back corner of the restaurant. Hugh, Jim, Father Jacob, and Father Bill were sipping Guinness drafts while Dora and Eric toasted one another with Coca-Cola, a Georgia favorite!

At 9:00 pm, after the food was eaten and another Guinness was downed, Hugh whispered to Jim. "We need to get Eric to bed. Let's get on with this!"

"This has been great fun, Father Bill, and thank you for it!" asserted Jim. "But Eric needs his rest, so do you mind if we finish up?"

"Oh my gosh!" replied Father Bill with a red face. "I'm so sorry! What was I thinking?!"

"No problem, my friend," responded Father Jacob as he gave Father Bill a pat on the back. "Anyway, here are another dozen St. Max's Premium Golf Balls. We can bless them here at the table. Let's join hands and bow."

Hugh was unsettled, but he needed to say something first. Eric was his protégé after all. "I know Eric has had very good success with St. Max's balls, but I think he should play with Titleist Pro V in the Masters. I believe it would elevate his game!"

The table became quiet, and everyone stared at Eric. The poor kid! He didn't know what to say. His coach wanted him to play a different ball, but his priest had conviction in St. Max's Premium balls. Personally, he really didn't care—he could hit either one of them straight and long! Fortunately, his mother could read the conundrum in Eric's eyes, and she took over the conversation.

"Hugh, you have been an exceptionally impressive coach, and Eric wouldn't be here without you!" proclaimed Dora. "But we are a family of strong faith and believe Father Jacob's blessing of golf balls made by our church would be the best option this weekend. We hope you understand!"

Hugh nodded in agreement, and Eric smiled and let out a deep sigh of relief. The group locked their arms in a circle, and Father Jacob and Father Bill's clasped hands were placed gently on the box of golf balls. Father Jacob said the prayer, then Hugh, Jim, Dora, and Eric departed for the hotel.

Father Jacob and Father Bill stayed for a couple more rounds of Guinness.

CHAPTER FORTY-SIX

April 2015

Hugh was shaking his head in disbelief. It was 9:08 am on the official clock at Augusta National. In six minutes, Eric would be teeing off in the seventy-ninth Masters Tournament, his first major ever played, and what was he doing? Getting autographs from his two golf partners—Vijay Singh of Fiji and Ernie Els of South Africa. They laughed and signed their John Hancock's on Eric's bag with a permanent marker. Tiger Woods had just finished with his signature and given Mann a high five. Eric was awestruck! He almost forgot that he was now one of them!

Hugh approached his mentee. These would be the last words he was allowed to say in person. After the first hole, Hugh was required to maintain a distance of twenty yards. He could only communicate with Eric via the boy's caddie. "Son, you need to focus! These guys you're playing with are no better or worse than yourself. Make them want your autograph!"

That was Hugh's best attempt at a pep talk. But it seemingly went through one ear and out the other. Eric's reply to Hugh was in the form of a question: "Why are all the holes here named after trees? And what's a Tea Olive?" Hugh rolled his eyes and walked away.

Vijay Singh and Ernie Els overheard the conversation and grinned. Vijay whispered to Ernie, "Cute kid! But why are we playing with this teenager?"

"Be careful, V, that cute kid won the Honda Classic. Evidently, he can play golf!"

As Eric approached the tee box, Ernie stopped him. "Hey, kid, this golf course used to be a nursery containing thousands of plants and trees imported from countries worldwide. Each hole was named after one of those plants or trees."

Eric beamed back at Ernie. "Thank you, Mr. Els! That's very interesting! I'll share that with my science class when I return to school on Monday."

As Ernie stood by Vijay to watch Eric's tee shot, Singh muttered under his breath, "I didn't know we would be babysitting today!"

Eric's one-wood landed 265 yards dead center on the fairway. He purposely played a mini slice as the hole slightly doglegged right. Eric's drive may have gone 300 yards had the fairway not been uphill! Els and Singh's mouths opened wide. Maybe this child wasn't so bad after all!

Ernie and Vijay's drives outdistanced Eric's, but both were lying close to the trees on the left. Eric's second shot was with a five iron, and the ball sailed perfectly onto the undulating green, rolled up and down, and straight into the cup for an eagle! Els and Singh weren't so lucky. Their approach shots were moderately punched onto the problematic green, and they two-putted for par. Eric was two strokes up as he headed for the second tee. Ernie and Vijay were dumbstruck!

Hugh radioed Eric's caddie telling him to ease up and take three shots on the par five, 575-yard, second hole. Eric pulled out a three-wood and placed the ball slightly left of center fairway but directly at the dogleg turn. A shot to the right would have landed in the bunker. Eric used a three-iron on his next swing for better control and landed 110 yards from the pin. Giant sand traps guarded both sides of the green, but Eric's lofty wedge shot landed a few feet from the cup and stopped due to the backspin. He one-putted for a birdie, as did Els and Singh.

Hole three, the Flowering Peach, was a deceptive 350 yards from the tee. Considered a short par four, the best pros don't even try to drive near the green because of all the obstacles. The problematic leaf-shaped green slopes sharply from right to left. Eric, Ernie, and Vijay hit irons off the tee to stay short of the ominous four bunkers on the fairway's left side. All three pitched onto the green and two-putted for pars.

Eric still had honors as the group strolled to the fourth tee. The 240-yard, par three was challenging due to deep bunkers that guarded both sides of the green. Ernie and Vijay pulled four-irons out of their bag. Eric yanked out his driver. Hugh was watching closely.

"No, no, no!" squawked Eric's coach loudly into the walkie-talkie. "Tell him to play up and hope for a good chip!"

A few seconds later, Hugh got a reply from the caddie. "Eric wants to drive it. The wind is blowing in his face, and the green slopes to the front side. I can't change his mind!"

Hugh turned his head away. He couldn't look. Later, though, he wished he had. Eric set the ball high on an extra-long tee and hit a gem! The ball started to hook, then magically turned back right and landed on the far side of the green. It stopped, then rolled backward directly into the cup! Eric never saw it, but a few seconds later, someone radioed his caddie. "A hole-in-one! Oh my God, a hole-in-one!"

Eric gently handed the driver to his caddie, then sprinted to Hugh, jumped up, and latched onto his coach. Hugh gave him a quick hug, then a soft push. "Eric, it's against the rules for you to come over here. Get back with your threesome!"

The PGA official gave Eric a warning instead of issuing him penalty strokes. Els and Singh smiled and agreed with the official's decision. You don't penalize a hole-in-one!

Shockingly, Eric's name popped up into first place on the leaderboard. He was five under par after four holes. Favorites Phil Mickelson and Jordan Spieth were waiting near the clubhouse, ready to tee off on one, when they heard the crowd roar. Both watched the big screen as it replayed Eric's incredible hole-in-one using a driver.

*****

Oliver Harwas was sipping a Bloody Mary at the Venetian Sportsbook in Las Vegas when Eric's drive rolled into the cup. His scream of joy annoyed those patrons sitting near him, and several departed for more peaceful surroundings. Oliver motioned for the bartender to come over. In a startling move, he bought drinks for everyone left at the bar. It had been a long time since he had made friends, but that generous move was a gracious beginning.

Meanwhile, Tommy Williams busily switched and moved video images on his computer screens. Cameras had been set up in trees at Augusta National so he could continue to monitor how well St. Max's Premium Golf Balls were performing. So far, he was thrilled with Eric's shots. The ball seemed to fly further than the Titleist Pro Vs, Callaways, and Taylor Mades the other pros were using.

*****

Mel Smith and Keith Malone were still floating several hundred yards offshore from the uncharted Plana Cay island waiting for Willy to finish making the bamboo raft. Mel switched his phone to speaker mode so Keith could hear Tommy giving a play-by-play analysis of the Masters tournament. The call was interrupted.

"The raft is ready, but Willy won't be getting very far," stated Bushman Jack with no degree of emotion. He was keeping a close eye on the video images from the drone. "A security team was deployed a few days ago with backpacks and automatic weapons. They are camped out in the shrubs and have surrounded him. I'm not sure why they are waiting for him. I would think they could rush at any time and overtake him!"

"How many?" asked Mel.

"I counted six."

"I think they know how dangerous and experienced Willy is with a weapon. They are probably waiting for him to put the raft in the water where he'll be isolated from the AK-47."

"Possibly. But who knows how much food and water they have in their backpacks. They can't stay there forever!"

"True. I guess we'll see. Thanks, Bushman!"

Keith shook his head when the call ended, then glanced at Mel. "Well, we probably can go back home now. It doesn't appear Willy will be around much longer."

CHAPTER FORTY-SEVEN

April 2015

Eric finished the first round with a nine under par sixty-three, tying the course record set by Nick Price in 1986 and Greg Norman in 1996. Jordan Spieth was two strokes back, and Hideki Matsuyama three behind the leader. As he held his post-match press conference in the clubhouse staging area, reporters from *ESPN*, *CBS Sports*, *Sports Illustrated*, and the *Golf Channel* battled their way to be the closest to Eric. Ernie Els, Vijay Singh, Jordan Spieth, and Tiger Woods hung around to hear what the young superstar had to say. The reporters ignored them.

Eric's speech was the shortest ever by a golfer who had just finished first in any opening round of the Masters Tournament. "Thank you for letting me play with all the greatest golfers of our time. I was lucky and blessed by God today. I wouldn't be standing here without the support of Hugh Kraft, my caddie, Mom and Dad, and my priest, Father Jacob. Love you all!"

Eric then stepped off the stage without answering questions and took a shower. In the locker room, Tiger Woods walked over with a Masters program and pen and asked the youngster for his autograph. Eric was so startled that he almost forgot his own name! After Tiger left him with a pat on the back, a line of PGA pros came to Eric with their own programs to sign. The youngster was in awe! So much so that he didn't sleep a wink that night.

Sleep deprivation, teenage anxiety, and golf do not mix. In round two, several of Eric's shots were mishit so badly that they never got more than five feet off the ground. However, when he did lift the ball, it soared long and straight as an arrow. What saved him was his putting. He one-putted a record fifteen holes. But his terrible tee and long fairway shots killed him. He ended the second round with a seventy-four, two strokes over par. His two-day total dropped to seven under. Eric still had a good chance to pull off a victory, but Jordan Spieth, Phil Mickelson, and Justin Rose were all tied on top of the leaderboard at ten under.

In the first two rounds of the Masters, golfers are grouped in threes. For the third and fourth rounds, they play two golfers per group. Pairings are based on their cumulative scores on rounds one and two. On Saturday, Eric was paired with Paul Casey, whom he was tied to begin the third round.

Eric was stressed. Hugh could see it in his eyes. His protégé was the talk of the town after the first round, then disregarded after the second. "***Beginners Luck***" was the headline in the *Atlanta Journal-Constitution* sports section. The article went on to describe Eric Mann's game as a case of "***fame to failure in twenty-four hours!***" Hugh, Dora, and Jim tried to keep the news from Eric, but during the middle of the night, he turned on *ESPN* to see what they were saying on Sportscenter. Big mistake!

After a second night of tossing and turning, Eric was constantly yawning as he warmed up on the driving range. His first tee shot sliced wickedly out of bounds, almost hitting a child standing with his dad. Fortunately, the father pushed his son to the ground and laid on him just in time. Eric wanted desperately to go over and apologize to the boy, but officials told him he needed to tee up his penalty shot. The second tee shot also sliced out of bounds. Eric was now playing his fifth stroke off the first tee!

*****

"What's wrong with that kid?!" yelped Oliver Harwas from the bar in Las Vegas. Other patrons simply chuckled at his fury. Not many gamblers had wagered on Eric beating the 200-to-one odds.

*****

"He's not lifting his drives," said a frustrated Tommy Williams on his cell phone to Mel Smith. "That's a problem."

"Keep us posted," replied Mel bluntly and hung up. He was juggling calls from Tommy and Bushman Jack, who kept tabs on Willy Banks' progress building the raft. The ex-cop appeared to be finished, but he was still lying low. Either he was planning to wait until morning to get a full day of sunlight for his float trip into the Atlantic, or he knew he was being watched by the security team.

*****

"Tell him to close his eyes, visualize a long drive, and don't swing until that happens!" squawked Hugh into the caddy's walkie-talkie. The caddy relayed the simplistic message to Eric.

His next drive lifted high, carried 250 yards in the air, then rolled another twenty-five. It was slightly past the dogleg turn and sitting on the edge of the fairway by the trees lining the left side. The caddy gave Eric a five iron for his 170-yard approach shot, then the youngster walked up to address the ball. Just before he swung, he stopped and stepped back a few feet. Remembering Hugh's advice again, Eric closed his eyes and visualized his eagle shot from this hole in the first round.

Impossibly, the shot landed on the edge of the green, rolled up and down the undulation, and dropped squarely into the cup! With the penalty strokes, Eric scored a seven. It was perhaps the best triple bogey ever played in professional golf! Fans surrounding the hole roared their approval.

Eric's confidence took a sharp turn, and he believed he could still catch the leaders. He birdied four holes and parred the rest, giving him a one-under seventy-one for the round. But Paul Casey bested Eric by a stroke. At sunset on Saturday, the new leaderboard had been established. Spieth was still in first place, fourteen strokes under par, followed by Mickelson (-13), McIlroy (-12), Rose and Matsuyama (-11), Dustin Johnson (-10), and Casey (-9). Eric was tied for eighth with Charley Hoffman at eight under par. His dream of winning the green jacket was fading, but he had no quit.

The sports writers were no longer hounding Eric. Hugh thought that would bother him, but he kept a positive attitude. A reporter for the *Sporting News* happened upon Eric as he and Hugh were headed back to the hotel. He stopped Eric briefly and said, "Great first round, kid! What are your thoughts going into tomorrow six back from Jordan Spieth?"

"Que sera, sera. My mom taught me that one. I'll give it my best shot. Whatever happens on Sunday happens." Hugh smiled and pulled Eric away before the writer could ask a follow-up question.

*****

On Sunday, Eric was in the clubhouse reading when Hugh expected the boy to be on the driving range. Frustrated, Hugh found him tucked into a chair in the corner. "What are you doing, son?! You need to warm up!"

"Oh, sorry, Coach. I'm just doing my homework. We're studying Greek Mythology."

"Well, that's just grand!" blurted Hugh sarcastically. "But right now, you're to be preparing for the biggest match of your young life!"

"I'm learning about King Midas. According to this book, Midas was known for being greedy and foolish. But one day, the king was generous to a man with ears and a tail like a horse, so the Greek God Dionysus granted him one wish. Midas wished that everything he touched turned into gold."

"Okay, that's good to know, but we've got to get going!"

"My point is, Coach, that Midas didn't know the wish was not a blessing but a curse. His daughter touched him and she accidentally turned into gold. The king's greed made me think about the bad consequences that come with it. So, what I'm saying is if I win the Masters, will I become greedy and somehow hurt other people during my life?"

"Eric, you chose to give your winnings to charity. That's as far from greed as you can get! So, when you play today, think about what a victory would do for those in need. Play for them, son!"

"That's a really good point, Coach. Thanks for the talk!"

As they exited the clubhouse, Hugh realized he may have given Eric the best pep talk he could muster.

*****

Eric was paired with Charley Hoffman for the final round of the Masters. Charley played well, but Eric was masterful—no pun intended! He landed on the green in regulation on the first six holes and one putted each for birdies. With one-third of his day complete, Eric was fourteen under par and tied for third with Justin Rose. Three holes behind him, Phil Mickelson and Jordan Spieth were tied for first at fifteen under.

Eric averaged 280 yards on his drives, significantly higher than usual. His approach shots were magnificent, and his putts were perfect. The sports media were again sitting up and taking notice of the teen superstar.

However, the flight of his balls was uncommon. Not only was the distance longer than usual, but the shot would also move left and right in the air, then land near the middle of the fairway. And weirdly, Eric's putts also rolled back and forth but ended up in the cup.

A PGA official stopped play to examine Eric's golf ball. The man radioed to the clubhouse and asked if St. Max's Premium balls had been PGA-approved. After a minute, the official received the news that the ball was definitely okay and for him to keep the action moving. They needed to finish before dark.

On his computer screen, Tommy Williams saw that the PGA official was examining the St. Max's golf ball. Talking only to himself, he muttered, "What's going on? There's nothing wrong with that ball!" He nervously watched the match resume and took notes.

Eric parred the next six holes. His ball continued to move erratically in the air but land perfectly on the fairways. However, he either didn't hit the green in regulation or two-putted. He was still fourteen under par with six holes to go.

Then Firethorn happened. The fifteenth hole. The 530-yard, par five has ruined many professional golfer's frames of mind. A drive off the tee must be exactly straight to avoid the forest of pines lining the very narrow fairway. A pond guards the front of the green, and there is a bunker to the right. For those who lay up, the wedge shot requires pinpoint accuracy.

Hugh was worried about Eric's next drive. The flight of his golf balls had been swaying, then self-correcting. He feared the youngster would graze a tree and go out of bounds. "Have him play a four iron off the tee," he radioed to Eric's caddy. "He needs to control this shot!"

The caddy relayed the message, and Eric glanced at Hugh standing in the shadows. He shrugged his shoulders and mouthed, "Sorry!"

Eric asked the caddy for his driver. The caddy reluctantly handed it to him. Then the teenager proceeded to wallop the drive of his life. Charley Hoffman watched the flight of the ball with amazement. It landed and rolled 300 yards dead center on the fairway!

Hugh was fist-bumping the sky, but a few minutes later, arrhythmia set in. He saw Eric pull out a two wood. Hugh was about to scream into his walkie-talkie but then turned it off. At this point, Eric was going to do what Eric wanted to do. All the coach could do was watch and enjoy.

Eric knew his next shot was a gamble. He needed 215 yards in the air to clear the nearest pond. But if he hit it too hard, it could easily bounce and land in the far pond. Virtually every professional golfer played up and wedged his third shot onto the green. All Eric was thinking was he needed a birdie to catch the leaders. It was time for guts over wisdom.

Miraculously, he launched the ball with precise loft and distance! It landed just over the pond, rolled up the green, then turned and inched into the cup for an albatross! A double eagle! The only other time that had happened on the fifteenth hole was in 1935 when Gene Sarazen hit his "shot heard round the world!"

Once again, Eric couldn't see the ball, but by the crowd's reaction in the bleachers, he knew it was close to the pin or in the cup. When he found out, he sprinted to the green, leaped into the air, then tossed his two wood into the pond. His caddy put on rubber waders and fetched the club out while Eric saluted the fans.

The leaderboard reshuffled. Eric was now in first place by two strokes at seventeen under par. Spieth and Mickelson were three holes behind him, so Eric knew he needed to regain his composure. Two strokes were nothing for Jordan or Lefty.

Number sixteen is a 170-yard, par three. To psych out their opponents, many golfers were heard uttering at the tee box, "This is where the men are separated from the boys!" The hole is played entirely over water and bends left. Two sand traps guard the right side, and the green slopes considerably from right to left. Even for the best pros, pars are rare. Eric was thinking about the well-known phrase as he approached the tee. Shoot, he was just a boy anyway—he didn't need to be separated!

Then he remembered Hugh's advice—step back, visualize, and take as many practice swings as necessary until it feels right. Eric did just that, then landed his ball on the green and one putted for a birdie. Phew!

With his confidence growing, Eric birdied the seventeenth, putting him nineteen under par going into the tournament's final hole. Hugh had told his caddy not to let Eric know the leaders' scores before he teed off. There was no need for additional stress.

But Eric would hear nothing of it! He wanted to know where he stood and demanded his caddy tell him!

Caught between Eric and his coach, the caddy sheepishly said, "Spieth birdied fourteen, and Mickelson parred it. Jordan is now sitting at sixteen under, and Lefty is still at fifteen under."

The eighteenth hole is a difficult 465-yard par four with an uphill dogleg right to start. On the left side are two deep sand traps that could bring a wayward drive to an immediate halt! With that said, a golfer must also avoid trees to the right. Eric's tee shot rolled into the landing zone right of the bunkers, 185 yards from the pin. Showing signs of nervousness as he approached the hole where his parents and priest were sitting, he topped his five-iron second shot. The ball lifted only a few feet off the ground and rolled into the front sand trap. Dora gasped and covered her eyes while Jim put his arm around her shoulders. Father Jacob whispered, "Have faith, my friends."

Eric's third shot didn't get out of the bunker. Sand flew, but the ball moved only a couple of feet. He could hear a collective groan from the crowd.

Just before he was to take his next swing in the trap, a gust of wind blew, sending sand directly into Eric's face. He closed his eyes, but it was too late. Tiny grains were lodged under his lids. He wanted to rub them but was unsure of the rules. Eric knew he couldn't lay his wedge down in the trap and wasn't sure if he was allowed to walk back out of the bunker. He decided to play it the best he could. The sand was stinging, so he closed his eyes and swung. What happened next was what Father Jacob later called a miracle!

Eric's golf ball rose out of the trap and appeared to be struck too hard. But suddenly, a wall of wind froze the ball in midair, and it dropped straight down onto the green. Bizarrely, the ball must have had a side spin as it turned left and rolled directly into the cup for par. The crowd cheered wildly as Eric lifted his cap, bowed, and saluted his frenetic fans.

He ended his first Masters with an amazing nineteen strokes under par. As he followed the electronic leaderboard with a high-definition video screen, he saw Spieth had birdied fifteen. Hugh escorted him into the clubhouse to watch the finish.

Justin Rose completed the tourney with a fourteen under par, 274. Phil Mickelson had bogeyed fifteen and was now even with Rose heading to the final tee box. Spieth had birdied the challenging sixteenth and seventeenth and was tied with Eric as he teed off on eighteen. One more birdie and Jordan would be wearing the green jacket.

His drive flew 320 yards and sat in the middle of the fairway, 145 yards from the pin. He followed with a masterful wedge shot that landed on the green, twelve yards from the cup. Spieth was a terrific putter, and Eric's victory looked like it would be grabbed from his clutches. Then Jordan's birdie putt missed the hole by a mere inch and rolled past it by two feet.

In the clubhouse, Hugh told Eric to get loose because he would settle the match in a sudden-death playoff. That's when the inexplicable happened. Jordan's par putt rolled slightly uphill and stopped less than an inch from the cup. He stared at the ball, trying to will it to drop into the hole, or hoping a wind gust would give it a tiny push. Neither materialized, and Eric became the youngest player to win the Masters!

He jumped into Hugh's arms, and his coach just about squeezed the life out of him! Then, his mom, dad, and priest all took turns doing the same thing! Cameras were clicking everywhere, and TV announcers were battling with newspaper reporters for a spot next to Eric.

Chills ran up Eric's spine, and goosebumps covered his body when Pete Burns, the PGA of America Chief Executive Officer, placed the symbolic green sportscoat on him. It was quite big, but Hugh whispered to him that a tailor would make it fit. Burns then presented Eric with a billboard-size check for $1,800,000!

The sportswriters and his coach were shocked when Eric said he was turning over all his winnings to Father Jacob for the excellent work St. Max's parish did for the homeless and poor. He had done the same thing after he won the Honda Classic. Jim, Dora, and Father Jacob gave Eric a long, tear-filled hug while flashing cameras caught every moment.

The headline on the front page of the *Palm Beach Post* read: ***The Most Generous Person in America is a 13-Year-Old Boy!*** The article told about the Honda Classic and Masters champion who donated his money to charity and refused to be interviewed because he didn't want the spotlight on himself. In a time when the world needed heroes, Eric had moved to the top of the list.

The story caught the attention of Bishop Brian O'Bailey, the head of the Diocese of Palm Beach. Bishop O'Bailey recently replaced Bishop Bob Kaiser, who unsuspectedly had been removed by the Vatican. O'Bailey didn't have the time to follow professional golf or read newspapers. Still, when Bishop Carson of the Miami diocese phoned to congratulate him on the positive news regarding one of his congregations, O'Bailey sat down in Starbucks and read the article with great interest.

CHAPTER FORTY-EIGHT

April 2015

Ursula Vero was livid. On Monday, April 13th, she and every one of her employees was escorted out of their Manhattan offices by fifty security guards hired by Oliver Harwas. They would be job searching soon. Harwas' corporation, OH Enterprises, was the new majority stockholder of Golf Country Superstore. Shea Hansen had reorganized one of her fake shell companies in record time and sold it to Harwas. Then, on Friday, April 10th, smack dab in the middle of the Masters tournament, the shell company purchased nine million GCS shares of stock trading on Wall Street at $31 a share.

As soon as Eric Mann was crowned champion of the granddaddy of all pro golf tournaments, stockbrokers were salivating at the chance to buy GCS holdings when the market opened on Monday. It was expected that the teenage advertising face of St. Max's Premium Golf Balls would help GCS's value soar to record levels. And they were right. Five minutes after the bell sounded on Wall Street, GCS stock rose to $70 a share!

Oliver Harwas was giddy with excitement. He had just won $50 million wagering on Eric to win the Masters, and now on day one, his newly acquired GCS investment doubled in value!. Perhaps it was time to retire, kick back, and live a life of luxury and extravagance!

*****

As dawn broke over the Atlantic, Willy pushed his homemade raft into the ocean. He had constructed a large paddle using bamboo, palm fronds, and a makeshift fishing pole. His two main concerns were water and sharks. Willy had a three-gallon liquid container from the seaplane, but he would have to sip the water slowly. The AK-47 had a high-capacity magazine with ninety rounds of ammunition.

As soon as he was ten feet from shore, the blasts started. Willy laid on his belly and fired back. He counted six people on the beach. They were all standing within three feet of each other with weapons unloading bullets in rapid succession. Big mistake thought Willy. He aimed low at the person on the left, pulled the trigger, and swept his gun to the right. All the security guards were hit below the belt, just what Willy wanted. They had let him live the past few weeks, so there was no reason to kill them. He sat up on the raft and paddled as fast as his monstrous biceps would allow.

Willy hadn't been at sea for more than a half hour when a yacht pulled up beside him. He watched curiously as two men dropped a ladder over the side. Willy tossed the AK-47 onto the boat, then scurried on board. He brushed himself off, put his hands on his hips, and gazed at the two men who may have saved his life for a second time.

"How did you know I came back here?" asked Willy, perplexed.

"That's a long story," replied Mel Smith.

*****

"Your hunch was correct, Mr. Burns," stated FBI Agent Cory Jones. "It's good you turned this over to us instead of looking for them yourselves. We found electronic golf cups in each hole at the TPC Craig Ranch in McKinney, Texas, and the Country Club of Jackson in Mississippi.

Pete Burns walked to his office window and stared out deep in thought. "The Byron Nelson and Sanderson Farms Championships," he muttered under his breath.

"What's that, sir? I couldn't hear you."

"I was just thinking to myself. Two of the upcoming PGA tournaments are at the TPC in Texas and the Sanderson Farms in Mississippi. Okay, so what about right here at the PGA National, or how about the Arnold Palmer Bay Hill course in Orlando? What did you find?"

"Nothing, sir. The cups here and at Bay Hill are normal."

"What about Augusta National? Did you check there?"

"No, sir. We were waiting for the Masters to finish. We will be looking at that course today."

"What does the FBI think about those electronic cups?"

"We are meeting in London with MI6 tomorrow about this situation. But based on phone conversations, we agree with their assessment."

"And that is what?"

"They are bombs planted by terrorists to kill PGA professionals. Sorry to say that sir! But we suggest you hire additional security for all your tournament courses and keep them posted year-round."

"Oh my God, Agent Jones!" yelped Burns. "That would cost us a small fortune! Plus, it's up to each course to hire their own security."

"Then I suggest you make it a requirement if they want to continue hosting PGA tournaments."

"The general managers aren't going to like this!"

"Better safe than sorry, wouldn't you say, Mr. Burns?"

*****

Agent Cory Jones assessed the situation and immediately called the Central Intelligence Agency. Had the golf cups been manufactured in the United States, the FBI would have handled it alone. But seeing a company in India was involved in possible terrorism, Jones thought it best to conduct a joint fact-finding mission.

India's internal security and counter-intelligence agency is the Intelligence Bureau. Founded in 1887, it is considered the oldest such organization in the world. Although it may be the elder statesman of espionage, it doesn't hold a candle to the CIA or MI6. However, they were happy to assist with the raid on Sharma Plastics in Rajkot, albeit from the backseat.

Because the initial blasts occurred on the Old Course at St. Andrews, MI6 took the lead. Scotland Yard and the FBI also joined in. Agent Jones and the FBI would later guide American PGA course investigations. But first, it was imperative to see what part Sharma played.

As it turned out, the incursion yielded nothing except frightened Sharma employees. They were following the specifications precisely and making plastic parts to be assembled by a company called TST Industries. Most of the employees interviewed didn't even know the pieces would become golf cups! They loaded their products onto a steamer and shipped them to Plana Cay in the Bahamas.

What the CIA found interesting was that there was no specific address on the shipment documents. Only GPS coordinates and Plana Cay were listed as the receiver. It was time to send the entire investigative force to the Bahamas!

*****

"The drone picked up CIA, FBI, and MI6 agents raiding Sharma Plastics today," said a concerned Bushman Jack. "They are all together in black limos pulling into the Rajkot airport."

"What?! Are you kidding me!" yelled Mel into his phone. Keith and Willy Banks were below deck and didn't hear his panicked frustration. It's time for Plan B—AGAIN! We need to act fast!"

CHAPTER FORTY-NINE

April 2015

Before the sun rose over the Atlantic, Mel cruised the yacht through Nassau harbor to the marina he had rented from a few days earlier. He had received permission from the owners to drop the boat off and leave the keys in the ignition if they returned during off hours. Stealing a boat from a marina was considered piracy in the Bahamas, and the thieves would be treated the same as murderers. There had been only one stolen boat in the past fifteen years, and the thief jumped overboard before being caught. Death by a shark seemed much more pleasant than death by a Bahamian court.

Mel and Keith woke Willy and told him they were all heading for the airport. Willy thanked them and said he would stay in Nassau for another day and catch a commercial flight back to Palm Beach. "What are you talking about?!" exclaimed Mel. "This is the second time we've rescued you, and we have no plans to do it again!"

"No one asked you to," retorted Willy. "There's a couple things I must do in Nassau before going home."

"Like what?!" asked Keith abruptly.

"Well, first, I need to tell the seaplane rental place I lost their plane. Then, one other thing."

"Mind telling us what that one other thing is?!" Keith had little patience for Willy.

"Mind telling me what the so-called 'long story' is? What were you two doing back at Plana Cay? I doubt you were on a fishing excursion! So, I'm assuming you were looking for me. Well, I ain't going back to Florida with you unless you tell me. The truth would be my preference."

Mel and Keith glanced at each other and shrugged their shoulders. Keith stepped back. He wasn't sure telling someone would be wise, but he wasn't going to argue with his partner. Mel said, "You're a great American hero, Willy. That's why I'm going to tell you. For the safety of many folks, I think you will keep silent about what I say. Am I right about that?"

"I ain't guaranteeing nothing, fellas." Then, with a swift motion, Willy grabbed the AK-47 and pointed it at Mel and Keith. His finger rubbed menacingly on the trigger. "There's something fishy going on, and it's time you talked, not me!"

"Can we both agree to a two-way conversation? Though, you need to trust us when we ask you to keep quiet. Just for the time being. It could be a matter of life and death."

Willy moved the rifle's aim from Mel's forehead to Keith's cheek and back. "I do believe, fellas, that I have the ace in the hole right here in my hands. But I'm willing to keep silent unless I find out you're breaking the law. Then all bets are off!"

"That works for us. Best we all sit down. This might take a while."

Mel and Keith moved to the table in the yacht's cabin and sat in the chair. Willy said bluntly, "I think I'll stand. Get on with your story!"

*****

"What do you mean all the cups are missing?!" asked a perturbed Pete Burns.

"What I'm trying to tell you is that someone dug up all the cups and removed them from the greens. None have been replaced!" answered Sam Mueller, head of maintenance operations for Augusta National. "This has never happened before. Someone must have dug 'em up in the middle of the night. Our security guards went on duty early this morning, like around 3:00 am. They usually get there at 7:00 am. I'm guessing they may have scared away whoever was stealing them!"

"Why did your security crew happen to arrive early this morning?"

"So, you probably won't believe this, but I got a call from an MI6 agent in London after the tournament concluded yesterday. They're like the CIA or something over in England. He wouldn't tell me why, but he advised me to have a security team watch the course until they talked to you about something. Three in the morning was the soonest I could get them out there. Sorry, sir!"

"Could you possibly have the course secured around the clock until the FBI investigates? And don't put in new cups, okay?"

"Yeah, sure. So, you're sending the FBI? Wow, them and the MI6! This must be important stuff, huh?"

"Yes, Sam. You might say that. I need to go. Thanks!"

*****

Eric didn't net the entire amount of $1.8 million presented to him on the billboard-size check. Once again, the IRS withheld forty percent, or $720,000. But the young phenom was still proud to hand over to Father Jacob a personal check for $1,080,000. That, with his Honda Classic and Arnold Palmer Invitational profit, now totaled $1,845,840 for St. Max's parish.

Father was surprised by the phone call he received from Ursula Vero. "A corporate takeover, you say?" he asked.

"Damn right . . . oh, sorry, Father. Darn tootin', I mean! It's a fake shell company incorporated by a crooked organization called OH Enterprises. Anyway, I wanted to give you a heads-up. The new owners will contact you about St. Max's Golf Balls."

"Hmmm. That's interesting. I'm so very sorry about the corporate takeover. I will pray that you get back on your feet soon."

"Thank you, Father Jacob, but I have an idea to run by you."

"What would that be, Miss Vero?"

"They have assumed my company, but according to my legal team, they have no rights to St. Max's Golf Balls. Nor can they force a covenant not to compete on me. I would like to start a new company. Would you be willing to give me a lock-tight contract to sell your golf balls? It would be exclusive. I would be happy to build a new factory wherever I start up the business and move your workers there as supervisors."

"Supervisors?! Really?! You're serious about this, aren't you, Miss Vero?"

"Darn tootin'!"

"Let me think about this. I'll get back to you."

CHAPTER FIFTY

April 2015

The badges contained a Nanochip tracking device that was a quarter the size of those used in mobile devices. The electronic integrated circuitry was designed, developed, and manufactured by a TST Industries factory in the Namib desert of southwest Africa at an abandoned diamond mine site. TST had purchased the entire ghost town of Kolmanskop from the Namibia government in the early 1990s and designed it as a tourist destination. They had no plans to make a profit from tourism; they just needed to find a way to export their product unsuspectingly. Who better than a cruise ship passenger to do that? TST was able to lure Norwegian Caribbean, MSC, and Holland America cruise lines to tender their ships in the nearby port of Lüderitz. From there, TST employees acting as tourists would deliver the goods to faraway places on the planet.

Henrik Frieder may have been the greatest salesman of all time. Representing Badgeworks International, a subsidiary of TST Industries, he sold metal identification badges to the CIA, FBI, MI6, Mossad, RAW, and even the KGB. The agents who wore the metal clip-ons had no idea Nanochips made in Namibia were embedded inside them! Specialized computers could track every movement of every agent all over the world!

One such computer had picked up a massive group movement by agents of the CIA, FBI, MI6, and RAW leaving Rajkot, India. They had boarded a jet there and landed in Nassau, Bahamas. The agents were now dispersed onto four large boats and heading east in the Atlantic Ocean.

"Twenty-four agents, six in each boat, appear to be heading for Plana Cay. They all arrived at the airport in Nassau and went to the Bahamian Coast Guard facility. I assume they have contracted armed Coast Guard cutters and will raid the island soon." The man paced back and forth as he talked on his Bluetooth cell phone.

"Get everyone out and blow up the whole damn island!" ordered the man who received the call.

"Their rubber emergency boats are no match for the Coast Guard. They'd be overtaken and quickly sunk, sir!"

"It's the only chance they have! Send them in the opposite direction—eastward into the Atlantic and make sure they stay a long distance from the island!"

"Okay, but God help them!"

*****

Twenty-seven TST workers, every person employed on Plana Cay, grabbed backpacks containing bottled water, protein bars, a multiuse pocketknife, and other provisions, including a SIG Sauer nine-millimeter pistol with thirty rounds of ammunition. Four eight-passenger life rafts with battery-operated motors were retrieved from an underground and camouflaged storage shed halfway down the retractable dock on the island's west side. Three rafts held eight men, and the other had three men and containers with extra food and water.

Since the underground factory began operations, the number one rule was it would never be found. If it was, that was a death sentence to the unlucky person or people who wandered upon it. Willy and his small party of four had escaped due to a lack of aggressiveness on the security team who was watching them. At significant personal risk, Willy returned to Plana Cay alone, was captured, and managed to break free. Although he had a stolen AK-47 to keep them at bay, the security forces should have rushed him. They didn't, and now the island was about to be attacked by international crime enforcement agents.

But they had an emergency plan. Get off Plana Cay and blow it to smithereens. Jimmy Tassett ran the factory his dad started way back when, and now under orders from his father, he would be the person to end his dad's prize possession. After the workers had exited the hole and were headed for the life rafts, Jimmy sat between separate containers of calcium carbonate and planacalum at the very bottom level of the factory. Each tub contained a half-ton of the minerals. One push of a button and the chemicals would empty into an iron tank. With the magnetic force of the iron working with the calcium carbonate neutrons, the chemical reaction would energize the planacalum to the point of dynamic combustion, and the island would soon be no more.

Jimmy hesitated as he pondered the outcome. The beach home he grew up in had already been destroyed by a group of unwelcome visitors. Their leader surprisingly returned and fled capture with one of TST's AK-47s. The products built in the soon-to-be-defunct factory had changed the course of history, although no one knew it because they weren't supposed to! Jimmy knew his father had been involved in life-changing events of the past, but he didn't know exactly what they were.

Jimmy never attended school. His mother was his teacher until she died in an accident, but during the time spent as his instructor, Jimmy learned to love reading about the great explorers of the world. Now, what was bothering him the most were the Christopher Columbus relics. If he pushed the dreaded button, no one would ever find evidence that Columbus landed on this island in 1492.

Jimmy didn't dare to defy his father's orders. His dad would punish him severely. Jimmy was the reason the four men who blew up his house were allowed to escape, and he was to blame for not rushing Willy Banks before he got off the island in a makeshift raft. Jimmy didn't believe in killing; he just hoped everything would work out and his dad would never find out. His security team was simply waiting for orders from their boss, who didn't give the directive. Thus, this was Jimmy's last chance to prove to his father he could be trusted to run the company with vigorous loyalty to the man who created TST Industries.

He pushed the button, and the two tanks spilled into the large iron vat. Immediately, smoke began to form, and Jimmy could feel the temperature rise. He hustled out of the room and dashed to the ladder, then climbed out of the hole and ran to the last life raft that was waiting for him on the shore. He dove headfirst into the lifeboat as the driver cranked up the electric motor to its highest level. The other three rafts were several football field lengths away, heading north. They would soon all turn east into the open waters of the Atlantic Ocean.

Just as the rafts were making their turn, it happened. A fireball shot out of the hole like a cannon, followed by intense smoke that started white, turned gray, and became black. The explosion was deafening and could be heard all the way to nearby islands. Dirt, trees, and shrubs shot sky high, and all wildlife melted instantly in the heat. Commercial fishermen twenty miles away later stated they believed the first-ever Bahamian volcano had erupted.

The shockwaves were enormous, and the TST employees hadn't considered that factor. The detonation caused a surge in wave activity, and soon the rafts were engulfed in thirty-foot crests. The four Bahamian Coast Guard cutters filled with international crime fighters killed their engines. They watched the demolition of the island from a distance of two miles.

Then perhaps the most bizarre occurrence ever witnessed on the high seas commenced. Metal items were yanked from boats and ships floating within a forty-mile radius of Plana Cay. Spears, scissors, loose screws, nuts, and bolts were dramatically lifted into thin air and pulled energetically toward the melting island. And the ferromagnetic substances in the coast guard cutters' structure began to tug the ships toward the flaming epicenter.

The four Coast Guard captains all shifted their motors into reverse to no avail. Then, they tried to circle around and move away, but the power of the magnetic force was no match for their mighty engines. Soon they would be heaved into the blazing core. The crime fighters quickly donned life vests as they stared fearfully at the island.

There was no way to survive the intense fire. Was there a way to survive hungry sharks?

CHAPTER FIFTY-ONE

April 2015

Tuesday, April 14th, was the tenth anniversary of Minn's Espresso Shop in downtown Nassau. To celebrate, every customer would receive a free medium latte or cappuccino. Willy, Mel, and Keith decided to take them up on their offer, and the three found a table in the back. Willy couldn't believe what Mel had told him on the boat, and now he needed some processing time.

Mel took a sip of latte, then stared directly into Willy's eyes. His lips showed no smile or frown. He was dead serious. "What we told you cannot be repeated." He motioned to Keith. "Our lives are on the line. Do you understand?"

"I spent many years in law enforcement, so I know the importance of keeping my mouth shut." Willy leaned forward so no one could hear. "But two CIA agents working in a church? It's baffling."

"The only reason we were in St. Max's was because of Tommy Williams. He contacted Father Jacob with a plan to raise money for the parish, and we smelled a rotten egg. Knowing Tommy like we do, he was going to use the church as a cover for bad deeds."

"How did you know Tommy?"

"Moylyn."

"Moylyn? Please explain!"

"We first met Tommy after Ovambo Airlines crashed in the desert west of Windhoek, Namibia. The CIA was called in because the accident killed King Achebe and his wife, Lesotho's rulers. President Obama was trying to smooth relations with the African continent at the time, so he offered our services to aid in the investigation.

"What we found were explosives inside a box of a dozen Titleist golf balls. The package was supposed to be loaded onto the airplane, but a luggage handler decided to keep it for himself. There were fifty boxes of balls to be loaded, and the man didn't think anyone would miss one. His brother golfed, and his birthday was coming up. The perfect present!

"I'm a golfer, and I noticed something wasn't right. I had bought many Titleist balls in my life, and I had never seen one called a Pro X. Pro V, yes, and even X-Outs, but never one called a Pro X. I knew then that Titleist hadn't made the balls. A technician cut one open and examined the inside. It was shocking! The ball had electric wires, a battery, a razor, and a tiny communications device inside. But the weirdest thing was two small plastic bags pushing against each other. Inside one bag was calcium carbonate. What was inside the second bag was an unknown substance. The technicians determined the communications device could be activated remotely, causing the razor to drop onto the bags and slice them open. When the two chemicals inside the bags touched each other, they began to smoke and then exploded. Right then, we were sure someone brought the jet down using a remote-control device."

A memory from the past was forming in Willy's mind: the downing of passenger jets in Florida. He was sure he saw remote-controlled radar jamming devices like the ones used during those terrorist events in the 1980s. They were on a shelf inside the TST storage room he was locked in and also on the island's trees. Remote controllers used to blow up jets? Was it just a coincidence? Willy needed more information to connect all the dots. "What about moylyn? You said moylyn. What's that?!"

"It's Tommy Williams' invention. The plastic-like material is impenetrable by imaging machines and X-rays. Whatever is wrapped inside a moylyn cover cannot be detected by modern technology."

"You're talking about airline security, right?!"

"Yep, that's correct. And although it wasn't easy, we traced moylyn back to Tommy because he made a mistake and patented the plastic. Our research indicated that no company has ever used moylyn in their products, probably because they didn't want to pay Tommy's exorbitant royalty."

"But why wasn't he arrested for terrorism?!"

"Because we didn't have enough evidence that he was the person shipping the balls. He was our only suspect, but we were worried we couldn't get a conviction. That's when we were assigned to follow Williams. We were ordered to make friends with him and watch him closely. So, Keith and I arranged to be in a foursome with him on a golf course one day. Afterward, in the clubhouse, we became friends. It only cost us several Scotch and sodas!

"Later, to gain his trust, we told Tommy we were ex-cons who had spent years in federal prison for fraud. We also told him we were aeronautical engineers in our previous life. So, when Tommy started his next corrupt mission, he invited us to participate in his plan. We now had a foot inside the door."

Mel needed some caffeine, so Keith took over the conversation. He explained to Willy about their friend, Bushman Jack, and how he helped them spy using a solar-powered drone capable of snapping sharp images from 100,000 feet up. That's how they discovered the secret island in the Plana Cays and Tommy's connection to TST Industries.

"The secret ferromagnetic substance mined in the uncharted Plana Cay is unofficially called planacalum," explained Keith. "It has extreme magnetic power. And mixed with calcium carbonate, it is highly explosive."

"Yes, I've seen what that mixture can do! That's how we blew up the beach house! But what do you mean by 'unofficially?'"

"It's not recognized by chemists or geologists as an official element. Also, it seems planacalum can only be found on that island. But going back to its explosive power when combined with calcium carbonate, there are plenty of seashells in the Bahamas that can be crushed into CaCO3. Anyway, our best guess was Tommy talked Father Jacob into ordering Bibles from TST to disguise the materials being shipped. Father Jacob didn't care where the Bibles came from; he just wanted a good price."

"So, what's Tommy's plan? Do you know his grand scheme?!"

Mel cut back into the conversation. "Yes, we do, and it's mind-boggling. But before I explain, I need another latte with a couple extra espresso shots!"

CHAPTER FIFTY-TWO

April 2015

With a tone of regret, Mel asked, "Jim Mann works for you, right?"

Confused by the question, Willy responded, "Yes. I hired him to improve trails in Loxahatchee Slough. Why? Is he involved in Tommy's plan?"

"No, no, no!" exclaimed Mel. "But his son, the now infamous pro golfer Eric, is a major participant."

"What?! No way! The boy is an angel! He may be the nicest and most respectable kid I've ever met! You must be wrong!"

"Relax, Willy. We're hoping Eric doesn't know anything about this, and he is just being used as a pawn."

"How so?"

"Tommy has developed an incredible system to control the outcome of professional golf. It borders on science fiction." Mel paused and glanced at Keith. If he spoke any further, Willy would be implicated. "Willy, if I tell you what Tommy did, your life could be in danger. We believe Williams is working with a criminal organization, but we don't know exactly which one."

"Fear is not part of my vocabulary. Keep talking!"

"The St. Max's Premium ball is constructed with planacalum, wires, a communications chip, and a GPS locator. All the minuscule pieces are neatly placed inside a moylyn cover. Eric is currently the only pro golfer using St. Max's Premium on the tour.

"Anyway, the ferromagnetic strength of planacalum is dynamic! Tommy developed golf cups for greens that contained the same robust ingredients as St. Max's Premiums. They, too, are extremely magnetized! Using a computer screen, he remotely controls the distance and accuracy of balls as soon as they are struck by a golf club. The ball is the positive conductor to the cup's negative polarized pull. Tommy could virtually make every shot go in the cup right from the tee-off if he wanted. But obviously, that would raise eyebrows, so he ensures that some of Eric's shots aren't so great. I videoed Tommy on my cell phone doing this without him knowing it. He helped the youngster win the Honda Classic. Still, he only let him finish in ninth place at the Arnold Palmer Invitational."

"Why ninth place?!" yelped Willy. "Why not let him win?"

"Eric only needed a top ten finish to qualify for the Masters. That was the tournament Tommy was gunning for to make big money. It would have been suspicious if he had won the Arnold Palmer after winning the Honda. Tommy wanted Eric to be respected, but not superhuman!"

"So, how does Tommy make money? From what I've heard, Eric has donated all his winnings to the church. Has he given Tommy some of the winnings no one knows about?"

"Once again, Willy, we're hoping Eric doesn't know anything about Tommy's plan, but we can't be sure. We also don't know if his mentor, Hugh Kraft, is involved. And perhaps even Wayne Siebold. We're guessing Tommy is involved in gambling. He's betting on Eric and winning big. But we haven't been able to prove it."

"How can Eric even use St. Max's Premium balls on the pro circuit. Don't they have to be approved by the PGA or something?"

"Excellent question, Willy! Tommy submitted the regular St. Max's balls for approval and not the premium ones that Eric uses. Those balls are good, thanks mainly to the moylyn cover and dimple design. Moylyn is okay by PGA standards because it's been patented. The core does contain planacalum, but it's not electronically energized. Planacalum alone still provides a lively get-up-and-go on the golf course. No one has questioned what the core is made of because the ball plays no better than a Titleist or Callaway. If it did, there might be some questions. But, once again, the planacalum ball and the moylyn cover work together to be just as good as the big names in golf."

"So, you're saying Tommy duped PGA officials into thinking that his electronically-controlled premium balls are the same as the regular ones?! Unbelievable!"

"Agreed! It was—"

"Hold on, Mel! Take a look at that!" Keith abruptly stood and pointed at the television hanging from the wall. "Holy crap!"

The CNN announcer spoke into a mike from a news helicopter rocking incessantly with turbulence. "Gene Talbot reporting live with breaking news from within the Bahamas archipelago, more specifically, the Plana Cays. An American Airlines pilot reported seeing an incredible explosion during his approach into Nassau. A massive volcano appears to have demolished an uncharted island about a half mile from our chopper. What is amazing is the fact that none of the Bahamian Islands were formed from volcanos. South of here, many of the Caribbean Islands were at one time volcanic, but none in the Bahamas.

"Fortunately, no lives were lost. Because this was an uncharted remote island, no one was living there. Strangely, the volcanic ash and rocks have already vanished into the sea, leaving nothing but palm trees and other foliage floating on the ocean. The US Geologic Survey has been called in to investigate. As always, we will keep you posted as soon as information is relayed to us! Gene Talbot, CNN."

"As usual, terrible reporting!" chided Keith. "That was TST Industries' island. No one living on the island? Right!"

"You're missing the point, Keith. That wasn't a volcano. Geologically speaking, it couldn't be. So, either someone blew up the island, or they blew it up themselves!"

Mel's phone rang just as he finished his sentence. "Sorry I'm late," said Bushman Jack. "But I wanted to get more information before I called. I'm sure you've seen it on the news by now."

"Plana Cay has vanished. We just saw the breaking news. What do you know?"

"Well, it's definitely not a volcano. That would be impossible. The drone has images of four life rafts floating on the northeast side of Plana Cay. Also, four Bahamian Coast Guard cutters with the international agents are now beached on what's left of the island. CNN didn't see them because of all the debris."

"Beached?! How?! They're all highly trained sailors?!"

"I'm just guessing, but I think the magnetic force of planacalum was stronger than their ships' engines."

"We need to rescue them! I'll get—"

Bushman Jack broke in. "You won't have to. The drone spotted a CIA helicopter that appeared to be heading their way from Langley. Well, I'm assuming it's Langley."

"From Langley! They'll never make it in time. They'll need to refuel."

"Not necessarily. Your CIA long-range choppers can fly 1,200 miles on a tank of gas. It's about 1,000 miles from Langley to Plana Cay."

Willy and Keith listened to Mel and heard what he had to say. Unfortunately, so did a few customers sipping coffee at Minns. Keith grabbed Mel's arm and led him to the door. "We need to get out of this place before all of Nassau starts posting your conversation on Facebook!"

A few minutes later, they were onboard their jet at an airport refueling dock. Mel and Keith were going through a preflight checklist when Willy walked into the cockpit. He was holding a piece of paper.

"I forgot to show you this. I found it in a security booth inside the TST facility. It's a log sheet I tore off a pad. The date and time on a twenty-four-hour clock are obvious, and by the way, all those dates are Mondays. However, under PRODUCT are GC and Bible. I know what a Bible is, but not GC. And the other abbreviations are a mystery to me! Take a look.

DATE/ TIME/ PRODUCT/ DESTINATION/ SIGNATURE

2/09/15:1342 Bible/ACT (PoFL/SMC)—CB
2/16/15:1114 Bible/ACT (PoSV/SMC) RP
2/23/15:1405 GC/18 (PoGV/HFCC)—CB
3/02/15:1220 GC/18 (PoNO/SJC)—RP

Mel and Keith scrutinized the form. They agreed something was shipped inside Bibles on the ninth and sixteenth of February. Then it dawned on Mel what ACT meant. "Activators. They packed activators inside the Bibles!"

"What are activators?" asked Willy.

"After the golf balls are finished, the planacalum needs to be activated to make sure it's fully charged. Tommy uses a tiny laser beam of some sort to do that. He told us about it, but we've never seen him actually activate the balls. He said he waits until one or two days before Eric uses them to ensure a full charge."

"Port of Fort Lauderdale!" blurted Keith.

"What? What are you mumbling about?" asked Mel as he gave a peculiar glance at his friend.

"PoFL in the destination column. I think it means Port of Fort Lauderdale. And I'm willing to bet that SMC stands for St. Max's Church! That's what Tommy uses as his business address."

"Okay, but your theory is shot with the next entry," inserted Willy. "Where is PoSV? I can't think of any Florida port with the initials SV."

"Good point. Unless SMC is the receiving party and Tommy, representing St. Max's Church, picked up the activators wherever they were sent."

Keith looked up from the log. "You're right, Mel. The Bibles that went to Fort Lauderdale were most likely picked up by someone representing St. Max's Church. And if you look at the date, I am guessing the PoSV stands for Port of Savannah, Georgia. That would probably be the closest shipping port to Augusta. Whoever picked up the activators there used them for the Masters!"

"What about the golf cups?" asked Willy. "The activated balls would do no good without cups placed in each hole, right?"

"That's it!" shouted Mel, pointing to the letters GC on the log. "GC must mean golf cups! That's why the number eighteen is right next to it. There are eighteen holes on a golf course, and TST must send a supply for each hole."

"Okay, I'll buy that," said Keith. "But there's no golf cup shipments to Fort Lauderdale or Savannah. Just activators. As Willy mentioned, the balls won't work without golf cups in place on the greens."

"The cups must have been sent earlier," stated Mel. "But I'd like to know what PoGV/HFCC and PoNO/SJC are. You'll notice that SMC isn't the receiver. Could other people be working with Tommy?"

"That's doubtful," responded Keith. "After all the time we spent with him, we would have known!"

"Hold on," said Willy as he was studying the entries. "All of the codes for the receiving party end in the letter C. If SMC stands for St. Max's Church, could it be possible that the last word for HFCC and SJC is church?"

Mel pondered that for a moment, then his eyes locked on Keith's. "How could we be so stupid?!" Keith nodded in agreement.

"You are absolutely correct, Willy!" declared Mel. "And I know where the ports associated with them are!"

"Huh? What did I say?"

"Think professional golf, Willy! That's what TST's mission is all about. PoGV is the Port of Galveston, Texas, and HFCC is Holy Family Catholic Church in Irving. PoNO is the Port of New Orleans, and SJC is St. Joes Church of Jackson, Mississippi."

"What in the world are you talking about?!" asserted Willy. "Okay, you may be right about the ports, but how did you come up with the churches?"

"Because Keith and I have been there. We delivered Christmas gifts to the priests of those parishes. The presents were crosses, and we're sure Tommy Williams planted activators inside them."

"Hey, wait! My brother Otis and I were supposed to deliver those gifts before our truck broke down in New Mexico! Then, they were confiscated at the Albuquerque airport! How did you get them?"

"When we heard about your mechanical problems, Tommy had us fly to Albuquerque to pick them up and deliver them to the parishes. He said he placed a friend inside the churches who would activate the balls a few days before the tournaments."

"What tournaments are you talking about?" asked Willy.

"The AT & T Byron Nelson Classic is in Irving, and the Sanderson Farms Championship is in Jackson. And we also delivered another cross to a church in Augusta, Georgia."

"So, those must be the next tournaments Eric is supposed to win, right?"

"Yes, most likely. But we need to put a stop to this now!"

"Do you think members of St. Max's parish are involved? They almost all work in the factory, you know."

"We think they're all innocent. Well, I should say, hopefully! But we suspect Eric's coach Hugh Kraft may be involved, and unfortunately, golf great Wayne Siebold. We followed them to the Whistler Golf Course in British Columbia while they prepped Eric on how to play in the cold and snow. They did that to help him qualify for the PGA in Scotland, but we thought they may have been actually there trying out the planacalum in cold weather. We didn't ask Tommy, so we can't be sure. While we were in BC, we saved Eric from drowning after he fell through the ice while ice fishing.

"Then, we were at St. Andrews when Eric qualified. We know Tommy had placed the golf cups on the greens and activated the balls. We disguised ourselves, but Eric recognized us in a coffee shop. We denied knowing him, but he was pretty certain we were the ones who rescued him. He may have seen us near St. Max's Church, too."

"I heard St. Andrews experienced some explosions shortly after Eric played the course," said Willy. "So, I'm assuming the planacalum was set off somehow. Is that right?"

"Yes. Groundkeepers placed fertilizer on the first green that contained calcium carbonate. The golf cup was broken, and the fertilizer became mixed with the planacalum and blew the cup sky high!"

"Where do we go from here?" asked Keith. "What's our next step?"

"I think we should let Father Jacob know what's happening before we turn this over to law enforcement. After the newspapers get a hold of it, St. Max's parish will become a crime scene."

"Is there any way we could do this without the news media or Father Jacob knowing?" asked Willy. "Father has done wonders for the poor and homeless in South Florida. All of society would benefit by keeping it under wraps."

"True. But it would be impossible to hide the indictments of such high-profile people like Hugh Kraft and Wayne Siebold. Then there's Eric Mann's rags-to-riches story being exposed. I feel for the poor kid, especially if he's innocent!"

Three heads nodded in agreement. The refueling ended, and Mel fired up the engines. Moments later, the Citation X lifted gently off the runway.

CHAPTER FIFTY-THREE

April 2015

John Barrett's office was on the top floor of the George Bush Center for Intelligence in McLean, Virginia. He was appointed Director of the CIA by President Barack Obama in 2013, and one of his first commissions was to prevent the corruption of professional and collegiate sports by foreign entities. President Obama was an avid fan of athletics and believed international crime organizations were involved in illegal gambling operations.

Barrett selected two of his finest agents to head up a special task force to investigate fraud and deception in sports. Mel Smith and Keith Malone were chosen to carry out this long-term mission and were provided complete secrecy status. In other words, no other CIA agents knew about Smith and Malone's activities. Only Barrett and Obama were privy to the quest.

Without blinking an eye, Barrett approved his agent's request for a black Porsche 918 Spyder for Mel and a deep blue Hennessey Venom GT for Keith to drive. And they were provided with a Cessna Citation X jet for business and personal use. It was only taxpayer money, after all!

Mel requested a conference with Barrett for Thursday, April 16th. This was the first in-person meeting with the director since the mission began. They would report in only as needed, which was seldom. Barrett trusted

Smith and Malone to do their job right, and he didn't want to be bothered with day-to-day details. Mel and Keith were given carte blanche authority to detain, arrest, or even kill to protect American freedoms.

Willy Banks joined Smith and Malone but was cautioned to say nothing unless asked. Mel introduced Willy to Barrett, and they shook hands. The director remembered Willy's heroics back in the eighties.

"Good to see you again," said Barrett to break the ice and start the meeting. He pulled a pad of paper out of his desk to take notes. "I don't have much time. What's up?"

Mel knew his boss didn't appreciate a long dialogue, so he tried to be succinct. "You may have heard about Eric Mann, the teenage golf pro who recently won the Masters. Casinos lost money, and we believe the tournament was rigged. As you know, we've reported that we were following Tommy Williams as a possible suspect in illegal gaming operations. Because we worked alongside him, we know for a fact that Williams used a ferromagnetic substance to create golf balls Eric used in the two tournaments he won. You are most certainly aware CIA agents teamed with MI6 and other international crime fighters to raid the Sharma Plastics facility in India, then tried to blitz TST Industries, which was located on an uncharted island in the Plana Cays. TST employees escaped and blew up the island—"

"Whoa, whoa," interrupted Barrett. "CNN is saying the explosion was a volcano. Four Bahamian Coast Guard cutters with our men onboard were lost at sea during the eruption. Our helicopters have rescued them and others. They are in Nassau now, but we haven't debriefed them."

"Sir, I assure you with the utmost confidence it wasn't a volcano that destroyed the island. Planacalum is the ferromagnetic substance I spoke about earlier. As far as we know, it can only be found on the uncharted Plana Cay island. We know when it is mixed with calcium carbonate, it becomes highly explosive."

"Wait a minute. I have a report on my desk about golf cups that contained calcium carbonate and an unknown substance exploding on the Old Course at St. Andrews. MI6 said terrorists were targeting professional golfers. Pete Burns, head of the PGA, confirmed finding the same type of golf cups where the AT & T Byron Nelson Classic and Sanderson Farms Championships are being played. Are you saying this is all related?"

"Yes, sir. But we don't think terrorists are trying to kill anyone. To make a long story short, Tommy Williams developed a way for Eric Mann to hit a polarized magnetic golf ball that could be pulled toward the golf cup. It's an unbelievably strong attraction and works every time."

"Wow! It sounds like science fiction. But how does this play into your mission, boys?"

"We believe Williams is connected to the mob or some other international crime organization and is gambling on Eric. Using his computer, he can control Eric's golf balls. He helped him win the Honda Classic and Masters and purposely had him finish in ninth place at the Arnold Palmer Invitational."

"Give me some names. Who is involved?"

"We think Eric's coach, Hugh Kraft, and Wayne Siebold may be part of it."

"Holy cow! What about Eric himself?"

"Maybe. We're hoping not, but maybe."

"Anyone else?"

"Not at this time. We—"

Although he knew better to speak until spoken to, Willy decided to break into the conversation. "One other man is involved."

Mel and Keith's mouths dropped wide open. Willy was only there if Barrett wanted to ask him something. What did he know that Smith and Malone didn't know?

"Go ahead," said Barrett. "What do you want to tell us?"

"I think Jake Tassett is a key player in the gaming operation."

Barrett thought a moment, then remembered. "Jake Tassett? Are you talking about the same Jake Tassett who was a lead investigator for the National Transportation Safety Board? The one who covered up the Florida airline disasters in the 1980s?"

"Yes, sir."

"He's been missing ever since the accidents. What makes you so sure he's part of this?"

"I was captured on the uncharted Plana Cay island that was destroyed. The underground factory there belonged to TST Industries. While locked up in a storage room, I saw radar-jamming devices like the ones used in the eighties to bring down those jets. Those same devices were also in trees on the island. That's the reason why the island and factory were never located. The devices jammed radio frequencies at sea and in the air. Because of the dead space for communications, airplanes were routed away from Plana Cay, and ships didn't get nearby. TST's imports from India were on freighters that could radio only the factory via a special, private frequency."

Barrett peered at Mel and Keith. "Why didn't you tell me about Tassett?" asked the director angrily.

"We were going to in a minute," replied Mel as he gave a disgusted glance at Willy.

*****

Barrett paused the meeting for a few minutes to hook up a video camera. Now that Jake Tassett was implicated, he wanted everything recorded in case President Obama needed to see it. Barrett asked Mel and Keith to start over from the beginning, then had Willy repeat what he knew.

Willy went into more detail about the island and why he went there in the first place. He told about renting the boat from Bongo Bay Marina in Fort Lauderdale to search for a port in Plana Cay where Bibles were being shipped to St. Max's Church. Willy mentioned being accompanied by his brother Otis, Jim Mann, and Bob Butler. And together, the four of them located a retractable pier, a subterranean facility, remnants of Christopher Columbus' voyage to the new world, and an empty beach house they believe belonged to Jake Tassett.

Willy pulled out the piece of paper he confiscated from the safe in the burnt house and handed it to Barrett. "I had planned to take this to a bank in Nassau because I thought it had something to do with financial account numbers. I never made it to the bank, so perhaps you can tell me."

With plenty of experience in this area, the director nodded. He knew immediately what the codes stood for:

BIBC-Nass-41379-Tassett-8976453570092*70094
BOSE-Gene-792231-Tassett-76100800748*81345
GCIB-BodT-4566547979-Tassett-88856723234*790213
HKMACINV-Jinw-396442-Tassett-20208080997*6984

Barrett punched a few keys on his desk computer, then smiled. "Just what I thought. This is bank account information. The first one is the Bahamas International Bank Corporation. Every letter and number before 'Tassett' identify the bank's direct deposit code."

"Don't banks have routing numbers for that?" asked Willy curiously. "You know, those nine digits before your checking account number."

"It's like a routing number, but international banks code things differently. The capital letters identify the bank name, and following the first hyphen is the city where the bank is located. A routing number of sorts follows the second hyphen. The customer's last name is next, followed by his account number and pin. So, in other words, the first line identifies the Bahamas International Bank Corporation of Nassau, Tassett being the customer, his account number and pin."

"Is the information I gave you helpful?" asked Willy.

"Helpful? Most certainly! We now know where Tassett stashed his cash! And all these countries will do that for wealthy clients without reporting to the IRS. The second account is the Bank of Switzerland in Geneva, the third is Grand Caymans International Bank in Bodden Town, and the last is Hong Kong Macao Investments in the Jinwan District of Macao."

"What will you do now?"

"We will request via international agencies to have those accounts frozen. Then, I'll put a team of CIA agents out to track down Tassett. He will—"

"We can find him!" stated Mel firmly. "Keith and I will locate him and bring him to justice!"

"You have your own mission, boys!"

"Tassett is producing the ferromagnetic golf cups and shipping planacalum to Tommy Williams, who, in turn, is fixing professional golf tournaments. I believe that falls under our mission's strategic plan!"

"You're right. But you will need more men."

"Too many people working on this task force will spook Tassett. Less is better. How about you, Willy? Would you join us?"

"I need some time to think about it! But thanks for asking!"

"Willy would need to be vetted first," stated Barrett.

"Seriously, sir?" asked Mel, somewhat respectfully. "This man's history in law enforcement and American heroics is all you need to know."

"Okay, you're right. Willy is a go if he wants to be part of the task force. But only as an outside contractor. It would take too long to blast through the human resources bureaucracy to have him approved and processed into the CIA."

"There's one other man we want to hire: Jack Boyer. And I know I will be in trouble for this, but we have already been using his services."

"Bushman Jack?! He works for the International Intelligence and Inquiry Agency. What would we need to pay him because I know he won't come cheap?!"

"If we could lure him into a tavern, I'm sure he'd settle for a pint of Balters XPA!"

"Alright, I'll sign off on Banks and Boyer to be employed as independent contractors for your task force. But you need to work fast. I don't want Eric Mann playing in any more fixed golf tournaments. Is that understood?"

"Yes, boss!"

After they exited the George Bush Center for Intelligence, Keith muttered, "Any idea how we're going to do that?"

"We'll think of something."

CHAPTER FIFTY-FOUR

April 2015

"What do you mean that was TST's island that blew up?!" yelped Tommy Williams at Mel. "How can that be?!" Tommy had been holed up in his apartment working around the clock and hadn't turned on the television or pulled up the news on his cell phone. Now he was beside himself watching CNN's continuing coverage of the Plana Cays uncharted island. It was Friday, April 17th, and today they were finally reporting it wasn't a volcano after all. Geologists were guessing an unknown chemical substance created enough heat to wipe out the entire island. But they believed it was an act of nature—not an act of man.

"It certainly puts a knife into our plans!" stated Mel. He and Keith were in Tommy's apartment, where a path had worn into the carpet from Tommy's nervous pacing.

"I have enough planacalum for several dozen golf balls, but only twenty golf cups are left. That means we can only rig one more course before the AT & T Byron Nelson. It's got to be The Players Championship at Sawgrass!" Tommy picked up his half-empty coffee mug and threw it at the wall. Then he pounded his fist on the table.

"You have it figured out, so why are you still angry?"

"No more planacalum, that's why! We were so close to a windfall profit! When Eric starts playing with regular balls and cups, he'll be a nothing! Our plan was to use him for three or four years, then move on to someone else! We need him to win the Byron Nelson, Sanderson Farms, and one other tournament to rake in as much as we can before it's all over!"

"So why the TPC at Sawgrass? There's other—"

Tommy cut him off as his face turned a bright shade of red. "Because Sawgrass makes the most sense. It's a top-dollar tournament and it's nearby, up at Ponte Vedra Beach. Why are you questioning me?!"

"Okay, okay, calm down! Set it up and let us know what we can do. Got to go; see you soon."

Mel and Keith made a hasty exit and entered Mel's apartment. When they closed the door, Keith plopped down on the couch, shaking his head. "What now, man?!"

"We have enough evidence, especially with the video on my phone, to convict Tommy. But we haven't nailed down the gambling. We need to find that connection!"

*****

On Sunday, April 19th, Father Jacob completed the New Testament verse and was ready for the sermon. "Good morning, God's children. May the Lord forgive me as I sidestep this morning's readings to make an announcement that affects the entire congregation. Some of you may know there was a hostile takeover of Golf Country Superstore last week. Although I have a strong opinion about what God would say to those who profit by using extreme force, I will not reflect on it. However, with new ownership, your jobs in the golf ball factory may not be secure." Father paused while there was a giant gasp and a dash of chatter. "But please hear me out. The Lord may have sent us an angel. Ursula Vero, the previous CEO of Golf Country Superstore, has approached me with an option. She wants to start a new company featuring St. Max's golf balls. Eric would be the face of their marketing, and the good news is she would offer you all new positions within the organization. She mentioned to me that you could be supervisors."

Several hands shot up in the congregation. Father pointed to Phil Carson. "Father, where would she build the factory? Would we have to move?"

"Excellent question, Phil. Most likely, the new company wouldn't be nearby, and those of you who decide to work would be required to move. I would feel horrible about losing lifelong members of our parish, but if it's God's wish for you to prosper, then I think you should jump at the opportunity." Father surveyed the congregation and pointed.

"Yes, Chris, did you have a question?"

Chris Johnson stood to speak. "Father, we have raised a lot of money for the poor and homeless by selling golf balls. And God bless little Eric for donating his winnings to the church. What will happen to our fundraising efforts if we go with a new company?"

"Thank you, Chris. I would only make this deal so long as Miss Vero continues to support our mission. Please have no worries!"

Willy and Otis Banks were sitting in the last pew, their usual seats for Sunday mass. Willy raised his hand, and Father nodded. "Father, do you happen to know the name of the corporation that initiated the hostile takeover?"

"Yes, I believe Miss Vero said it was OH Enterprises."

Willy ripped out a blank page from the Bible he was holding and scratched ***OH Enterprises*** on it.

*****

Mel and Keith were sipping coffee in the teacher's lounge at St. Max's School, trying to devise a plan to find Jake Tassett. Willy didn't find them in their apartment, so he guessed they would be in the lounge where they always drank java on Sunday mornings.

"Perhaps you two should attend Sunday mass more often! You might learn something." Willy sat in a folding chair at the table while Otis plopped down on the couch and was soon snoring.

"Noah loaded a pair of each animal into the Ark and saved them from the flood. What more do we need to know?" asked Keith sarcastically. "Then again, I'm not sure why he bothered to save skunks."

"Don't mind him," said Mel. "He's in a perpetual bad mood. What brings you down here?"

"Did you know a company called OH Enterprises completed a hostile takeover of Golf Country Superstore last week?"

"You can't be serious, can you?" replied Mel. "How did you hear that? I was so absorbed in watching Plana Cay dissolve and our future in the CIA that I didn't think about anything else. I wonder why Tommy didn't tell us?"

"Tommy may not know either. At least that's what I'm assuming. But according to what Father Jacob told us in church today, it sounds like nothing may change. Golf Country Superstore's previous CEO, Ursula Vero, is forming a new company and wants to take the St. Max's golf ball business with her. In fact, she's offering any of our parish members a new, highly-paid supervisor position in the new factory. But they would have to move because the new plant wouldn't be in Florida. At least I don't think so."

"Really?! Wow! What was Father's take on all of this?"

"Calm as usual. Nothing seems to bother him. He's a man with strong faith and knows the Lord will watch over him."

"So, I can tell by the look in your eyes you have something else to tell us. What is it, Willy?"

"No, not tell. But I have a favor that would require the investigative powers of the CIA."

"And what would that be?"

"Can you find out who's running OH Enterprises? The CEO, board of directors, anything you can find."

"Sure thing. When do you need it?"

"Yesterday!"

CHAPTER FIFTY-FIVE

April 2015

For the fifth time in his life, Burt Merriman was arrested for tax evasion. The previous four apprehensions were brief, thanks to his legal team. But this time, an accountant for Merriman Enterprises died suspiciously on the job, and additional charges were brought forth making the Attorney General hopeful Burt would be put away for good. Merriman's lead lawyer, Vince Menderelli, was the only person the mob boss was allowed to communicate with while awaiting trial for murder and fraud. His first visit was held in a private cell in the back wing of the Federal Detention Center in Miami. No recording devices were permitted by either the legal team or prison officials.

Merriman had no fear about the government's charges. His lawyers would once again find a way to get him released, and he would soon be free. But he was incensed with his right-hand man!

"What the hell?!" shrieked Burt angrily. "Oliver wasted ten billion dollars of my money on a hostile takeover of Golf Country Superstore? What gives him the right, damn it!"

"You signed a Power of Attorney for him, Burt. And, as you remember, it was against my strong advice not to. He also took five million in cash to gamble with."

"I don't care about the gambling money. Oliver always pays it back with interest. But a ten-billion-dollar investment without my approval is loathsome." Merriman's legs were shackled, and he was secured to the brick wall with a ten-foot chain, but he could still stand up and pace, which is what Merriman did to help himself think. "So Tassett told you about the takeover, and you said he was ticked off? Why did he even care? The golf balls can be distributed by anyone."

"Because Tassett was profiting from the sale of the balls, and now Oliver has taken a cut of those profits. Plus, Oliver is gambling on Eric Mann, so he is actually making more money, which is upsetting Tassett."

"Why doesn't Tassett gamble, too?"

"He's not a gambler. I don't think he would know what to do."

"So why come to me? What does Tassett think I can do?"

"He thinks you still have power over Oliver, and he wants you to make him sell the stock back to Golf Country Superstore on an even exchange. It is your money, after all! And Harwas always follows your orders."

The guard unlocked the door. "Time's up!" he shouted. He then unchained Merriman from the wall and escorted him back to his cell.

*****

On Monday afternoon, Mel and Keith decided it was best to meet with Willy at his home on the PGA National Golf Course. They didn't want Tommy Williams to see them together at the apartments. Otis answered the door and showed them to the patio, where Willy was sipping iced tea.

"We found some answers," said Mel. Willy nodded but didn't speak. "OH Enterprises was most recently Merriman Enterprises. It was just a corporate name change."

Willy perked up. Everything was starting to make sense. "Let me guess. Burt Merriman is the owner?"

"You obviously have heard about the infamous Burt Merriman, right?"

"The mob boss who never sees prison time for his multitude of crimes! Of course! Everyone in law enforcement is appalled by the court system that lets Merriman roam free! I thought I heard he was just arrested again and is awaiting trial down in Miami. How can he make decisions from a jail cell, such as changing corporate names?"

"Well, as an ex-cop, you should know, Willy. You're innocent until proven guilty in this country. But he signed over a Power of Attorney to a man who completed the hostile takeover for him."

"And I'll wager my house and everything in it that the man's name is Oliver Harwas. Thus, the initials OH before Enterprises. Am I correct?"

"You're a smart fella, Willy! I'm not sure how you knew that! But Burt Merriman isn't so intelligent. He must not have thought a simple POA would ever be traced. If he had, he certainly wouldn't have given it to someone who is number one on the FBI's Most Wanted List. Regardless, Harwas has never been caught or brought to trial; thus, he, too, is innocent until proven guilty. We need to find him. But, how did you know OH was Oliver Harwas?"

"Let me give you boys a history lesson. Oliver Harfield, **f-i-e-l-d**, was one of your own—a CIA agent who broke bad back in the eighties. He was the leader of the pack, so to say, when it came to downing the passenger jets in South Florida. He even tried to blackmail the president. Well, anyway, Harfield had an illegitimate son who he gave the same name—Oliver Harfield. Years later, after his dad died, the son didn't want to be associated with the world's worst criminal, so he changed his last name to Harwas, **w-a-s**. And, yes, you guessed it—Oliver Harwas is now the FBI's most wanted criminal!"

Mel looked at Keith and frowned. "Harfield, Harwas, why didn't we put two and two together?!"

*****

"Stupid move, Oliver," spoke Vince Menderelli firmly into his cell phone. "Spending Burt's money for a hostile takeover without his knowledge could prove deadly if you know what I mean! But now, after what's happened in Plana Cay, your investment looks pretty woeful!"

"You say the entire island blew to pieces, and there's absolutely no planacalum left on this earth?!" Harwas was so upset spittle was flying everywhere. "What's Tassett's plan now?! With no rigged golf balls or cups, Eric Mann stands no chance of winning!"

"Perhaps you should call Tassett and ask him," replied Menderelli, smirking. He was happy to have Oliver on the ropes.

"Something tells me Tassett wouldn't want to speak to me."

"You should have thought of that before spending Burt's money to take over Golf Country Superstore, you fool!" Vince was walking a fine line with his language, but he was sure Oliver couldn't do much about it.

"So, what do you think I should do?"

"I'm not your lawyer, Oliver. But for a small retainer, I could help you out."

"What would you do for me?!" shouted Oliver. His anxiety was growing deep inside.

"Sell your shares back to Ursula Vero on an even exchange. Then Burt will pretend this never happened. I will take care of all the paperwork. You won't even need to speak to her."

"If there's no planacalum, why would she want the company back?"

"I'm going on the assumption she never knew St. Max's balls were magnetically juiced. Her company was ethical—much the exact opposite of Jake Tassett's!"

*****

Vince Menderelli had a plant inside the Securities and Exchange Commission that Burt Merriman paid handsomely to do some dirty work. So, by mid-afternoon on Wednesday, April 22nd, Golf Country Superstore again belonged to Ursula Vero. Remarkably, the original takeover was canceled upon further review due to incorrect filing procedures. Although she was thrilled to death to have her company back, Vero lambasted Vince

Menderelli for representing crooks in a court of law. All that took place at Carmine's Restaurant in Times Square over endless Chianti and pasta.

It's what Italians do.

CHAPTER FIFTY-SIX

April 2015

Father Jacob delivered the worst possible news to the congregation on Sunday, April 26th. "I'm so very sorry to tell you I received word that Deacon Ollie succumbed to cancer and passed into the spiritual afterlife yesterday. His family has invited me to be the priest for his private funeral next week in Jacksonville. I offered to preside over a memorial service here at St. Max's, but the family wished to have it there in Northern Florida."

Tears and sighs filled the church, and Father could see it would be difficult to conduct a full service. Instead, he read Psalm Twenty-Three in memory of his friend, said a few prayers, rushed through communion, and dismissed everyone for the day.

Jim called Hugh Kraft and said Eric was so distraught about Deacon Ollie that he didn't want to ride to Ponte Vedra Beach for a practice round at the TPC Sawgrass. Church was at 8:00 am, and Hugh had made a tee time for 1:15 pm. He hoped to get two rounds in before sunset, which was at 7:59 pm.

Dora was thrilled Eric wasn't going because, with a four-hour drive, the earliest her son would be home would be after midnight. She wanted him bright and alert for school on Monday! The seventh graders were starting a new unit on statistics and probability in math that Dora didn't want him to miss. On the other hand, Hugh was beside himself with anger. Eric needed to play Sawgrass before competing in two weeks.

Dora had gained much respect as a teacher through the years, and Father praised her efforts constantly. Next month, April Carson would be her first student to graduate from high school. April had been in a grade level all by herself since the beginning of St. Max's School in 2007. Keith and Karen Johnson, Bill and Chris' kids, would be next. Keith was a junior, and Karen a sophomore.

Eric's closest friends had become Ben and Betty Butler, Bob and Becky's children. Betty was in eighth grade, and Ben was in ninth. Whenever Eric wasn't golfing, he would go with the Butlers into the Loxahatchee Slough to fish. Eric would walk past the area where he lived in his car as a toddler, and it would bring shivers to his body. He was donating all his professional golf winnings to the parish to try and keep other homeless kids from growing up in the backseat of a broken-down automobile. He wasn't sure he was making a difference, but he believed the money helped at least a little bit!

On that Sunday, after canceling the trip with Hugh Kraft, Eric went fishing with the Butlers to try and keep his mind off the sad news from church that morning. He returned home to his apartment and shocked his parents with the first words he spoke after closing the door. "Mom and Dad, I don't think I want to be a professional golfer when I grow up. I think I want to be a deacon or a priest."

Dora cried as she hugged her son and held him tight. Jim patted Eric on the back and said, "We'll talk about it later, son. You need some time to grieve Deacon Ollie."

*****

Bob Butler invited Jim Mann and Willy and Otis Banks to play poker in Bob's apartment on Sunday night. Willy was tired and was going to decline the offer until Bob said pointedly, "There's something important we need to discuss." Willy wondered if St. Max's Director of Security had figured out Mel and Keith worked for the CIA. With those thoughts swirling around in his mind and the implications it could cause, he guessed it would be best to be present at the table. But Willy's worries never evolved.

Instead, while dealing the first hand of Texas Hold Em, Bob said, "I think we should clean out Deacon Ollie's trailer over in Pahokee and notify Myra Rother about his death. It would be one less thing Father Jacob would have to do."

"Who's Myra Rother?" asked Jim.

"You remember, she's the old lady who runs the trailer court."

"Oh yeah. So, how about tomorrow? Is everyone available?"

"Sure! Why not?" voiced Willy. "I'll rent a U-Haul and pick everyone up at nine."

*****

"Y'all say he's dead?! Naw, can't be. Just saw him a week or so ago." Myra was shaking her head and spilling coffee all over herself and on the office floor.

"A week or so ago?" asked Jim as he scrunched his face. "Are you sure? He's been fighting cancer for quite a while. He would have been on his deathbed just recently."

"Well, I sees him go into his trailer where he stayed most all day. Then, I sees him leave. Yessiree Bob. That was him. He be here sure as my hair is whiter than a snowball!"

"Hmmm. Okay. Well, could we go in and get his things?"

"Sure can, if y'all got his keys."

"Oh, sorry. Deacon Ollie had the keys with him when he died. Could you open his trailer up for us?"

"Ha! What if youze all a bunch of crooks trying to rob the place? What do ya take me for, a chump or something? Nope, can't let ya in. So, you best be going away, or I'll call the cops!"

The four men gave a puzzled look at one another. Then, Willy spoke up to save the day. "Ah, excuse me, ma'am, but I am a cop. Let me show you my badge." Willy pulled his US Fish and Wildlife Service Park Ranger pin from his pocket. Myra's eyes weren't the best, and she thought it looked like an official police officer's badge.

"Well, well, well! Why didn't ya tell me that before? I should have guessed you was a copper with them humungous arms and legs! I'll go get the spare key for y'all!"

"Willy, you ain't no cop no more," said Otis. "Were you just bluffin' her, or did you sign on with the police again?"

"Shut up, Otis, and pull the U-Haul over to the trailer." Willy hoped Myra hadn't heard his brother.

As they walked out the office door, Bob asked, "What do you suppose she meant when she told us she saw Deacon Ollie a week or so ago?"

"Myra is an old lady with vision problems. Either some maintenance dude went in to fix something, or she was looking at the wrong trailer." Willy tried to sound confident, but deep down, he wasn't all that sure.

A few minutes later, Willy opened unit number thirty. Everything appeared to be in order. The kitchen was neat and clean—no dirty dishes anywhere. Bob and Jim walked to the only bedroom in the back of the trailer and found a queen-size mattress on a metal frame. There was no headboard, but the bed had been made. One dresser sat against the wall, but there were no clothes there and none in the closet. Bob shouted to Willy through the open door, "No clothes in here. Ollie couldn't have been living here."

Willy didn't respond, so Bob yelled it a little louder. Once again, nothing from Willy. Jim and Bob went out to the living room and found Willy sitting at a desk with two computers hooked up. He was totally focused on trying to get past the password and didn't hear Bob's voice.

Along with the computer desk, there was a lightly used couch and reclining chair made of leather and a fifty-inch LED television on a stand with BOSE speakers. Otis was busy playing with the remote control.

Bob was scratching his head. "Where did Deacon Ollie get the money for all of these electronics?"

"The deacon liked to gamble; we all know that," stated Jim. "So he took a little of his winnings and bought a computer and TV. Who can fault him for that after all he's done for the church?!"

"Yeah, you're right, Jim. This is no big deal. Knowing Father Jacob, he probably told Ollie to buy something nice for himself!"

Willy was still ignoring the group. He carefully undid the plugs on the computers and carried the system to the truck, then placed the components gently near the rear, covering the whole thing with blankets.

"Load 'em up, boys!" ordered Willy smiling. Two hours later, everything was in the U-Haul, and the trailer was clean. If it was okay with Ollie's family, they planned to sell everything on consignment except the computers, with the proceeds going to St. Max's parish.

One final gift of charity from Deacon Ollie.

Chapter Fifty-Seven

April 2015

After school on Monday, Eric, Jim, and Hugh were hiking down a path in the Loxahatchee Slough. All three were carrying fishing poles. Jim was holding a tin can full of night crawlers they had dug when they entered the park. This would be Hugh's first time fishing, and Eric said he would give him some pointers to make up for all the coaching tips in golf.

"I know Deacon Ollie was your friend, Eric," said Hugh sadly. "And when someone close to you dies, you don't feel like doing much. I get that. And I think becoming a deacon or a priest is an honorable career goal. But I just want to say you have a very special talent for playing golf. Tiger Woods said after the Masters that you would crush all his records someday! Let me ask you something, Eric."

"Okay. What is it?" replied the teenager timidly, a tear slowly rolling down his cheek.

"If you became a deacon or a priest, what would be your purpose in life?"

Eric thought about it momentarily, then said meekly, "To help God by helping people who need help, I guess."

"So far, you've donated all your winnings to the church. Don't you think you're helping people that way?"

"Yeah, I guess so."

"I think by being a professional golfer, you could do so much for your church, community, and even the entire world!"

Eric stopped in his tracks, put the fishing pole on the ground, and sat on his haunches, covering his face with his hands. Tears were now flowing rapidly. Jim sat cross-legged next to him and wrapped his arms around Eric's shoulders.

"Son, Coach Kraft is right, but I want you to know your mom and I will support you no matter what you want to do. Now, I have a question for you that might help you decide."

"What is it, Dad?"

"What would Deacon Ollie and Father Jacob want you to do?"

Eric waited another minute, wiped his face on his shirt, then smiled at Jim and Hugh. "Yeah, I bet they'd want me to keep playing golf, wouldn't they?"

After a group hug, the three fished until past sundown. Hugh caught four largemouth basses and a couple of bluegills. Eric said he would teach his mentor the art of fileting next.

When school ended on Tuesday, Hugh and Eric met at PGA National to begin prepping for TPC Sawgrass. After a good night's sleep, Eric was fired up once again to hit the links!

*****

"You need to know this," said Bushman Jack into the phone. Mel had asked him to track the rafts loaded with TST employees after they escaped the island, just before Jimmy Tassett blew it to smithereens. "A US Sugar Corporation freighter rescued the men in the TST rafts yesterday. It looks as though everyone survived. It is now headed eastbound into the Atlantic."

"East? Where did the ship originate, and where was it going?"

"I just follow things on my drone, Mel. I'm not a soothsayer."

"Yeah, sorry, I was just talking aloud to myself!"

"Can your drone read the Hull Identification Number?"

"Well, of course. I thought you'd never ask!"

"Smart ass! Just tell me what it is."

"US-613449-87FL"

Mel wrote the number down and gave it to Keith. Using a dedicated CIA line, Keith punched the keyboard. Immediately, the computer screen read: *Error-NNA.*

"It might be a fake hull number, Mel," announced Keith. "Got an error message. The number is not assigned."

"You sure about the hull number, Jack?"

"My picture is clear as glass. No doubt about it!"

"Anything else written on the ship?"

"Across the stern is *US Sugar Corporation, Clewiston, Florida.*"

"If it's legit, US Sugar ships eastbound out of the Port of Miami and westbound from Tampa. Based on where they rescued the TST men, the freighter must be headed to Europe or Africa."

Keith interrupted. "True. But where will they drop the rescued men off? There's not much between the US and Europe."

"Most likely the Azores or Canary Islands, depending on their destination."

"Possibly. Jack, please have your drone locked on the ship and follow it. But we need to be prepared for the worst possible scenario."

"What's that?" said Jack into his phone while Keith blurted it out in the apartment.

"The freighter is hijacked. All those TST employees have guns!"

*****

Mel waited for Willy to arrive at the apartment before making the call. This could be important, and Mel wanted his team assembled in case a group decision needed to be made.

"What do you mean you have no ship with that HIN?!" asked Mel rather rudely to the assistant director of Global Logistics for US Sugar in Clewiston. He had identified himself as an agent for the CIA.

"Exactly what I just told you, sir. We don't have a ship with that number. And we don't identify our freighters with *US Sugar Corporation,*

Clewiston, Florida. All our ships are identified as *US Sugar, USA*. Simply that!"

"Okay, thanks! Sorry to bother you!"

Mel hung up and called Bushman Jack. "Keep a close eye on that ship. We'll take the jet and fly east. When we're mid-Atlantic, radio us their GPS coordinates, and we'll head to either Ponta Delgada or Tenerife so we can be close when we find out where it's going."

An hour later, Mel had filed a flight plan from the North Palm Beach airport to Lisbon, Portugal, with a refueling stop in Ponta Delgada. He would change the stop to Tenerife if the ship appeared to be headed to Africa.

Meanwhile, Willy lied and told Otis he was flying to Tallahassee on business.

CHAPTER FIFTY-EIGHT

April 2015

CIA Director John Barrett's contacts in Nassau, Geneva, Bodden Town, and Macao froze TST bank accounts simultaneously at 8:00 am Eastern Standard Time on Tuesday, April 28th. He wanted a perfectly coordinated timing of the shutdowns to prevent Jake Tassett from catching wind of what was happening and trying to prevent all the accounts from freezing. Tassett no longer had access to credit cards or wired cash from any of those banks.

Mel hadn't informed Barrett about the fake US Sugar freighter that had picked up the TST employees who escaped on rubber rafts. As usual, he didn't want to bother the busy man until he had solid evidence to provide. However, Barrett had sent a secure text letting Mel know Tassett's international bank accounts were frozen.

While Mel prepped the jet and Willy packed a few clothes, Keith told Tommy Williams he and Mel were taking a short beach trip to Bermuda. Tommy was beside himself. "What in the world! Next week is Sawgrass and you're taking a vacation?! What if I need you to help me with something?!"

"The balls are ready, and you plan to place the cups in the holes yourself during the night. What would you need from us?"

"You guys need to make sure my computer lines, video, and radio controllers are secure. But most of all, you need to ensure we have a backup generator in place in the event of a power failure. Remember the Honda Classic? We lost control of everything when the power went out! Eric could have blown the match. Then where would we be?!"

"Okay, Tommy, settle down! We'll only be gone for a brief time. We'll have everything set up at Sawgrass before the tournament begins!"

An hour later, Keith, Mel, and Willy were climbing through the blue skies over Palm Beach and whisking east over the Atlantic Ocean. At the same time, Jake Tassett found out his assets were frozen.

*****

"It's a weird freighter," stated Bushman Jack into the satellite radio.

"What's so weird about it?" asked Mel impatiently. He only cared about the ship's direction so they could determine which refueling stop to make.

"The drone was able to zoom in on the doors when they were opened. The mass of steel is really incredible! If my measurements are correct, the bulkhead and hull are thirty inches thick! And it must be as cold as ice inside. There are five massive refrigeration units surrounding the berthing. With the insulation from the walls, it could be zero degrees or less in there!"

"Well, we know it's not sugar they're carrying. So, I wonder what exactly is their cargo?"

"Stating the obvious—something cold!"

"Any chance you know what direction the ship is sailing?"

"Looks like it's Europe-bound, fellas."

"Thanks, Jack. We'll land in Ponta Delgada and wait until we know their destination."

*****

"You have enough fuel to get to Italy, right?" asked Jake Tassett.

"No problem, Dad," was Jimmy's reply.

"The CIA has frozen our overseas assets. We still have our US bank accounts, but they're not loaded with cash. With nothing left on Plana Cay, your cargo is our last, best hope for rebuilding our fortune. Protect it with your life, son!" Tassett hung up before Jimmy could respond.

Thanks to a strong tailwind, Mel landed the jet at João Paulo II Airport earlier than expected. The airport was named after Pope John Paul II, on the island of São Miguel, in the Azores. A large monument memorialized perhaps the Vatican's most popular leader of all time at the center of the main terminal. Mel, Keith, and Willy needed to pass the time, so they started by reading about the Polish hero, Giovanni Paolo, who had been canonized a saint the previous April in 2014.

When Willy finished Pope John Paul's biography, he stood and walked to the window that looked out into the parking lot. He appeared to be in a daze when Mel came over and patted him on the back.

"What's the matter, big fella?" asked Mel. "Jet lag got you down?"

Willy shook his head no but didn't say anything for a moment. Then he turned to Mel and said, "Something's bothering me, that's all."

"What is it?"

"Aw, nothing that I can't take care of myself."

*****

May 2015

Hugh was able to lock in back-to-back tee times for 1:00 and 5:00 pm on Saturday, May 2nd, at Sawgrass. Thirty-six holes should give Eric a good feel for the course. Hugh wanted to stay overnight and play on Sunday, too, but Eric wanted to go home and be in church with his parents on Sunday. He was still distraught over Deacon Ollie's death.

The course was a beautiful par seventy-two woven around small ponds, thick palmetto trees, and a sprinkling of alligators here and there. The Player's tees were rated at 76.8, slightly less than Augusta National. Hugh told Eric the rating should be 80.8 based on how he had played throughout the years! Eric didn't have a clue about course ratings or slopes; he just hit the ball the best he could when it was his turn!

The course record was sixty-three, achieved first by Fred Couples in 1992, then by Greg Norman in 1994, Roberto Castro in 2013, and Martin Kaymer just last year. Eric's first practice round was perfectly executed, and he shot an amazing sixty-five. In the second round, he dropped another stroke to sixty-four. Just past midnight, while traveling south on Interstate 95, Eric claimed he would break the record next weekend! Not could but would! Hugh offered up no argument!

Tommy Williams drove up on Monday and planned to place the cups in the holes the next three nights. This was always a last-minute mission before a tournament. Six on Monday, six on Tuesday, and six on Wednesday. He had to make sure they were flawlessly set into the ground and superbly manicured. The pros practiced on Tuesday and Wednesday; thus, he knew the landscaping crew wouldn't be shifting the cup placement again until the following week. PGA rules didn't allow pin placements to be moved once the players assembled for practice rounds. That way, the players could read the slope of the greens while their caddies took notes.

But Monday night there was a problem Tommy hadn't encountered before—night security roaming the course! Pete Burns had ordered all PGA courses to have twenty-four-hour officers on guard. TPC Sawgrass employed five men to work the night shift, and they were to constantly move about looking for suspicious activity.

Fortunately, the guards didn't split up. They walked in one group of two and the other a group of three. How stupid, thought Tommy. With all his practice, he could remove an old cup, set in the new electronic one, and manicure the hole in a half hour. The video cameras were the real challenge. Tommy had to climb nearby trees and secure them to branches. The cameras were wireless, which meant there were no cables to mess with, but they had to be paired with one of three Wi-Fi booster boxes Tommy hid in shrubs. Without Wi-Fi, Tommy wouldn't be able to maneuver the cameras, nor could he magnetize the golf cups.

One team of guards hiked around the front nine while the other walked the back nine. They all were burning flashlights, so Tommy knew where they were at all times. This is when he could have used Mel and Keith. They could have run around in opposite directions making noise so the guards would follow them. But no, they were on vacation in Bermuda! Damn them!

It took three full nights with no breaks for Tommy to finish prepping the course. He could only operate the equipment remotely from his apartment in Palm Beach Gardens, which meant he had to drive like the dickens to get back before the first tee-off on Thursday. Something would need to change before the next tournament now that security guards were posted all night long.

Mel and Keith were supposed to check the computer lines, video, and radio controllers to ensure they couldn't be discovered or hacked. They were also to ensure a backup generator was in place in the event of a power failure. With no sleep, Tommy walked into his apartment, turned on the computer and video system, and took a deep breath. He wasn't sure he could do this all day with no coffee.

*****

Oliver Harwas was confused. He returned home to find his place turned upside down, and he guessed the vandals were FBI agents. He knew he was number one on their Most Wanted List, and law enforcement was getting closer. He never should have used his real name on the Golf Country Superstore takeover documents! Oliver should have known better than to leave a paper trail.

Now he was tucked away in an off-the-strip sportsbook in Las Vegas. Everything in his home had been confiscated, so he couldn't gamble online without purchasing a new computer system. Might as well return to Sin City and make some money the easy way. But betting on Eric to win the Players Championship at Sawgrass was risky. With Plana Cay blown up, did the boys in Palm Beach Gardens have everything fixed for this tourney?

Eric's opening odds were +2200, or twenty-two to one. Oliver decided to place the small casino's limit of $5,000 for the young golfer to win. He could leave Las Vegas $110,000 richer if Eric pulled out a victory.

*****

Tommy knew better but he was tired and frustrated, so what the hell? He decided to let Eric win by shattering the course record. Now that Plana Cay was gone, Tommy knew the mission was about to end, so why not let the kid go out with guns a blazing?!

In the Honda Classic and the Masters, Williams purposely made matches close to divert suspicion. He even made sure Eric played well enough in the Arnold Palmer Invitational to qualify for the Masters but not win it. The last thing Tommy wanted was an investigation, like the one in Scotland, after the damn landscapers sprinkled fertilizer on the cups before he had a chance to remove them. He learned a big lesson with the explosion on the Old Course—remove the cups immediately after a tournament! So, he hired an unemployed man who loved to golf to replace the cups in the middle of the night.

Tommy's new employee had no problem at PGA National and the Bay Hill Club and Lodge, but things got a bit dicey after the Masters. Pete Burns, PGA of America Chief Executive Officer, ordered Sam Mueller, head of maintenance operations for Augusta National, to hire night security guards. But the security crew arrived too late, and by the time they got there, the cups had been removed. Unfortunately, there weren't enough hours or minutes to replace the cups, so the golf course was left with empty holes on the greens! Tommy almost fired his new man but decided to give him one more chance at Sawgrass.

For the first round, Eric shot an amazing nine under par, sixty-three, to tie the course record. Rickie Fowler and Sergio Garcia were six strokes back at sixty-nine. Eric's golf balls hooked or sliced when they needed to, and his distances were perfect. He one-putted twelve holes. Tommy thought about having him one-putt all eighteen, but he didn't want to get too out of control. He would ensure Eric broke the course record on Sunday.

Eric finished the second round with a sixty-four and the third round at sixty-three once again. Going into the final match on Sunday, Eric was twenty-six strokes under par, leading Fowler by fifteen shots! ESPN's Sportscenter spent a full two hours replaying each hole on Saturday night.

CHAPTER FIFTY-NINE

May 2015

At the Marina Ponta Delgada, Mel purchased a new fifty-two-foot Cranchi Evoluzione yacht using the CIA credit card. The Marina usually limited credit card purchases to $5,000, but when they saw the piece of plastic was backed by the full good faith of the United States government, they gladly made an exception. Mel knew he would have some explaining to do when the $2,500,000 charge hit the books in Langley!

Willy had plenty of experience maneuvering an ocean-going vessel all by himself, so his assigned task was to follow the fake US Sugar freighter in the yacht as it sailed past Ponta Delgada. He would continually radio Mel and Keith, who would fly their jet to the next probable location. They removed the galley inside the boat and replaced it with three additional 1,570-liter gas tanks, so Willy didn't have to stop to fill up.

On Sunday morning, May 10th, at 6:00 am Italy time, the freighter pulled into the harbor in Genoa. Mel and Keith landed at Genova City Airport, which was only a short distance from the boatyard. Willy arrived twenty minutes later.

While Willy's yacht was closely inspected from bow to stern, strangely, no customs agent boarded the US Sugar freighter. Mel and Keith rented a Fiat 500x Sport. They arrived at the docks, pulled out their CIA credentials, and the thorough inspection of Willy's boat and documents ended immediately.

The three men sat on a wooden bench on the wharf and kept a close eye on the freighter. But no one got off, nor did they even open the door! Two hours later, a large truck parked on the dock next to the ship. A cargo door on the freighter opened, and things were moved from the boat into the truck. Although they were using binoculars, Mel, Keith, and Willy could not determine what was being unloaded. Everything was in metal crates. One man exited the ship and got in the passenger seat of the Renault Premium 380DXi Pritsche.

They followed the truck through the maze of city streets that had no pattern to them whatsoever! Using the drone, Bushman Jack had been tracking the Renault, too, in case Mel lost the truck in the heavy traffic. It didn't take him long to determine where they were headed.

"Based on the roads they're traveling, the truck is probably going to Christopher Columbus' home," said Jack. "It looks like a new structure is being built behind the house. Just guessing, but I wouldn't doubt it's a new museum."

Willy, whose enormous body forced him to sit lengthwise across the backseat of the Fiat, let out a loud yelp. "That's it! Now it makes sense!"

Mel looked in the rearview mirror. "What makes sense?"

"Everything! Let the truck be. We need to go somewhere else."

Confused, Mel slammed on the brakes and pulled over to the curb. He and Keith looked at each other in bewilderment. Mel turned around to face Willy and asked, "And where would that somewhere else be, my friend?"

"Vatican City!"

*****

Eric felt minimal pressure during the final round of play at The Player's Championship. With a fifteen-stroke lead over his golf partner for the day, Rickie Fowler, he could afford a few bad shots. But deep down, he wanted to break the course record of sixty-three. Twice he tied it, and this would be his last chance.

After birdieing the first eight holes, the game and match were virtually over. Unless he hurt himself and had to withdraw, the tournament was his. But he could tell his balls were doing wacky things in the air and on the green. Eric didn't believe he was swinging all that well; however, his golf balls were ignorant of his beliefs. They stayed out of the mass of water and thick foliage and constantly landed on the fairway. The balls would start to fade but miraculously straighten themselves out.

Eric parred nine, ten, and fourteen. He birdied eleven, twelve, thirteen, fifteen, and sixteen. That's when he approached the infamous seventeenth hole. World-renowned golf course architect Pete Dye must have had a lapse of sanity when he sketched out the design for the par three signature hole! He created an island green that has become one of the most recognized in golf and been the doom and gloom for many players' hopes of winning!

The green is not only surrounded by water but also by stadium seats. Thousands of screaming fans add to the anxiety at the tee, where perfection is demanded to avoid penalties. A family of gators glide through the pond in hopes a Reddish Egret will decide to land to watch the show and become dinner for the reptiles.

With two holes to go, Eric was thirteen under par, and breaking the course record seemed in the bag. Rickie Fowler was shooting a fantastic round himself and was eight under par going on seventeen. Even though he was losing, Fowler was an excellent role model for sportsmanship! He had cheered and encouraged Eric the entire day after each of the teenager's shots.

Eric felt guilty he hadn't been a better sport. Winning the tournament by an unheard of twenty strokes would be gloating, something that appalled him! So he decided to show himself he could be a good sport, too. He would land his ball in the water, then hit another ball into the pond from the drop zone. With penalties, his next shot would be his fifth. Then Eric would purposely three-putt on the green for a quintuple bogey eight. If Rickie could somehow par the hole, they would be tied going onto the eighteenth. Then Eric could make sure he hit one more stroke than Fowler. Rickie would win the fourth round and feel good about his remarkable comeback, and Eric would feel good about being a good Christian! Sure, his dream of breaking the course record would end, but he believed it was the right thing to do. When the reporters congratulated him on winning

The Player's Championship, Eric would simply tell them Rickie Fowler was the better player!

Fowler had honors and teed off first. His ball landed on the edge of the green and rolled about fifteen feet from the cup. The fans applauded but were really waiting for Eric to complete his round with a record that might never be broken. Listed at 137 yards on the scorecard, seventeen required a carry of 132 yards to the front of the green, while it was 158 yards to the back edge. The wind was in his face, so the caddy pulled out a nine iron. Eric shook his head and asked for the wedge. His caddy approached and told him the wind would be a major factor and to use the nine iron. Eric smiled and grabbed the wedge from his bag.

He planned to have the ball land short into the water on both the tee and drop zone. Eric purposely lofted the ball high so the wind would blow it down, but something weird happened. The St. Max's Premium reached its peak, then pulled itself toward the green. Eric frowned as he watched the ball land on the green, take two bounces, and end up in the cup for a hole-in-one!

The crowd was so wild with excitement that even the gators perked up! Rickie Fowler ran over, lifted Eric off the ground, and gave him a huge hug! Oliver Harwas pounded the table in the sports bar in Vegas, spilling beer everywhere and shouting, "Yesssss! That's my main man!"

Eric smiled meekly but was frustrated deep down inside his soul as he walked to eighteen waving at the fans. How could that happen? Now he was fifteen under par and leading Fowler by seven strokes. He played the final hole without thinking about ball placement or clubs. The caddy would take care of that. He finished with a par giving him the new course record of fifty-seven!

After an hour of interviews where Eric claimed to fans worldwide he was just plain lucky, he made his way to the locker room. A few minutes later, he was swamped with hugs from Jim, Dora, Hugh Kraft, and Father Jacob, who, of course, had blessed the golf balls each day.

The headlines on the front page of Monday's *Palm Beach Post* read: *"Eric Mann—The Best Ever?"*

CHAPTER SIXTY

May 2015

Mel, Keith, and Willy slept on the jet at the Genoa airport. They needed to sell the yacht before they could travel to the Vatican, so on Sunday, they visited each boat dealer near the port. Three offers were on the table, and Mel chose the best one from Giuseppe Russo, owner of Nautica Russo, for $200,000. Now he really had some explaining to do, seeing he took a loss of $2.3 million on the sale. But Willy wasn't about to navigate the yacht back to America, so easy come, easy go.

For some reason, Willy wouldn't tell Mel and Keith why he wanted to go to the Vatican. All he would say is, "Trust me!" Mel did have faith in Willy's investigative skills, so he accepted those two words. However, Keith simply rolled his eyes and shook his head. Forever a naysayer!

Plans changed drastically when the three men awoke on Monday morning and heard the news that thirteen-year-old Eric Mann had shattered the TPC Sawgrass course record while dominating the tournament from start to finish.

"What the hell was Tommy thinking?!" screeched Mel as they listened to Hugh Kraft's interview being broadcast via sports networks around the globe. "He's going to ruin the integrity of the game! No legit player will ever be able to break Eric's record!"

"We need to do something," stated Keith firmly. "We've let this go on too far."

Mel paced the Citation's cabin, grimacing with disgust and disapproval. Finally, he plopped down on a couch and stared out the porthole in deep thought. "You're right, Keith. It's time to put an end to Eric Mann's heroics and arrest Tommy Williams. Hopefully, he can lead us to Jake Tassett!"

"I hate to state the obvious, but you realize there's a good chance Eric is knowingly involved in this racket," mentioned Keith. "I mean, how could he think he was good enough to win the Honda Classic, Masters, and TPC Sawgrass at his age?! Come on! Really?!"

Shockingly, Willy jumped up from his seat, grabbed Keith's shirt with his fists, and slammed the CIA agent to the floor. While Keith was opening and closing his eyes to regain focus, Willy kneeled on his upper torso to prevent him from moving. Then, purposely mustering as much spittle as he could salivate, Willy leaned his head down a few inches from Keith's face. "Eric wouldn't do that! Do you understand me? Eric would not be part of a fraudulent crime! I dare say the boy has a moral uprightness ten times what you have!"

With that, Mel pulled Willy off Keith and asked, "Why won't you tell us why we need to go to the Vatican?! Does it have something to do with Eric?"

"Because I'm a trained officer of the law. I believe I have the answer, but I don't want to say anything until we get there."

"Why not?! Wouldn't it make more sense for the three of us to mull over what you're thinking and brainstorm solutions?!"

"I'm not sure."

Keith stood up, brushed himself off, then howled, "You're not sure! Why not, you foolish dimwit?!"

Willy looked at Mel and then at Keith. "Because I'm not sure you two aren't rogue CIA agents who are in cahoots with Tommy Williams. I dealt with two CIA agents back in the eighties who were con artists!"

"Okay, Willy, how fast you forget," said Mel bluntly. "We saved your life out at Plana Cay. However, I'm not getting into that again. Keith and I are heading back to Palm Beach. You're welcome to come along, or you can find your own way to the Vatican. But let me assure you if we find Eric was involved in defrauding the PGA, he will be arrested."

Willy didn't respond or even glance at Mel and Keith. He strutted down the gangplank, walked into the airport, and rented a Citroen C4 hatchback. It would take him about five hours to travel the 315 miles, which should give him enough time to plan exactly what he would say and ask. But one thing was bothering him the most.

Would the pope even give him an audience?

*****

"Twenty-five million euros, Dad. That's the best they would offer." Jimmy Tassett was standing in the street so he could talk privately on his cell phone.

"Take it. Our overseas assets are frozen, and I closed our American bank account today to be on the safe side. I'll open a new account soon with an investment firm and text you the online number where they can wire the funds directly. Once it clears the books, I will also close that account. Any questions, Jimmy?"

"Nope, I think I understand. I'll wait for your text."

The call ended as it usually did between Jimmy and Jake Tassett—no thank you, goodbye, or have an enjoyable day! Just a simple "Call Ended" on the iPhone. Jimmy never knew where he stood with his father.

CHAPTER SIXTY-ONE

May 2015

CIA Director John Barrett touched down at the North Palm Beach County Airport five minutes after Mel and Keith landed. Over the Mediterranean Sea, Mel radioed his boss and asked for a meeting in Palm Beach Gardens. He wanted to show Barrett the apartments next to St. Max's Church. Mel also asked his boss to bring a federal search warrant for Tommy Williams' office. They met at a card table in the back of the hangar. Mel thoroughly presented his case to Barrett.

"Okay, Mel, I need to make a decision. And by the way, when this is all over, we'll discuss why you purchased a yacht for $2.5 million without my approval." Barrett smiled slightly and winked at him. Mel let out a sigh of relief!

"What options are you pondering," asked Keith. "Perhaps we can guide you in the right direction."

"If I need your navigation, I'll ask for it!" snapped Barrett. Keith lowered his head.

Barrett continued, "The quandary here is Eric. He's a thirteen-year-old youngster who may be caught in the middle of all this. The way I see it, there's a chance, a small one at that, that the kid didn't know anything about the planacalum, magnetized golf cups, or rigged balls. But if we charge him and we're wrong, we'll totally ruin his life. Sure, he'll never golf again, but he will be marked a fraud for as long as he lives. Eric will be the butt of jokes for many years to come."

"The kid had to know!" blurted Keith. "Even he could see his ball move this way and that way while it straightened out and landed perfectly on the fairways. And how many one-putts did he have?!"

Barrett glared at Keith. "How about you sit back and let me talk this through? I assure you, I'll ask for your input if I need it!"

Keith dropped his head again. "Yes, sir. Sorry!"

"Okay, we need to interview Eric. We can do that later today. Obviously, his parents will need to be present." Barrett pointed at Keith and said, "You will let his dad know to have a lawyer present, but you WILL NOT tell him why. Is that understood?!"

"Yes, sir!"

"Next, I have a search warrant for Tommy Williams' apartment. The three of us will go over the place tooth and nail. Confiscate the computer system, video equipment, and any other electronic devices that appear to be evidence. If Tommy is in the apartment, we'll arrest him first. If he's not there, we will arrest him later. No one must see us. Do you follow me?!"

"Yes, boss," replied Mel, "but I'm not sure why."

"Some, or all, of the church members who live in the apartments and work in the factory could be involved in this. We don't want to spook them so they will run."

"What about Father Jacob? Shouldn't we tell him?"

"Later. There's no reason to worry him until we know more. Now, make sure your weapons are hidden, and let's get over to Tommy's place."

*****

"There's nothing in here!" howled Mel. "No furniture, no computer or video equipment, nothing in the fridge!"

"And no Tommy Williams," added John Barrett sarcastically. "I thought you worked closely with him. Why didn't you know he was leaving?!"

"Someone tipped him off!" replied Mel, his face red with embarrassment. "It had to be someone who knew we were chasing that freighter. We told Tommy we were going to Bermuda on vacation. He must have figured out we were lying and put two and two together!"

"Who knew about your Europe trip?"

"No one!" Mel paused a few seconds in thought. "Okay, wait a minute. Bushman Jack knew. He was operating the drone and updating us on the ship's location. But Bushman wouldn't tip off Tommy. He was playing it straight—I swear!"

"How about Eric Mann or Hugh Kraft? Did they know?"

"No! No way we would have told them!"

Mel paced the empty apartment, then looked in closets and cabinets for anything Tommy may have left behind. Barrett stared out the window at the building used as a factory to make St. Max's golf balls. A few minutes later, Tommy walked into the apartment and smiled as Mel and Barrett grabbed their pistols and aimed them at Williams.

Director Barrett didn't waste time or ask questions. "You're under arrest, Mr. Williams. You have—"

Tommy laughed and cut him off. "For what? I've done nothing wrong!"

"Do you know how many guilty criminals I've brought to justice in my life who've said the exact same words? Yep, like all of them! Right now, you're under arrest for fraud. Once we find a connection between you and Jake Tassett, expect more charges to follow. In the meantime, you have the right to an attorney and to remain silent. Do you understand, or would you like me to clarify it?"

Barrett approached Tommy with handcuffs. He stopped in his tracks when a voice behind him shouted, "Hold on! Those cuffs aren't going on Tommy's wrists! Nope, nada!"

Barrett and Mel quickly turned around. Keith was pointing a Glock Nineteen at them.

"But I'm sure they will fit just fine on your wrists!"

Tommy approached and cuffed Mel and Barrett to each other. Then he stepped backward and looked them over as if they were clothing in a men's store. He turned to Keith and chortled, "What should we do with these two has beens?!"

CHAPTER SIXTY-TWO

May 2015

Willy dropped his car off at Rome's Fiumicino Airport and took the train to Roma Termini. He wasn't about to try and conquer the crazy traffic of the Eternal City! He found a business center in Rome's rail station and rented a computer and printer for an hour.

Willy searched his own name on Wikipedia and found a three-page biography for a time in his life he wished he could forget. He printed out the article, folded it, and then stuffed it in his front pocket. It was his only chance to possibly get an audience with the pope!

Willy flagged down a cab and asked to be dropped off at Castel Sant'Angelo. That way, he could be genuinely absorbed in the moment. As he strolled down Via Della Conciliazione to St. Peter's Square, he paused to take in the breathtaking site before him—St. Peter's Basilica, the largest church in the world and the final resting place of the great apostle for whom it's named. Goosebumps popped up all over his skin. Most of his friends didn't know the big fella was an art enthusiast. He wasn't sure it was a macho hobby for a man his size. But he really didn't care all that much. He read many books on art history and would sneak away to museums whenever he could get the chance.

As Willy entered the square, he was in awe of the numerous columns and pilasters flanking the colonnades. Above the columns, Willy stopped to count the 140 statues of saints created by Bernini's students. He was amazed by the obelisk and the two fountains in the center of the square. He remembered from his readings that the obelisk was carried to Rome from Egypt in 1586.

Willy crossed his arms and gazed at the spectacular St. Peter's Basilica. He seemed to become frozen in time. Before him stood the headquarters of the Catholic Church, and to the side, Pope Francis' residence.

Finally, he ascended the marble steps and entered the cathedral through the grand, holy doors. Built during the Renaissance period, the magnificence of the basilica was created by the hands of tremendous artists such as Bramante, Michelangelo, Bernini, and Maderno. Those lucky enough to roam the foyer and see the chapels are taken on a journey through history, artistry, craftsmanship, hope, truth, and otherworldliness. Willy cried and muttered a short prayer as he admired Michelangelo's Pietá.

He longed to visit the Vatican Museum and behold the glorious Sistine Chapel, but that's not why he came here. Willy knew it would be a challenge to speak to the pope, and he was right. The Pontifical Swiss Guards chuckled at his request and pointed to the exit. Willy walked and strolled around St. Peter's Square until an idea occurred to him.

Pope Francis was world-renowned for his charity. He had dedicated his life to ending extreme poverty and providing for victims of natural disasters. Perhaps this could be Willy's foot in the door.

The pope had just established a new office called the Dicastery for Charity Services, better known in Italy as Elemosineria Apostolica. It was the Holy See's special office for charity enterprises serving the poorest and most disadvantaged people on earth. Willy walked into the office, showed the secretary his Wikipedia biography, and said he represented a philanthropist from America who wanted to donate a billion dollars to the pope's charity fund. He hoped lightning wouldn't strike him for his little white lie!

Sure enough, the secretary perked up when she began to read his biography. She looked at his picture and nodded. She could see the resemblance from a photo taken in the eighties. Wow! Sitting in front of her was perhaps the greatest American hero ever! She was speechless.

In English, which was her second language, the secretary stated the obvious, “Ah, er, you are no longer a police officer, Mr. Banks.”

Willy shook his head no. She hadn’t asked a question, so he decided to wait until she did.

“What do you do now, sir? Are you all over the history books? Do kids learn about you in the United States?”

“Yes, ma’am, I guess they do. But I quit law enforcement a few years ago. Now I am an agent for millionaires who want to give to charity to help the poor and homeless.” Willy paused a moment for it to sink in. Then, not knowing what to say next, he lied again. “Not only do I represent the rich people, but I also represent churches that want to provide aid to the poor. As a matter of fact, I’m working with St. Max’s Catholic Church in Florida. You may have heard of them, too. They started a company that manufactures golf balls, and all the proceeds go to helping the poor and homeless. Their balls are being used by Eric—”

The secretary cut Willy off. “What?! St. Max’s Church?! Just a minute, Mr. Banks. Please wait here!” She stood up quickly and ran down the hallway. Willy wasn’t sure what he said, but maybe now he was only a few minutes away from visiting with Pope Francis in person! OMG!!

*****

Meeting Pope Francis didn’t happen. But when he shook hands with Archbishop Milo Guidan, Willy knew it was the next best thing! Something was up. He felt it in his bones. Bishop Guidan was the pope’s personal advisor and head of the Dicastery. He motioned for Willy to come to his office.

Willy had barely plunged into the thick leather chair in front of the archbishop’s desk when Guidan asked him a perplexing question. “My secretary says you represent St. Max’s Church in Florida. May I ask how involved you are with them?”

“I guess you might say I’m a parish member.”

“What do you mean by ‘I guess?’”

“Okay, so I go to church at St. Max’s. But I’m not Catholic.”

"So, I assume your wife or significant other is Catholic?"

"I'm not married. You might say my significant other is my brother, Otis. We live together. I'm a park ranger in South Florida."

"Do you know, or have you met Bishop O'Bailey?"

"Bishop who?"

"O'Bailey. He oversees your congregation."

"Really? We pray for Bishop Bob Kaiser during the service. I thought he was our bishop!"

"Mr. Banks, may I call you Willy?"

"Yes, by all means! Please do!"

"Okay, thanks. Willy, there's something I need for this meeting to continue." Archbishop Guidan stood, and out of respect, so did Willy. "If you don't mind, I'll be right back."

"Yes, sir."

The archbishop moved swiftly to the door and down the hallway. Willy was confused. There were many things he wanted to get off his chest, but it seemed the feelings were mutual.

CHAPTER SIXTY-THREE

May 2015

Willy almost collapsed when the archbishop reentered the office. Moving slowly in front of Guidan was the supreme pontiff, the highest priest of the entire Catholic religious order! Pope Francis was rarely seen without his coat of arms or white cassock. However, today he wore a white, button-down short-sleeve shirt under a red sweater and a pair of khaki dress pants. The light sweater had frayed edges, and the color of his pants had faded from umpteen washes. Willy remembered Francis grew up in poverty and shunned excess, and after looking at him today, he knew the Holy See was a man of conviction who truly walked the talk!

Having no clue about proper decorum when addressing the pope, Willy genuflected to show respect. Pope Francis approached and gave Willy a warm hug, then stepped back and said, "Bless you, my son."

"Thank you, Your Holiness."

"I have read all about your heroics, Willy. As rector of the Colegio de San José in the early eighties, my students were assigned to interpret the historical impact the events in Florida created for the rest of the world. I also prayed daily for the victims of the incomprehensible airplane disasters. Today, I believe your visit was an act of the angels as Archbishop Milo and I have been contemplating how to proceed with St. Max's Church."

"How to proceed? I don't understand, Holy Father."

"The archbishop will explain." The pope motioned to the leather couch in the back of the room. "I will sit there and listen."

"Please, Your Holiness. Please take my chair." Willy backed away from the comfortable chair in front of Archbishop Guidan's desk.

"No, thank you, son. I just want to be a fly on the wall, so to say." He smiled, sat on the couch, then winked at Guidan.

"Willy, we need you to sign this form before we begin. It's a legal document saying nothing discussed in this room will ever be repeated to anyone: Not to clergy, law enforcement, news reporters, or even your next-door neighbor, without the Holy Father's approval. And we will reciprocate the order, as well."

"I'm not sure why all the secrecy, but I will gladly sign the form so we can begin." Willy scratched his name quickly and handed it back to the archbishop.

Pausing to formulate his thoughts, Guidan shuffled through some papers on his desk. Then he looked at Willy and said with a serious tone, "Earlier, you mentioned you prayed for Bishop Bob during your church service. Is that correct?"

"Yes, sir. Why?"

"Well, I'll get right to the point. Bishop Bob Kaiser is no longer the ecclesiastical dignitary of your diocese."

"Eccle—what? Sorry, I didn't understand that term."

"I'm talking about the chief pastor of your diocese."

"Okay, well, I never knew the man anyway. Perhaps you can tell me more."

"Bishop Kaiser was recently removed from his position. Actually, he has been excommunicated from the Catholic church. To cut to the chase, he was misappropriating money."

It didn't take Willy long to perceive what the archbishop was probably talking about. He spent many hours the past few years wondering about church finances. "Let me guess. Does this have anything to do with the Catholic Charities Foundation?"

Archbishop Guidan perked up. "What do you know about the Catholic Charities Foundation?"

"Well, a lot, you might say. It is one of the reasons I'm here today. Indirectly, I should say. The Catholic Charities Foundation was used to pay for St. Max's School, which included buying a bus and providing clothing and supplies to the school kids. The foundation also subsidized the apartment complex for poor church members and then the golf ball business. It seemed the fund was a bottomless pit! I'm sure you know about all of that, though. Right?"

Hesitantly, Archbishop Guidan responded. "There's no such thing as the Catholic Charities Foundation approved by the Vatican. There is an organization called Catholic Charities USA, but not Foundation."

"Huh. I don't understand. Then how was all that stuff paid for?"

"We're just in the initial phase of our investigation. Bishop Brian O'Bailey replaced Bishop Kaiser a few weeks ago. However, Father James Nealy, a retired priest from Canada, handles all the paperwork within the diocese. You see, O'Bailey is not a real bishop. He's a private investigator from Dublin, Ireland. We placed him in that position after he told us what happened in St. Patrick's Cathedral." The archbishop stopped speaking. He wasn't sure he should say anymore.

"What took place?!" Curiosity was killing Willy!

Archbishop Guidan glanced at Pope Francis, who nodded. "For one month, Bishop Kaiser falsely claimed he was sent by Pope Francis to Ireland's national cathedral to raise money for the poor and homeless people on the Aran Islands, and to build them a massive church on top of the cliffs of the Dún Aonghasa stone fort. Kaiser claimed anyone who donated 100,000 euros to the cause would have a private audience and blessing with the pope here at the Vatican. The Holy Father knew nothing of it. The wealthy folks of Dublin gladly pitched in, and the money was funneled to the Catholic Charities Foundation, which we found had a registered offshore bank account in Nassau, Bahamas.

"After a month of raising millions of euros, Kaiser moved on to Madrid, Spain, and lied about funds going toward a church for the poor and homeless somewhere along the Camino de Santiago. According to Kaiser's propaganda, folks on their pilgrimage to Santiago de Compostela could spend a night there and worship. Once again, donators were promised an audience with Pope Francis, and obviously, the Holy See knew nothing about it.

"Anyway, several people who were bilked in Dublin complained to authorities, and Brian O'Bailey came to visit us. We washed our hands of Kaiser and asked the detective if he would work undercover for us in America. After approval from his bosses in Ireland, Brian accepted the temporary position. His first assignment was to take over Kaiser's office and see what he could find in the files.

"We didn't hear from O'Bailey until last night. He reported to my secretary that he was suspicious of unusual activities taking place at St. Max's Parish in Palm Beach. For instance, they are manufacturing golf balls and selling them. My secretary told me what O'Bailey said this morning, and I immediately relayed the information to the Holy Father. And now you're here, Willy, telling us you have concerns about St. Max's Church. That is quite a coincidence, wouldn't you say?!"

"Yes, sir, no doubt about it! Have you had time to research anything O'Bailey told you?"

"Just one thing. And this may come as a surprise to you."

"What's that?!" Willy was on pins and needles with anxiety.

"According to our records, a Catholic church in Florida called St. Max does not exist!"

CHAPTER SIXTY-FOUR

May 2015

"Why did you come to us?" asked Pope Francis politely from the leather couch.

Willy struggled to find comfort in his chair. He wrestled with his conscience about how to tell the leaders of the Catholic religion what he knew. Mainly, how would this affect young Eric Mann? He believed the boy to be innocent, but he wasn't sure. Regardless, the teenager was a good person, as were his dad and mom.

"I think I need to start at the beginning, if you don't mind?"

"We wouldn't have it any other way," replied Archbishop Guidan. "My secretary is rearranging our appointments as we speak." Both Guidan and Pope Francis started taking notes on clipboards.

Willy cleared his throat and began. "I am the South Florida director of the United States Fish and Wildlife Service. In the early 2000s, I hired Jim Mann to work for me to repair hiking trails in the Loxahatchee Slough near Palm Beach. He, his wife Dora, and son, Eric, were homeless and living in a beat-up car in the park, and I wanted to help them the best I could."

"You are a blessing to humanity!" offered Pope Francis. Archbishop Guidan smiled and nodded.

"Thank you, Your Excellency, but I'm far from who I wish to be. You see, I should have known."

"Known what, Willy," asked Guidan.

"St. Max's Church was built inside an airplane hangar at the North Palm Beach County Airport. Then, an apartment complex was constructed next door for church members to live, seeing they were either homeless or on the verge of homelessness. Finally, another hangar was purchased and converted into a golf ball factory. All of this was supposedly paid for by the Catholic Charities Foundation. I suspected for years the fund didn't have enough money to support all of that. Then, to top it off, my brother and I were sent to deliver newly packaged balls to our distributor, Golf Country Superstore, in various cities, ending in San Francisco. When our truck broke down in New Mexico on the way home, we abandoned it. A few weeks later, a new one was purchased; thanks again to the Foundation!"

This time, the archbishop glanced at the Holy See, and both were shocked. "So, Bishop Kaiser built a church, apartments, and a factory using this money! I wonder why?"

"It takes money to make money, sir. You see, the contract with Golf Country Superstore was large. However, that's not how the parish made most of their money."

"Please, go on."

Willy wanted to leave. Perhaps, he shouldn't have come. This needed to end, and he couldn't do that without mentioning Eric's participation. "Jim Mann's son, Eric, has become world famous as a teenage professional golf prodigy. He is—"

The archbishop interrupted, "Yes, by all means, the entire planet has heard of Eric Mann! Most importantly, we learned he donates his winnings to the church for aiding the poor and homeless!"

"Are you aware of the church he donates to?"

The archbishop stood abruptly and strutted to the window. He was beginning to see the whole picture. "Let me guess. St. Max's Catholic Church?! We read that it was a Catholic parish, but we didn't research any further! As a matter of fact, His Holiness was going to send the boy a plaque with a letter of thanks from the Vatican for his selflessness! Being busy here, we just hadn't gotten around to doing it."

Willy then told about Plana Cay, planacalum, and Tommy Williams' setup inside the apartments. He thoroughly explained how the doctored St. Max's Premium golf balls and golf cups for the greens were manufactured and how the balls were magnetically attracted to the cups. He mentioned Mel Smith and Keith Malone were CIA agents who were about to arrest Tommy Williams.

"And now all that I told you brings me to why I came to the Vatican today. Mr. Smith and Mr. Malone knew I was coming here, but I didn't tell them why. I wanted to be certain before I put anyone in harm's way with the law, and I knew the truth would be in the Vatican records."

"What is it you're not telling us, Willy?"

"After I escaped from the storage room in the Plana Cay factory, I saw an employee who appeared to be the boss. At least he was supervising by checking out each room. I hid, and he didn't see me. Later, Mr. Smith told me the man in charge was Jimmy Tassett. In the 1980s, Jimmy's father, Jake, was part of the conspiracy to take over America by downing jets in Florida. Jake Tassett was the National Transportation Safety Board Lead Investigator at the time. He escaped the United States with Judge Maximillian Boone, a corrupt magistrate from Okeechobee County. To make a long story short, we believe Jake Tassett is alive and well and funding the St. Max's golf ball project."

"So, ex-Bishop Kaiser had several forms of revenue! Interesting!" The Archbishop put down his clipboard and pulled a tape recorder from his desk. "Do you mind if I use this? I don't want to miss anything."

Willy nodded his head. "Anyway, we heard Jimmy and the other workers on Plana Cay were rescued by an eastbound freighter, but after checking the registration, we found it was an unknown ship disguised to look like it was owned by the US Sugar Corporation. Using a CIA jet and an oceangoing yacht, we followed the freighter to Genoa. Then it dawned on me what the cargo was being shipped: Christopher Columbus relics obtained on Plana Cay. During our two visits there, we found actual items from his first sailing across the Atlantic. We believe the uncharted Plana

Cay island was where Columbus first landed in the new world. Over the years, I think the relics were periodically moved to a storage location in South Florida. And after Plana Cay was blown up, they were placed on the freighter and shipped to Genoa."

Willy paused to give the archbishop and Pope Francis a moment to digest the story. "This is all quite complex, Willy! But I'm still unsure why you needed our help here at the Vatican."

"Tassett's financial assets have been frozen by the CIA in America and throughout the world. We believe the Columbus relics were being sold to a new museum in Columbus' home city to keep him and his criminal organization solvent. It was when they were unloading the cargo at the museum that a vision slapped me in the face, and I had a hunch I figured everything out. But I needed someone here at the Vatican to confirm my suspicion."

"Well, go ahead. What is your intuition?"

"Jimmy Tassett. And from what I remember about his father, Jake Tassett."

Archbishop Guidan stood up again. He was perplexed. "What about Jimmy and Jake Tassett?!"

"They both look very much like St. Max's priest, Father Jacob."

*****

Willy wiggled restlessly in his leather chair while Archbishop Guidan pulled records from a large oak file cabinet in the corner of his office. Pope Francis remained speechless but was scribbling something frantically on his clipboard.

Guidan sat back down at his desk and formed a tent with his hands. "Just as we don't have diocese approval for St. Max's Church, we also don't have an ordained priest named Jacob in Florida. The closest one is Father Jacob Keating in North Carolina. He has been in Charlotte for many years, and His Holiness knows him personally."

"How could this happen, Milo?" asked Pope Francis calmly to his right-hand man.

"I'm not sure, Your Holiness. We place a lot of trust in our bishops to oversee their diocese. Bishop Kaiser obviously fooled us. Going forward, I will ensure our staff scrutinizes every parish throughout the world. This will never happen again!"

Pope Francis didn't respond verbally. He smiled and nodded, then gave Willy another hug before leaving. The big man dropped to one knee and bowed his head in respect.

"I would like to keep in touch with you, Willy," said Archbishop Guidan. "We will thoroughly investigate all of this, and we may need your help down the road. Is there anything we can do before you leave?"

Willy read between the lines and assumed the meeting was over. "Yes. Just one thing. Please don't move forward with your investigation until the FBI has had the chance to arrest Father Jacob—I mean Jake Tassett. If he caught wind of this, he would be gone in a heartbeat!"

"Yes, of course. Lest you forget, we signed an agreement to that effect. When the arrest is completed, please inform us immediately."

Archbishop Guidan walked Willy to the exit and shook hands. Despite his lifelong desire to visit the Vatican Museum, Trevi Fountain, and the Colosseum, Willy hailed a taxi to Fiumicino Airport. He had about twelve hours to come up with a game plan. Father Jacob was highly respected by the parish, and this news would come as a shock to everyone!

CHAPTER SIXTY-FIVE

May 2015

"This is the earliest I could get here, sorry!" huffed Pete Burns, out of breath. He had sprinted from the taxi to the clubhouse at TPC Sawgrass. An hour earlier, Pete's personal pilot had landed the corporate jet at the Northeast Florida Regional airport near St. Augustine.

"Actually, I appreciate you coming so fast!" exclaimed Karl Ballontine, manager of the country club. "Our groundskeepers just found them today when they were repositioning the holes on the greens." Karl passed one of the eighteen golf cups to the PGA Chief Executive Officer.

Pete scrutinized the cup and weighed it with both hands. "Same damn cup!" He looked at Ballontine and scolded, "Didn't you have security guards hired around the clock for The Players Championship last weekend?!"

"Yes, sir, we certainly did. They didn't see anyone all night long."

Pete paused to organize his thoughts. "Okay, sorry, I snapped. This is a very stressful situation. And very dangerous! I believe these cups contain explosives. Please clear the clubhouse while I call the FBI!"

Karl hustled all the employees and customers out, put a closed sign on the door, and used his cell phone to call the upcoming golfers who had tee times to notify them the course would be temporarily shut down.

*****

FBI Agent Cory Jones arrived at Sawgrass two hours later. He had been working in the Orlando office when the call from Burns came in. With lights flashing and siren wailing in his Ford Expedition, Jones scurried up I-4 and I-95 with the accelerator buried most of the time. Suspecting the golf cups were loaded with explosives, he deemed this a national emergency!

Ten agents and a bomb squad from the Jacksonville office met Jones upon arrival. The cups were carefully placed inside a protective solid-plate steel container that was towed behind the bomb squad's van. Quickly, the team of experts moved the cups to a safe room located on the Mayport Naval Station grounds, which was wholly waterproof and radiation-resistant. Navy explosives experts offered to assist the FBI with the golf cup dissection.

After four hours of examination, Lieutenant Commander Paul Dow entered the conference room with the FBI's bomb squad to discuss the findings with the FBI agents and Pete Burns.

The Navy lieutenant was holding a cut-up golf cup in one hand. "We found no explosive material," stated Dow, seriously. "There is an unknown substance enclosed inside the base of the cup, but it didn't react to heat, acid, or other chemicals. However, the substance is extremely, and I mean extremely, ferromagnetic! Let me show you."

Dow laid the cup on the floor by a wall. He walked to the opposite wall fifty feet away and removed a nickel from his pocket. He lifted the coin above his head so everyone could see it.

"Now, I'm going to flip this nickel up in the air like we were having a coin toss at the start of a football game or something. In case you don't know, a nickel is only twenty-five percent nickel, which is a magnetic metal. The other seventy-five percent is copper, which isn't ferromagnetic. What I'm trying to say is there's only a small amount of magnetic material in this coin. But watch what happens."

Dow flipped the nickel two feet above his head, and nothing happened. The coin fell to the floor.

"Huh? What's that supposed to prove?" asked Jones inquisitively.

"It proves that the magnetic material in the golf cup needs to be activated." Dow walked back to the other wall and grabbed the cup. He showed the agents and Burns the electric wires wrapped around the cylinder, as well as the tiny battery and minuscule computer chip. Pointing to the battery and chip, Dow said, "The energy in this thing is released remotely. In other words, the battery is turned on and off by someone who controls it from a distance. For the sake of this experiment, I will hook up the electric wires to one of my batteries."

Everyone in the room was startled by what happened next. As soon as Dow touched the electric wire to a live battery, paper clips flew from a desk in the corner and clung to the golf cup. But even more incredibly, staples were ejected from a stapler and shot across the room like bullets!

Dow then walked back to the far wall and flipped the nickel once again. This time, in midair, the coin zipped across the room and stuck to the golf cup. The observers' mouths were wide open, and there was stunned silence. Everyone was too shocked to speak!

Dow broke the quiet with a statement that intrigued all who were present. "Remember, the coin is only twenty-five percent magnetic. Same with the paper clips and staples. Both are steel-centered but covered with a non-magnetic zinc alloy. Now watch this."

The lieutenant removed a small amount of the unknown substance from the base of the golf cup. He rolled it in a ball and covered it with Kleenex tissue, then put Scotch tape on the Kleenex to keep it from coming off. Dow then walked back to the far wall and placed the wadded ball on the ground. Surprising no one at this juncture, the ball rolled across the floor and into the cup that was lying on its side, already full of paper clips, staples, and a nickel coin!

"What the—?" expressed Burns. His brain was spinning out of control!

Agent Jones nodded as if he could read Burns' mind. "Are you thinking what I'm thinking?"

Burns paused momentarily, almost afraid to say it. "If a golf ball was made from that unknown substance, it would be attracted to the golf cup.

A person with a remote could turn the magnet on and control the trajectory of the ball both in the air and on the ground!" Burns paced briskly across the room, shaking his head no. He was thinking about Scotland's Old Course at St. Andrews and, of course, the Honda Classic, the Masters, and the Players Championship. Rhetorically, Burns asked the question everyone wanted to know, "What does this mean?"

Agent Jones frowned and lowered his head, "It means I need to put out an arrest warrant for Eric Mann and Hugh Kraft."

CHAPTER SIXTY-SIX

May 2015

"Has the money been wired?" asked Jimmy Tassett to Stefano Marco, the Chief Executive Officer of Historical Galleries International, the private company that owned the Christopher Columbus Birthplace and Museum.

"No, sir. We agreed on Friday. We will complete your transaction once our holding company deposits the funds into our account.

"I've had a change of heart. I would like to keep the relics for myself. You may display them here free of charge for a year, then I will rent them to you for future years."

"That's not what we agreed on, Mr. Tassett!" Marco was upset HGI might not retain ownership. He knew twenty-five million euros was a steal for what he was getting. Customers paid thirty-five euros to get into the museum, and there was always a steady stream of visitors. Marco also charged five euros to park and averaged an additional twenty euros per customer in the souvenir shop. The twenty-five-million-euro price tag for the ancient artifacts Tassett brought in would be paid off in a year or two.

"According to Italian law, the items are mine until the cash disbursement occurs. Now, if you want to keep them free for a year and then rent them from me after that, I will leave them here. If not, I will load them up in my truck and haul them away. Which is it?"

Marco was stuck between a rock and a hard place. By displaying the relics free for a year, his income would still grow. But he didn't like the idea of a loan for future years. Perhaps Tassett would change his mind after twelve months and sell them to HGI. "Okay, have it your way, Mr. Tassett. We'll keep them here for a year while you work out the loan terms beyond that!"

"Good choice, Mr. Marco. I need to photograph and inventory my artifacts before I leave."

Marco nodded and said, "Go for it."

Jimmy wandered around the museum with the cell phone's camera. When his father and his friend, Judge Maxiillian Boone, arrived on the uncharted Plana Cay island, they found a manor house built sometime in the late fifteenth century. Judge Boone held both a law and an archeology degree from the University of Florida. The judge was a master at carbon dating, and it was Boone who determined the relics were from Columbus' first voyage. Apparently, Columbus had planned to eventually live on Plana Cay, and so he built a home on the island and filled it with items that were onboard the Nina, the Pinta, and the Santa Maria ships.

As Jimmy snapped pictures, he felt a sense of reverence for the array of antiquities before him. There was a well-trodden oak admiral's desk, fifteenth-century paintings, and various medieval marble, bronze, and wood statues. Columbus' coat-of-arms was lying on top of an oversized chest of drawers, and inside were silk religious vestments embroidered with gold. On a shelf in a closet were robes with skull-and-crossbones used as funeral garments for all of Columbus' crew who didn't survive the trip across the Atlantic.

King Ferdinand and Queen Isabella of Spain sponsored Columbus in his pursuit to find a westerly route to China and India. However, the monarchy would only agree if Columbus spread Christianity along the way. Thus, Columbus carried a variety of precious religious items to use for trading. Jimmy photographed a silver reliquary that contained two pieces from the cross of Jesus certified for authenticity by a Spanish bishop.

Twenty minutes later, Jimmy finished his photography and flipped through the pictures to ensure he had recorded all his possessions.

Technically, they were his father's chattel, but Jimmy tried to scratch that from his mind. He would need to come up with some kind of falsehood to tell his dad when the money wasn't wired into his father's investment account on Friday.

Or, perhaps, it was time to finally leave Jake Tassett once and for all. And, of course, that meant finding a permanent hiding place!

*****

The hangar that was converted into St. Max's golf ball factory was locked. There was a note on the door giving all employees the rest of the week off because of the hard work they had put in. It even had a complimentary close. Not "Sincerely" or "Best Wishes," but simply "Vacation Time!" It was signed by Tommy Williams.

Most of the parish workers began grumbling. First, many had kids still in school, so they couldn't do anything with their families. Second, none of them earned and saved enough money to go anywhere. They decided to see if Father Jacob would conduct a Bible session. When they got to the church, there was a note on the front entry doors: *Dear Parishioners – I have been invited to a religious conference out of state. Unfortunately, we will need to cancel church services for the rest of this week and next week. God bless you all! Father Jacob.*

"I've never heard of canceling a Catholic mass," stated Sue Carson disappointedly. "Don't they usually find a substitute, like a retired priest or someone?"

"Yes, Sue, you're right," replied Chris Johnson. "But I know there is a shortage of priests right now."

The group dispersed. Some went back to their apartments to read, some decided to take a hike in the Loxahatchee Slough, and a couple drove to Walmart for groceries. Bob Butler and Jim Mann decided to play cribbage in Bob's apartment. By habit, Butler briefly checked the security video cameras.

"Holy cow!" shouted Jim as he gazed at one of the computer screens. "Tommy, Mel, Keith, and some other dude are talking to someone out front of Mel's airplane hangar."

"What's so surprising about that?" asked Jim softly. "That's where Mel and Keith keep their cars."

"No, no, no! Not them. It's the person they're talking to, and rather vehemently, I might add. They are definitely arguing about something! The screen is a little bit hazy, but I'm sure I know that man!"

"Well, who is it?!" Jim stayed put in his chair and shuffled the deck of cards.

"Come over here and look, Jim! I swear it's Deacon Ollie!"

Jim let out a small chuckle. "You're seeing things, my friend. Deacon Ollie is dead."

*****

Ten minutes later, Mel lifted the Citation X gently off the North Palm Beach County Airport runway. Keith was sitting in the copilot's chair, pointing a gun at him. According to the rapidly-filed flight plan, the jet would be touching down three hours later in Minot, North Dakota. In the cabin, CIA Director John Barrett was sitting cross-legged, chained to the fuselage floor.

Tommy Williams was chatting with the man next to him who looked just like recently deceased Deacon Ollie.

CHAPTER SIXTY-SEVEN

May 2015

The FBI could have waited a half hour until school was out, but Cory Jones wanted to make a statement. He, and four other agents, burst into Dora Mann's classroom at 3:00 pm with their pistols out of their holsters. They hustled to where Eric Mann was reading the assigned pages in his science textbook and surrounded him.

"What are you doing?!" screeched Dora. She wasn't sure if the men wearing FBI windbreakers were legitimate agents or fakes who disguised themselves to kidnap Eric.

Jones flashed his badge at Dora, then ordered Eric to stand up. His arms were pulled behind his back and handcuffs snapped onto his wrists. The students in the class were silent and flabbergasted as Jones read Eric his Miranda rights and said he was under arrest for fraud and extortion. As they led Eric to the FBI van, Jones gave Dora a business card with the address to the holding cell in West Palm Beach where her son would be taken.

Eric cried throughout the process. He had no idea what was happening, but he remained respectful to the agents. "Please, sir, what did I do wrong?" he muttered softly. His face was deep red with embarrassment. What were his friends thinking?!

Dora didn't know what to do. She couldn't let the kids leave school early without notifying their parents. She had one student go and try to find her husband, Jim. Using the classroom phone, she called Hugh Kraft's cell phone. There was no answer, so she tried to call Willy Banks at home. Otis answered and said his brother was in Europe somewhere. Dora asked Otis if he would run over to Hugh Kraft's house and see if he was home.

Ten minutes later, Otis called back, huffing and puffing from running. "Oh my God, Miss Dora! The FBI is at Mr. Kraft's house, and they got him in cuffs. What did he do, ma'am?! Do you know?!"

"Sorry, Otis. I don't know anything. But thanks for checking." She hung up as the bell rang for dismissal.

The stunned students hustled to their apartments. None could wait to tell mom and dad about Eric's arrest! Jim Mann caught wind of what happened and sprinted to Dora's classroom.

"What's going on?!" yelled Jim as he ran and hugged Dora.

"I have no idea! But we need to find a lawyer fast. Do you think Father Jacob would help us pay for one? I mean, Eric did donate all his winnings to the church!"

*****

When Willy's taxi pulled up to the curb at his house, Otis ran out to meet him. Willy smiled and chortled, "What's up, Otis? I've never seen you run so fast!"

"Something's happened to Mr. Kraft, Bro. The FBI arrested him up a few minutes ago and put on handcuffs! And Miss Dora said they took Eric right from school!"

"Damn!" Willy ignored his brother. Quickly, he jumped into his park ranger pickup truck that was in the driveway and cranked the engine. Otis watched in total confusion as Willy sped away.

Twenty minutes later, Willy raced through the doors of the West Palm Beach FBI Headquarters on Flagler Drive. He threw his cell phone, keys, and wallet on a plastic tray, moved through the security scanner, and then hustled to the front desk. After identifying himself, he was led to a small room outside the interview room where Eric and Hugh Kraft were being held.

There was a man who looked familiar sitting in a chair, and Willy sat down next to him.

"Hi, I'm Willy Banks." He shook hands with the man. "I'm sorry, but you look like someone I should know."

"I'm Pete Burns, the CEO of PGA America."

*****

A few minutes later, agent Cory Jones walked in. "Willy Banks, they told me you were here. May I ask why?"

"I believe I have some important information you should hear regarding this case. Would you mind if I sat in on the interview?"

"How could I say no to America's greatest hero!" chuckled Jones. "I look forward to what you have to tell us!"

They were led past the two-way mirrored holding cell to a conference room down the hall. Eric and Hugh were there, still in handcuffs. Jim and Dora Mann were sitting next to Eric. Agent Jones had warned them not to hug Eric or even touch him. Two FBI agents guarded the door, and another one was setting up a video camera and tape recorder. Hugh and the Mann family all perked up at the sight of Willy Banks. But not so much when they saw Pete Burns enter the room.

When everyone was seated, Jones looked at the camera and began. "Today is Wednesday, May 13th, 2015. The time is 6:00 pm. We are interviewing Eric Mann and Hugh Kraft regarding possible fraudulent activities directly affecting the Professional Golfers Association of America. Seated at the table are Jim and Dora Mann, parents of Eric, who is a minor. Also, Pete Burns, CEO of the PGA, is in attendance, as is Mr. Willy Banks, who has information to share with the FBI. Both Mr. Kraft and Master Mann have waived their right to counsel.

"Let us begin with—"

Willy coughed and cut in on Jones, who didn't appear happy about the interruption. "Before you begin, Mr. Jones, I have a question. Where are CIA agents Mel Smith and Keith Malone?"

The Manns and Hugh Kraft glanced at one another with puzzled looks on their faces.

"From now on, I will ask the questions, Mr. Banks. Please don't speak unless I indicate that it's okay to do so."

"Sure, sorry, Agent Jones. However, now that it's on the table and recorded, why not answer my question? Where are CIA agents Smith and Malone?"

Rolling his eyes, Jones replied, "I have no idea. This is my case, not theirs. The CIA isn't involved! Now, please, let's move on!"

Willy found the reply very strange. He thought it was Smith and Malone's case, not Jones'! He decided to sit back and listen.

"Mel Smith and Keith Malone are CIA agents?" questioned Dora Mann quietly. "We're confused. We thought they were engineers."

Agent Jones ignored Dora's bewilderment. "Okay, I'm going to skip the preliminaries and cut to the chase," he stated without guile. "Eric, in the Honda Classic, Masters, and TPC, you used a doctored golf ball filled with a magnetic substance. That substance was strongly attracted to the golf cups on those courses you played and won! Did Golf Country Superstore put you up to this? Did they manufacture the balls? We know the cups were made in India and distributed to a company on an island near the Bahamas, which, coincidently, was recently destroyed. But we're guessing GCS created the balls. We have a warrant issued for CEO Ursula Vero's arrest once you confirm what we're saying. So, well, son, please come clean!"

"I didn't use no doctored balls! I don't know about anything you're saying! I really don't't!"

Willy was beside himself with anger. These clowns who call themselves FBI agents don't have a clue! Meanwhile, Pete Burns was also fuming. How dare Eric lie during an official interview with law enforcement?

Jones looked up from Eric and over to Hugh. "Does he or doesn't he, Mr. Kraft? We're certain you are behind this. We just want to know Eric's involvement."

"I'm behind nothing!" exclaimed Hugh. "The boy is a natural golfer. You are mistaken! I don't know what evidence you have, but Eric and I had absolutely nothing to do with fraud!"

Pete Burns stood up, red-faced, "Bull crap! Hugh Kraft, you two can rot in jail, for all I'm concerned! And Eric, I expect you to return every dime of your winnings back to the PGA, as well as the green jacket from the Masters! As of this minute, your PGA titles are stripped!"

Eric slouched down in his chair, his face flooded with tears. Dora leaned over and gave him an enormous hug, one that only a mother could give.

"No touching!" yelped an agent who was guarding the door.

"Jump in a lake!" yelled Dora, and she squeezed her son even harder.

The scene was about to become chaotic when Willy stood up. "Okay, enough of this, all of you. You need to hear what I have to say." Willy paused to glare at Agent Jones. "And unlike you, sir, I have proof! But I need to make a phone call before we begin."

*****

Jones called Hoagie Harry's to have some sandwiches delivered while Willy was out of the room. He hoped a light dinner would get everyone back under control. Jim and Dora were too strained to eat. Hugh calmed down after a few bites of the ham and cheese sub, but Eric sat still with wet cheeks and soft sobs.

Willy called several times and left messages on Mel Smith's and Keith Malone's cell phones. Why weren't they answering?! Then he dialed Bob Butler at his apartment next to the church. "Hi Bob! Hey, it's Willy Banks. By any chance—"

"Willy! Wow, so glad you called! Have you heard about Eric Mann being arrested at school today?!"

"Yes, Bob, that's why I'm calling. Will you check and see if Mel Smith or Keith Malone are in their apartments?"

"Don't need to, Willy. I saw them on the security cameras earlier. They got on Mel's jet with Tommy Williams and someone in a suit. And, oh yeah, there was another guy with them who I swear looked just like Deacon Ollie."

"Deacon Ollie? He's dead, Bob! You know that!"

"Yeah, tell me about it! I can't tell you where they were flying off to. Sorry! Hey, by the way, where are you?"

"Long story. I'll fill you in later."

Willy plopped down on the wide ledge of a window that overlooked the Intracoastal Waterway and the Atlantic Ocean beyond the strip of land known as Palm Beach. He was in deep thought about Mel and Keith. Speaking only to himself, he muttered, "How could I be so stupid?!"

*****

"You've got it all wrong!" said Willy firmly. He was back in his seat in the conference room. Eric was still crying. "Now, first things first. You need to back off this young man." Willy winked at Eric, who, in turn, smiled slightly back at him. "Eric is more honest than the total sum of every FBI agent in this room! And that's not a putdown, fellas; it's a fact. You all, and I'll even include myself, couldn't hold a candle to Eric's integrity. Shame on you for accusing him of fraud without proof of his involvement in the plot. That goes for you, too, Mr. Burns! Eric was a pawn to some very unscrupulous people, that's all!"

The FBI agents and Pete Burns were red-faced from their scolding. Eric saw the embarrassment and spoke up. "Please, Willy, they are only doing their jobs. I don't want you to hurt their feelings." Then Eric motioned to Hugh and added, "Please, also know Mr. Kraft had nothing to do with the golf ball problem. He never wanted me to use St. Max's balls in the first place! In fact, he wanted me to switch to Titleist every tournament!"

Willy smiled, then stood up and gave Eric a hug of his own. The FBI agents didn't say a word about touching.

"Now, I will be happy to tell you everything I know, but on one condition."

"What's that?" asked Agent Jones.

"Take off Eric and Hugh's handcuffs immediately! It's a disgrace to your profession they even had them put on!"

Jones nodded and uncuffed them.

Willy then told the whole story of his trip to and from San Francisco, finding Plana Cay, stumbling upon Jake Tassett's home and business, and how the highly explosive and magnetic planacalum destroyed both. He described the factory at St. Max's and how innocent parishioners were making the golf balls. Willy talked about some of the people he met along the way, including Mel Smith, Keith Malone, and Tommy Williams. But Willy didn't mention his visit to the trailer home in Pahokee and dropping in on the pope at the Vatican. All of that he wanted to save until the end.

When the follow-up questions were done, and it appeared the FBI had a grip on the situation, Willy unloaded his grand finale.

"Fellas, I've just returned from Vatican City, where I met with Pope Francis and Archbishop Milo Guidan." Everyone in the conference room looked stunned, then listened carefully as Willy resumed. "I've confirmed the former bishop of Palm Beach, Bob Kaiser, was linked to Jake Tassett's criminal organization. The current bishop, Brian O'Bailey, is actually not an ecclesiastical dignitary. He's a private investigator hired by Archbishop Guidan to scrutinize the workings of Kaiser and the diocese.

"Also, and this will come as a shock to the Mann family, I'm sure, but you all need to know. I am certain that Father Jacob is really Jake Tassett."

Willy waited until the groans and mumbled words dissipated. It was then that Jim and Dora Mann began to cry right along with Eric.

"On the airplane ride back from Rome, I thought of something else. Not only did Tassett basically keep his first name when he became a fake priest, but he named his church after his best friend—Judge Maximillian Boone. The judge also escaped prosecution from the airline disasters in

Florida back in the eighties and left the country with Tassett. Now, St. Max's golf balls are named after him, too!"

Agent Jones yelled an order to one of the agents guarding the door. "Mack! Quickly, call Judge Barker and get an arrest warrant issued for Father Jacob! I'll organize a team and move in fast on the church, so he can't escape!"

"It's too late for that," said Dora softly. "He's attending a religious conference somewhere unknown."

"I have a gut feeling Father Jacob is going to be wherever Mel Smith is flying his jet," said Willy. "I hate to say it because I trusted those two, but I think Smith and Malone are rogue CIA agents. I'm not sure what their motive is, but I think they were bluffing me for some reason!"

"Right from the beginning, I never believed they were engineers," inserted Jim Mann. "They owned a jet and expensive cars, and I doubted they would come to work at a church!"

Willy paced the room slowly, then dropped another bombshell. "I think Father Jacob is planning on reconnecting with his deacon."

"But Deacon Ollie is dead, Willy!" screeched Eric.

"No, son, I think he's alive and well."

"What do you mean by that, Willy?! Can it be true?!"

"Yes, Eric. It's the name game, once again."

"What do you mean by that?" asked Jones.

"Jacob is Jake. Judge Maximillian Boone is St. Max. I'm now certain that Deacon Ollie is really Oliver Harwas, the FBI's most wanted criminal!"

CHAPTER SIXTY-EIGHT

May 2015

Within an hour, an all-points bulletin was issued for Mel Smith, Keith Malone, Jake Tassett (aka Father Jacob), and Oliver Harwas (aka Deacon Ollie). If the FBI got lucky, they would find all of them in one location, making it a much easier arrest. Agent Jones called the Federal Aviation Administration to see if a flight plan was registered for Mel Smith. Fortunately, there was one, but it could have been a false plan just to allow the Cessna Citation X clear space for takeoff. The jet was due to land in Minot, North Dakota.

Meanwhile, CIA Director John Barrett hadn't checked with his office the entire day, which was against policy. For safety reasons, even on Saturdays and Sundays, the director was required to phone or text his assistant, Steve Bergenstein, at Langley. However, Bergenstein received a copy of the APB issued for Smith and Malone, and he knew his boss was supposed to be with them. He phoned Agent Jones and asked to be updated on the FBI's progress.

A corporate jet owned by the FBI arrived at the Minot airport from Minneapolis with twenty agents onboard. Meanwhile, eight vans loaded with six agents in each vehicle raced down I-94 from Grand Forks. State Police from Bismarck drove four empty paddy wagons for the FBI agents to use. Five other state patrol cars, with two officers in each, were already in the Minot area and would assist in any way they could.

Sure enough, the Citation X was parked next to a private hangar at the airport. But which way those on board went after landing was a mystery to all the law enforcement personnel who had gathered. They were ordered to wait at the airport until Agent Jones arrived from West Palm Beach to take over command of the mission. A few minutes before midnight, Jones touched down, and the group assembled in an empty hangar owned by Minot State University Athletics. The Beavers' baseball team was playing Wisconsin-Parkside, and a well-used 1975 Embraer 120 twin turboprop had flown the team to Kenosha.

*****

Mel had installed a special GPS tracer next to the nosewheel tiller before he, Keith, and Willy departed for Europe. It was so Bushman Jack could easily track their flight and move the drone into position. No one but Jack had access to the tracer, and Keith simply forgot it existed.

As Mel conducted the preflight routine in the cockpit with Keith's pistol pointed at his head, he punched the activation button on the tracer. Fortunately, Keith didn't notice. But Bushman Jack's computer was beeping. A notification displayed that the Cessna Citation X was available for tracking. Jack wasn't happy about waking up in the middle of the night in his mountaintop office in Uluru, Australia. Still, he was sure curious about where Smith and Malone were headed now. Obviously, Mel wanted him to know, or he wouldn't have activated the switch.

The drone's phenomenal camera locked in on the Citation as it reached its cruising altitude over Ocala, Florida. Jack zoomed in through the cockpit windows and was startled by what he saw. The copilot, who looked like Keith Malone, was aiming a gun directly at Mel!

Jack tried to position the drone so he could see through the side windows of the cabin, but the jet was moving too fast. Bushman watched as the Citation headed in a northwesterly flight path. Three hours later, it landed in Minot, North Dakota.

Jack saw five men deplaning. The first two were Mel and someone who looked just like CIA Director John Barrett. Both were cuffed as Keith

Malone followed them with his weapon held discreetly at his side. Behind them were Tommy Williams and the notorious Oliver Harwas. What was going on?!

Keith flashed a badge at a security guard who was posted at the entrance to the charter terminal door. He yawned and waved them all through. The guard must have thought two criminals were being transported to the courthouse. The drone lost sight of the men as they entered the terminal but picked them up again at the front door exit.

Jack expected them to rent a car or hail a taxi, but strangely they walked to the back of the parking lot where three twenty-six-foot white box freight trucks were waiting. There was no writing on the trucks. The men entered the cargo hold of the first truck, and all three drove away together.

Bushman had seen enough. With Keith pointing a gun at Mel, he didn't want to call Mel on his satellite phone. He wasn't sure if the other guy was Barrett, so he tried to call him at Langley but was told by a receptionist that the director was gone. When he asked to speak to Barrett's assistant, the gal responded, "That's not possible!" She then hung up before Bushman Jack could explain himself.

Jack didn't want to lose sight of the trucks, so he had the drone continue to focus on them. He decided he would call Willy when the trucks came to a halt. Banks would know how to get through to the CIA!

Bushman Jack zoomed in on the Minnesota license plates and wrote the numbers down. He had a link to police, FBI, and CIA records, so he should be able to track where the trucks had originated. Typing on a second computer with only his right hand, the answer rapidly popped up on the screen. The trucks were registered in Duluth by TST Industries.

The cargo caravan drove north on US 83 to ND 256, then continued straight towards the Canadian border. Just a mile from US Customs, they turned right onto a dirt road and headed east for four miles, then turned left onto a tractor path in a wheat field. Bushman Jack watched closely as the three trucks stopped next to a barbed wire fence. The drone zoomed onto a sign on the barrier that read:

United States-Canada Border: DO NOT CROSS!

The driver of the lead truck got out and used wire cutters to slice through the thin metal cords. The trucks then entered Canada and stopped for the driver to reattach the wires to a pole. Bouncing up and down through a patch of open grass, the trucks entered a dense forest of trees that the drone couldn't penetrate. Jack combed the area for twenty minutes, hoping they would exit the woods, but without luck. Did they get out of there without the drone seeing them? He decided to slowly sweep north, northwest, and northeast. It was challenging because the trucks didn't need an asphalt road for travel.

Finally, Bushman Jack picked up his cell phone and called Willy, but the line was dead. He didn't know Willy had lost his personal cell phone weeks earlier. So, Jack tried Willy's house, and Otis answered. "Yah, so who did you say you were?"

"A friend of Willy's. When will he be home?"

"Dunno. He's at the FBI office in West Palm."

"What's he doing there?"

"Can't tell ya. Some things are private, ya know!"

"Please have him call Bushman Jack right away! It's very important!" Otis wrote down the strange-looking set of numbers and went back to bed.

After leaving FBI headquarters, Willy went to Hugh's house to chat and didn't get home until past midnight. Unfortunately, he didn't get Otis' message until he woke up the following day.

*****

The cabin in the woods was actually a metal shed covered with nonflammable, fake pinewood plastic panels affixed to the interior and exterior walls. Attached to the metal were electrical wires looped together in a circuit to generate heat. On the floor, an aluminum cylinder the size of a soup can was filled with planacalum and sealed with a plastic cover. Next to it was a bag of fertilizer.

The thirty-by-thirty-foot cabin had a small sink, gas stove, and tiny refrigerator. On a cupboard was a Mr. Coffee machine and a can of Folgers. There were two single-sized cots against the wall with sheets and a comforter lying on top of the mattress. One oak dresser loaded with reflective orange and camouflage green clothes was placed between the two cots. In the middle of the room was a card table with four chairs. Everything in the cabin was designed to look like a hunter's retreat.

But underneath the shed was a basement loaded with five-gallon barrels of planacalum. A rug was lying on top of the subterranean entrance in the middle of the floor. The swinging door opened easily, and a ladder was secured extending sixteen feet down to the concrete base. The underground vault was six times the size of the cabin. It took several years to gradually fill up the basement with planacalum. Once a year, while a flatboat delivered material to Florida and other southern ports, a fake US Sugar Company freighter shipped raw planacalum north to Quebec, then westward, following the St. Lawrence Seaway through the Great Lakes, to Duluth, Minnesota. From there, it was trucked to this desolate location on the Canadian-American border. The entire operation was meant to be a backup plan if someone discovered the factory on Plana Cay. Today was the day the backup plan went into effect!

A portable conveyor belt was lowered into the hole, while a second belt went from the hole through the front door to a loading area outside. Throughout the night, the hired drivers loaded the barrels of planacalum into the three cargo trucks. Early on Thursday morning, once the trucks were full, Oliver Harwas bolted two metal chairs to the floor, then chained Mel Smith and CIA Director John Barrett to them.

The trucks moved away from the cabin, then parked near the north edge of the patch of forest. Oliver opened the plastic top from the cylinder of planacalum in the shed and spread it around the floor. When he went to grab the fertilizer, Keith stopped him. "Hold on, Oliver! Let me do the honors!"

Oliver looked at Keith and chuckled. "Sure, why not! You just want all the fun, right?"

"Yes, of course! But I was thinking you should get the trucks well away from here before we blast this place. Once someone sees the smoke, a fire department will be on the way, along with policemen."

"So, how are you going to escape? You don't even know where we're going!"

"Tommy can call me when you get to your destination. I'm a long-range hiker. That's what I do for exercise. I can easily make my way to a road, then hitchhike from there." Keith paused momentarily, then chortled, "It makes more sense than being caught by the Royal Canadian Mounties!"

"Good plan, Keith! I'll make sure Tommy calls you!" Oliver exited the cabin and made his way to the first truck. He shook his head and smiled. There was no way he was going to tell Tommy to call Keith. One less person to share the profits was okay by him!

*****

Bushman Jack flew the drone all the way to Regina, Saskatchewan, but he still couldn't locate the cargo trucks. When he was about to give up, Willy called him. "I got your message! What's happening?!"

Jack filled him in on everything he knew. Then Willy said, "I thought both Mel and Keith might be rogue agents! So, Mel is legit, but Keith is working with Tommy! I never did like that damn Keith! Anyway, I'm going to fly the Fish and Wildlife Cessna up to Canada. Are you sure about the GPS coordinates for that patch of forest the trucks went into?"

"Yes, I'm certain. How do you plan to land?" asked Jack.

"I'll deal with that when the time comes!"

*****

"Okay, let's get the hell out of here!" screeched Keith to Mel and Barrett. Using a bolt cutter he found next to the cabin in the grass, he opened the lock on the chains.

"Why didn't you shoot them?!" yelped Mel.

"My gun wasn't loaded!"

"Why wasn't it loaded, you idiot?!"

"Because I didn't want it accidentally going off when I had it pointed at your head! This decoy mission of yours wasn't very well thought out! Well, okay, except for me using the code words 'nope' and 'nada' to execute the plan."

"Tommy had been bragging about this extra planacalum for quite some time. We didn't know where it was, so by pretending you were breaking bad, they would lead us to it! Who would have guessed it was in Canada?!"

"Okay, stop the argument, boys!" exclaimed Director Barrett. "We now know where the excess planacalum was stored, but that does us little good. The sad thing is we let Oliver Harwas get away!"

"Not a problem," stated Keith. "Oliver assured me he would have Tommy call me. He will let me know where their destination is."

"Yeah, good luck with that! Do you really think Harwas cares if you are part of their scheme?! Rather naïve for a CIA agent, wouldn't you say?!"

Embarrassed by his boss' comment, Keith changed the subject. "Let's get this thing done. If they don't see the explosion, they won't believe you two were killed."

Mel sprinkled fertilizer on the planacalum, then flipped the switch that started the electrical circuit. The combination was lethal, and they knew they had to sprint vigorously to escape. The smoke began to rise on the floor as they exited hastily.

A hundred yards away, the three men dove for the ground and covered their heads with their hands. The blast was enormous, sending everything in the cabin sky-high. A pillow from the cot landed squarely on John Barrett's back.

They stood up, brushed the dirt off themselves, and watched the smoke and flames until only embers remained of the cabin.

Mel looked up at the clouds and muttered, "Now what?"

CHAPTER SIXTY-NINE

May 2015

NASA developed the most powerful cell phone in the world that utilized six completely private satellites for earth-to-space communications. US astronauts have the cells built into their helmets while on spacewalking missions. President Obama ordered NASA to provide the same satellite phones for high-level agents from the National Security and Central Intelligence Agencies. Mel Smith, Keith Malone, and Bushman Jack all had one in their possession.

As part of the ruse he and Keith devised, Mel had turned his sat phone off and hid it in the jet's cockpit. He didn't want it ringing in midair, which would raise suspicions with Oliver and Tommy. Meanwhile, Keith's battery was running low, but he had enough juice to speak quickly to Bushman Jack in Australia. "Bushman, Keith Malone here. How long would it take to get your drone into position to video along the Canadian border near North Dakota?"

Mel and Keith hadn't said a word about their risky gambit to Bushman. Remembering what he witnessed inside the CIA jet's cockpit, Jack wasn't sure how to respond. So, in reply, he asked, "Where is Mel?"

"Next to me. But we need to know about the drone."

"Let me talk to Mel!" demanded Bushman. Keith was taken aback.

"Why Mel? Why can't you tell me what you want to say?"

"Is Mel your prisoner?!"

"Prisoner? Hell no! What's gotten into you?!"

"The drone focused on you holding a gun to Mel's head while he was flying the Citation X! Care to explain?!"

Keith was startled, but he was even more surprised the drone's camera could see through the cockpit windows of a jet going 700 miles per hour! "That was all a scam! The pistol wasn't loaded. I can tell you about it later, but we need the drone to search for three cargo trucks that—"

"The drone is already combing Saskatchewan for those cargo trucks. It's searching for them because I thought you were inside the trucks! Now, let me speak to Mel to make sure you're telling me the truth!"

Keith rolled his eyes and handed the phone to Mel. "He thinks I kidnapped you, the dumb fool!"

"Bushman, this is Mel. Keith's right—it was all a decoy. We hoped Oliver Harwas and Tommy Williams would lead us to Jake Tassett. Tassett had stockpiled tons of planacalum underneath a cabin in the woods north of the Canadian border."

"Yes, I was able to follow you from Minot until you became hidden in the forest. I had assumed the trucks left there without the drone seeing them. Why didn't you stay with them?"

"Director Barrett and I were chained to a chair. After the planacalum was loaded into the cargo holds, Oliver spread some of it on the cabin floor. He was about to sprinkle fertilizer on top of the planacalum and blow us to pieces. Keith saved our lives by offering to create the explosion, which would give the trucks time to get away. Tommy is supposed to call Keith with their new location, but I doubt that will happen. We blew up the cabin to make it look good, but we have no idea where they're going. Do you think the drone can find them?"

"Maybe. But meanwhile, Willy Banks is flying his company's Cessna to North Dakota to try and find you. It's a small plane. I gave him the coordinates for the patch of woods so he can fly close, but is there an accessible area near you where he could land it?"

"Sure, if he has the skills to land in a wheat field!"

"I'll relay your message to Willy. By the way, I told him what I saw with the drone's camera through your cockpit window. So, I'll explain to him that Keith's not a kidnapper. Otherwise, he might step out of the aircraft with guns ablazing!"

"Yeah, good call. Keith might not think too highly of that!"

*****

The cargo caravan traveled eastbound for 104 miles on a tractor path cut through multiple fields of golden wheat. They skirted around the many tiny lakes and ponds of Turtle Mountain Provisional Park. The drivers and passengers were hoping to be more concealed, but winter had ended not long ago, and the grain was relatively short. It didn't matter. For some reason, Bushman Jack assumed the trucks were headed west to Alberta. The drone was going in the opposite direction.

When they reached the small community of Holmfield, the drivers continued on asphalt backroads northeast to Headingley, a western suburb of Winnipeg. Their destination was the Motley Corporation, located next to the Canadian Pacific Railway tracks. Iron ore was transported by Burlington Northern freight trains from Hibbing, Minnesota, to Winnipeg, then switched to CPR engineers who muscled the trains west to Vancouver. The first stop was at Motley in Headingley.

The Motley plant converted raw ore into pig iron, then shipped it to a steel factory in Calgary. They also had one other recent customer—TST Industries. Motley never knew what TST did with the pig iron, and they never asked. TST paid five times as much per pound as the Calgary factory. Twice in the past two years, they bought a ton of pig iron and hauled it away in a semi.

"We need one more ton," said Oliver Harwas to the salesclerk, who sat in an office the size of a walk-in closet in a modest home. Papers were everywhere—on the desk, on the chairs, and on the floor. Everywhere except in the metal filing cabinet where they belonged!

"Okay, may I ask the destination for the bill of lading?" queried the clerk.

Oliver smiled and winked. "No, you may not. The semi will be here a week from today. Is that a problem?"

"No, sir. We'll have everything ready. But we need payment upfront, as you know." This time the clerk smiled and winked.

"Don't have it with me. Our driver will pay you." Oliver turned sideways to reveal a pistol stuck in his belt.

The clerk noticed the gun and began to perspire. "Ah, yes, sir! No problem! No problem at all!"

"I didn't think so." Oliver exited the building and stepped into the cargo truck.

"All good?" asked Tommy.

"Yep, all good." Oliver nodded at the driver. "Get moving."

*****

Grand Rapids, Manitoba, is a small community 265 miles north of Headingley on MB-6 N. It is known for a power plant that generates electricity for much of the province, as well as producing two National Hockey League superstars and providing extensive boat access to Lake Winnipeg. At 11:00 pm, when most of the town was sound asleep, barrels of planacalum were loaded onto a barge with the insignia *Canadian Sugar Corporation* printed on the hull. Many fishermen had seen the freighter cruise Lake Winnipeg, but none of them ever thought twice about it. The company never existed.

The barge departed Grand Rapids at 5:15 am on Friday, the fifteenth of May, shortly before the sun rose. Cruising due east for thirty-one miles, it came upon its destination precisely at 11:15 am. The deserted island was a half mile wide and one mile long. The Canadian government had placed four navigation lights on each side of the island many years ago. A Royal Canadian Mountie had been assigned to live on the island to maintain the lights. Along with a two-bedroom home, he was given a twenty-six-foot runabout with dual 200 horsepower Mercury outboards for the Mountie to assist boaters with mechanical problems in the lake. He could also use the boat to travel to Grand Rapids for supplies or just weekend R & R.

Seven years earlier, when the economy was tanking, the Mounties told provincial leaders they could no longer afford to support their employee on the island. The government took out an advertisement in Toronto's *Financial Post* and New York's *Wall Street Journal* to sell the island with the requirement the new owners must maintain the navigation lights. TST Industries offered twice the asking price, completing the deal in a month. The runabout was included.

An underground vault and factory were built, and a sand bar was dredged that gradually extended a small beach outward for fifty yards. New navigation warning lights warned boaters to stay away due to shallow water. However, the sand bar became a perfect landing location for the *Canadian Sugar Corporation* barge because its bow dropped down, and goods could be unloaded from the front.

Jake Tassett employed ten men who would put the finishing touches on the vault and factory and one day head up the operation, whatever that operation might be. He had several ideas, but a clear vision hadn't popped into his head. When Plana Cay was destroyed, that vision became crystal clear!

The ten employees and three truck drivers unloaded the barrels of planacalum and placed them inside the vault before the sun set on Friday. Another storage area was separated from the vault by a three-foot-thick titanium and concrete wall. It was filled with pig iron. The barrier was designed to keep the planacalum and iron from magnetically clinging to one another.

Luckily, no fishermen or boaters saw the workers unloading the barge. The middle of the lake was rarely traveled.

Oliver Harwas and Tommy Williams sipped whiskey sours and fished from a dock while the hired men did all the manual labor. As the bright orange sun slowly sunk below the western horizon, the runabout arrived and tied up to cleats.

When the boat driver stepped onto the dock, Oliver Harwas walked over and embraced him.

"Praise to you, Deacon Ollie," said the man.

"And praise be to you, Father Jacob."

CHAPTER SEVENTY

May 2015

The drone was unable to find the cargo trucks. Bushman Jack apologized profusely, but Mel handled the letdown very well. "It's not your fault, Bushman. My plan didn't work, so it's on me!"

"No man, don't blame yourself. It just happened, mate! Anyway, I need to recall the drone to Australia for maintenance. I can have it fully serviced in two weeks.

"Sounds good. Let me know when you're back in action!"

An hour later, Keith heard a buzz and looked up to see a Cessna circling overhead, waving its wings. "It must be Willy! Let's get out in the field so he can see us better."

It turned out Willy had the skills to land a small plane in a wheat field. Flying out would prove more challenging! The men had to pull wheat stalks from the ground with their hands to clear a 1,000-foot path for a runway. They worked through the night using only the light from a full moon.

On Saturday morning, the Cessna blew a tire during a shaky takeoff, but with a strong headwind and a little help from God, Willy got the plane airborne. The plan was to stop in Minot to refuel and fix the flat. Unfortunately, the landing didn't quite cooperate. The Cessna struck the runway hard and flipped end-over-end. Mel broke four ribs and pulled several muscles, Keith dislocated a shoulder and cracked his right patella,

John Barrett broke both arms and one leg, and Willy was knocked unconscious. Miraculously, they all survived. However, the search for Jake Tassett would need to be postponed for an undetermined amount of time.

*****

"Dang nab it! I don't care if the kid knew about it or not! He didn't win those tournaments honestly!" asserted Pete Burns. "We need to strip him of his titles and remove him from the PGA tour! Plus, he needs to refund all his winnings! And Hugh, I hate to say it because we've known each other for quite some time, but I'm still not sure you weren't a part of all this!"

Pete was at his office desk in Palm Beach while Hugh Kraft and Jack Nicklaus sat in chairs. Jack was confident his lifelong friend would have nothing to do with cheating, and he was there to support him. The Golden Bear was someone you wanted by your side if you had an issue with the PGA.

"Pete, get off your high horse and start thinking rationally, my friend," said Nicklaus. "First of all, Hugh Kraft is a gentleman of honor, ethics, and morality. His blood flows with integrity instead of hemoglobin! And from what I know of Eric Mann, the teenager is created from the same mold!"

"That may be, but—"

"Ah, ah, ah, no interruptions, please. I haven't finished."

"Okay, sorry, Jack. Go on."

"Secondly, there's a better way to solve this fairly. Let Eric play in the AT&T Byron Nelson tournament. If he finishes in the top five, he gets to remain a pro golfer and keep his titles. If not, you can take them from him."

"Why top five. He won big money, so let's say top three!" Pete was willing to give in to Jack's demand but still wanted the last word. "If he doesn't place in the top three, he returns all the money to us! Also, he's no longer allowed on the PGA tour!"

"Pete, he donated all his winnings to charity," said Jack. "But I believe so much in the kid, I'm willing to pay back the money for him if he doesn't finish top three. I'm sure Hugh will chip in, too!" Nicklaus smiled and winked at his friend. Hugh returned the grin but just about choked on the Starbucks coffee he was sipping!

Hugh and Jack shook hands with Pete, then left his office. On the way out of the building, Hugh said, "This isn't going to be easy. Not only is Eric finishing school, but he has been traumatized since being arrested in front of his friends. He hasn't touched a golf club in several days! Top three at the Byron Nelson? Chances are way beyond slim, my friend!"

"I'll help you coach him," responded Nicklaus. "All I need to know is if you believe in him."

"Of course I do! He was playing incredibly well on the junior circuit before all the bad stuff started to happen!"

"Well, then. Let's help make him a champion!"

Hugh and Jack walked to their cars with arms around each other's shoulders.

*****

Dora and Jim Mann didn't want to put any more stress on their son. After Eric's parents said no to what seemed like a thousand times, Hugh dropped his head and started to walk out of their apartment. He paused at the doorway and said, "Okay, I fully understand. I really do. Eric will need to return all his winnings. Jack Nicklaus and I will take care of that, though. Don't you worry about a thing."

Instantly, Jim uttered, "Hold on, Hugh!" Kraft turned and looked at him. "You would pay my son's debt?! I can't have you do that!"

"It's not a problem, Jim. We'll take care of it."

Without asking Dora, Jim changed his tune. "Okay, so Eric can play if he wants to. But it's totally up to him. Right?"

Hugh glanced at Dora. She wasn't thrilled but understood why her husband relented. She smiled softly at Hugh and nodded. "Just please be careful with his feelings. He's fragile right now, Coach."

Eric was all in after Hugh gave him the pep talk of the century. Just knowing the Golden Bear stood up for him to Pete Burns, and was willing to help coach him, he couldn't say no. Eric was fired up to play his best ever round of golf!

But things changed when the sports were broadcast on the nightly news. From his bed, Eric could hear the TV in the living room.

"Breaking news in the golf world," announced the local NBC sports anchor Ben Houghton. "Teenage prodigy, Eric Mann, is under suspicion of cheating in both wins at the Masters and Honda Classic. Due to possible legal ramifications, Pete Burns refused to provide details but did say that Eric would be allowed to play in the AT&T Byron Nelson Classic in Dallas in a couple of weeks. Strangely, he would need to finish in the top three to retain his two previous tournament victories and stay on the PGA tour. If we get more particulars, you will hear it first right here at WPTV, Channel Five!"

Eric ambled out to the living room and sat down on the couch between his mom and dad. All three were fighting back tears.

*****

The phone call from Jack Nicklaus to Pete Burns wasn't pretty. "How could you leak this to the news!" shouted Jack angrily. "You're a bad person, Pete!"

*****

May 19, 2015

"This is tough, son, but we only have ten days to get you ready," said Hugh as he sat on a bench at the practice range with his arms around Eric. "But you can do this! We know you can!"

"I didn't cheat, Mr. Kraft and Mr. Nicklaus; I hope you believe me."

Jack patted him on the head while Hugh squeezed him. "Of course we believe you! Just remember, you were sensational when I first started coaching you. That was a long time before you went pro!"

The practices were shortened because it was the last week of school, and Eric wasn't going to miss it. His classmates gave him the cold shoulder, but out of respect for his mother, who was their teacher, no one harassed Eric in the hall or outside. But finding someone to play with during his free time wasn't going to happen. He was as lonely as he used to be when he lived in the family car in Loxahatchee Slough!

On Saturday, May 23rd, Jack Nicklaus flew Eric in his corporate jet to Dallas, and they rented a suite in the Las Colinas Four Seasons Resort where the AT&T Byron Nelson tournament would be held. Jack and Hugh played four practice rounds with Eric on Saturday and Sunday, then the teenager joined the field of pros for practices on Monday through Wednesday.

That's when the badgering and insults began. None of the PGA Tour professionals knew what happened, but they all heard Eric had somehow cheated. They weren't about to let the kid walk away unscathed from his sins.

Hugh and Jack saw what was happening, and they continued to pump Eric full of self-confidence with every stroke he took in preparation for the tourney. When he would be down in the dumps from words spoken both to his face and behind his back, Hugh would console Eric. "Ignore the ignorant!" his coach would say—over and over and over again!

On Wednesday night, Eric paced around the suite, stared out the window to the golf course, then paced some more. There was no chance for sleep, something he badly desired! Soon enough, dawn broke, and the sun rose over the great state of Texas.

CHAPTER SEVENTY-ONE

May 2015

Las Vegas oddsmakers scratched Eric Mann from the field of wagers for the AT&T Byron Nelson tournament. Simply put, you couldn't bet on any professional athlete accused of sidestepping the rulebook. That included every sport played worldwide. Meanwhile, Pete Burns had every golf cup and pin replaced early in the morning at Las Colinas and hired eighteen security guards to watch each hole. In his mind, he was taking every precaution to ensure an honest tournament.

While the other pro golfers were checking their shoes and loosening up in the clubhouse, Eric was swarmed by the press. Three PGA officials were examining and weighing every club of his, much to the frightened teenager's total embarrassment! Hugh attempted to deflect the reporter's questions, but they didn't want to hear from the coach. They only wanted the words coming from the cheater's mouth.

Golfers were placed in groups of three for the first round, and Eric drew Dustin Johnson and Jimmy Walker. A few minutes before their 8:50 tee-off, Dustin and Jimmy pulled Eric over and patted his back. "Hey, buddy, neither of us cares about what's being reported," uttered Jimmy softly. "We've all been attacked by ruthless media, so we know what you're going through. If they allow you to play this weekend, it means you're legit. Just play your game, and good luck!"

With the encouragement from Jimmy and Dustin, Eric smiled and approached the first tee. But when the fans started booing, his enthusiasm gave way to fear. What would Hugh want him to do? Step back and gather his thoughts. Don't step up to the tee until you are focused. Yep, that's what his coach taught him!

Eric stepped back and was greeted with even more jeers and catcalls. "Get off the course, cheater! Go play hide and seek with your toddler friends somewhere!"

Eric tried to ignore it, then stepped back up to the tee. As he was about to swing, a dead mouse hit him square on the cheek. The thrower was escorted away by security guards while fans cheered the bully!

Shaking, Eric's first shot bulleted left, one hundred yards out of bounds. The fans jumped up and down cheering, then settled on laughter. As he teed up his penalty shot, tremors commenced once again. Then, out of the corner of his eye, he noticed Jack Nicklaus had walked over to stand in front of the crowd of fools. He had said something to them, and silence fell upon the tee area. Jack then winked and gave a thumbs-up to Eric.

Wow! Eric's emotions were all over the place! This time he approached his ball, closed his eyes, and thought only of Hugh, Wayne Siebold, and Jack Nicklaus. The all-time greats were on his side! He could do this!

Eric's tee shot flew straight for 285 yards and landed dead center in the middle of the fairway. Still, the only applause came from Hugh, Jack, Jimmy Walker, and Dustin Johnson. Eric thanked his partners and smiled. He truly believed he could tune out the naysayers and focus on what he needed to do. But starting off with a penalty made a top three finish seem impossible.

The holes at Las Colinas were dotted with moguls that would put a black run at a ski resort to shame. Plenty of sand traps and elevated greens added to the challenge. Eric was 173 yards from the pin and decided to use a six iron to ensure he lifted over the erratic landscape. And if ever there was a well-needed perfect stroke, Eric made it! The ball landed on the edge of the green and rolled into the cup! It was a fantastic par four considering he teed off hitting his third shot because of the penalty!

Suddenly, his joy ended as he pulled the ball from the cup. A PGA official was waiting on the green and asked to examine the Titleist Pro V. He shook it, scratched the cover with his fingernail, and, to add insult to injury, placed a magnet on the dimples. Fortunately, it didn't stick! He gave the ball back to Eric without saying a word.

The Golf Channel announcers had a field day with what they saw. Never in PGA history has a ball been checked on a green! Still, no one, including the media, knew exactly why Pete Burns thought Eric had cheated. However, the use of a magnet by officials raised suspicions, and announcers assumed the balls contained iron shavings, an illegal ingredient for the pro circuit because metal reduced drag inappropriately. Interestingly, it was called the Anti-Aristotle effect in the rule book.

Amidst another layer of boos, Eric approached the second tee. On the walk over, Dustin Johnson handed him a pair of foam earplugs. "Here, try these. I use them when the crowds are loud."

Eric smiled at Dustin and said, "Thank you, but what if you need them later? I don't want to ruin your game."

"You won't ruin my game!" chuckled Johnson. "I do enough of that on my own! Now give the earplugs a try."

They helped, but Eric had never played without noise. He loved hearing the wind blowing through the trees and the birds chirping. At least the unruly fans' jeers were muffled.

From the corner of his eye, Eric noticed Hugh motioning left with his arms. He guessed his coach was trying to tell him to aim that direction on the second tee. He was right. Stay left on the fairway to have a better angle of approach to the narrow green.

The hole was a 422-yard par four. The pin was placed on the bottom, right hand side of the green where four bunkers awaited those who played long, short, or to the right! Eric's drive landed exactly where Hugh was hoping—262 yards and on the left side of the fairway. His six-iron approach landed dead center and rolled toward the pin, stopping inches short of an eagle. Eric tapped in for a birdie while the crowd hissed their disapproval.

While throwing dead mice was an offense that would get a fan the boot, beginning with the third hole, tossing pecans at Eric was okay. Many times during the front nine, Eric had to step back from addressing his ball when the Texas State Nut hit him in the back, neck, or legs. It wasn't until the eleventh hole that a pecan hit him in the temple, and his legs collapsed beneath him. Amazingly, he had birdied six of the first ten holes and parred the other four. While attempting to stand, he fell again. Then, Eric was penalized for not completing the stroke within the forty-second time frame.

Hugh was beside himself with anger as he confronted a PGA official on the sideline. Although it wasn't in the rule book, Eric received another penalty because of his coach's temper. That clearly violated PGA rules because only a caddie and player can receive penalties for unsportsmanlike conduct!

The 599-yard, par five hole, was layered with sand traps. It was monstrous to begin with, so Eric didn't need two penalty strokes added to his score! After being hit with the pecan, his vision was blurry. He finished the hole with a nine, which moved him off the leaderboard.

As difficult as it was to play a round of golf with cloudy eyesight, being pelted with pecans, and a boisterous crowd who hated him, Eric parred the final seven holes and was sitting at two under with a sixty-eight. No one spoke to him in the clubhouse except the relentless media who wanted Eric to explain how he cheated at the Masters. Hugh stepped in front of the cameras and microphones and said succinctly, "That didn't happen!"

Dora met Eric at the door, gave him an enormous hug, then said, "Come on, son. We're going back to Florida. There's no need to play any more golf amongst a bunch of putrid bullies!"

Eric broke away from the hug and looked at Hugh, Jack Nicklaus, and his dad. All had sad facial expressions, and all nodded in agreement with his mom. "There's no need to put yourself through this baloney," stated Hugh with compassion. "And it's too dangerous. Who knows what these nincompoops have planned for the next three days."

Pete Burns overheard the conversation, then came over and joined the group. "I want you to play, Eric. I saw the incredible shots you made today, and I realized you probably had nothing to do with the cheating. Plus, Dustin Johnson and Jimmy Walker said they would drop out of the tournament in protest if you quit.

Hugh pulled Eric back, stooped down to come eye to eye, and uttered so everyone could hear, "Don't do it, son! Not until Mr. Burns changes his sentence from 'probably had nothing to do with the cheating' to 'definitely had nothing to do with the cheating!' Then, he needs to publicly announce the same thing during a press conference. Also, he needs to provide enhanced security so no more pecans are thrown at you! Lastly, he needs to give you a heartfelt apology!"

Pete Burns heard every word along with the others. Red-faced, he nodded and said, "I am very sorry, Eric. I made a rush to judgment that was wrong. Please forgive me. I will most certainly provide better security on the course for your protection."

"What about the requirement for a top-three finish in order to continue as a PGA golfer?" asked Hugh bitterly.

"I'm sorry to say I can't change that. The board has already approved the motion. Because Eric only qualified thanks to the challenge we established at the Old Course in Scotland, he technically didn't meet all the requirements in junior golf to get him elevated onto the PGA circuit."

"That doesn't matter, Pete! We had a contract stating if Eric shot at least par at St. Andrews, he would be allowed on the tour!"

"Yeah, but that round of golf was fixed, wasn't it? You and Eric may not have known about it, but it doesn't lessen the fact that it was perfidious."

Eric cut in, "Perfi what?"

"Deceitful," replied Burns. "Not that you were dishonest, but whoever rigged the Old Course was traitorous towards the PGA."

"So, you're saying I still need to place in the top three here at Las Colinas to stay on the PGA tour?" asked Eric meekly.

"Yes, son, that's what I'm saying. Sorry."

"You can't be serious," inserted Hugh. "If it wasn't for the abuse Eric took on the first round, he would be leading the pack right now! You can't make him—"

“It’s okay, Coach! If that’s what the rules say, then I will abide by them. Mr. Burns is a good person to tell me the things he said just now. If I was helped somehow in Scotland, he’s right. I shouldn’t be allowed to play on the circuit.”

“A top three finish will be very difficult, Eric. I don’t want you thinking otherwise.”

“I know, Coach. But I’m up for the challenge!”

CHAPTER SEVENTY-TWO

May 2015

Pete Burns woke up at 4:00 am to write the speech he planned to present to the media before the second round of play in Irving. But he never had the chance to speak. In his hurry to prepare for the day's events, Pete slipped in the shower and knocked himself unconscious. He awoke to find himself covered in blood, which drained from his nose. He wrapped himself up in a towel and called the front desk asking if they had a doctor on staff. No, but they would call an ambulance on his behalf. Twenty minutes later, he was transported to Medical City Las Colinas, the closest local hospital, and diagnosed with a grade four severe concussion.

Dr. Zeb Barnett, a neurologist at Medical City, was placed in charge of Pete's care. At the hospital, the PGA CEO lost consciousness once again, had multiple seizures, and vomited several times. When he was finally stabilized and alert, Pete looked at Dr. Barnett and whispered, "Where am I?"

"You're at Medical City Las Colinas hospital. You suffered a severe concussion. How do you feel?"

"Alright, I guess. But, um, who am I?"

*****

Hugh couldn't understand why Pete Burns didn't show up for the pre-tournament press conference. Did he plan to renege on the promise he made the night before? Hugh never cared much for Burns, but this was about as low as it could get!

The boo birds seized positions on the first hole as Eric, Dustin, and Jimmy Walker approached the tee. Today, they had an 11:00 am start, and Eric assumed Pete Burns would have made his speech to the media by then. After that, all would be well! Eric's fans would return and cheer him on louder than ever! When the catcalls began, Eric guessed the fans hadn't got the message! And where were the extra security guards he was promised?

As Eric was taking practice swings, two pecans hit him. One on the cheek and the other on his leg. Then a chant began that would gradually get louder each hole and haunt Eric for the rest of the day. "Cheater, cheater, cheater!"

Dora was going to pull her son away from the maddening crowd, but Jim held her back. "Dora," he said softly, "let him decide. If he wants to walk away, I'm all for it. But let it be his call."

Eric put in the earplugs and addressed his ball. Today, it was a Taylor Made. He didn't want anyone to think Titleist was involved in unsportsmanlike conduct. Tomorrow he would use a Callaway.

At each hole, a few more spectators would join the crowd of Eric haters. The heckling and scorn were deafening, and the teenager was pelted with pecans. Eric did his best to remain focused on his swings, but anytime he hit a fantastic shot, a PGA official would ask to check his club!

Eric bogeyed three holes and double-bogeyed two on the front nine. He was seven over par going into the turn, and he was well aware he was in danger of not making the cut. Eric's two-day total now stood at five over par after twenty-seven holes, and he was near the bottom of the pack.

That's when Willy Banks showed up. Willy had watched the first round on TV and saw what the fans were doing. Although he was still smarting from injuries when the USFWS Cessna crash-landed in Minot, he wasn't about to let those obnoxious idiots in Texas mess with one of his best friends! He and his brother Otis caught the first jet out of Palm Beach to Dallas. They both arrived at Las Colinas wearing old sheriff's uniforms, complete with holsters and pistols Willy had stored from the eighties. No one at the entrance noticed the badges were from Okeechobee County, Florida! They just waved Willy and Otis through the gates!

Eric was a nervous wreck when he took the club from his caddie on ten. The cheater chant began once again, and pecans started flying. Then, like roaring thunder, someone yelled, "Stop this now, you punks!"

Eric turned to see Willy with his hands raised high above his head, staring at the crowd with the meanest look on his face! Next to him was Otis, who had taken his gun out of the holster and was holding it in his hand down by his waist. A security guard and two PGA officials stood and watched like frozen snowmen! Everyone was sure the policemen were legit and told to keep law and order on the golf course!

The crowd became eerily silent, except for one young man wearing a cowboy hat and holding a can of Budweiser. "Hey, this here's a free country, ya know. We can hoot and holler all we want, and y'all can't stop us!" Then the obtruder grabbed a pecan from the ground and threw it hard at Eric.

Willy grabbed the man's chest, lifted him off the ground, and shoved him into a garbage can. The crowd backed up and opened their mouths in awe. Willy then turned to the fans and bellowed, "You all think this young boy cheated. Please, tell me how. If you can do that, I'll leave you alone. If not, then get the hell out of here!"

Someone, who was hiding behind several other folks, spoke up. "The newspeople said he cheated."

Willy couldn't see the speaker but glared into the group. "That didn't answer my question! I asked how he cheated!"

"Well, the newscasters didn't tell us. They just said he cheated, that's all."

"Okay, so none of you can answer my question. Then, I strongly suggest you go follow another golfer. Now, all of you, GET LOST!!"

The crowd dispersed quickly. The man in the garbage can was stuck and pleaded for Willy to get him out. Otis smiled at him and muttered,

"We'll be back when the round is over. You might want to take a long snooze."

Dustin Johnson patted Eric on the back and asked, "Any idea who that cop is?"

"America's greatest hero!" he announced with a grin. Eric took several practice swings, addressed his ball, then dropped it perfectly onto the par three, split-level, tenth green. A short putt later and Eric had his first birdie of the day.

Willy followed the PGA's youngest player for the final eight holes, never getting more than twenty yards away from him. Twice, the huge ex-deputy sheriff with arms like tree trunks carried pecan throwers off the course and tossed them into wooded areas. Eric could hear the branches snapping as the unruly fans landed hard on the ground.

With his security blanket nearby, Eric's game turned sensational. He birdied six of the final eight holes and parred the other two. After the second round, he was two under par and tied for seventeenth with a host of other players, all sitting six strokes back of the leader, Adam Schenk.

But the good news—Eric had made the cut!

*****

May 30, 2015

The news that Pete Burns was in a local hospital suffering from a concussion and amnesia was finally reported by the media at sunrise on Saturday. The first tee times of the day were held up five minutes for a prayer to be broadcast over the loudspeaker. Hugh chatted with Jim and Dora Mann and deduced that Pete's accident was the reason Eric's injustice hadn't been retracted. The teenager was scheduled to play the back nine first, and he was teamed up with Matt Jones and Brandt Snedeker for a 10:15 am start. All three were two under par after thirty-six holes.

With Willy standing just a few feet away and in front of the crowd, Eric smiled and approached the tee confidently with his driver. The tenth hole was a 435-yard, par four, but straight as an arrow from tee to green. His drive knocked off 275 of the yards, and he landed two feet from the cup on his fairway approach shot. An easy tap in putt, and Eric had his first birdie of the day.

Eight more birdies, seven pars, and a bogey would follow, giving Eric a sixty-two for the round. He was now sitting at ten under par for the tournament, but moving up the leaderboard was a challenge as other golfers performed well on Saturday, too. Steven Bowditch and Charley Hoffman were shooting out of their minds, both tied for the lead at fourteen under. Scott Pinckney was a stroke back, and Jimmy Walker and Jon Curran were tied at twelve under. Eric was alone in sixth place, but he knew full well he needed to finish in the top three, or his career would be over.

*****

May 31, 2015

Bowditch, Hoffman, and Pinckney would be teeing off last on Sunday. Eric was teamed with Curran and Jimmy Walker, his new friend from the first two rounds. Jack Nicklaus was standing next to Willy Banks, and the two were the sum total of Eric's cheering section! But the buzz around the first tee had nothing to do with golfers on the leaderboard.

The *Dallas Lone Star* sports columnist, Gene Attley, had published a scathing online article on Sunday morning blasting Pete Burns for not coming clean to news outlets regarding Eric Mann cheating to win the Masters and Honda Classic. The column's tone held no empathy for Burns' amnesiac condition, and Attley suggested Eric be arrested for fraud and tried in court as an adult! After all, he golfed on the PGA circuit with adults, so he should be considered one, too!

Then, to top it off, Attley pleaded with fans to boycott the final round if PGA officials refused to clarify precisely how Eric cheated. Because of the article, the attendance was lower than any previous finale in the past fifteen years! The ones who showed up weren't about to allow the teenager to win again. No siree Bob!

With Willy ready to pounce on them, no one in the crowd made a sound as Eric teed up his first shot. It soared straight above the fairway and landed dead center. His approach dropped onto the green, and Eric two-putted for par.

The result of hole two was the same as one. Using a five wood, Eric ran the ball onto the green, then two-putted for a par three. Shooting par in golf was a blessing for amateurs, but Eric was losing ground. Steven Bowditch followed up with a birdie on one, as did Charley Hoffman. Scott Pinckney birdied both holes and was tied for first at fifteen under. Eric was now five strokes back of the leaders.

Hugh knew the par-four third hole would make or break his teenage prodigy. For even the most outstanding professional golfers, the 528 yards were unreachable in two. More bogeys were recorded on the third hole at Las Colinas than any other on the pro tour. Water runs the length of the right side, and a pair of fairway bunkers are obstacles on the left side. Sand traps flank the heart-shaped green, and today the pin was located in the back right, making it nearly impossible to get close to the flag upon landing. Eric's caddie advised him to not overswing and settle for a bogey five.

"No way," he thought. "No risk, no reward!" Eric had been taught that for quite some time!

The drive was his best ever! It landed 240 yards from the tee, then skidded forward for another fifty! Eric's three-wood shot was long but rolled into the trap on the right front side. Unfortunately, the ball was lying only three inches from the grass behind it, meaning Eric had a limited backswing out of the bunker. Worried his teenage boss would top the ball and plow it deeper into the sand, Eric's caddie suggested he hit it backward onto the grass. Eric knew that meant a probable bogey or double bogey, and he shook his head no.

Lifting the wedge high and using a narrow arc, Eric dropped his knees, dug into the trap, and immediately punched upward and out. As if in slow motion, the ball elevated in a cloud of sand grains, bounced on the green, and rolled steadily into the cup! Willy and Jack Nicklaus were seen on television cameras giving each other a high five! The other fans let out a loud and boisterous boo!

Jimmy Walker parred the hole, but Bowditch, Hoffman, and Pinckney all bogeyed the monster. Jon Curran's drive had hooked left into the water, and he finished with a triple bogey. The three leaders were still tied but had dropped to fourteen under. Jimmy Walker gained a stroke and was one back at thirteen under. Eric had moved into fifth place at twelve under par.

Eric played his best, but he couldn't catch the leaders who were playing the hole directly behind him. His caddie was giving continual updates on their progress, so Eric always knew where he stood. For the remaining six holes on the front nine, Bowditch, Hoffman, and Pinckney matched Eric's three birdies and three pars. To make things even more complicated, Jimmy Walker birdied four holes. Going into the turn, four leaders were tied for first at seventeen under par. Eric was still two back with nine to go.

The tenth hole yielded pars for the frontrunners, so nothing changed on the scorecard. However, two holes back, Jordan Spieth had played a tremendous front nine and was now tied with Eric, two strokes behind the leaders.

Although the eleventh hole was perhaps the easiest one at the TPC Las Colinas, it turned out to be a nightmare for Eric. Nicknamed "birdie time," the 323-yard par four was joyous for the long hitters who could drive the green! The fairway had a slight dogleg left and featured water bordering the entire left side. Eric wanted to take the shortcut, but he and his caddie knew he didn't have the strength to do it. So, Eric played the hole to the right side of the fairway, then chipped onto the green in two.

Behind him, Bowditch and Hoffman ripped their drives over the stream and hazardous landscape, landing on the green in one. Pinckney played it safe, like Eric had, and parred the hole, but the others birdied it. When his caddie informed him, the dream of a career on the PGA tour seemed to be slipping away!

Eric had shifted up into fourth place after Pinckney lost a ball on fourteen and triple-bogeyed the hole. Scott was now two strokes behind the teenager. But Eric gained no ground on the top three playing holes twelve through fifteen. A birdie and three pars moved him to sixteen under par. However, things changed at the top. Bowditch was now alone at nineteen under, while Hoffman and Jimmy Walker were tied at eighteen under par.

Charley should have known better. He had played Las Colinas many times. The 546-yard, uphill par five dogleg hole is laced with sand traps, but the most distinguishable and dangerous one lies dead center on the fairway, 105 yards from the green. Instead of laying up his second shot behind the bunker, Hoffman tried to reach the green in two. The ball cleared the perilous trap but landed in a smaller bunker directly in front of it. The Calloway was buried in two inches of sand, and while trying to dig it out with a wedge, Charley launched his third shot over the green. A bogey six dropped his score to seventeen under. Bowditch, Walker, and Eric had parred in.

Eric was ready to tee off on the par-three seventeenth when a PGA official ran up and stopped him. He ordered Eric's caddie to turn his golf bag upside down and empty out all his clubs, balls, tees, towels, etcetera. Shocking everyone watching, including the sports reporters, the caddie obeyed the orders and dumped everything on the ground! The PGA official picked up six clubs, then let out a loud cackle and took off running into the woods. It didn't take a Rhodes Scholar to realize the man wasn't an official but another one of Eric's haters!

The pitiful incident stopped play for twenty minutes while the actual PGA officials tried to figure out what to do. Meanwhile, the golfers became backed up on the seventeenth tee. Now Bowditch, Hoffman, and Pinckney were together with Eric, Walker, and Curran. Willy took off chasing the club-stealing scoundrel through the course!

Officials decided the sixth golfers would all play the final two holes together. Eric had been intimidated and embarrassed by the crazy episode. His entire body became spasmodic, and he knelt on the grass, shaking. The youngest pro golfer was still in fourth place, three back of leader Steven Bowditch. Walker was in second, one shot behind Bowditch, and Charley Hoffman was third, two shots from tying for the lead.

"Nothing short of a miracle will help now," muttered Hugh to Jack Nicklaus. "Eric's a mess, and Charley's too good to overtake with two holes to play."

"And a par three seventeenth isn't going to help him gain strokes!" Jack smiled and patted Hugh on the back. "You gave it your best effort, my friend! You always have!"

Willy had returned, puffing from exertion. He couldn't catch his prey and was very disappointed. When he overheard them talking, Willy glared at Hugh and Jack with a stern look. "It ain't over 'til it's over! I know Eric. He ain't about to give up." Willy glanced up to the clouds and pointed toward heaven. "Miracles do happen, you know!"

*****

Sure enough, a miracle did happen on the very next hole. Officials had drawn straws for honors, and Eric would hit first. The 198-yard par three played downhill from the tee to a green highlighted by a pond on the right, a trap on the left, and bleachers in the back for fans. The fake official stole Eric's three iron, so he teed off with a five wood. The ball lifted and carried perfectly, landed gently on the green, and rolled next to the cup, hanging slightly over the edge. Fans were clapping and stomping their feet, thrilled not that Eric hit an exceptional shot but that the cheater's ball didn't roll in for a hole-in-one! However, it all backfired when due to their foot-trampling, the earth shook just enough for the ball to fall in before the time limit. Eric had aced the hole and dropped two strokes off his score!

The other five golfers watched in awe! This kid was absolutely sensational! He was the real deal, no doubt! Steven Bowditch was still planning on victory, so he played it safe and hit left. The ball landed in the bunker. Walker and Hoffman smiled, both thinking if they hit a phenomenal shot, they could gain on the leader. Curran went next and landed in the middle of the green. Then Charley Hoffman made a fatal mistake by trying to go over the water and land the ball next to the pin, which was tucked in on the right side, only a few feet from the pond's edge. His ball landed in the water!

Jimmy played it safe, like Curran, and landed the ball on the center of the green. Bowditch chipped out but was still fifteen feet from the pin. He two-putted for a bogey. Walker one-putted and was now in the lead, one stroke ahead of Bowditch and Eric. Charley Hoffman finished the seventeenth with a double-bogey and was virtually out of contention, sitting at fifteen under. All Eric needed was to maintain his three-stroke lead over Hoffman, and he would secure a top-three finish!

A PGA official announced honors for the final tee. "Mann, Walker, Curran, Pinckney, Bowditch, and Hoffman. Good luck, fellas!" The eighteenth hole was Las Colinas' signature. It was a 429-yard par four, highlighted by a dogleg left that plays around a gorgeous pond with a series of stunning waterfalls. Eric aimed at the bunker on the far side opposite the pond. His drive was perfection—275 yards and lying high on the grass on the right side of the fairway. But Jimmy Walker bested him. And so did Curran, Pinckney, Bowditch, and Hoffman! All were ten to twenty yards ahead of him.

Eric had hoped his ball wouldn't be back because he didn't want to hit the uphill approach shot to the green first. Water lined the left side of the green, and a bunker protected the right side. The pin was on the left, only ten feet from the pond. This would be Eric's most challenging shot of the day! His caddie said to stay right because the ball would roll left. But Eric could see if it rolled too much, it would end up in the pond!

Eric asked the caddie for a nine iron. He was 140 yards away, and that was his prime club for that distance. "Uh, sorry, Eric," mumbled the caddie. "You don't have a nine iron. Or an eight or seven or even a wedge. That dude stole them from you!" Eric looked out into the crowd trying to find Hugh. He needed guidance. His coach saw him but didn't understand what he was asking, so he shrugged his shoulders.

"Okay, well, do I have a six iron?"

"Yep, here ya go." The caddie handed him the club and, when Eric wasn't watching, shook his head in dismay.

Eric tried a half-stroke but chili-dipped the ball, and it sailed hard into the sand trap on the right side of the green. The crowd in the bleachers hollered their approval. "Ain't no way a cheater is going to win this tourney!" yelled a man, and those around him turned and gave him high fives. When Eric was heading to the bunker, the same man bellowed, "Go bury your head in the sand, right there with your ball, you baby-faced imposter!"

Curran and Pinckney landed their second shot in the middle of the green and were looking at twenty-foot putts. Jimmy Walker's second shot was masterful! It landed mid-green, spun left, and rolled two feet from the cup. The simple birdie putt would give him the championship! The crowd let out a thunderous applause! Steven Bowditch had no choice but to try and chip in to stay even with Walker, but he landed the ball too far right, and it rolled into the water. Disaster!

Then Charley Hoffman sent the fans into a frenzy. His ball soared sky high, then plopped down on the green and literally bounced into the cup for an eagle! Bowditch was given a penalty stroke, then hit his fourth shot from a drop area behind the water. Like magic, it, too, bounced on the green and rolled gracefully into the cup for par.

Hugh began to sweat on the sidelines. Jack had told him Eric's critical clubs had been stolen. He glanced up at the scoreboard and saw Bowditch had finished at eighteen under par, and Charley Hoffman completed the tourney at seventeen under. Doing the math quickly in his head, he realized Eric couldn't afford a bogey. That would put him in a tie for third with Hoffman, and who knew what the PGA would do in that case.

Eric's ball was buried deeply in the bunker, and he had no wedge to dig it out! Well, not exactly. He did have a left-handed sand wedge he used for balls that were lying next to a tree when he couldn't take a clean right-handed stroke. But he hadn't used it since Hugh taught him how—over two years ago! And not once had he practiced using the wedge in the sand!

"I have no advice, Eric," whispered the caddie. "A six iron or left-handed wedge from here both seem devastatingly awful. Sorry."

Eric patted his caddie on the back, smiled, and said confidently, "It's only a game. I'll give it my best shot no matter which club I use. The rest is up to Him." Eric pointed to the heavens.

Eric took the left-handed wedge, stepped into the trap, and looked extremely awkward as he addressed the ball. He was careful not to let the club touch the sand as he reeled off a few practice swings. A penalty now, and his career would be over. Hugh and Jack had the ultimate nervous looks on their faces. Jim and Dora huddled together in a deep hug. Willy looked up and gave the sign of the cross.

Eric's stroke was smooth as silk! He entered the sand two inches behind the ball, struck it perfectly, and followed through with precision! The Titleist landed softly, rolled flawlessly to the cup, and dropped in. The crowd booed relentlessly as Eric's score was posted on the leaderboard. The birdie gave him a nineteen under par 261 for the tournament. He was in second place, one stroke ahead of Steven Bowditch. He walked to the edge of the green and took a deep breath!

Curran and Pinckney each two-putted for pars, and that left Jimmy Walker with an easy two-footer for a birdie and the championship.

But Walker's gimme putt amazingly rolled past the cup and stopped eighteen inches on the other side! The fans collectively sighed from the bleachers. Instantly, Eric realized what that meant. With a par, he and Walker would compete in a sudden-death playoff for the championship. Oh wow!!

Jimmy knelt on the green and lined up his effortless putt. An amateur golfer could tap this in with his eyes closed. In fact, an amateur's buddies wouldn't even make him putt it. This was a gimme anyway you look at it!

Walker stood over his putter, ready for the tap-in. Then, he turned his head slightly toward Eric and winked. Hugh and Jack saw him and knew exactly what that meant. Jimmy pulled the putter back an inch and lightly tapped the ball. It stopped two inches short of the cup! He tapped it again for a bogey. The crowd couldn't believe it! A three-putt from two feet away! How could it be!

The crowd was upset Eric had won the tournament, and they began pelting him with water bottles, candy bars, and anything else they could find. Willy grabbed and sheltered him with his body as they hurried into the clubhouse. Eric's joy turned quickly to tears.

Meanwhile, Hugh and Jack approached Jimmy Walker, and each gave him a soft hug. "You are the epitome of a good sport, Jimmy," said Hugh. "I'm not sure why you did it because it cost you over a half million dollars in winnings, but you have gained our utmost respect!"

A tear rolled down Walker's face as he replied, "I watched and listened to what that poor kid had to endure this entire weekend. And still, his shots were astonishing, and his attitude was even more incredible! He deserved to win much more than me!" Jimmy smiled and headed to the clubhouse to congratulate Eric. Because of the obnoxious fans, he hadn't had the chance to do so on the green.

When Jimmy entered the clubhouse, Eric ran to him and gave him a hug. "What you did, Mr. Walker, was wonderful! But I can't accept winning this tournament because you let me win. I'm going to tell the press that you are the true winner."

Walker broke away with a slight push. "You'll do no such thing, Eric Mann! I messed up those putts on my own. You had nothing to do with it! And to any of the naysayers who think you are not the PGA's best golfer today, I say bunk! You are the greatest, young man! Don't ever forget that!"

A PGA official grabbed Eric's arm and yanked him to the podium in the center of the room. There, he was to be interviewed by a reporter for the Golf Channel. Other sports analysts were waiting their turn in line. The first question posed had nothing to do with his victory. "How did you cheat at the Masters, Eric?" asked the reporter.

Right away, Hugh ran in front of the cameras and blocked his young champion. "He didn't cheat. These interviews are officially over!"

Hugh rushed Eric into the locker room, stuffed his belongings into his duffle bag, then dashed for the back door. Jack Nicklaus was waiting inside a limousine with the door open. "Hop in, Eric. We're taking you to the airport. It's time to go home!

CHAPTER SEVENTY-THREE

June 19, 2015

Willy, Mel Smith, Keith Malone, Bushman Jack, and Pete Burns huddled in CIA Director John Barrett's office with British PGA President Winston Helms, two Scotland Yard police, and a handful of MI6 agents who had traveled across the pond for three weeks of logging evidence that could be used in a United States federal trial. Pete Burns was beginning to get his memory back but still hadn't made an announcement vindicating Eric Mann. Archbishop Guidan had declined the offer to attend the meetings but said he would fax information that could lead to the arrest of Bishop Kaiser.

Every member of St. Max's parish was interviewed in person, as were Golf Country Superstore CEO Ursula Vero and Eddy Gambo, owner of Electro Eddy's in San Francisco. Willy could kick himself now for not fully listening to Eddy's metallurgical analysis of the St. Max's golf ball. Had he acted then and been a good investigator, this whole mess could have been prevented, and Jake Tassett would be locked up in prison! Myra Rother, the manager of the Pahokee trailer court, came in to talk about Deacon Ollie.

Today was Friday, June 19th, and all the facts and observations of the case had been presented to Federal Judge Clyde Dahling. After a brief review of the evidence, Judge Dahling handed down indictments for fraud, tax evasion, and various other criminal actions. And to no one's surprise, he swore in Willy Banks as a federal marshal and appointed the ex-sheriff to head up investigations and make arrests. Willy was given a temporary leave of absence from his US Fish and Wildlife Service position. He could use the new Cessna, which had replaced the damaged plane following its rough landing in Canada and North Dakota. Insurance covered everything except for a $1,000 deductible.

Highest on the priority list for arrest warrants was Jake Tassett, better known by locals as Father Jacob. Next were Oliver Harwas, or Deacon Ollie, and Tommy Williams. Although nobody knew where they were hiding, the Canadian government offered their assistance in finding the crooks.

The computers taken from Oliver Harwas' trailer in Pahokee were directly linked to online gambling casinos. Harwas violated the *Unlawful Internet Gambling Enforcement Act of 2006,* which prohibited any person engaged in wagering online from knowingly accepting credit, electronic fund transfers, checks, or any other payment involving a financial institution to pay for Internet gambling bets. It was also shown that Harwas paid no taxes on his gambling wins. But seeing he was already America's Most Wanted felon by the FBI, the latest charges just added to his lengthy list of crimes.

*****

June 29, 2015

Bishop Bob Kaiser was the first to be arrested. Actually, he gave himself up. When he lost contact with Jake Tassett and Oliver Harwas, he assumed things weren't going well for TST Industries. He stopped by St. Max's Church and saw it was empty. The golf ball factory had yellow crime scene tape wrapped around it. He knew it wouldn't be long before an investigation led to him. One phone call to the Vatican by authorities would take care of that, so he lawyered up and walked into the Palm Beach police station to capitulate.

A few phone calls were made to determine if this man was a wanted criminal and, if so, who was the lead detective on the case. The police chief called the local FBI headquarters, which in turn called CIA Director Barrett in Virginia. Barrett called Willy, and he made the arrest. Willy escorted Kaiser and his attorney to a vacant St. Max's apartment, where Barrett had set up Willy's office. Willy wanted to be close to his Cessna in case he was needed elsewhere. Mel Smith and Keith Malone were present for the meeting, as well.

After a morning of haggling over legal matters, Willy received permission from Barrett to offer Kaiser a deal in exchange for information that would solidify the case and lead to the arrest of Tassett and Harwas. In the end, following several calls to authorities in Great Britain and Ireland, if Kaiser could deliver condemnatory evidence, he would be a free man and avoid extradition to the Emerald Isle. However, it was made very clear should Kaiser ever set foot again in the UK or Ireland, he would be prosecuted to the fullest degree of the law!

Kaiser's first testimony was to identify Jake Tassett's corrupt priest buddies in Irving, Texas, Jackson, Mississippi, and Augusta, Georgia. He knew exactly where they were living because he was the one who recommended their placements to the Vatican. Kaiser explained that none of the priests were ordained, nor were they ever enrolled in collegiate religious studies. As a matter of fact, none had ever gone to college! Kaiser falsified their documents and persuaded Vatican officials to place them in parishes that happened to be strategically close to PGA golf courses holding major tournaments: The Masters in Augusta, the AT&T Byron Nelson Classic in Irving, and the Sanderson Farms Championship in Jackson. The fake priests' job was to bless Eric Mann's golf balls before each tournament. What they really were doing was activating the balls with a tiny laser embedded into a cross. Activation gave the balls immense ferromagnetic attraction to the golf cups on the greens. Father Jacob also gave Eric false blessings that activated St. Max's balls before his golf matches, including the Honda Classic in Palm Beach Gardens.

Tassett had grand plans to build a five-star golf resort in the middle of the desert east of Albuquerque, New Mexico. Once the PGA approved it, he hoped to host major tournaments there. Because of that, he needed Bishop Kaiser to place one more priest somewhere in the area. Tassett's high school friend was Michael Cole, who became Father Michael of Holy Spirit Catholic Church in Clines Corners, New Mexico.

The golf cups couldn't be activated simultaneously, or when a ball was struck, it might be attracted to any green on the course. Thus, one cup would be targeted at a time and controlled remotely. To turn the golf cups on and off, Tassett needed Wi-Fi boosters placed on the golf courses. He asked another high school friend who had later earned a Bachelor of Science degree in Electrical Engineering to create the boosters and hide them inside solid, crystal-clear glass crosses with beveled edges. Tassett wanted a sculpture of Jesus encased inside each booster to give a three-dimensional effect. The glass crosses were placed on wooden bases about four inches thick. Father Jacob's priest friends would install the crosses on the roofs of the PGA clubhouses. If anyone noticed, they would appear to be random religious symbols for golfers to pray to before playing a match.

Willy ended the meeting. He needed to make some phone calls and visit a judge.

*****

June 30, 2015

On Tuesday morning, all of Jake Tassett's fake Catholic priests received warrants, were handcuffed, and led away from their churches in disgrace. Parishioners were stunned and were given no information about the arrests from church employees. They watched the nightly news hoping to understand the situation but with no luck.

Wednesday, Bob Kaiser was called back to provide more intricate details of Jake Tassett's life since escaping prosecution in the 1980s. When he hesitated, Kaiser was reminded that if he wanted his freedom, he must cooperate. That's when Bob said he was in fear for his life.

"You've taken enormous risks!" declared Willy emphatically. "You don't seem like a man who is afraid of much! So, who are you frightened of?"

"If Tassett finds out I have a deal with you, he will send Oliver Harwas out to end me! And he won't miss his mark. He never does!"

"One call to the FBI, and I can have you in the Witness Protection Program by tonight. You'll be safe and can start a new life."

Kaiser scribbled some words on a piece of paper and drew a rough picture of a house. The doodling was a nervous reaction to Willy's offer. What choice did Kaiser have? If he didn't lay out all the facts, figures, and particulars, he would spend the rest of his life in prison. His whole body began to shake, but the decision was a no-brainer. "Okay, but can I choose where I'm placed?"

"Within reason. You realize an undercover FBI agent will need to live nearby. We would have to provide arrangements for him, too."

The fake bishop nodded, and a video camera was set up. Bob Kaiser's testimony would be recorded and used in court. Tense with trepidation, he asked to use the restroom. Kaiser leaned against the wall in the bathroom, on the verge of hysterics. Mel came in five minutes later to calm him down and show him back to the table.

*****

With the video recorder whirring and the power button on the camera glowing red, Willy fired away with the first question. "Mr. Kaiser, when did you first meet Jake Tassett? Bob's response sounded like an autobiography.

"I was just a beach bum when Tassett and his friend Judge Maximillian Boone approached me on Paradise Island in Nassau in the mid-1980s. I owned a fly-by-night SCUBA business and a twenty-two-foot wreck of a fishing boat I got free in a divorce settlement. Me and my ex-wife were bartenders at a resort's poolside joint on the island when my ex decided to run off with a dude who hung out at the pool. He offered me his boat and business in exchange for my wife. That way, none of us would need to pay for a lawyer. Sounded reasonable, so I took the deal. But it came with one rather large condition: I needed to take our six-month-old baby son, Jimmy, and raise him. His mom and her boyfriend wanted nothing to do with him!

"Not wanting to work next to my ex, I quit the bartending job and started a SCUBA business at a marina. I had eight rusty air tanks and other shabby dive equipment. The boat had a small leak, and I constantly had to run the bilge pump to stay afloat in the ocean. I hired a Bahamian babysitter who watched Jimmy all day for ten dollars and free food and lodging. She stayed with me in a two-bedroom apartment that cost $125 a month.

"That's when Tassett and Boone found me and asked if I had come across any uncharted islands anywhere in the Devil's Triangle. It was crazy they should use that term because natives around there were superstitious and didn't want to hear it! Anyway, I had seen an island once that wasn't on nautical maps, so I thought maybe it was deserted.

"They offered me a thousand bucks to take a look, so I said yes, but I told them they would need to pay for a new bilge pump first, as my old one was wearing out. They agreed, and off we went. And yes, the island ended up being deserted and uncharted. Instead of just dropping them off and going back to Nassau, Tassett and Boone offered me a permanent job. They said they would buy me a new thirty-five-foot yacht and give me $50,000 a year if I would transport them to and from the Bahamas when needed. I told them I had an infant son, so I couldn't do it. Tassett said to bring him and the babysitter along, and he would build a house for all of us to live in. I had nothing going for me in Nassau, so I said yes!

"While probing for a location to build, Tassett found evidence of someone living on the island in the past. He had me take him to the University of the Bahamas in Nassau, where he could research the area. In the library, he read about Christopher Columbus landing somewhere in the Bahamas, but there was no definitive location other than one of the Plana Cays. After reading, he knew the relics he found belonged to Columbus' landing party!

"Tassett traveled back to Florida and hired a handful of sugar cane workers and four of their bosses to be his employees. The men were single and earning diddly squat, so they gladly followed Tassett to the uncharted island. Tassett wanted them to find ancient relics and dig a vault to keep them in. That's when the men discovered a powerful magnetic substance. Tassett later named it planacalum, after Plana Cay. Many of Columbus' weapons were made of iron and clung to the planacalum in the vault. It was so powerful it took five men to break the weapons away! It was then that Tassett had the idea he could use the substance to make money—criminally!

"One night, one of Tassett's new employees was using a flashlight in the vault to look for a watch he had misplaced. The light went out, so the worker had to change the two size D batteries. It was dark, and he dropped one of the batteries. It skidded across the floor. Shockingly, the man watched as sparks rose, and suddenly planacalum rocks and dust flew across the room and clung to the battery. He yelled for a friend to come into the vault and see it. Both of them rubbed the positive stem of a different battery rapidly on the floor, causing friction, and sure enough, planacalum again shot through the air and clung to the battery! The employees told Tassett and Boone to come take a look. It was evident the magnetism of the planacalum was enhanced by electricity.

"Jake Tassett's network of wrongdoers lined him up with Burt Merriman, a mob boss who lived on a private island in the Caymans. Merriman had employees in every line of work imaginable. Tassett needed an electrical engineer for some guidance with what he witnessed in the vault. Merriman said he would rent a guy out for $100,000 a month. Tassett made the deal and sent someone to the Caymans to pick him up.

"It only took a week for the electrical engineer to discover the already super strong ferromagnetic properties of planacalum could be enhanced one hundred-fold by stimulating it with electricity or even a specially designed laser beam that produced radiation. To demonstrate what he was saying, the engineer used a laser to activate a small planacalum rock with radioactive energy, then tossed it high into the air. Instead of falling to the ground, the rock shot three hundred yards to a container of planacalum hooked to a battery with electrical wires running around it.

"That's when Judge Boone had an idea. It was the middle of October in 1991, and the Major League Baseball semifinals had just finished. Through a series of phone calls, Boone found out a shipment of Rawlings baseballs stamped with a special logo of the 1991 World Series was headed to Minneapolis and Atlanta in company cargo trucks. The one heading north out of St. Louis on Highway 61 would be stopping overnight in Dubuque, Iowa. Jake Tassett immediately sent all his Plana Cay employees, including myself, on a private jet to Dubuque with planacalum nuggets infused with small batteries created by Merriman's engineer.

"We broke into the trucks and worked through the night injecting the nuggets into the baseballs. Afterward, we applied innovative magical leather patches over the holes and smoothed them with the tip of a hot iron. Some core material was extracted so the baseballs would weigh almost the same after inserting the tiny nuggets and batteries. The balance was a bit off, but after close examination, you couldn't tell the balls had been doctored.

"Judge Boone was given a metallic cross containing planacalum, wires, and a battery that he sewed into the pocket of a baseball glove. The glove would need to be strapped to the Judge's arm, or it could fly away and strike the targeted ball in midair. All he had to do was flip the switch on the outside of the cross, and the planacalum would be activated.

"Had the World Series only gone four or five games that year, the whole scheme would have been wasted and postponed for the following season. But fortunately for Tassett and Boone, the Twins and Braves played game six at the Metrodome in downtown Minneapolis. Should the Twins win, a decisive game seven would follow the next evening. Atlanta was favored by all oddsmakers to close out the series in six. Jake Tassett flew to Las Vegas and wagered two million dollars throughout various casino sports books betting on the Twins to win.

"Judge Boone bought a priest costume and roamed around the stadium talking to scalpers until he located a ticket in the left field bleachers. Knowing his targeted ball would be a homerun, he paid ten times the ticket price for the seat. The police didn't even look twice at him making the deal on the street. Why should they? A priest wouldn't buy an illegal ticket from a scalper, right?

"When the game started, Boone wasn't sure what hitter he would select to help him hit a homerun. Actually, he wasn't totally sure the plan would work. But knowing how much Tassett was gambling on the game, it better perform as it was intended!

"The game was close throughout, and Judge Boone, who had changed his name to Father Max for the night in case anyone sitting nearby had asked, thought maybe he wouldn't even need to activate the cross in his glove. The Twins scored two in the first, and the Braves tied it up in the fifth, but the Twins went ahead by a run in the bottom of the inning. The Braves picked up the tying run in the top of the seventh, and soon the game was headed to extra innings. Hoping the Twins would pull it out in the tenth, Father Max held back. Then, worried that everything might fall apart he decided to target a pitch to Kirby Puckett in the bottom of the eleventh. All Kirby had to do was hit it in the air, and the magnetic cross would do the rest.

"The strategy worked like a charm, and after watching the homerun on a large screen monitor in a sportsbook, Jake Tassett danced around Vegas collecting his winnings!

"Next up, he and Boone thought they would try messing with collegiate women's softball games. Then, they targeted cricket. It was easier to insert planacalum with batteries attached into a Kookaburra ball than an MLB baseball. But as technology improved, the ploy changed a bit. The electrical engineer found a way to activate the pulling magnets remotely using pocket radios. That way, Judge Boone didn't need to be there. And when Wi-Fi came out in the early 2000s, Tassett switched to the Internet. The balls would be doctored at the factory in Plana Cay and shipped to Europe and Australia encased inside Bibles. Father Max would be at the ports of entry with a truck to unload the Kookaburras. Then he would surreptitiously switch them with the actual balls at night. The remote-controlled magnets would be installed into the outfield fences and used when needed.

Willy stood up and pounded his fist on the table. "Are you telling us that all those Bibles meant for the homeless contained Kookyberries and were sent to England and Australia?!"

"The word is Kookaburras, and yes, that's what happened."

Willy, Mel, and Keith were blown away by all the information Bob Kaiser was giving them. They needed a break!

*****

Kaiser continued his deposition a half-hour later. "Judge Boone's younger sister, Alma, still lived in Seminole Bend, and he called her once a month to check up on her. She worked as a night custodian for Father O'Shea at the Catholic Church and was unhappy because she had few friends. Alma had never been married but, at Father O'Shea's request, was raising a boy who had no parents. The boy was named Oliver Harfield, after his dad who—"

Willy interrupted Kaiser. "Wait! What?! Judge Boone's sister was raising Oliver Harfield's illegitimate son?! What a coincidence!"

Willy looked at Smith and Malone, then spoke into the microphone so what he had to say could be documented. "Harfield was a CIA agent who was the mastermind behind the downing of the two jets over Florida in the 1980s! Tassett was the NTSB lead investigator who helped with the coverup. Harfield died when his private jet crashed, but I never knew what happened to his illegitimate son!"

Mel nodded and said, "Yes, we know all about Oliver Harfield and how Tassett worked for him. Harfield was a rogue CIA agent—a black eye to our organization!"

Bob Kaiser continued. "Well, anyway, Boone moved Alma and young Oliver to the Plana Cay island. Alma lied to Father O'Shea and said she had a job offer in California and would take the toddler to live with her.

Little Oliver became best friends with my son, Jimmy, during those years on Plana Cay. Later, after discovering who his dad really was, Oliver broke bad and became a criminal. It must have been in the genes! Anyway, he changed his last name to Harwas to avoid harassment by legal agencies who would recognize his real name."

Kaiser stood up and paced the room. Willy, Mel, and Keith could see he was struggling to say something. Finally, Bob sat back down and muttered softly. "After only a year on the island, I made a huge mistake."

"Go on," said Willy. "What was it?"

"Tassett and Boone polished up their grand scheme to fix professional sports by using the magnetic force of planacalum. Seeing it worked during the World Series, they believed they could control sports gambling and make tons of money. That's when Judge Boone's sister came up with the idea to use religion as a decoy for the operation. She liked how her brother had dressed up as Father Max and fooled the police and fans in Minneapolis. She thought that theme could become a perfect strategy for their enterprise.

"So, they came up with a plan for me to become a bishop in the Catholic church. It required falsifying documents and college transcripts, then fooling the Vatican into hiring me somewhere in the United States. The diocesan bishop of Palm Beach passed away, and Tassett knew he had to make his move within nine months because that was the timeframe given to pick a new bishop. He bought a couple of hangars right here on the grounds of the North Palm Beach airport, then quickly hired an architect to draw up plans for a church. He facetiously called it St. Max's Church after Judge Boone's disguise as Father Max. The building of the church would come later—all he needed was to register it with the county. By the time the church was built, Judge Boone had died, so Tassett decided to name the golf ball factory after him, too!

"Tassett had me act as the pastor of St. Max's Catholic Church and introduce myself to all the priests in the Palm Beach diocese. None had any clue where my church was located, and had they come to visit, they would have found an empty airplane hangar! Thankfully, none did stop by. Meanwhile, I visited every priest almost weekly in their own parishes. I would tell them I had friends in the Vatican who could provide funding for their congregations. 'Just let me know what you need,' I would say. Then, I sent a bunch of Tassett's money to their churches!

"There soon became a buzz around the diocese that I should be the new bishop. Who else had financial connections to Vatican City? When the nine-month waiting period was over, I was the unanimous choice. My falsified documents had been snuck into a filing cabinet in the pope's offices by one of Burt Merriman's Mafia men, who was a master at breaking and entering! He drove up the Italian coast from Sicily to Rome, broke into the Vatican offices one night, and poof, my fake bio and resume were tucked neatly away!

"When the recommendation from the Palm Beach diocesan priests arrived, there was most likely only a cursory glance at my file, and then a stamp of approval for me to be the next bishop. I doubt the pope even knew!

Willy shuffled through his notes. "Earlier, you said you made a big mistake, Bob, but you never told us about it. What was it?"

Kaiser teared up and waited a moment to gather his thoughts. "Because I was going to be on the road, perhaps for a long, long time, and I was going to be a Catholic bishop, I couldn't bring my son along with me. To try and make me feel better, Tassett offered to adopt Jimmy. My mistake was that I said yes. I didn't have much confidence in Jake's ability to be a good father! But my options were limited. If I didn't become bishop after all the finagling they did to get me the position, they would send me back to Nassau to live on the beach. Or, in the back of my mind, I thought they might kill me. As long as my Bahamian babysitter was there to look after Jimmy, I thought he would have a better chance in life if he stayed and grew up on the island.

"When Tassett moved to Florida to become Father Jacob, he placed Jimmy in charge of the Plana Cay operation, which had become, as you well know, a huge money-making venture. He treated him terribly!" Kaiser paused a second, then glanced at Willy. "As a matter of fact, when you were hiding out on the island, Tassett was thinking about killing Jimmy because he let you get ahold of an AK-47!"

"Hmmm. This is starting to make some sense. Go on."

Bob Kaiser talked for hours about making the factory and how Tassett built up the business by using his networks of corruption throughout the world. Kaiser testified how he set up fake charities, including the one at St. Max's Church in North Palm Beach, and swindled the Catholics in Ireland. He also placed Tassett's friends into priest positions so they could help control the illegal gaming efforts.

Lastly, Kaiser identified Tommy Williams as the engineer and conductor of the nefarious train that would corrupt the Professional Golfers Association. "Do you remember me telling you about the electrical engineer on Plana Cay who experimented with planacalum and electricity?"

"Yes, of course," replied Willy. "The man Burt Merriman loaned to Tassett for $100,000. The guy who discovered the super strength of planacalum. What about him?"

"His name was Thomas Williams. His only son was Tommy Williams. Tommy had worked for Titleist and invented new covers and cores but was never given any credit. So, he decided to head up the St. Max's golf ball project and make a lot of money. He hoped to overtake Titleist as the top-selling golf ball in America. After I was removed from my duties as a bishop, he hired me to bury the electrified cups laced with planacalum on the greens and to replace them immediately after the tournaments ended.

Mel broke into the conversation. "Yes, because we worked clandestinely with him, we certainly knew about Tommy Williams, and along with your testimony, we can put him away for a long time. But we didn't know his father discovered the ferromagnetic capabilities of planacalum."

Everyone in the room looked at one another and nodded. It was time to end the deposition. They had gathered plenty of evidence necessary to lock up Jake Tassett, Oliver Harwas, and Tommy Williams for life. All they needed now was to find them!

"An FBI agent will be arriving soon to move you into the Witness Protection Program. We appreciate all the information you provided. We'll see you again as soon as we catch Tassett, Harwas, and Williams and have them in court. Until then, are there any requests for us?"

"Yes," said Kaiser. "Just one. Could you use the services of the CIA to find my son, Jimmy? He was just a pawn for Tassett and had no choice but to carry out his boss' orders. I'm sure he would also testify against Tassett if you could find him. I would love to restart my life with him and finally be the dad I should have been."

Mel nodded at Willy, then said to Bob, "We'll do our best to make that happen."

CHAPTER SEVENTY-FOUR

July 5, 2015

Pete Burns' occupational therapist provided daily sessions of memory training to help him learn methods to organize new information and replace details and particulars that were lost. Although he hadn't gained back all that had vanished, he did remember Eric Mann was innocent. The day after Independence Day, Eric was exonerated from all wrongdoing. Burns spent most of the day giving interviews to the Golf Channel, ESPN, and Associated Press reporters who forwarded his message worldwide.

The two main points Burns stated were comforting to Eric and Hugh: First, Eric is the best golfer ever on the PGA circuit, and second, the rude fans who pelted the teenage phenom with boos and pecans should be ashamed of themselves and never be allowed to attend a professional sports contest again! Never again, any sport! Harsh words and truly unenforceable but nevertheless consoling to Hugh Kraft.

After presenting Eric with a check for $1,278,000 as the prize money for winning the AT&T Byron Nelson Championship, the youngster shocked the golf universe. "First of all," he expressed, "I forgive the PGA fans who attended the tournament in Irving. A cheater has no right to play in any athletic contest—pro or amateur. They thought I had cheated and reacted to it. My only advice would be to throw something that didn't hurt so much, like foam balls instead of pecans."

The reporters and cameramen all began to laugh, thinking Eric was being sarcastic. But Eric didn't smile because he was dead serious. "I know you are assuming I was joking, but I'm not. My dad taught me 'sticks and stones can break my bones, but words can never hurt me.' Well, a few weekends ago, I discovered that pecans should be added to the saying, along with sticks and stones! I also found out the hard way that words can actually hurt you. They can hurt your feelings, that is.

"Wouldn't this be a much better world if people would be nice to each other? And wouldn't it be better if the saying 'it's not whether you win or lose, it's how you play the game' were true? Mom taught me that one. It's from the poem, *Alumnus Football*. A poet named Grantland Rice wrote it in 1908. You all should know him. He was a sports columnist for the *New York Herald-Tribune* and the first World Series play-by-play announcer in 1922. I believe Mr. Rice was just as heroic as the pro athletes he wrote and spoke about! Why? Because he dared to express in words how sports idols can affect the physical, mental, and social well-being of their fans, which should be their main goal in life. Not winning contests simply for their own personal gain!

"Mr. Burns said I was the best golfer ever on the PGA circuit—but he is wrong. I wouldn't have won the tournament without Jimmy Walker's support and encouragement when I was down in the dumps. Jack Nicklaus showed up to cheer me on. Both of them are tremendous golfers, but more importantly, they are wonderful human beings! I can't hold a candle to them!

"My hero isn't in the world of sports. My hero is my mom! She's a teacher. Mom goes to work each day with one goal—to make life better for her students by giving them knowledge. And to also be a role model of fairness, honesty, and compassion.

"The Catholic Church I go to is about to be shut down and leveled to the earth because the priest was a bad person. If that happens, my school will also be closed, as will the apartments that are provided for low-income families. The church members are hardworking, decent people who are my friends. We are going to appeal to the pope to let St. Max's parish continue and to find us a new priest—someone who is honest and caring.

"I am donating every penny of my prize money to keep St. Max's church, school, and apartments open. I will continue to play professional golf until I'm old enough to attend college. All my earnings will go to helping underprivileged people have a better existence on earth. Then I will retire from the PGA and pursue a degree in education. I want to be a teacher like Mom and dedicate my life to helping homeless and oppressed kids succeed."

Eric thanked the media and waved. Astoundingly, every reporter rose from their seats and gave Eric a standing ovation. In the back of the room, Eric saw his coach nod and wink at him.

Hugh thought to himself, "Golfers will come and go who will be better than Eric. But finding someone more honorable, principled, and generous will be highly unlikely! The kid has redefined good sportsmanship!"

EPILOGUE

August, 2016

Jake Tassett, the new president and CEO of Lake Winnipeg Enterprises of Canada, was an incredibly aggressive capitalist who would try any strategy to gain a prospective customer's business. During the summer of 2015, LWE outbid Inglasco, Incorporated, for the rights to supply pucks to the National Hockey League. Inglasco had been the NHL's supplier of hockey pucks since 1976 but had no way to match LWE's offer. Shea Hansen, who had been hired as LWE's Director of Sales, negotiated the contract, but Tassett knew before the meeting that it would be a slam dunk. It's difficult to outbid free! Yes, LWE would provide the NHL with pucks for the first five years of the agreement at zero cost!

Produced on a small island in the middle of Lake Winnipeg, LWE pucks are made of granular rubber, antioxidants, and coal dust, all bonded into a two-part mold using superior-strength glue. The rubber is three inches wide and one-inch thick. The NHL logo is silk-screened onto the pucks with ink that won't diminish with constant wear and tear by sticks and ice. Before the pucks are molded, four other ingredients are inserted: planacalum, electrical wire, a battery-operated activator, and a remote-controlled GPS guidance system.

The NHL commissioner was ecstatic about making a deal for free pucks! LWE offered to provide hockey goals free for all the league's stadiums once the NHL's contract with Heartland Sports expired after the 2015-16 season ended. Heartland Sports, the NHL's goal supplier since 1982, was devastated. How could they offer a price better than zero?!

Voila! Easy money! Tommy Williams would be sent to various NHL arenas while Oliver Harwas wagered absurd sums of money on whoever Jake Tassett chose to win the contest. Life was good! However, that was the future—it would be a year later! The pucks had to be tested during the upcoming season, meaning something innovative was needed to rig the goals with electronics and planacalum.

*****

June 2016 (A year later)

Some who have followed professional hockey for many years would say that Gordie Howe was the best skating stickman ever. Sure, others would say it was Wayne Gretzky or Bobby Hull or Bobby Orr. But Gordie, better known as Mr. Hockey, won six Hart Memorial trophies, a Lester Patrick trophy, six Art Ross trophies, and the coveted NHL Lifetime Achievement Award. Those honors were nice and very much appreciated, but Gordie cherished one prize even more: Howe's teams won four Stanley Cups, the summa cum laude of professional ice hockey. The NHL's grand championship!

It was fitting that Gordie, who passed away on June 10th, 2016, should be memorialized during the Stanley Cup finals. The Pittsburgh Penguins held a three-to-two advantage over the San Jose Sharks and hoped to wrap things up at the SAP Center in San Jose. Game six was in progress, and Penguins defenseman Brian Dumoulin got things started in the first period with a power play drive. After the period ended and teams headed for their locker rooms, a sound and light system was attached to the base of both goals to ensure they were equidistance apart from the center of the rink, thus producing a perfect stereo effect. Then, the arena lights were dimmed. A hologram of Gordie Howe was illuminated and a tribute to the Detroit Red Wings star was played.

The sound and light technician was in a frenzy! The tribute was supposed to be done before the game started, but the equipment hadn't arrived in the cargo van in time. Traffic on Highway 101 in the Bay Area can be a nightmare!

Pittsburgh had taken a one to nil lead. Playing on the visitor's ice, they were the underdogs. The Penguins, who had lost game five at home, were given little chance of winning by bookies. They opened with plus 120 odds for game six. Oliver Harwas had spent the last two days wagering ten million dollars online and in casinos. The next day, he hoped to collect $12,000,000 in winnings! But Pittsburgh needed the victory.

Harwas, watching the game in the Venetian Sports Book, pounded the bar table with his fist after Sharks center Logan Couture fired a shot past Penguin goalie Matt Murray, which tied the game at one. "What's going on in San Jose!" muttered Harwas. "Why was the tribute at the first intermission and not the beginning of the game, damn it?!" Those sitting at a table nearby wondered why that angry fellow cared more about Gordie Howe's tribute than the game!

Tommy Williams had attached the cylinder of planacalum and electrical wires to the base of both goals during the time he was setting up the sound and light system. No one noticed him, and no one thought twice because it appeared the small cylinder was being used to hold the goal in place.

Now, sitting in the top row of the SAP arena, Tommy activated the cylinder behind the Sharks' goal. Seconds later, Pittsburgh regained the lead when defenseman Kris Letang ricocheted the puck off Sharks' goaltender Martin Jones, and it went in. Jones was beside himself. He had stopped the shot with his glove and sat on it, but somehow it wiggled out and went into the goal! Impossible!

As the game continued and the Sharks had plenty of breakaway opportunities to score, the puck would strangely turn like a boomerang and be intercepted by Penguin defensemen! The Sharks managed only two shots on goal in the third period, and Pittsburgh ended up winning their fourth Stanley Cup in franchise history! In Las Vegas, Oliver Harwas waved both hands in the air, then bought a round of drinks for everyone in the sports bar!

*****

September 25, 2016

Five professional golfers have achieved a career slam, a feat that requires winning four major tournaments: the British Open, the Masters, the PGA Championship, and the US Open. Those Hall of Fame golfers were Gene Sarazen, Ben Hogan, Gary Player, Jack Nicklaus, and Tiger Woods. Only one golfer had ever won a calendar year slam: Bobby Jones completed the gigantic triumph in 1930.

All of Bobby's scores in those tournaments were shattered during the 2015-16 PGA tour when fourteen-year-old Eric Mann became the second player to win a calendar year slam. The teenager also won five other invitationals and never placed lower than third the entire season! He was officially crowned King of the Links and became recognized globally as the crème de la crème of professional golf.

Eric Mann would have been a multimillionaire had it not been for the fact that he gave away every penny of his winnings to St. Francis of Assisi Catholic Church, the new name for St. Max's parish. Eric himself petitioned the pope to keep the church and attached K-12 school and rename it after St. Francis, who was the patron saint of the poor.

The parish grew to one-thousand members because of Eric. Everyone wanted to get to know him personally since he was the most famous professional athlete playing today. He loved chatting with his fellow parishioners and signed personalized autographs for each of them. Eric offered free PGA tour tickets to anyone who donated food or clothing to the *Eric Mann Fund for the Homeless*.

Meanwhile, at Archbishop Milo Guidan's demand, St. Max's golf ball enterprise was permanently shut down.

*****

June 28, 2017 (The following summer)

Two years after being appointed a federal marshal and lead investigator, Willy was released from his position and returned to his previous job as South Florida Director of the US Fish and Wildlife Service. Keith Malone retired from the CIA, but Mel Smith offered to stay on part-time in a consultatory role. To keep from being bored in semi-retirement, Mel offered to manage the apartment complex next to the church free of charge. Keith said his goodbyes and was never heard from again.

An exhaustive search for Jake Tassett, Oliver Harwas, and Tommy Williams proved fruitless, but a week earlier, a private jet registered to TST Industries back in 2009 crashed during a storm near Pakwaw Lake, Saskatchewan. The plane had taken off from a private runway east of Grand Rapids, Manitoba, on the western shore of Lake Winnipeg. The female operator of the Mission Point Lighthouse adjacent to the runway said three men got into the aircraft, and she gave detailed descriptions to the Canadian Royal Mounted Police. The police surmised that the three men could possibly be the ones who were on the FBI's Ten Most Wanted list in the United States. Willy flew his Cessna to Grand Rapids with a variety of pictures of Jake Tassett, Oliver Harwas, and Tommy Williams. The lighthouse operator, who strangely looked somewhat familiar to Willy, confirmed those were the three men who got into the jet.

The FBI closed the case on Thursday, July 6th, 2017. On Friday, Bob Kaiser was released from the Witness Protection Program because no one was alive who could harm him. Kaiser's biological son, Jimmy Tassett, who had been living with him, was happy to hear that his adoptive father and the madman, Oliver Harwas, were dead.

*****

July 14, 2017

After it was reported a private jet owned by TST Industries had crashed in Canada, Mel called Bushman Jack and asked him to provide drone surveillance at the site where the plane went down. He reported back to Mel that the aircraft was in pieces, and no one could ever survive an aviation disaster such as that. It was precisely what the FBI, CIA, and Canadian Royal Mounties assumed.

After the case was closed, Mel forgot to tell Bushman Jack he could call off the search. A few days later, the drone picked up something very unusual: Three parachutes were lying on the ground near Turnberry, Manitoba.

Sitting in his office on top of Ayers Rock in the Australian desert wasteland, Bushman Jack pondered a terrible thought: Was it possible Tassett, Harwas, and Williams jumped out of the plane and purposely crashed it to make it look like they were all dead? That idea was very doubtful. Most likely, the parachutes belonged to the *High-Flying Jumpers Club*. This organization offered first-timers the chance to skydive. Jack tried to call Mel, but Smith had accidentally turned off his satellite phone. Bushman didn't know how to reach him.

Jack shook his head and muttered to himself, "Naw, they couldn't have staged something like that. It would cost a fortune to acquire a new jet, and now that they were no longer fixing golf tourneys, Tassett had no money. All his assets had been frozen around the world! And to top it off, they would have needed an accomplice to cover for them."

Bushman Jack put the thought to rest and frowned. Why was he always talking to himself, he wondered? He drank a glass of milk and went to bed.

Meanwhile, Ursula Vero removed her wig and fake glasses, then climbed down from the Mission Point Lighthouse. It was time for a morning coffee break.

ACKNOWLEDGEMENTS

Interesting characters make for a compelling story. My favorite authors use captivating protagonists surrounded by an irresistible supporting cast to enhance their novels. John Grisham creates Deep South personalities so perfectly believable that you can envision yourself living in Mississippi even if you haven't set foot in that state. Wilbur Smith does the same for Sir Francis Courtney's family on the African continent. And Dan Brown has developed Robert Langdon's character so ingeniously that only one of the greatest actors of all time, Tom Hanks, could portray the Harvard symbologist who successfully solves mysterious religious codes.

Although I can't hold a candle to Grisham, Smith, or Brown, I have tried to make my novels more appealing by using real people, places, and historical events. I also try to ensure that the real people are portrayed in a positive light. I mean, who said it better than Disney's famous rabbit, Thumper, when he spoke about Bambi? "If you can't say something nice, don't say nothing at all."

With that said, it's time for a few disclaimers. Jack Nicklaus was not a friend of Hugh Kraft or even young Eric Mann. Why? Because Hugh and Eric do not exist in real life (at least not that I'm aware of!). However, Nicklaus is a wonderful man who was an incredibly talented professional golfer! And the same can be said of the lengthy list of PGA and other professional athletes (baseball, cricket, and hockey) I used to enhance the story. Kirby Puckett was very much the hero of the 1991 World Series Game Six, however, planacalum had nothing to do with it!

Pope Francis became the head of the Catholic Church in 2013. He always has been and continues today as champion for the poor and oppressed, which is why I used his real name in the book. However, Archbishop Milo Guidan is a fictional character.

Okay, now for a disclaimer of my own disclaimer. As I have done in all my novels, I have used actual friends or relatives as characters. Most have asked me to do this so they can live forever in infamy! Yeah, right, we can only wish! But the agreement I make with them is to not guarantee what type of role they will portray: hero or villain! Can you hear Thumper sighing?! So let me tell you a little about *Bold Expectation's* oldie but goodie and the newest chosen few.

First, and yes, you've seen his name in print before: Oliver Harwas. But no, it's not on the FBI's Most Wanted List pinned on the post office bulletin board! Although he's one of my most wily and corrupt characters once again, he has petitioned me umpteen times to become a well-liked, friendly, and honest guy like he is in real life. But until he lets me win a game of tennis, that will never happen!

Second, Wayne Siebold's wife, Kay, served up her hubby to be a professional golfer in my book without his knowing about it. Wayne was my high school basketball coach and has remained a lifelong friend. His actual nicknames in college were Speedboat and Siebs, but his high school players only knew him as Coach. We always admired Coach Siebold for teaching his players to play ethically and live responsibly. Sometimes on the golf course when I wavered between gamesmanship or winning at all costs, he would put the hex on my putts and force me to lose. That brought me back to earth!

The other two on the list are college roommates and volleyball teammates from Pace University in New York: Ursula Vero and Shea Hansen are both successful business ladies, which is why, of course, they are portrayed as such in the novel. However, Ursula is not an exploiter. Rather, she is a cheerful, polite, and respectful young gal raised by two big-hearted Italian parents in the Bronx. And Shea is not a corporate raider! Instead, she is a thoughtful, caring, and fun-loving woman. I can attest to that—she's my daughter. Nevertheless, after her Aunt Linda, Uncle Randy, and three cousins had been characters in previous books, I was threatened, er, I mean, graciously reminded that I overlooked her turn.

Thanks to my neighbor, Dave Taylor, who taught me a lot about the rules of golf. He is a retired coach for Adams State College in Colorado. Until I golfed a round with him, I didn't think it was possible for an amateur to play the game with complete honesty. If you golf with Dave, you get no mulligans, no gimme putts, and no moving your ball for a better lie. Say what??!!

A big thank you to my wife, Meg, who tirelessly edited and scrutinized my rough draft several times and provided excellent advice. Why is it she seems to enjoy catching my mistakes?!

And last, but not least, thanks to Luke Hansen, for his creative ideas, design of the cover, and ensuring the final product meets the print shop's very precise requirements!

APPENDIX

CAST OF CHARACTERS

Alphabetized by LAST NAME & CHAPTER he/she first appeared

NAME	DESCRIPTION	CH
Archbishop Martin	Archbishop of Melbourne, Australia	15
Attley, Gene	*Dallas Lone Star* sports columnist	72
Ballontine, Karl	TPC Sawgrass manager	65
Banks, Otis	Willy Banks' younger brother	2
Banks, Willy	Director of the South Florida US Fish and Wildlife Service	1
Barnett, Dr. Zeb	Neurologist at Medical City Las Colinas	72
Bergenstein, Steve	Assistant to CIA Director Barrett	68
Berger, Daniel	Pro golfer	35
Boone, Father Max	Priest that St. Max's Catholic Church is named after	Prol
Bowditch, Steven	Pro golfer	72
Barrett, John	Director of the CIA	53
Brùn, Fergus	PGA official in St. Andrews, Scotland	24
Burns, Pete	PGA of American Chief Executive Officer	45
Bushman Jack	Genius scientist who works for III in Australia	15
Butler, Becky	Member of the church—wife of Bob	3
Butler, Ben	2nd grade son of Bob & Becky Butler	3
Butler, Betty	1st grade daughter of Bob & Becky Butler	3
Butler, Bob	Member of the church—hired as chief of security for parish	3
Canadian Tourist	Found golf cup on the Old Course at St. Andrews	38
Carson, April	5th grade daughter of Phil & Sue Carson	3
Carson, Bishop	Bishop of Diocese of Miami	47
Carson, Mike	2nd grade son of Phil & Sue Carson	3
Carson, Phil	Member of the church—worked at Dunkin Donuts	3
Carson, Sue	Member of the church—wife of Phil	3
Casey, Paul	Pro golfer	47
Cauldwin, Omar	Neurologist who helped Hugh Kraft to walk again	4
Collins, Gibby	*Palm Beach Post* sports reporter	16
Couture, Logan	San Jose Sharks' center	Epi
Cramer, Doug	Vice President of Golf Country Superstore	41
Curran, Jon	Pro golfer	72
Dahling, Clyde	Federal judge	73
Davis, Milton	Mayor & Chief of Police of Blister Rock, New Mexico	10
Davis, Morton	Operator of Morton's Motel of Glory—brother of Milton	10
Deacon Ollie	Deacon of St. Max's Catholic Church	3
Dumoulin, Brian	Pittsburgh Penguins' defenseman	Epi
Dow, Paul	Lieutenant Commander at Mayport Naval Station	65
Egbert & Johnny	Two men at the Old Union Coffee Shop in St. Andrews	23
Els, Ernie	Pro golfer	46
Every, Matt	Pro golfer	41
Fareesh, Abdul	South Florida Container Terminal clerk	5
Father Bill	Priest of St. Mary's Catholic Church in Augusta, GA	45
Father Jacob	Priest of St. Max's Catholic Church	2
Father Michael	Priest of Holy Spirit Church in Clines Corners, NM	10
Finch, Aaron	Australian Cricket Team Captain	15
Fowler, Rickie	Pro golfer	58
Frieder, Henrik	ID badge salesman for TST Industries	50
Gambo, Eddy	Owner of Electro Eddy's in San Francisco	9
Garcia, Sergio	Pro golfer	32
Goodell, Roger	NFL Commissioner	34
Guidan, Milo	Archbishop and Pope Francis' personal advisor	62
Hansen, Shea	Real estate mogul and investor in San Francisco	9
Harfield, Oliver	Rogue CIA agent who created air disasters in the 1980s	2

Harrington, Pádraig	Pro golfer	32
Harwas, Oliver	Son of Harfield – changed name & is FBI's Most Wanted	2
Helms, Winston	President of the British PGA	38
Hoffman, Charley	Pro golfer	47
Houghton, Ben	NBC Sports Anchor	70
Howe, Gordie	Hologram of the great NHL hockey player	Epi
Johnson, Bill	Member of the church—repaired trailers in Pahokee	3
Johnson, Chris	Member of the church—repaired trailers in Pahokee	3
Johnson, Dustin	Pro golfer	47
Johnson, Karen	3rd grade daughter of Bill & Chris Johnson	3
Johnson, Keith	4th grade son of Bill & Chris Johnson	3
Johnson, Zach	Pro golfer	41
Jones, Cory	FBI agent	48
Jones, Martin	San Jose Sharks' goaltender	Epi
Jones, Matt	Pro golfer	72
Kaiser, Bob	Bishop of the Palm Beach Catholic Diocese	6
King Achebe	King of Lesotho	51
Kohler, Herb	Owner of American Club and a friend of Hugh Kraft's	23
Kraft, Hugh	Eric Mann's golf coach and best friend of Jack Nicklaus	4
Letang, Kris	Pittsburgh Penguins' defenseman	Epi
Liebrandt, Charlie	Pitcher for Atlanta Braves	Prol
MacGavin, Clydell	PGA official in St. Andrews, Scotland	24
Maglia, Dale	Head of US Customs for Port of Miami	5
Malone, Keith	Aeronautical Engineer—consulted for St. Max's golf balls	6
Mann, Dora	Eric Mann's mother – wife of Jim Mann	1
Mann, Eric	Son of Dora & Jim Mann – becomes a pro golfer	1
Mann, Jim	Eric Mann's father – husband of Dora Mann	1
Marco, Stefano	CEO of Historical Galleries International	66
Martin, Ben	Pro golfer	41
Mason, Earl	ESPN reporter	34
Matsuyama, Hideki	Pro golfer	47
McIlroy, Rory	Pro golfer	47
Menderelli, Vince	Burt Merriman's lawyer	55
Merriman, Burt	Mob boss	44
Mickelson, Phil	Pro golfer	32
Minter, Art	Kangaroo Sportsbetting GM & Head Bookmaker	15
Mueller, Sam	Head of maintenance operations for Augusta National	49
Muggins, Trevor	Commissioner for the US Customs & Border Protection	44
Murray, Matt	Pittsburgh Penguins' goaltender	Epi
Na, Kevin	Pro golfer	41
Nicklaus, Jack	PGA superstar and best friend of Hugh Kraft	4
Obama, Barack	President of the United States	51
O'Bailey, Brian	Bishop of Diocese of Palm Beach	47
Perkins, Stu	Port Everglades Port Authority Director	26
Pinckney, Scott	Pro golfer	72
Pope Francis	Leader of the Catholic Church worldwide	63
Poulter, Ian	Pro golfer	35
Puckett, Kirby	Outfielder for Minnesota Twins – hit game-winning HR	Prol
Renko, Mark	TSA Director for Albuquerque International Airport	11
Rose, Justin	Pro golfer	47
Rother, Myra	Manager of the Pahokee Trailer Court	18
Roy & Rick	Men who saved Eric's life when he fell through the ice	21
Russo, Giuseppe	Owner of Nautica Russo in Genoa, Italy	60
Schenk, Adam	Pro golfer	72
Siebold, Wayne	One-time PGA MVP—friend of Hugh Kraft	12
Siebold, Troy	Wayne Siebold's son	12
Singh, Vijay	Pro golfer	46
Sister Nancy	Nun who delivered Eric Mann	1
Smith, Mel	Aeronautical Engineer—consulted for St. Max's golf balls	6
Snedeker, Brandt	Pro golfer	72
Spieth, Jordan	Pro golfer	46

Stenson, Henrik	Pro golfer	41
Stewart, Bram	Head horticulturist for the Old Course at St. Andrews	38
Talbot, Gene	CNN reporter	52
Tassett, Jake	NTSB Lead Investigator in 80s – CEO of TST Industries	2
Tassett, Jimmy	Plana Cay factory director	43
Tunley, Abbot	Owner of Atlanta Braves	Prol
Vero, Ursula	CEO of Golf Country Superstore	6
Walker, Jimmy	Pro golfer	71
Wells, Spencer	Geneticist and Inventor	15
West, Billy	Reno's Super Bowl MVP QB—died in car crash after game	25
Williams, Thomas	Tommy Williams' father; Electrical Engineer on Plana Cay	73
Williams, Tommy	Golf ball designer & HS friend of Father Jacob	6
Woods, Tiger	Pro golfer	46
Zayer, Marvin	Lawyer who investigated TST Industries	20

www.ingramcontent.com/pod-product-compliance
Lightning Source LLC
Chambersburg PA
CBHW060600310726
48982CB00008B/1187/J

* 9 7 9 8 9 8 8 9 6 6 2 1 0 *